Praise for

When Two Feathers Fell from the Sky

"Combining meticulous research, a fresh point of view, and vivid imagery, Verble's third novel does what historical fiction does best: folds a compelling story into a snapshot of time before life changed. . . . A wholesome story of hope for the future, the search for justice, and ultimately a tale of human connection."

—*Atlanta Journal-Constitution*

"Verble beautifully weaves period details with the cast's histories and enthralls with the supernatural elements, which are made as real for the reader as they are for the characters. This lands perfectly."

—*Publishers Weekly* (starred review)

"*Two Feathers,* tough and warmhearted, clear-eyed and funny, captivates from the first striking scene. Margaret Verble has created a remarkable world, rich with vibrant characters and layered histories, long obscured, that emerge to shape their lives in surprising, thought-provoking, and moving ways."

—Kim Edwards, bestselling author of *The Memory Keeper's Daughter* and *The Lake of Dreams*

"Verble is an immensely gifted writer."

—NPR

"Themes of death, belonging, and our distance from the past make this a good choice for book groups who like historical fiction. This utterly memorable, beautifully written story will linger with readers."

—*Booklist* (starred review)

"A blend of historical fiction and magical realism makes this an unforgettable story."

—*Book Riot*

"Margaret Verble, a citizen of the Cherokee Nation, surrounds Two Feathers' story with a concise history of the area and an in-depth look at the social culture and mores of the times. . . . She will have you believing and cheering. . . . Great fun."

—*Florida Times-Union*

"Pulitzer Prize finalist Margaret Verble has written a singularly unique story of a Cherokee horse diver named Two Feathers. Alternately funny and touching, this novel has a distinctly original and unconventional feel."

—*Ms.*

"A compelling, haunting read. . . . Read it if you're into ghost stories, mysteries, Native American history."

—*Hey Alma*

"An ambitious novel that's impressive in its scope and concept: Glendale Park Zoo and the 101 are rife with narrative possibility and give the author a chance to examine a fascinating cross section of race and class, and the uneasy relations between all manner of characters."

—*Kirkus Reviews*

"*Two Feathers Fell from the Sky* is a rich and lively novel, steeped in place and history. Verble's meticulous research and generosity of spirit shine through, lending her characters and their adventures a fullness that lingers."

—Kelli Jo Ford, author of *Crooked Hallelujah* and winner of the Plimpton Prize

When
Two
Feathers
Fell
from
the
Sky

Margaret Verble

MARINER BOOKS

New York   Boston

P.S.™ is a trademark of HarperCollins Publishers.

HarperCollins books may be purchased for educational, business, or sales
promotional use. For information, please email the Special Markets Department
at SPsales@harpercollins.com.

A hardcover edition of this book was published in 2021 by Houghton Mifflin Harcourt.

FIRST MARINER BOOKS PAPERBACK EDITION PUBLISHED 2022.

Designed by Greta D. Sibley

Library of Congress Cataloging-in-Publication Data

Names: Verble, Margaret, author.
Title: When two feathers fell from the sky / Margaret Verble.
Description: Boston : Houghton Mifflin Harcourt, 2021.
Identifiers: LCCN 2021004083 (print) | LCCN 2021004084 (ebook) |
ISBN 9780358554837 (hardcover) | ISBN 9780358581727 |
ISBN 9780358581895 | ISBN 9780358555094 (ebook)
ISBN 978-0-06-326910-1 (pbk.)
Subjects: BISAC: FICTION / Literary | FICTION / Southern
Classification: LCC PS3622.E733 W48 2021 (print) |
LCC PS3622.E733 (ebook) | DDC 813/.6—dc23
LC record available at https://lccn.loc.gov/2021004083
LC ebook record available at https://lccn.loc.gov/2021004084

ISBN 978-0-06-326910-1

22 23 24 25 26 LSC 10 9 8 7 6 5 4 3 2 1

For Joe Shaver,

my wonderful father,

and for Pepper (Vince) Parrish,

my lifelong, true friend

My mother used to tell us that Nashville was fought for against the Indians by the early white settlers and that it was the spirit of the slaughtered Indians hovering over the place that made everybody there so queer.

— Peter Taylor, *A Summons to Memphis*

When
It
Was

≋

It was long after the buffalo thundered toward a great salt lick in lines, bellowing, snorting, and flicking flies. Long after their path, beaten like a drum, had grown four feet wide and two feet deep and had been there for eons. It was after a civilization of tens of thousands of people settled in a large, fertile basin, built a city near the old buffalo trace, and thrived there for over three hundred years. After they laid their dead in stone box containers stacked in mounds thinly covered by dirt, tucked in clusters in caves or, occasionally, hidden alone in groves. After that entire culture was decimated by a change in the climate. After the rains came again, and seeds scattered by wind grew into oaks, hickories, walnuts, chestnuts, sourwoods, maples, pines, catalpas, and cedars; a forest, thick, wide, and high.

It was after the Cherokee, Chickasaw, Shawnee, and Muscogee agreed to share the forest, the creeks, and the salt lick as a common hunting ground for the good of their families. After the braves stalked game every fall and winter, won an occasional scalp in a fray, brought home meat, and enjoyed the fires of their women, played with their children, danced, smoked, and prayed.

It was after the white people came, saw the land was better than what they'd previously stolen, and proclaimed it was theirs. Said no Indians lived there, so nobody would, or should, object to their staking it. Said their big God-in-the-Sky in His goodness had reserved it especially for them. After they reinforced that God's goodness with guns and dogs, and spread out all over the basin in fortified stations — French Lick, Freeland's, Barton's, Buchanan's, and Robertson's. It was after John Rains camped on that very spot and, in a single winter, slaughtered thirty-two bears in the knobs eventually named the Overton Hills. After the few bears that managed to survive had scattered.

It was after the allied tribes passed through on their way to the stations. After they explained to the whites (again) that this land was held in common and shared. After those Indians were bribed, humored, and shot. After other Indians hid in the trees and cane, killed who they could, and tried starving out the rest. After they stormed the big stockade and the smaller fortifications. After they were attacked by smallpox, canines, better weapons, and a cannon. After the stream of whites became never ending. After the Indians retreated, were cheated, and removed. After the few remaining buffalo were shot for meat, oil, and sport. After their path filled in with weeds and soil.

It was after Tennessee became a state, and a great Indian fighter became its first governor. After one of his grandsons-in-law built a lovely home for the governor's granddaughter and started a plantation. After the Northern invaders arrived, the plantation owners fled, and an occupying army took over Nashville. After the Federals freed the slaves and worked hundreds of them to death. It was after General Hood's army retreated from Atlanta, was decimated at Franklin, and, regrouping in and around that lovely home, wrecked it and all of its surrounds. It was after the Battle of Nashville snaked back and forth over that ground. After soldiers of both sides hid in the giant trees, in the cane, and among the mounds of that ancient civilization.

It was after the peace brought general poverty, hunger, and humiliation. After some former plantation owners sent their darker children north for educations, and started universities for them right there in Nashville. After one former owner bequeathed his dusky children their fair portion of his land, trying to give them a head start in the new order.

It was after a few enterprising entrepreneurs took advantage of the overall destruction, and created new wealth from honest hard work, and from scheming and double-dealing. After they promoted high standards for themselves and, especially, for others. After they developed a new hierarchy, almost identical to the one they replaced. After they invested in railways and electricity, and wanted to make more money by selling rides and wattage by transporting people to places other than work. After trolley parks became that business-problem solution and the new recreational rage in progressive cities all over the country. After the next owner of that formerly lovely home revived and expanded it, and donated two hundred acres of his land to build such a park for Nashville and christened it Glendale. After the laying of the tracks to Glendale was blocked by running into that ancient, prehistoric burial ground, which, aside from being in the way, contained pots, effigies, ear spoons, and whatnots, all worth a lot. After four thousand of the graves were destroyed and robbed, the bones broken and tossed. After the loot enriched several universities, museums, and private collections.

It was after Nashville Railway and Light ran electric lines out to Glendale. After lights were strung all over the place and amusement rides were erected. After both children and adults rode horses, zebras, a red goat, and a unicorn around and around and up and down to a calliope's sound. After they spun in the Roulette Wheel's screechy seats and dipped on a wobbly roller coaster that threw their hearts into their throats. After those delights were torn down and replaced with cages even taller than the surviving old trees and used to house a collection of exotic fowl.

It was also after a school for young ladies of higher culture was built abutting the park zoo, and provided instruction in Greek, Shakespeare, math, and archery. After it declined due to the death of its patron. After the Great War was fought, killed millions of people, and destroyed the old world order. After the global influenza pandemic killed millions more.

It was while buffalo, carrier pigeons, and other species were on their *way to worldwide extinction, and a few forward-looking people became convinced that locking animals up was better than slaughtering them by the millions. After new pens for monkeys, bears, alligators, sea lions, tortoises, and buffalo were added at Glendale, to exhibit the animals and preserve them from total extermination.*

It was in a time of a deep national disagreement over whether people were descended from monkeys. And a time when it'd been decided that even the children of Adam and Eve couldn't be trusted to drink spirits, beer, and wine in public (or in private, if caught). It was also an era of dangerous racial and social divide. When men in white hoods expanded their tradition of terrorizing Negros to include Catholics, Jews, adulterers, and anybody else they didn't particularly like.

But it was also when people were trying to shed their grief and get some relief. When the Shriners built a golf club next to Glendale, and hundreds came to the park zoo every warm weekday, and thousands came on the weekends. When people picnicked in droves, enjoyed concerts and shows, swung tennis rackets and croquet mallets, and ran separate races for fat folks and skinny ones. When they chased tickets dropped from aeroplanes, hunted Easter eggs for pony prizes, and joined civic clubs to socialize, fulfill their duties, and erect monuments to the past as they cared to recall it.

It was also a time of real work for those at Glendale who managed the animals, the people, and the living arrangements. For those who maintained the grounds, handled the horses, mucked the cages, and performed in the shows. When motion pictures were rumored soon to get sound, but vaudeville acts and Wild West shows were hanging around, and diving horses and their riders were still quite thrilling.

It was also when one of the star attractions at Glendale took a terrible fall. When an heir to part of an old plantation embarked on a difficult romance. When the zoo's manager struggled with demons brought home from the Great War. When the patron of the place was trying to outwit his wayward children. And when strange, inexplicable occurrences began intruding upon daily living. It was also when the hippopotamus fell sick. Specifically, it was the summer of 1926.

The
Main
Act

$$\equiv$$

Two Feathers looked forty feet down into the pool. The water was peaceful and slightly brown, the color of the canvas containing it. Beneath the canvas was wood. Two looked at each hook securing the lining and at the boards they were nailed into. A few people were already on benches beyond the pool's edges, but Two didn't glance toward them. She was meticulously professional in checking her equipment, and, also, being mysterious.

She stepped back to the middle of the diving tower where the audience couldn't see her, and eased down to the floor to pull off her cowboy boots. She was wearing her swimming costume under her robe, but diving required long socks and clunky shoes she didn't like to be seen in. It required, also, a diving helmet that was hard to get on, and not particularly attractive. Two was on the floor because there were no benches up there. Her mare, Ocher, would come up the ramp alone, usually walking fast, but occasionally running, and sometimes at an angle. A knock into a bench would shake the whole tower, and although it'd never happened, everybody in the horse diving business (which wasn't many people, but more than you'd expect) worried that someday a horse would run into something and bring an entire structure down. Horse diving was risky business. That's why people liked it so much.

After Two changed into her shoes, she rose, closed her robe, and peeked out at the benches. They were filling, but not enough for her to yet step into the sunlight and wave. She retreated to deeper shade and flexed her fingers and wrists to loosen her joints, limbered her legs by stretching, and visualized Ocher coming up the ramp, hooves slapping the planks. She imagined grabbing hair and harness, swinging her leg. She saw Ocher carrying her to the edge of the platform and stopping abruptly. What was next was harder to gauge. It depended entirely on Ocher's mood. Sometimes the horse liked to snort and prance. Sometimes she wanted it over. Two believed her steed's decisions had to do with the size of the crowd. The bigger and louder, the more prancing around. Horses have pride. And show horses have more than most.

But, eventually, Ocher would dive. Always the extreme plunge, not a safer one. It was the dive both Ocher and the audience preferred, but for Two the most difficult. Ocher would go in headfirst, at a completely vertical angle, and it was easy to be tipped off her into the air. Also Ocher would jerk her head back at their landing to keep water out of her nose. It wasn't uncommon for a diver to get hit in the face as the horse went in. Two would have to dodge, but not so far as to tilt over. The trick was to hang on at an angle while underwater, avoid getting hit or kicked, and come out straight, smiling, and in control. Like she'd done nothing more difficult than ride a bicycle to the end of the street. That illusion had helped make Two a star.

Two wiggled her helmet down over her hair. And she was tucking strands in when she spied Crawford leading Ocher down the path to the ramp. Both children and adults were reaching out to pat. One boy was skipping along close to Crawford, clearly chatting, asking questions. Crawford shook his head, nodded, or, maybe, replied. He was too distant for Two to hear. But she saw Ocher was alert and not overly excited. The ideal mood for a jump.

Two lifted a board in the floor and dropped her robe and cowboy boots straight down into an empty washtub for Crawford to retrieve and have for her after her dive. She walked to the front of the platform, smiled, and waved. The crowd waved back and clapped. Some men put their fingers between their teeth and whistled. Music piped through speakers started up: "I'm Sitting on Top of the World," the current number one on the charts, and the song most often chosen while Two was on the platform. Two waved more. The clapping, whistles, and Al Jolson continued. Then Two turned her back, walked under the roof, and hopped onto a rail with extra padding and a plank that would keep her from falling should she lean back. By the time she was settled and calm, Ocher was at the end of the ramp and the music had stopped. Crawford shouted, "Three." Two cupped her hands around her mouth and shouted, "Three," back.

Two flexed her fingers. Crawford shouted, "Two." Two flexed her neck. She heard "One" and hooves on wood. She turned. Saw nostrils flaring, ears alert, muscles churning. Ocher was coming up fast. Pounding, nearer and nearer. When Two smelled her horse, she reached. Grabbed her mane, then the harness, and threw her leg over her back. She landed square and tightened her knees. Tucked her fingers under the leather. Then Ocher stopped. They were out in the open. The crowd cheered. The water reflected the sun. Drums started up. A bad imitation of an American Indian beat. Two flung her head back. Appeared to be praying to the sun. Really, she was limbering her neck.

Ocher snorted. Then backed up. Went forward. Eyed the crowd. Whinnied and nickered. The audience clapped louder. Ocher tossed her head. Shimmied down her back. But not from fear. Horses that didn't like diving didn't do it. There was no forcing after the initial try; a panicky horse is a danger to itself and its rider. And though a few animal protection activists complained, most folks still believed animals should work for their livings, just like people.

Ocher had been diving for five years before Two got her. She had the plunge down, and wanted to excel and have the pleasure of a jump done well. But she'd also developed a craving for recognition, a lust for attention, and a taste for the crowd. In short, Ocher was basking in the applause, and Two was becoming slightly impatient. Ocher could keep that up for a while. She didn't have an accurate nose for when an audience was tiring of clapping and wanted to see the jump. And Two sensed this crowd was getting restless. She pressed her heels to Ocher's sides.

Large, alert ears turned back, then forward. Ocher took a step to the edge of the hanging ramp. She inched down slowly; her muscles tensed, she pushed off hard. The crowd leapt to their feet cheering. Two ducked into Ocher's mane, snuggled, and dived in unity and freedom. Two leaned in time to keep from getting knocked by Ocher's head, and the splash was smooth and the water warm. Ocher hit the bottom with her front hooves evenly placed, and she pushed off strong. Two centered herself on Ocher's back, and they rose together, dripping in sunshine, sparkling with water, and to great applause and more drums. Two undid the strap of her helmet, gave it a tug, and pulled it away from her head while Ocher climbed the ramp out of the water.

Two hopped off. Waved, grinned, and clicked her heels. The drums died, the claps grew. Two slung tassels, shed water, and flung drops. She waved more, grinned and glistened; her costume reflected the sun. The audience was eating her up. And Two loved the attention. Radiated in the admiration. And was thankful to have made it out of the tank alive and uninjured after another dive.

Crawford was on the other side of Ocher, holding her harness, gazing over the crowd at the Overton Hills. He'd camped in them as a boy, still rode through them as a man. But his mind wasn't on the knobs, or at the diving tank either. It was on his past Saturday night. He didn't show that. Or move. But Ocher shimmied like Two. She shook her mane, slung water, and sprinkled Crawford. It wasn't an intentional slight. Ocher loved Crawford as much as she loved her rider.

Two moved to Ocher's head, spread her fingers, and firmly grabbed her mane. She nuzzled her horse's muzzle, and kept waving her free hand. The audience had clapped nonstop. And they didn't let up. But

Two never waited until the din abated. She said to Crawford and Ocher, "That's all," snatched her robe from a rail, slipped her arms in its sleeves, and picked up her boots. She waved once more. Then she lowered her head and walked off. She gave Ocher the last of the claps.

She stopped just past the ramp to sign autograph books held out in female hands. She also scribbled on newspaper ads where she and Ocher were lauded as "The World's Most Thrilling and Daring Act." But many of her fans were men, angling their shoulders to get in the front of the crowd, angling their smiles to get Two's attention directed on them. She answered questions she heard every day she dived: "Are ya a real Indian?" "Do ya ever get water up your nose?" "Does your horse like diving?" "What are ya doing tonight?" The answers were "Yes," "Yes," "Yes," and, "Working." Two rarely added details because the questions were simple, white people didn't expect chatty Indians, and she had no intention of starting a romance.

Backstage

After Two wiggled away from her fans, she walked a graveled path toward the casino, sat down on the first unoccupied bench, and took her diving shoes off and put on her boots. She felt both exhilarated and relieved. She'd been kicked in the middle of the previous season. A swift underwater accident while she and Ocher were trying to rise to the top, break the surface, and breathe. Coming up occasionally entailed thrashing, and the rectangular tank was only eleven feet deep. Horses have four long, strong appendages. Those kinds of mishaps are bound to happen. Still, the kick had broken Two's ribs and left her unable to work.

She'd returned home to Oklahoma, to the Miller Brothers' One Hundred and One (101) Ranch, on a torturous trip by train, taped so she could hardly breathe. Too bound up to argue, she was relegated to a colored car until she reached St. Louis. For the next leg of the trip, she managed to get a glossy photograph of herself in buckskin and feathers in front of the conductor. She settled in a cleaner, less-crowded car, but the last half of the trip wasn't easy either. When she disembarked at Ponca City, she was so pale from pain and fatigue that she looked like a white.

The women in her family were accustomed to nursing cracked ribs. They knew there wasn't much to be done except to avoid exertion, laughing out loud, and coughing. So Two had minded her nieces and done the mending. Lifting the wash was too heavy. Even lifting a skillet hurt. But just when you think they never will, ribs heal. They get better all of a sudden. Two spent her winter at the 101 doing her normal chores, riding a horse, practicing her shooting, and sparking with the first serious male suitor she'd ever made time for.

Come March, she'd headed back toward Nashville, again through St. Louis, where she laid over a night and indulged one of her favorite vanities, the buying of scarves. All cowgirl performers — white ones, Indians, Mexicans, and the single Negro performer ("Rope 'em" Sherry) — crafted their individual styles with a few basic pieces of clothing. And none were more important than scarves, which proclaimed their femininity when their other attire was so practical it looked and felt masculine. For daily wear, Two sported cotton bandanas, bought in the ranch commissary. They were red or blue, but came in a variety of patterns. Two preferred paisley, but also liked flowers or, when she could get them, feathered fans. But for the arena, courting, or just dolling up, Two wore silk scarves she purchased in St. Louis or Tulsa. They could be ordered from catalogues, but she didn't like buying things she couldn't touch with her fingers. And, besides, St. Louis's Famous-Barr department store was one of her special places. Clothes that weren't daily or costume she often bought there, and on her way to Glendale that year (and the last) she spent her day in St. Louis on the different floors of that store, deciding on scarves and supplementing her homespun lingerie with apparel she didn't wear around her parents and brothers.

There on the bench after her dive, she was still in her swimming costume, but she did have a scarf in her robe's pocket, and after she got her second boot on, she pulled it out and tied it around her neck. It was one of her cotton ones, as she didn't want her silk ones getting wet. After that, she continued toward the casino, a large building encircled by verandas and sporting corner cupolas capped with red bonnets sprouting flagpoles doubling as lightning rods. In spite of the building's name, there was, officially, no gambling inside. But there were lots of dances, concerts, and shows.

There were also dressing rooms for performers. They were never private, but were segregated; men to the left, women to the right, coloreds over there. Two Feathers, though not white, headed to the women's, opened the door, and found, as she'd expected, the Juggling Juggernauts.

The tall Juggernaut, Marty Montgomery, said, "How'd it go?" as soon as Two came in the door.

Two said, "Smooth as silk, except for those drums." She went directly to the other side of the screen the women used for undressing.

Franny, the short Juggernaut, said, "They're still playing 'Sweet Georgia Brown' for us."

"I like that," Two said, while removing a boot with a jack.

"You wouldn't if you were from New York and heard it twice a day for a month." The Montgomerys had grown up performing on the East Coast and in the Catskills and spoke with Northern accents. But, except for the repetitive songs, they liked Glendale because it was clean, the people there more polite than in the North, and they could stay the whole season.

Marty said, "A kid came around here looking for you. A boy." She was seated at a mirror, putting clasps in her hair. She and her sister were bottle blondes.

"What'd he want?" Two had both boots off and was working on a bathing costume strap.

"Don't know. I shooed him off. He probably just wanted a peek in the women's dressing room. Franny wasn't dressed."

Franny snorted. "Not that he'd see much." She was swinging her arms, limbering them up, but was, Two knew, referring to her chest. Both Montgomerys were flat-chested, and Franny often joked that "naught" was the accented syllable in the second word of their act. However, flat, at the time, was fashionable. And on the Juggernauts, big breasts would've been a bother. In addition to needing straight arms and straight aims, tossing rubber balls, batons, and dishes doesn't tolerate impediments. Fortunately, straight noses are not a requirement. Both their noses had been broken multiple times. Their cheeks once apiece. Their faces, really, were rather uneven. But not enough to mar their appeal. Just enough, in Two Feathers' estimation, to look, upon close inspection, slightly beat-up. A professional hazard. She recalled her broken ribs, and rightly reckoned a rubber ball to the bridge of a nose was survivable, whereas a horse's kick to the head sometimes was not.

Marty and Franny left for their act, and Two came out of the dressing room and the casino with her bathing costume slung over her shoulder, swinging her diving helmet and shoes. She again walked gravel paths bound by red fences, blooming flowers, and old trees. She passed women with children, couples holding hands, boys running races, sulphur fountains, the concession stand, and six-story-high bird cages in the near distance. She passed, too, peacocks and cranes walking free, screaming as they pleased. And cages of foxes and coyotes, the former hidden from view; the latter, sitting like dogs, inspecting visitors, licking a chop or two.

Two was headed toward Chambliss Hall, a dormitory left over from a defunct women's college. And her dorm was, by comparison to Glendale, relatively peaceful. The old Buford College stood far enough away from the park's bandstand and casino that only the most animated tunes floated over. Even the crane and peacock screams were muted. But the grounds had grown a tad ragged since the school's demise. In its heyday, sheep had grazed its twenty-five-acre central campus. Neat creatures, careful eaters. Now those acres were chawed by cows. Spotty clumps of weeds too briary or bitter to eat stood like green gophers surveying the landscape. So did clumps grown around patties. But, still, the old-growth magnolias, maples, and oak spread majestic branches, squirrels scampered, and songbirds tweeted.

The building itself was uncommon, two stories high and peaked with an attic dotted by single square windows on the front and the back. Both floors below sported long windows every four feet. Those provided for the circulation of air and generous views of the vistas. Even more unusual,

the entire building was ringed by wide verandas on both floors that to-
taled a half mile in length. Those shaded porches were used by the residents as extra living space. During the days, they provided a gracious,
high-minded retreat. On hot nights, the women hauled their quilts and
pillows outside and slept on their planks.

As soon as Two hit the front door, she was greeted by Helen Hampton, the dorm's mother, who often sat at the desk at the entrance. Out of
twin intentions, Two stopped to chat. She knew she made Mrs. Hampton
uncomfortable, and she got a little pleasure from that. But she was also
trying to educate the older woman out of her bigotry. She remarked on
the weather.

Helen replied, "We've been lucky. I've seen far worse Mays."

Two, who didn't think people in Tennessee had ever actually seen
hot weather, said, "I'm sure ya have. Ya seem to be getting a little breeze
here today."

Helen looked out over the lawn. She didn't feel like she could get
as familiar with Two as she could with the other residents. The Indians had been run out of middle Tennessee long before the Negroes were
freed. The only ones Mrs. Hampton had ever seen were in the Wild West
shows that toured the country and had come to town when her husband
was still living. Those Indians were quite thrilling. They chased buffalo
around fairgrounds, attacked wagon trains, beat drums, and performed
war dances. Mrs. Hampton, who knew Two was on loan from the 101, the
last Wild West show in existence, assumed that she was a Wild Indian
and Two Feathers was her real name. But she didn't know if Two should
be treated like a white or a Negro. And that was important. Standards
had to be maintained. The mixing of races was the subject of a national,
heated debate that had, in the past few years, grown rather nasty.

But Mrs. Hampton was literally a daughter of the Confederacy, so
her views weren't quite as new as those of people in the North who'd only
recently given race much thought (except when it came to Greeks, Ital-
ians, and Jews). She'd settled on treating Two like a mulatto. Which is to
say, she treated her like a house Negro, to whom one once, not that long

in the past, could actually bond with affection (as long as she kept her place). She'd assigned Two a room to herself the previous year and gave her the same one when she returned because she didn't know if any other woman would want to room with her. She said, "If you left your windows open, your room should be quite pleasant."

Two understood Mrs. Hampton was reminding her that she had a prized corner room with two windows to herself. She felt that as a specialty act, a dangerous one at that, her status alone should have ensured that. It would have, had she been white. But Mrs. Hampton's motivation for her room assignment wasn't a mystery to Two. She'd faced plenty of prejudice on the road, and even some on the ranch. She just didn't complain on the rare occasion when it gave her a privilege. Although, to be accurate, Mrs. Hampton was wrong about her heritage, and Two Feathers was a stage name. Two's real name was Nancy Benge, a combination of common Cherokee monikers not colorful enough to be helpful in shows.

Two said, "I hope so. But I'm starving. I didn't buy anything in the park. What was dinner like?"

"Light. Just sandwiches. But we're having spaghetti and meatballs for supper." Helen knew Two couldn't eat supper before her evening dive, but it was something to say, and she prided herself on ensuring good meals for her residents.

Two's stomach growled. She hoped Mrs. Hampton didn't hear it, and hoped there was at least one leftover sandwich in the refrigerator. She said, "Has the mail run?"

It had. And Helen knew there was a letter for Two. She wished she'd thought to get it out when she'd seen her walking toward the dormitory. She liked handing out mail. Most of the residents were hungry for news from loved ones, and when she got to deliver it herself, she felt like some of the happy feelings it produced floated over and landed on her shoulders. Helen had had more unhappiness than she should have at her (middle) age, and did get genuine pleasure in producing it in others and feeling some of the residue. She said, "I believe your mother has written to you." She picked out mail from a pigeonhole on the wall behind her, and thumbed through it, squinting, because she had developed a need for glasses she hadn't quite yet come to terms with. She said, "Here!" and handed over a letter addressed to "Two Feathers."

Two smiled, thanked Helen, told her she would see her later, and rushed off toward the kitchen, still carrying her diving shoes and swimming costume. She did find two ham sandwiches in the refrigerator, and she doctored them with mayonnaise and mustard, and took them on a plate to the dining room, where she'd left her diving paraphernalia and letter. She ate an entire half of a sandwich just looking at the envelope and chuckling to herself.

Two Feathers was a Wild Indian name her mother would write on letters but didn't like using. On the ranch, they lived and worked with the Ponca, Osage, Otoe, Kaw, Kiowa, Pawnee, Sioux, Cheyenne, and Arapaho. Cherokees were rather rare on the 101, even though the ranch was on the old Cherokee Outlet, which had been conceded by force in the Treaty of 1866, chopped to pieces by the U.S. Government, and given to other Indian tribes and to whites. That treaty had put distance between the Cherokees and the rest of the 101 Indians, and so did cultural differences and historic hostilities. So her family didn't like her Wild Indian stage name, and didn't call her by it at home, but realized she had to make a living, and went along.

When Two opened the letter, it was filled with news. Her Aunt Sis, who was a cashier in the ranch's general store, had caught a guest stealing beef jerky by concealing it in his hat. He'd made the mistake of tipping the hat to her, and the jerky had flown out and dropped to the counter and floor. The customer had tried to explain that he was carrying the jerky in his hat because he hadn't picked up a bag when he'd come in the store and he hadn't intended to buy the jerky. It'd just reached out and overtook him. They'd all gotten a big laugh about that.

In a more serious paragraph, there had been a storm on the ranch. Her father, both of her grandfathers, and one of her brothers, all cowboys, had been on the range at the time. They'd escaped uninjured by riding hard to cover, but every woman in the family agreed they were idiots, who didn't have sense enough to watch the sky, and could have just as easily been killed. Two's mother didn't elaborate on that, but Two's imagination filled in the spaces. The men would've tried to get some sympathy, and would've been given silence. Then they would have asked for food. They would have been given that, but the plates would have been set down hard on the tables.

Probably her Uncle Steak would have broken the silence in one of the two houses they occupied. He was white and gregarious, and fond of his father-in-law. Two could picture him filling the quiet in her maternal grandparents' house by talking about their employers, the Millers. Individual Poncas were suing the brothers for stealing Indian land. Talk about those lawsuits was constant in both houses, and everybody agreed on the subject.

Two wished her mother had written about those developments. Maybe there were none, but more likely there were and her mother had left them out of her letter. She didn't entirely trust white mail, and the family's whole livelihood depended on the ranch. They all lived in ranch housing built for Indians who preferred square rooms and plumbing to tipis, wigwams, and huts. Her mother managed the ranch cannery. Her maternal grandmother tended a flock of two thousand chickens; her paternal one cooked in the mess hall. Her Uncle Steak was a mechanic at the Marland Oil service station on the ranch. Rooster, her brother who wasn't a cowboy, was a butcher in the meat processing plant. Two's older sister, Sally, pregnant with her third child, was married to the manager of the ranch's dairy. Her younger sister, the baby of the family, was still in school. That was on the ranch, too. The families aired their true feelings about the Millers only around their own kitchen tables.

So, except for the storm, Two's mother's worries didn't come through in the letter. But they all knew the era of the 101 was coming to an end. They just didn't know when. Nor did they know what they would do when it did. They hadn't held on to the allotments of land the Government had given them (and the rest of the Cherokees) when they'd broken their treaties (again) and created the state of Oklahoma. And it was clear to the whole family that cars would replace horses, buggies, and wagons. Those vehicles already had done so everywhere, except in the West. But only Steak knew anything about motors.

When Two finished her sandwiches, she tucked her letter into a pocket in her robe, returned her dish to the kitchen, and drank a big glass of water. After that, she retrieved her shoes, socks, and bathing costume, and climbed the stairway to her room. As soon as she got in there, she raised both windows higher. Out one was an old hen house, a covered cistern, crumbling tennis and croquet courts, and a virgin forest. The other window overlooked another hall, Burgess, which was still very much in use. It also caught the late afternoon sun and faced the southwest. Two was especially glad to have that window. Raised in Oklahoma, she knew the direction most tornadoes come from.

That same window also framed an ancient, twisted, and damaged catalpa tree. Its trunk was hollow, and its top had been sawed off long before Two had arrived, maybe before she was born. The tree had survived by the luck of a limb sending down a smaller bough that grew into the ground and became a new second trunk. It fed the damaged old tree and formed, with the mother limb, a bridge with the original trunk. The tree had captured Two's imagination; she'd often wondered how it had gotten into its peculiar situation. The year before, she'd decided that lightning was the most likely explanation. But that gave her the creeps. She didn't know an Indian of any tribe who entirely trusted a lightning-struck tree, and as many times as she'd looked at that one, she'd never touched its bark. While dressing, she glanced at the tree, and recalled her mother's letter. Range cattle go blindly wild in lightning and rain. Cowboys are killed by them all the time. She felt a little anger at the men in her family, and actually said out loud, "Idiots."

Two set her shoes and helmet on the porch outside her southwest window to dry, and set her bathing suit and socks on a towel on a radiator to get some sun. Like all cowgirls, she made her own costumes and many of her everyday clothes. Aside from the bandana she'd kept on, she'd changed to a homemade blouse and a pair of men's jeans she'd bought in the ranch commissary and altered to fit. Riding for the 101, she wore split leather skirts or twill pants. But the women's trousers in stores pooched out in the thighs and had generous rear ends. And, as Two Feathers was as flat in back as the Montgomery sisters were in the front, the extra cloth in those slacks fit her derriere like an empty sack. Jeans were uncommon in the East, even for men, but they suited Two's temperament. And clearly not white, she could get away with sartorial choices paler women could not.

She spent the next half hour at her desk writing a response to her letter that would be passed around at home. She envisioned her mother reading it silently first. Then again aloud to her father, who didn't read much, and certainly not when he could have anything read to him. The letter would then be read by her grandmothers, probably together in the evening, as they were great friends, and in some way distant cousins. Her grandfathers would get summaries, as would her aunt and uncle. So would her brothers, Lefty and Rooster. (Really, Martin and Grant.) They could read well, but didn't. Her sisters, Sally and Liz, would read the letters, and Sally would write back. Also maybe Liz, whose heart was set on being a teacher if she could save enough money to get to Tahlequah to college.

Two was sending money home every two weeks to help Liz's goal. And she missed her whole family, and often fell homesick between dives, particularly when she got a letter. But Two was glad she had the showbiz bug. By the time she was six, she could ride better than the Wild Indian children. And she knew early on that she didn't want to tend chickens, stand over boiling water canning vegetables, or cook for people. She wanted to ride horses and shoot guns. Like the men in her family. And like Lucille Mulhall, Fox Hastings, Leasey McFarlin, Ruth Roach, and Juanita and Ethyle Parry. All women she knew and admired growing up. Women who could ride Roman style, or standing up in a saddle, or standing on their heads (at least Ruth Roach could), or rope anything, or shoot anything, and get money and applause in return.

Unfortunately for Two's ambitions, the Wild West shows had waned with the Great War and the movies. But the Millers (Joe, Zack, and George) had kept theirs alive longer than had W. F. "Doc" Carver, Buffalo Bill Cody, Pawnee Bill, and the rest. And when the show left the road in 1918, they continued to perform on the ranch. After a few years of that, Two, who'd already been given her stage name by "Colonel" Joe, got into diving horses, a fad Doc Carver had started after his Wild West show had closed. Two had been raised swimming like a fish in the Salt Fork River, along with her brothers, sisters, parents, friends, and assorted horses and cows. She was a natural.

She liked excitement, and was addicted to danger, crowds, and clapping. Also to horses and diving. Too, she was good with a rope and a gun. She could lasso anything running. She'd also developed a specialty of shooting a rifle backwards over her shoulder by using a mirror. But among cowgirls, the competition in trick shooting and lassoing was stiff. Horse diving won out when Carver came to the ranch, saw how well she could swim, took her under his wing, and taught her how the diving was done.

It demanded fearlessness she'd already developed or had been born with. But that courage didn't extend to all areas of Two's life. She was leery of white people she didn't know. Of some men on the ranch who were a little too rough and ready. And of anything dead. That last fear was a natural Cherokee reaction, as was the first one. But many of the girls on the ranch preferred men's men or goofy Indians. Not Two. She was attracted to males who had some education and showed a little refinement. There weren't many of those on the 101, and the first one she had fallen for had scorched her badly.

Two's letter to her mother talked about the size of her crowds, how well Ocher was diving, and not much else. There wasn't much else to tell. Two was really rather lonely, and didn't want her mother to know that. She got up and retrieved from her trunk a five-dollar bill she'd tucked away for Liz's education, and she'd already stuffed it in the envelope and licked that when Marty Montgomery appeared in her doorway. Marty said, "For you," and handed an envelope to Two. She plopped down on the end of the bed and said, "Franny dropped another plate."

"How many this week?" Two sliced the envelope using an opener Ruth Roach had brought her from the 1914 trip when the show had been trapped in London.

"One this week. And one last. Four already this season."

Two was reading. Said, "Hum. That's a lot. Who gave you this?" She sat down at the head of the bed, propped up on a pillow.

"A kid."

"Boy or girl?"

"Boy. I think he was the same one who knocked on the dressing room door."

"No grownup with him, I guess."

"No. Why?"

"Someone wants to meet at the bear pit."

"Who?"

"Strong-Red-Wolf." Two grimaced.

"That some sorta Indian name?"

"A baloney Indian name."

Marty tucked a strand of hair behind an ear. "Men always want to meet at a pen or a cage."

"Maybe that's because we work in a zoo. What're ya gonna do about Franny?"

The conversation flipped to the slippage of dishes. It was becoming an issue. And not like Franny, who'd been throwing objects from the time she could walk. The Montgomery sisters had grown up in vaudeville and had the same show business values as Two. Theirs had been acquired on grubby stages in the East rather than in sunbaked squares in the West, but none of the three fit in anywhere normal. Certainly not in the South or around Southern women. But they all felt thankful to have settled at Glendale. It was an idyllic park engineered for joy, recreation, and relaxation. And it provided steady work while the other streams of employment for vaudeville and Wild West performers continued drying up.

Two and Marty chewed on what could be causing Franny's misses. Unsteadiness related to her cycle? Boredom with the same tricks? They chewed quite a bit. But as much she really did care, Two's mind wasn't solely on Franny and dishes. Part of it was on the letter, now wadded up and thrown in a basket. All female entertainers got notes. Most expressed admiration; a few asked to meet. They were sometimes handed in person, sometimes slipped under the dressing room door, or often, as this one, delivered by a child who'd been sent. That wasn't unusual.

But this note felt different. It wasn't the rendezvous point. The pit was a romantic destination for couples. Everyone loved the bears. Zerle and Zana, Zip and Zora, and especially Tom Noddy, the cinnamon juvenile, brought from the Cincinnati Zoo and adopted by Zana, his biological grandmother. The bears were behind bars — but not entirely. The pit was actually the mouth of a cave below a limestone outcropping of rock that was slippery with the slow drip of a spring. A giant oak grew up in the middle of the enclosure. Except for a curve of bars in front of the cave, the pen looked natural. A place where bears would live if they could choose. A place wild bears did actually hibernate, before they were killed and turned into oil, hats, and coats.

Two bit her bottom lip. That made-up Indian name bothered her. It was a lame way to get attention. Not a strategy that would win her affection. An outright deception. And Two had been deceived all winter. By the 101's new botanist, who'd come from California to improve the ranch's fruit trees and vineyards. She'd kept company with him on long twilight rides through orchards. Been romantic beneath naked branches of apple trees reaching like webs to gray skies and night ones. Horses tied, they'd walked under arches of arbors so thick they'd seemed lost in a maze. He'd sworn she was the woman for him, the one he'd waited for. Until she found out that he was romancing a fourteen-year-old Osage who lived in Pawhuska.

In a fury, she'd told her mother. Her mother had told her father. And her father had set out to beat him up. Her brothers prevented that. Said things like, "Daddy, settle down. He ain't worth it," and, "Ya can't risk busting yer fists." They whipped him themselves. Two hadn't seen the fight. But others had. Lefty hooked him without warning and spun him around. Rooster uppercut him in the ribs. They both piled on as soon as he hit the ground. Thrashed him to unconsciousness before bets could be taken. Then Rooster jerked the cad's saddle off his horse. Threw it on his chest as he was struggling up. Lefty spit in his face. Told him, "Ya got 'til sundown 'fore we kill ya."

George Miller had been a little peeved. He was serious about the 101's fruit trees. Had thousands of acres in apples, peaches, and figs, and thousands more in grapes, and he wasn't as prone to fighting as his brother Zack. In fact, George tried to discourage pugnacity at every opportunity. But he liked Two, and would've done the same for his own sister if he'd needed to. So he took the side of her family, wrote the botanist off, and called Luther Burbank for another hire.

However, Two had yelled at her brothers for their behavior. And had sulked for three days. But that was from a broken heart and embarrassment, not from real anger at Lefty and Rooster. She was thankful for their protection. Thankful for blood-kin men upon whom she could depend. She wound up apologizing to each of them separately, and endured their lectures with only a slump in her shoulders and a promise to be more careful in the future. It was her Aunt Sis who'd asked if they needed to start sewing a new quilt. Two turned crimson, told her she didn't think so, and slunk away thankful her mother hadn't asked that. Turned out Two was right. She and the botanist had been careful. He was, after all, an expert in propagation.

Marty brought Two's mind back to the conversation with a nudge to her leg. Two suggested trying a new routine. Maybe with different objects—like tomahawks? Marty frowned. Like lighted sticks? Put a little danger in it. Keep Franny's attention.

Marty said, "Easy for you to say. You just dive twice a day. There're over two hundred throws in a routine. Besides, it could be her mind's on a man."

"Who?"

"I don't know. But she's been hanging around the band some. Two or three of them aren't married."

Two's mind went to the musicians. She didn't know which of them were hitched. Thought only one was a cutie. But not that cute. Two knew the sisters well enough not to suggest Marty ask Franny if she had her eye on a band member. The siblings got along. Shared parents, memories, and looks. But they also worked together and shared a room. They could rub each other raw with familiarity and get into spats. Two asked about that: "Y'all getting along?"

"Same as usual. I don't tell her anything. And she doesn't tell me anything. Works pretty well. Still, she's my sister. And we've got the act. I can't trade her for a new horse."

Two toe-tapped Marty. "I've never dived on any horse except Ocher. Never will."

"I know. I meant horse trading in general."

After that, they stopped talking about Franny. She'd be back soon. And they needed to get on with the grooming and costuming which occupied their late afternoons and readied them for their evening shows. Two did that thinking only once again about the note wadded at the bottom of her wastebasket. She had no intention of meeting a mystery fan at the bear pit, sea lion pool, buffalo pen, or hippopotamus den.

After
the
Evening
Dive

The evening show went off with a big splash and no hitches. After sign-ing autographs, Two went to the horse barn. Crawford was already there, brushing Ocher. Two picked up another brush, complimented Ocher on her dive, and said to Crawford, "I been thinking about what ya said yes-terday. Working on her mother might help." She started brushing Ocher's other side.

Crawford started on Ocher's mane. "Would in my family, but I think he runs the show." He was talking about the father of his romantic inter-est. The interest so consumed him that they often started conversations about her just out of the blue.

Crawford kept talking. The object of his affections, Bonita Boydstun, lived with her parents in a large house in downtown Nashville with sev-eral younger siblings and a great deal of printing equipment. As Bonita's parents were religious, the couple had been quarantined in the parlor for their dates. Bonita's younger siblings were shooed away, so they usu-ally carried on semi-private conversations. However, there was no telling who could be listening around what corner, so the chats were held with decorum. That frustrated Crawford to no end.

And though Two didn't say it, she doubted the romance would last. Crawford, who was fairly forthright, had taken some time working up the courage to call on Bonita. And she was younger, and had those strict parents. Also, Nashville was a full eight miles away. Crawford had to take the trolley to spark her, as he didn't want to ride his horse downtown and have it spooked by automobiles. He lived close to the park with his mother and two of his brothers' families as neighbors. His father was deceased and had been, Two thought, some sort of politician with no narrow reach—even though Crawford was a Negro. He was lighter than a brown paper bag, but Two was used to people being mixed and had never asked about his ancestry.

Two listened to Crawford's troubles like she would have a woman's, but she hadn't told him about her winter romance. She felt a little guilty about that. Crawford, Marty, and Franny were her only real friends at Glendale, and she hadn't told any of them. She believed in sharing troubles, but she hated thinking about that lost love herself. It was done, and in the past, and really he would have made a terrible husband. She told herself that several times a day, but fewer times than just a month ago, so she was making progress. And she really didn't want to dampen Crawford's hopes with a sad story.

As they settled Ocher for the night, they talked about a bird Crawford was carving for Bonita, when he should give it to her, and how she might like it. Then Crawford saddled his horse, and Two left the stable for the concession stand. She bought a peanut butter sandwich and a small bottle of milk. She took them to a secluded, unlit bench, where she could eat unbothered, but still watch the visitors at the fountain in front of the casino. She'd already changed from her costume, and she'd left her diving shoes, suit, and helmet in the dressing room. She was wearing jeans, a pair of sandals, and a Western-style shirt. Her black, straight hair was bobbed. Its strands framed her face and curled toward her mouth at the start of each day. But they got damp during performances. By night, after two helmeted dives, they were drooping enough to tuck behind her ears, and she wore a folded bandana headband to help people identify her out of costume. She wasn't a fullblood, but dark enough in the summer to raise suspicions she might be a Negro.

She thought over Crawford's predicament. Wished he could bring Bonita to the park. It wasn't totally segregated. Negros worked all over it at tasks they'd always been allowed (or forced) to do — hard labor, food, entertainment, and animal tending. And they also commonly escorted and cared for small white children. They could even, if well-behaved and accompanied by a white, ride the rides. The park was liberal that way. But Negros couldn't come by themselves, or in a group, without a white escort and real good excuse. So bringing Bonita there, really, was out of the question and, to Two's mind, a shame. But she was aware that Negros had their own park, Greenwood, a few miles northeast of Glendale. She'd never been to it, but Crawford said it had fountains, gardens, a club-house, theater, skating rink, roller coaster, merry-go-round, shooting gallery, swimming pool, and baseball diamond. Two was getting some pleasure thinking about Greenwood having a swimming pool, and Glendale not, when she smelled rain on the wind.

She quickly threw her milk bottle and napkin in a bin, and hurried toward the casino to retrieve her costume. A slow waltz was playing, but the saxophonist was packing his horn. Lights were blinking their ten-minute warning. Only three couples remained on the floor. One pulled apart mid-dance; the female patted her forehead with a hankie, the male looked for his jacket. The casino wasn't far from the station and the last trolley ran at eleven fifteen during the work week. If missed, people were stranded. Although automobiles were beginning to abound in town, Glendale was out in the country, and few people, except heads of house-holds, knew how to drive.

Two gathered her belongings from the dressing room and headed back out. Glendale's wider paths were generously lit. Those bulbs were flickering off or dimming. The narrower paths, just as graveled and smooth, were dark but more comforting to Two. Even though the 101 had an electricity plant, her family lit coal oil lamps at night because her grandparents didn't like false light.

Two turned off onto one of those secondary paths as the wind was becoming moist. In the shadows, ancient trees, scattered randomly by nature and survival, loomed like ghosts of another era. And, indeed, the land could've been filled with apparitions from several ages. A lot of the park's acreage was in a stone box Indian burial ground. And after those people disappeared, the Cherokee, Chickasaw, Muscogee, and Shawnee often retreated there to the trees and weeds to die of their wounds. Then, during the cold, bleak battle of the North against the South, the ground was trampled by armies shooting each other and, in spots, stacked high with bodies.

It's just as well that Two didn't know any of that. She favored life over death, and the dark was growing, the wind rising, and the music dying. But the night would soon rumble. The trolley would come from behind, clacking and whining. Having hopped from the back of one horse to another since a tot, Two was expert at jumping and catching a ride. But that night she got to the tracks while the trolley was still at the park's entrance. She crossed the rails and, trying to beat the rain, hurried off the path into the grass.

As she did, her mind shot to Glendale's buffalo, pastured on the far side of the zoo. She envisioned them enjoying the showers, if thunder and lightning didn't follow. The bison were her friends, and she was as accustomed to them as other people are to cats and dogs. At least three times a week she visited their pen. She didn't approve of caging buffalo in, but understood Glendale didn't have the resources of the 101. Didn't have thousands of acres for them to graze upon. Knew if it weren't for places like Glendale, only a couple of protected herds would still be in existence.

Thoughts of buffalo turned Two's heart toward home. She'd been born inside the three hundred miles of the 101's fences, and knew very little of the world beyond them and show business. She'd started touring at ten, and was, fortunately, in Omaha with the American show in 1914 when the Millers' European cast was in London. The British impressed most of that show's horses and all of its mules to use in the war. Zack Miller; 1,100 entertainers and staff; and numerous buffalo, elephants, camels, longhorns, and oxen finally escaped via a mail boat bound for New York. They returned to Oklahoma weary and disheartened. The American tour was pulled in then, and, after that, the show was severely diminished. In 1916, it was plagued by bad weather and a national outbreak of infantile paralysis that made people afraid of exposing their children to crowds. Then in January of 1917, Buffalo Bill Cody, the major Miller draw, died of hard living and damaged kidneys. The show folded. From then on, until Two spent her year with Doc Carver learning horse diving, she performed her trick riding and sharpshooting only for the crowds that flocked to the ranch.

Two began to feel lonely again. She'd been training at Glendale since mid-March, practice-diving into a cold pool twice a day, except for the three days when it snowed. The park opened to the public on Easter (that year, April 4), and since then the weather had turned considerably warmer. But she was away from her parents, siblings, and extended family, and still feeling betrayed. A croaking frog called in the rain. The trolley rumbled in the distance.

Then Two thought she heard something else. Her ears sharpened. She heard it again. Someone was treading behind her. Rustling the grass. Stopping. Rustling again. Two's back muscles tightened, her shoulder blades folded to her spine. She controlled her breathing like when she'd first started diving. Horses sense fear and take advantage. So do humans. Two quickened her step. When she entered the lights of the dormitory's porches, she turned and looked out into the lawn. The shades of darkness varied. Trees and their shadows loomed large. Yellow light from the windows rectangled the yard. A far pool of spotlight bathed the trolley stop. The trolley's headlight arced toward it. Two hoped it would illuminate the lawn. And it did sweep against trees that lined the tracks. But they threw only more shadows.

The trolley stopped. Nobody got on, but Marty and Franny hopped off and hurried up the walk. Rain had begun falling in scattered, large drops. Two asked the sisters if they'd noticed anybody lurking on the lawn. They hadn't, and they all peered into the darkness and saw nothing unusual. They rushed inside together, talking about how spooky the park could be when the visitors went home.

Picking
a
Racing
Spot

≡

The rain wasn't hard or long, and the next morning, Two headed out past seesaws, slides, climbing contraptions, and animal cages, toward a hillside and meadow used for picnicking and romancing. She'd been asked to meet with Duncan Shelton, the groundskeeper, and with Mr. James E. Shackleford, a man she'd rarely been around and didn't intend to be around much in the future. But Two, and everyone else, did what Mr. Shackleford asked (or told) them to do. He'd donated the land for Glendale and was the chair of its board, and a founder and major stockholder of Nashville Railway and Light, the park and zoo's corporate owner. His home, Longview, a mansion and old plantation, abutted the park.

Mr. Shackleford was also walking to the meeting. Whenever he was vexed or perplexed, instead of being driven, he habitually strolled from Longview down one hill and up another to the park to try to shed his cares on the way. He did that quite often, as he had a lot of worries. At any given time, he could be embroiled in a dozen or so lawsuits, some of his own innovation, and some initiated by others who felt he'd skinned and deboned them. He was the president of the largest bank in town, the chair of the board of Peabody College, and also of Cumberland Telephone and Telegraph, a company he'd built, sold, and made a fortune from. He was, additionally, a breeder of livestock and an owner of insurance companies. Most recently, in collusion with one of his sons, he was moving bonds, securities, and small banks into and out of various corporate entities, much like other men move checkers from black squares to red ones.

Mr. Shackleford was the patriarch of a family that was also often worrisome. It extended to grandchildren, nieces, nephews, and in-laws of two generations, though six of Mr. Shackleford's own offspring had sadly predeceased him. Some of those dead had left children to be supported, and one living child, a wastrel widower with two little girls, had come home to live with his parents and had been lingering for years. Mr. Shackleford was one of the wealthiest men not just in Tennessee, but in the entire nation. He enjoyed, and suffered from, all that went with having *real money,* including supporting dependents.

Two was used to being around the Millers' wealth, at least at a distance. And Mr. Shackleford knew that. He'd been on the 101, as had everyone who was anyone. He'd also personally called George Miller to hire Two's act because he'd seen what a draw it was. However, Mr. Shackleford didn't envision turning Glendale into anything as rowdy as the 101. As interesting as it was, it was no place for the genteel (or even the plain) people of Nashville. He considered everything on it in poor taste, no matter how entertaining. But Mr. Shackleford did yearn for a little of the glamour of the 101, and, of course, for the crowds and the fame.

He'd asked to meet with Two because he was looking ahead to another new lure that garnered large attendance and generated lots of goodwill: a box turtle race, the national rage ignited by the Millers two years in the past. Mr. Shackleford intended to hold a race on the Fourth of July, and had been informed that the young Indian woman knew how to conduct one, as she'd casually mentioned that to the casino manager a few days back, and he, Frank Greer, had stuck that nugget into Mr. Shackleford's ear the next time he'd seen him. Shackleford had wondered, for a moment, why he, himself, hadn't realized Two Feathers was a turtle-racing resource. But he'd shaken that doubt from his head as a weakness akin to giggling in men, and had asked Greer to arrange a meeting for him with Two, and to pull Duncan Shelton in.

Greer had envisioned the turtles racing on the dance floor, as it was commonly chalked for cakewalks and other contests and recreation. But provoking turtles into racing isn't easy, and Mr. Shackleford already knew that the 101 ran their tortoises outside. So he, Two, and Duncan were on a slope that'd been a concert field in the past when Two explained, "What ya want, sir, is an open spot, circled by trees. Turtles need a clear, flat hundred feet at least."

Mr. Shackleford looked out and around. Said, "This way," and started marching downhill through grass trimmed by mowing machines. At seventy-two, he was stiff, more by temperament than age, but he did carry a cane. Whether that cane was an accoutrement affected for show, a needed support, or a weapon was hard to say on any given day. Two assumed he needed the cane for stability, but she didn't know him very well.

However, Duncan did. He'd worked for Mr. Shackleford for twenty years. Mostly in the park zoo. But also around Longview, and in the gardens between it and two other mansions, a new one built by Shackleford's son, Meredith, and the other, Wayside, built by his brother, Alex. Alex was deceased, and his widow, Maggie (who was also Mr. Shackleford's wife's sister), traveled quite a bit. She'd turned Wayside over to her children as they'd started their families, but lodged there in an apartment when she was in town. All three homes were connected by paths through flower gardens that Duncan, Maggie, Mr. Shackleford, and his wife, May, all oversaw, took pride in, and in Maggie's case, made money on.

Duncan knew of several places in the park that fit the requirements of the hundred cleared feet of flat earth in the sun that Two recommended. But he was content to let his boss pick a space that suited him best. Duncan took orders well, gave advice sparingly, and said "that's a shame" when things didn't work out. He did have strong opinions, but only on horticulture and Indian and Civil War relics that, in his line of work, he quite naturally found scattered around.

With Duncan and Two following, Mr. Shackleford marched until he passed an ancient oak and emerged from its shadow. There he stopped, planted his walking stick, and spread his legs a bit. After bouts of inflammatory rheumatism when young, he was still as straight as his cane. He'd been one of seven children, and his father had been struck down by yellow fever when he was quite small. His mother was left to run a Mississippi plantation that, within the next two years, was trampled, looted, and burned by both Confederate and Federal soldiers. After the war, she was cheated by carpetbaggers, gave up trying to survive on ruins, and moved her children to Memphis and in with friends. From there, when James was thirteen, the family relocated again, this time to Franklin, Tennessee, where his mother took over raising the children of a newly widowed Presbyterian minister. Somehow, she found the time and energy to be courted and remarry. All of which is to say, Mr. Shackleford did not have it easy growing up. He started in ruins and wound up in a mansion as a result of hard work, intelligence, an eye for opportunity he'd inherited from his mother, and various crooked dealings.

Shackleford squinted into the sun, Duncan pursed his lips, and Two surveyed the trees, calculating the distance to the far ones. She was quite accurate at that, as her profession required quick estimations of the speed of galloping steeds. She said, "This would do, sir."

Duncan, who was bug-eyed and bald, but wearing a cap, said, "Will the watchers get hot?" The temperature had dropped into the fifties because of the rain. That was unusually cool for late May, and it'd be hot and humid by Independence Day. Duncan wondered, too, if ladies would risk standing in the sun. They'd stopped carrying parasols, but pale was still the ideal. He bit his tongue. The Indian girl might not appreciate mention of that.

"They can stand in the shade," Two replied, as though she'd read Duncan's mind.

Shackleford was in his suitcoat, his collar stiff and tight. He put a finger between it and his neck. Then he drew a paper from his front trousers pocket and unfolded it. He said to Two, "I made a drawing. Based on my recollections." He handed it over.

The drawing was concentric circles, drawn with a compass and divided by straight lines into eighths. Two was impressed. It was an exact replication. But Mr. Shackleford was smart. And part of smart is a good recollection. She said, "That's it, sir," and handed the paper back. Mr. Shackleford passed it to Duncan.

"What are the lines for?" Duncan asked Two.

"Depending on how ya score, sometimes judges stand where the straight lines cross the circles. A bunch of turtles are hard to track."

Duncan frowned. "How many turtles are we talking about?"

"First year, we had a hundred and fourteen. We did all those in one race. But last year, the field was over sixteen hundred. They held elimination races. Drew it out. Made it more fun."

Duncan frowned. "I don't know offhand where we can get that many turtles."

"Ya can order 'em from the 101. We got a turtle pit there."

Duncan was mulling what he'd need to do to house a horde of turtles, when Mr. Shackleford said, "We could put them over there." He was pointing to a grove of trees ringed by a low white fence. "Reinforce the fence with wire so they can't get through."

Two had never seen the grove. Or, if she had, didn't remember it. But she could see it sloped in, and assumed a little cave or spring was in the center, as those pocked the entire park. She said, "If there's a cave in there, ya could lose turtles to it."

"There is a cave, as best I recollect," Mr. Shackleford said. "But the mouth's not very big. And there's sort of a crypt in front of it." He put a finger in his collar and avoided looking at Two. But then he avoided looking at most people, assuming they'd look at him. He did raise an eyebrow in Duncan's direction.

Duncan said, "They ain't hard to dismantle. I helped my pa on the Noel Cemetery." He put a hand to his throat and fingered a lump.

Shackleford knocked a rock with the tip of his cane. He'd also helped dismantle those graves. Some had been on his land, but even more on Oliver Noel's, his neighbor, business partner, and friend; another now dead. The cemetery had covered acres and acres. The excavation was huge, and led by Gale Thurston, who'd been a lawyer by degree, a businessman by necessity, and an archeologist by heart. Thurston, the son of a senator, had been a Yankee officer, but a decent one. He'd married a Southern lady and had stayed in Nashville when the war was done.

Shackleford's memory moved from Thurston's character to bones stacked all over the ground as far as the eye could see. Skulls in piles, long bones in others. Rib cages tangled so badly they had to be broken by stomping. The slabs that had housed the bodies were piled in long rows, lifted by Negros, and carried off in wagons. Years of work. Over four thousand burials. And thousands of grave goods — effigies, gorgets, whistles, pots, pipes, knives, hooks, and tools. Many taken to homes, set on mantels or used as doorstops. But cart after cart taken to museums, as near as Vanderbilt, as far away as Harvard.

Shackleford had ridden over to the excavation mostly on Saturday or Sunday afternoons. He'd even shoveled dirt, lugged stones, and picked through bones. But he was embroiled in business ventures and had a wife and young children at home. He depended on an accomplice to squirrel away some of the best spoils and bring them to Longview for him to sift through. He'd wound up with quite a collection. Had previously displayed, and would again in the fall, his best artifacts at the State Fair. An urge to describe them to Two arose in his throat. He hesitated and swallowed that inclination. Still, memories of dismantling the graves were some of his most common recollections.

Duncan, too, had temporarily retreated to the past. He said, "I don't expect to ever see the likes of that cemetery again. I help pile them skulls. Lost count of them. Got me a perfect stone pipe. Made like a bird. Still have it." He smiled. Muscle memories of hooking his fingers through eye sockets and throwing skulls made his arm twitch.

Two looked up the hill toward the zoo. She stood still and thought about riding the range. She stirred only when Mr. Shackleford said, "I've been in that thicket. My boys liked to run off in here to play. I've always thought that's the grave of an important person. Buried away from the crowd." Shackleford cleared his throat. His own plot was picked out and paid for. "I told them not to disturb it. Had that fence built."

Duncan wasn't as eager to destroy a grave as he'd been as a youngster. Since then, he'd lost a wife to the Spanish influenza and had developed a thyroid disorder. Besides, his boss didn't seem to want to dismantle that particular grave. The fondness important people have for other important people extends over centuries and cultures. He said, "We could leave the box alone. Stretch wire over the mouth of the cave. Put the turtles in there anyway. The fence is already there. Just add the wire to it and reinforce it near the ground. Give 'em some water to sip."

"Have you any advice, Two?" Mr. Shackleford asked that.

The turtles on the 101 lived in a gully below a cliff where the earth dropped a good forty feet. Where, at one time, buffalo, chased by Plains Indians, had jumped off, died, and been butchered. Their bones still protruded from the earth like long, thin mushrooms. Some of the Wild Indian children played with them before the turtles were housed there. But Two considered the pit a place of death. Would ride up to it, watch the turtles, but wouldn't go in it. The thicket would do, and she was glad to know what it hid. She wouldn't go in it either. She told Mr. Shackleford, "It should work, sir."

After that, she was excused and the men turned toward Longview, where they would telephone the 101, order turtles, and figure out the details of securing them. That job done, Mr. Shackleford would walk across the street to his sister-in-law's, join her and his wife for afternoon tea, and worry about one of his boys. Mr. Shackleford's mind was neverceasing. He believed idleness, mental or physical, was a plague on the entire population. That he dabbled in running a trolley park and zoo devoted almost entirely to play was an irony lost on him. Most were. He was neither ironic nor easily amused. He believed a certain amount of pleasure was important for sustaining hard work. It was a practical necessity, often overdone.

Visiting
the
Animals

≡

Any conversation with Mr. Shackleford made Two uncomfortable, and after that one she decided to settle down by visiting the animals. She walked up the old concert hill toward the heart of the zoo, shaking Mr. Shackleford off and trying not to imagine what exactly was hidden in the grove. She also wondered about the sounds she'd heard the night before. She felt like she needed to be alert, and she looked more directly at the people she passed than she commonly did. She had no real idea who she was looking for, but her thoughts traveled back to the note signed "Strong-Red-Wolf." When she got back to her room, she'd get it out of the wastepaper bin and look at it again.

The first animals on her course were a giant tortoise and a young hippopotamus. Their den was encircled by a bank of dirt lined on the inside by cement pavers that in theory (and, so far, in reality) prevented its residents from waddling or rampaging out. The interior consisted of dirt, spotty grass, and a concrete pool. Looming on the north side was a relatively new platform, mostly used by the keepers. Beneath it was the filtration unit, encased in a woodshed painted red. The large turtle,

Methuselah, had lost his mate a couple of years back, and she'd been replaced by the hippo. Though visitors couldn't tell a healthy hippo from an ill one, Two knew from Crawford that the zoo's manager and attendants were worried about the behemoth.

When new to Glendale, the hippo had been named in a contest open to the zoo's visitors. The winning moniker, Dinah, was submitted by a musical instrument salesman known for playing sheetless any song you could pull out of the air. "Dinah," an Ethel Waters hit, described a Southern woman who couldn't be finer. The connections between the wildly popular tune, the South, an African animal, and a hefty Negro singer made the entry soar above others like a chestnut tree over a forest of dogwoods.

Dinah, still a juvenile, was gentle for her species and the source of unusual sounds visitors found more amusing than threatening. The first hippo at Glendale, she was a draw for the crowds. But of late, she'd grown picky in her eating and listless at night. She appeared to be losing weight, although it's fairly difficult to tell if a hippo has dropped pounds until one has dropped quite a few. Additional wrinkles are natural and don't provide much of a clue. Then too, there wasn't an abundance of hippos around to compare a sick, wrinkly one to. However, there was the matter of food not taken and muck not produced.

As a child, Two had been taught to start downwind from animals she was hunting and upwind from those she wanted to befriend. She approached the southwest side of the pen, joining two boys still wearing knickers. One was chewing a stick, the other throwing pebbles at Methuselah. The gravel bounced off his shell into the mud. The thrower said, "Ducks do." The other said, "Turtles aren't ducks, stupid." Two tuned out from there and focused on Dinah.

At rest in shallow water, the hippo seemed more reddish than usual, and appeared to be sweating blood on her back. Two didn't know if that was normal or odd. Dinah's shoulders were really quite pink. She'd soon need deeper water than that in the pond. In Africa, hippos live in rivers; their heads protrude like rocks. Two dredged up a memory of a newspaper article about a man who'd stepped on one of those rocks and was eaten leg first. Or maybe not. Maybe chomped in two. Dinah was fed vegetables and reeds. And most big animals that attack humans rarely consume them. Two's mind wandered to buffalo, elephants, camels, and oxen. All she knew from the 101. Not a human-eater among them.

She was trying to talk spirit-to-spirit with Dinah when the pebble-throwing boy threw an actual rock. It bounced off Methuselah's shell. The turtle pulled his head in. The boy threw another. Said, "Take that!" Near the platform, an older woman wearing a floppy hat put a hand to a little girl's back. She said, "Let's go see Tommy, the llama."

The other boy threw a stone. Methuselah, close to the pond, backed into the water. He stopped, partially submerged, near Dinah's front leg. A third rock bounced off his shell and made a small splash. Both boys bent to pick up more stones.

Two said, "Watch out for the turtle's father."

The boys straightened up and looked to Two. Their eyebrows lifted to their foreheads. One raised his lip in a snicker.

"His father carries the world on his back. Look at the ground." Two lowered her eyes. "It's his shell. Have you heard of earthquakes?"

Both boys nodded.

"They're caused by boys like you who bother turtles."

The taller boy squinted. The shorter boy's eyes widened. The taller said, "I don't think that's right."

Two pulled herself to her full height, which was five foot ten. She raised her chin and nose and folded her arms over her breasts. "I am Two Feathers. My grandfather, Geronimo, often spoke of the great Earth turtle. Passed the pipe with him as a friend. When the next earthquake shakes, it will be the angry Earth turtle wreaking revenge. That will be the fault of you."

The boys exchanged glances. Geronimo, though dead, was still very famous. And the woman suddenly looked like the picture of an Indian on a poster, the side of a can, or a box of cigars. She, also, was young (or old) enough to be Geronimo's granddaughter. The shorter boy bit his lip.

He said, "Let's go see the monkeys. These dumb animals aren't any fun." He put a rock in his pocket. The other dropped his stone on the path.

Two, trying to keep from smiling, turned away from them and back to the animals. Methuselah blinked a small wink. Dinah yawned. The pair seemed to relax. Two realized then that she often found them near each other and wondered why she hadn't noticed that before. She knew animals of different species frequently were friends. Knew a goat who hung out with chickens, a crow who kept company with a sow, and several cats who slept with horses. She decided to go visit her pal in the buffalo pen.

The bison lived across the park from Two's dormitory, on a hillside overlooking a creek. But of all the zoo's residents, Two was most drawn to them. The 101 was home to the largest herd left in existence, and she had acted with buffalo in shows. The bison brought her closer to home. Particularly when she could entice one near enough to the fence to peer in its eye, discern the swirls in its fur, watch the saliva drip from its working lips. The smell she could easily sense at a distance. Everyone could. However, without a doubt, Two was the only person in the park whom the odor made homesick.

And she was close to the enclosure, savoring the buffalo scent, when she heard steps behind her. She turned quickly. It was only two women. They had on jackets; it was getting warmer, but was still unseasonably chilly. Two turned back around, relieved, and hoped the water would warm some before her dive. She walked up to the fence, propped her elbows on a board, and cupped her palms to her mouth. She called, "Haba, haba."

A buffalo's ears turned. He was the largest and eldest in the enclosure, and he was bored. The grass was tall, but he held out for hay. And the only things he had to do were monitor the six other buffalo, flick flies, smell people, and keep his ears perked for the creak of the gate or the thud of bales thrown to the ground.

The haystacks and gate were on the east side of the pen. Two had walked all the way to the west, resisting the temptation to open the gate and free the buffalo by not going near it. Cranes and peacocks pranced in the park, but a loose buffalo could rampage and pose a problem. Two called "haba, haba" again, trying to attract the large old buffalo, Adam, whom she personally knew. He'd been Buffalo Bill's pet. The Millers had housed him for a couple of winters. "Haba, haba" was how Mr. Cody had called him.

And Adam recognized both his old call and Two. Although it's hard to say if he recognized Two from as far back as the ranch. Maybe, but probably not. What is certain is that he liked her smell, which didn't remind him of any other of the two-legged animals. He lifted his nose slowly. Inhaled her scent. Momentarily pretended disinterest. Looked right and then left. Shook his head. Then turned around and slowly sauntered in Two's direction. About six feet from the fence, he plopped down on the ground and folded his legs.

Two looked to her sides, just as Adam had. She saw the two women in deep conversation fairly far away, not even looking at the buffalo. Which was good. As much as Two loved Adam, she didn't want to get caught talking with him at Glendale. And she harbored some guilt over that. She was certain animals have minds, spirits, distinctive personalities, preferences for work, and senses of humor. Are like humans, only in different bodies. On the ranch, Indians of every tribe knew that, and talked to, and about, particular animals like they talked to, and about, particular people. But Two had observed that white people didn't do that. And had figured out that whites thought that all living creatures were on a ladder. Them at the top, of course. Everybody else on the rungs below. In the trolley park and zoo, only Mr. Lovett, the general manager, the animals' attendants, and visiting children talked to animals. Adult visitors watched, pointed, smiled, and talked to other humans. Two didn't want to reinforce whites' meanness about Indians being several steps down on the ladder and just as well killed or penned up.

So, like Adam, she engaged in pretense. And while they silently tried to determine each other's mood and attitude, on the far side of the pen, a redheaded man in a khaki uniform approached the haystacks. He was holding a pitchfork, but didn't stick it in a bale. He climbed the bales to the top, and he looked out over the pen. Even though he did that for several minutes and the wind shifted direction, neither Adam nor Two noticed him.

But, eventually, children's shouts broke their mental conversation. Adam's ears turned at the same time as Two's shoulders. A gang of boys was running toward them. Pointing branches, shouting, "Bang, bang." The boys reached the fence, aimed their sticks, and banged some more at Adam. His rump was toward the attackers. He didn't turn his head. One eye focused out in the distance, as far as he could see. (Which wasn't that far in reality.) The other focused on the stacks of hay. He couldn't see them clearly either, but he suddenly smelled them, and he was fond of their aroma. He concentrated on that to drown out the bangs. He caught a whiff, too, of the man in the khaki uniform.

The boys irritated Two the same way the pebble-throwing ones had at the hippo enclosure. But shouted bangs didn't, in Two's estimation, really bother buffalo. However, they do interrupt peaceful conversation. She whispered goodbye to Adam and turned from the fence. She still didn't notice the man, now without the pitchfork, walking toward her from the other side of the enclosure. She didn't see him put a hand to the corner of his left eye, trying to tame its twitch.

Another
Letter

$\equiv$

As the day progressed, the weather warmed enough for Mrs. Hampton to take up her station behind the desk at the open front door of Chambliss Hall. She enjoyed that particular position because she could gaze out onto the lawn when she wished, read a novel when she was unbothered, and have agreeable conversations with women residents who were coming and going quite a bit. She also relayed pieces of information, some verbally, others as notes. When Two came in, she plucked an envelope from a pigeonhole on the wall, said, "Good morning, Miss Feathers," and extended her hand. "This is for you."

Two was hoping for a letter from her sister, but there wasn't a stamp or an address. "Thank ya. Who's it from?"

"A fan, I suppose." Mrs. Hampton didn't really know. She'd been in the ladies' when the note was dropped.

Two flipped the envelope over. "Did ya talk to him or her?"

Mrs. Hampton blushed only slightly. "No. It was left on the desk. I was tied up with a delivery." She paused. "In the back of the building."

Two recognized the handwriting from the note the day before. She tore the envelope with her thumbnail before Mrs. Hampton offered an opener pointed up. The words said,

> Dear Miss Two Feathers,
>
> I think you will like me when we finally meet. I understand you're playing hard to get. That's how most decent women are. But I want you to know I have a university education and a good reputation. I've watched your dives many times, and admire you greatly. I know you often visit the buffalo. I do, also. Ironically, there used to be a buffalo trace running near where the pen is now. It was deep and wide, and used by the bison for centuries.
>
> I will be near the pen at 11:00 a.m. If you wish to meet, please signal me by picking a wildflower and placing it behind your ear.
>
> Most sincerely,
> Strong-Red-Wolf

Two didn't own a watch. She asked Mrs. Hampton for the time, as the house mother was wearing a pocket watch on a chain around her neck. The watch had belonged to Mrs. Hampton's dear, deceased husband and had a top she enjoyed springing open. She retrieved the timepiece from the warm, often moist, slit between her bosoms, and did just that. "It's eleven thirty-four."

"When did this note arrive?"

Mrs. Hampton had acquaintances who were overly concerned with regularity. Who tried and discussed the latest remedies. She was thankful not to be among them, and didn't keep track of the times of her visits to the ladies'. She said truthfully, "I don't know. I was detained." She added, "There was a laundry delivery. It took quite a while." That, too, was true, but had happened after the note had appeared.

Two didn't attend closely to the laundry explanation. She asked, "Has the trash been taken out?" The trash was emptied from the rooms once a week. Always on Thursday. Mrs. Hampton told her it had been.

Two frowned. She wished she'd come directly back to the hall after talking with Mr. Shackleford. She shook her head. Read the note once again. Pictured the buffalo pen, Adam, the two women, the boys shooting their sticks, and the hay. Recalled nothing else. She read the signature again. *Strong-Red-Wolf.* Two knew Rattlinggourds, Walkabouts, and Redbirds, and was, herself, a Sixkiller on her maternal grandmother's side. But she didn't know any Strong-Red-Wolfs. Besides, those dashes were out of fashion. Nobody used them anymore. And people had first names. Even fullbloods. Whoever had written the note wasn't a Cherokee, and probably wasn't an Indian at all.

There were, at the time, some whites who pretended to be Indians. But that had happened more frequently during allotment days, and was solely for the purpose of fraud. The ruse had tapered off when Indians had nothing left worth taking, but when it did occur, it was to divide the public from their money. Two held those frauds in low regard, unless they were forced into their deceptions by their employers. The Millers did that occasionally. But attendees at Wild West roundups knew they were watching fiction. And those whites playing Indians didn't play them out of costume. Two Feathers couldn't fathom why a white would pretend to be an Indian for any reason other than criminal.

She returned to her room and tucked the note and its envelope into *The Bandit of Hell's Bend,* a novel she was sort of stuck in. She picked up her kit and felt the anxiety of running behind. She needed to eat quickly so her food would digest and she'd have her time with Ocher before their three o'clock dive. Ocher liked to jump. Enjoyed the excitement and crowd. Only occasionally shimmied around, and had refused to leap only once. That next day, she'd been the picture of obedience. However, Two believed in preparation and attention. Knew they prevented mistakes. Her father's friend, Dan Christy, flashed into her mind. Dan rode once too often while drunk. Slid out of his saddle as the performers were pulling into the circle for the grand finale, waving their hats to the crowd.

Dan's own horse hadn't put a hoof to his face, and, thankfully, neither had hers. But someone hadn't been paying attention. Dan survived, but his cheek was crushed. He was prescribed alcohol for the pain, and afterwards stayed drunk all the time. Eventually, was given his saddle and told to skedaddle.

Strong-
Red-Wolf

Strong-Red-Wolf had been tracking Two for some time. She was the first real Indian he'd seen outside of a Wild West show or a motion picture. But he'd been fascinated with Indians ever since he could remember. His secret Indian name had tiptoed into his noggin when he was about ten and had stayed trapped in there. He'd joined the archery team in high school and won some ribbons. He'd also competed at county fairs and beat his competition. With every ribbon, he became more convinced that he was an Indian. But he wasn't sure what kind. So he began reading history. And that was when he discovered that his parents' farm sat on land that once belonged to the Cherokees. Instead of concluding the land had been stolen, he decided the Cherokee must be his tribe. By this time, his notion, fantasy, delusion, or whatever, was fully formed and baked like a brick into his mind.

He'd gotten a job at the zoo because his university major (anthropology) was, since the Scopes trial the year before, seriously out of vogue in Tennessee, and because he had studied a little about the Noel Cemetery in college. He knew about the late-1880s excavation (or pot hunting, plundering, and desecrating, depending upon your perspective). He'd been hired in February, while the heat-loving animals, like the alligators, snakes, parrots, pheasants, monkeys, and armadillos, were still in their winter quarters (either a heated barn or the casino). So he was there when Two came in from Oklahoma and started practicing her diving. But he was busy with the animals, and didn't become aware of her until he read about her daring act advertised in the paper shortly before the park opened in early April.

Seeing Two dive for the first time was a new high in his life. And when he was told she was a Cherokee, she seemed like his destiny. He'd been watching her ever since, trying to engineer a meeting. He'd also managed his duties so they'd coincide with her activities and routines — which were as firmly planted in his head as the tall trees of the park were stuck in the ground. And like all true obsessions, Strong-Red-Wolf's seeped into other competing urges; in his case, sexual. He stirred between his legs just watching Two stride down the walk swinging her diving shoes. His desire for her was so strong that it dragged him like a tethered calf in her direction. As the weeks went on, it was all he could do to attend to his work, take orders from Mr. Lovett, and go where he was told. And when he first used his Indian name in writing to Two, he experienced an emotional release that erupted into a sexual emission. He poured a bucket of water over the front of his pants to disguise that situation.

When Two didn't signal him at the buffalo pen, his left eye, which twitched when he was nervous or, sometimes, when it pleased, had fluttered rapidly. He'd been determined to approach her, nevertheless. Was headed in her direction when the noisy boys arrived and she started walking away. He'd stopped, watched her leave, and spent the rest of his day mired in despondency, irritation, and irrationality. By suppertime, he'd decided only a late night excursion could lift his spirits. He had some trouble determining where that should be. To go back to the park and watch Two in her dorm room was his first inclination. He had, on a few occasions, climbed into the lightning-damaged catalpa and sat on its bridge for hours. Twice, he'd seen her undress. Both times, it'd been dark enough for him to relieve his stress without soiling his clothes.

But Strong-Red-Wolf was cross with Two. He felt personally snubbed. He didn't know Two had left Chambliss that morning to meet with Mr. Shackleford, and he assumed she'd gotten his note, and had come to the buffalo pen and not signaled just to humiliate him. Somewhere inside, he thought that theory might not be quite logical, but he was in too much of a dither to sort out another explanation, and he did indulge in another kind of nighttime excursion in the park.

He'd made that same type of exploration since childhood, but then in broad daylight, as there was no reason at the time to hide what he was doing. But Glendale was different from the farmland and woods he was accustomed to. He kept in his apartment a burlap sack, a crowbar, a small shovel, a few rags, and a lantern-shaped battery torch of a modern design. A month in the past, he'd discovered his mark while sussing the park, so near midnight when he crept onto the grounds, he knew where to enter to avoid Bobby Minton, the watchman, and to stay away from the wider paths, which were illuminated dimly at night by lights atop tall poles.

The place he headed to was in a dark part of the park. Specifically, it was the same copse covering the cave that Mr. Shackleford, Duncan Shelton, and Two had visited earlier that day. Only after he slipped into the thicket did he switch on his light. His heart beat hard in his chest. His eye twitch, twitch, twitched. Though it was the coolest night in several, his undershirt stuck to his chest with sweat. Strong-Red-Wolf was nervous about getting caught, and even more afraid of lurkers beyond himself. Mr. Lovett had all uncaged snakes removed to the Overton Hills as soon as they were spotted. But that was fairly often. And copperheads, in particular, like shrubbery, and retreat to its warmth to sleep. Strong-Red-Wolf used his crowbar to rattle bushes and fallen leaves. Even though the snakes would be sluggish because of the weather, he listened for movement. When he was sure what he heard was only his breathing, he turned his attention to his mission.

Which was to pry open the casket in the thicket, see if it contained treasures, and steal them if it did. Strong-Red-Wolf had an East Tennessee contact who was willing to pay for any artifact he could find, and he had, during the day, heard about the new plan for the turtles. As Mr. Shelton usually quickly did whatever Mr. Shackleford ordered, he needed to get in there before the fence was reinforced with wire. He slid deeper in between bushes toward the cave before finding the grave.

Like many of its kind, the stone box partially protruded out of the ground. Strong-Red-Wolf set his sack down by his feet and rested his battery-powered lantern on the flat stone top. He lit a cigarette and took long drags to steady his nerves. When he finished smoking, he knelt and lowered the light. Inspected the edges where the standing sides met the slab top. He wanted to pry the lid off at a place that wouldn't be easily detected. He fingered the edges and found a spot where a side slab dipped, picked up his crowbar, and shoved it in that dent. He stood up and pushed forward.

The top slab moved a little. Strong-Red-Wolf pulled, tugged, and shoved more, but the slab moved too far. It hit the ground and cracked. Strong-Red-Wolf froze. Listened for sounds outside the thicket. Heard none. Then picked up his light, walked around the casket, and looked down. The slab was in two pieces. Strong-Red-Wolf rubbed a hand over his eye. Stretched the lid to keep it from twitching. He set the light down and lit another cigarette. He turned his back to the crypt and smoked until he was calm and had decided two slabs would be half as hard to lift back into place.

Strong-Red-Wolf stubbed his cigarette out on a piece of broken slab and peered into the open grave. He lowered his light in. He'd expected to see dirt. Most of the boxes were filled with it; but all weren't, and not this one. Instead, the empty sockets of the skull looked up. The hole of the nose seemed like a lower third eye. Strong-Red-Wolf shivered and pulled his lantern back. He hadn't expected to see a head without digging. It gave him the creeps. It also made him worry that his effort was foiled; that the grave had already been robbed.

He peered back in and saw the head again. Twitched from his eyelid to the base of his spine. Looked quickly at the feet. The phalanges and metatarsals lay flat on the earth. Some were detached from others, but the bones of the ankles were still connected. The tibias and fibulas, also. And beyond them, up, the patellas and femurs were still joined. The length of the legs made the body seem male. But Strong-Red-Wolf had learned at the University of Tennessee that pelvises are key, and that inspection would take more time than he had to devote. He moved his lantern to his left hand and used it to block the face. Then he spied something in the rib cage. A round shell. A gorget cut with a design. What was it? Strong-Red-Wolf twisted his head. Two carved rows of circles; in the center, perhaps a snake. He reached in and gently lifted the ornament from between the bones. Softly pressed it with his thumb. It was still sturdy. He let out a long sigh. Then he set the light down, wrapped the gorget in rags, and slipped it into his sack.

Strong-Red-Wolf's confidence was ignited by his find, and he examined the remains of the face without any more fear than he'd had looking at the feet. The head was brachycephalic, as he'd expected and had learned in school. If he turned the skull over, its occiput would be flat. He knew that, too. So he didn't hook a finger through a socket. He lifted the scapula closest to him and checked under it for small treasures such as beads. Finding none, he lifted the second scapula and then the pelvis. He was about to give up when he saw, in the dirt between the ribs, an arrowhead peeking out. He carefully pinched it up. The back of his hand brushed against only one bone.

The arrowhead was unbroken, but he found nothing else. If the Indian had been buried with a pipe or effigy vessels, those had been already taken. Still, he felt lucky. He sat back on his haunches, pushed his glasses up the bridge of his nose, and congratulated himself for work well done. He even said to the bones, "Thanks, brother. You did well for me tonight. Happy hunting."

Up
at
Longview

≡

The next afternoon, about an hour before Two was scheduled to dive, Mr. Shackleford finished a conversation with one of his attorneys and carefully replaced the receiver in its holder. He crept to the door of his study, looked around his large living room and dining room, up the staircase, and out a window to the front porch, trying to assure himself he hadn't been overheard. He couldn't see every nook and cranny because he didn't want to stray far and get engaged in some sort of conversation, and his home was quite large.

The oldest part had been built in 1845 by Henry Norvell for his wife, Laura, a granddaughter of John Sevier, the first governor of Tennessee and a proficient Indian killer. Even then, the house had been big for its time, and it was situated on a hill overlooking a creek, and close to an ancient, great mound. Henry's slaves had planted extensive orchards and vineyards, and Laura had overseen their bedding of rows and rows of roses. The slaves did excellent work, and nature took care of the rest. The grounds grew lush, and Henry and Laura grew proud of their home and its surroundings. They christened the estate Leafy Lot.

But along came the Civil War. The Norvells fled Leafy Lot ahead of the Federal invasion. Nearly three years later, the house was confiscated for the Battle of Nashville and occupied by Confederate General John B. Hood and his officers. The ragged, war-weary Army of Tennessee camped all around on its grounds. By the time Hood's men retreated in defeat (again), the house was worse for the wear, and the property was pocked with trenches and dirt breastworks girdled by newly hewed planks from the orchards and the old-growth forest. The destruction was so great that for a decade thereafter the estate was referred to as Hood's Waste.

When Mr. Shackleford bought the waste in 1878, he renamed it Longview and felt proud because he'd gotten it cheap and it already had an interesting history. Slowly, as he and May accumulated money, children, and assorted resident relatives, they had the house expanded, the trenches filled in, and the breastworks dismantled. They also had the stumps dug up and replaced with new trees, and had new gardens planted. The children collected the Minié balls, buttons, and buckles strewed around the grounds; however, to dig out the cannonballs, the Shacklefords brought in professionals.

By 1926, the house had been expanded even more, updated, and decorated with the finest furnishings available. It was large enough to accommodate parties of six hundred guests. Even on guestless days, the house was rarely empty or silent. Fortunately, Mr. Shackleford's widower son, Charles, and his two daughters had decamped to their summer home on the Mississippi Gulf, but grandchildren and grandnieces and nephews who lived in the neighboring houses ran in and out. And, of course, there were the maids and the cook. But on that day, after he hung the telephone up, from his study's door, Mr. Shackleford didn't see anyone who could've overheard his conversation, so he straightway started to the kitchen to escape out that door. He'd gotten about ten steps when a voice behind him said, "Your mail's on the tray."

His muscles tightened. He turned around and found Adelaide, their housekeeper and head maid. He said, "Hum." His eyebrows lifted, his eyes widened, he tried to keep his fingers from moving. "You don't say."

Adelaide had known Mr. James a very long time. She said, "I do say. It ran early today."

"Did you just bring it in?"

Adelaide shook her head. "Waz a few minutes ago."

Mr. Shackleford wanted to say, "So you heard my conversation?" But he didn't, as he didn't want to hear a yes, and, anyway, Adelaide heard a great deal and was expected to keep it all to herself. He said instead, "Do you happen to know the whereabouts of Mrs. May?"

"I believe she's visiting Miz Maggie. There's some sort of committee over there."

"Hum," James said again. "I'm going to take some air. If she comes in looking for me, I'm in the gardens."

"Yes, sir. It's a nice day. Enjoy yourself. Take the burden off."

James breathed in. Was Adelaide hinting she'd heard the conversation? She was often indirect. And the conversation had been about Lewis, and he was her favorite. He breathed out hard. It never paid to get in too deep with Adelaide. She could be like a swamp, and did have opinions. He said, "I will," exited the room for the kitchen, and was relieved not to run into his cook. He left the house by that door without retrieving his jacket.

James walked an iris-lined path to a secluded bench overlooking the creek. There he sat down to soak in the solitude. The babbling stream soothed him, but, presently, he began fiddling with the stub of his left hand's middle finger. Rubbing that stub was practically a lifelong habit, as he was only four when he lost the finger to a hatchet-wielding six-year-old sister. Not a murderous act; a playful one. She'd been chopping sticks, and his finger had darted out in the way. Perhaps, also, in an effort to play. In 1858, Mr. Shackleford liked to say, children had to make do because they didn't have many toys.

The adults made do, too. James's mother snatched the finger from the planks of the porch and tried to reattach it. But they were out in the country near Yazoo, Mississippi, and there wasn't a hospital or, really, an actual medical professional anywhere around. People, even rich ones, doctored with home remedies and concoctions rooted in voodoo and shared by their slaves. Not surprisingly, the finger didn't stick. Soon after the stub healed, James developed a habit of rubbing the remnant while worrying.

Which is what he was doing that day about Lewis, a middle child, and one of only four he had left. The other six had died at various times. Two daughters, born one right after the other, and dead just as quickly, each at two years. Then, three adult sons gone within an eighteen-month span during the first decade of the century, one death expected, two certainly not. Then in 1918, Danny, their youngest, on the mend from the Spanish influenza, died suddenly of meningitis in an army hospital. Mr. Shackleford grieved his dead children every day. Often the three boys together, as those deaths came like rapid punches from a robber in a dark alley at night. But Danny he grieved alone, as he was his favorite and the most recently deceased. His little girls had been dead a long time, but they still ruined his sleep by crying in their cribs at night, and awakening him so thoroughly that he invariably checked their room, and then often had to read until light.

But Lewis was very much, sometimes too much, alive. And Mr. Shackleford could find him severely irritating. As a tike, Lewis had seemed similar to his siblings. A tag-along to his older brothers. Mostly obedient, and kind to his mother. But then there was the mule incident. James rubbed his stub harder while reflecting on that. The mule had gone missing from Oliver Noel's farm. Probably taken only to ride, from someone considered an uncle. But not returned. And it was a working mule, prized for its intelligence, diligence, and willing spirit.

Oliver's men began searching for the animal. High and low. Far and wide. But to no avail. Finally, Oliver, who was particularly fond of the mule, advertised a reward in the paper. Two days later, the mule appeared in the drive ridden by Lewis, who claimed he'd found it down by a spring, munching grass, as mules do in their leisure. Lewis asked for the reward, and Oliver, who was famously tight with his money, paid it, but warned James, "I'd keep an eye on that one."

Mr. Shackleford tried, but never got the particulars of the mule crime. However, he didn't need them. He knew the outline; also knew the writing that warns on the wall. He would've begun watching Lewis even without Oliver's advice. He determined while the boy was still in knickers that he had a shifty disposition. Watched that guile grow as Lewis added inches. Had to admit a sprinkle of shiftiness in his son was an asset. One he was currently exploiting in creative business endeavors and, perhaps, one inherited from himself. But his wasn't excessive in his estimation. He'd worked for his money. Worked in the cold, worked in the heat, worked while others had cavorted.

Lewis had not. He'd always charmed and cajoled his siblings, the help, and his friends into doing his work for him. Made everybody feel special and needed. Harvested the big rewards for himself. But it wasn't that Lewis was greedy in the traditional sense. He gave away far too much money for that. It was that he was ... James rubbed his stub again and experienced a moment of self-doubt. Was he jealous of his boy? He'd wondered that previously. He bit his lip and thought not. But why, then, did it cross his mind again? Maybe it was because he was, by nature, introspective, careful in drawing conclusions. Which was true. But it was also true that Lewis, though still only in his thirties, was more successful than he. He was president of Shackleford and Company, a municipal bond concern that dealt in eight-digit figures in seven Southern states. He also owned insurance companies, a tractor company, an oil company, and the Bank of Tennessee, a shell which he'd cleverly set up to sift money. He was referred to, both in private and in print, as "the J. P. Morgan of the South."

Mr. Shackleford's fingers moved from rubbing his stub to smoothing his beard, though there wasn't a hair out of place. He didn't like that comparison. Bristled when it was mentioned in his presence. He'd known Morgan. Thought he didn't have an honest bone in his body. Could list his swindles in detail. Often did. And, anyway, the comparison felt diminishing. It lessened his own accomplishments. He'd been the one who'd erected a financial empire out of the ruins of the Civil War. Created something from nothing. Supplied Lewis with his capital and connections.

However, at the moment all of that was beside the point. The present problem was a yearling Lewis had bought in Lexington, Kentucky. He'd paid forty-five thousand dollars for the horse. Entirely too much. Particularly for a colt out of a mare with no proven pedigree. And that wasn't the half of it. The sire, Zev, though a Kentucky Derby winner, was an unproven stud. But, still, that wasn't the full extent of the problem. Zev was owned by Harry Sinclair, who couldn't stay out of court, congressional hearings, or headlines. Mr. Shackleford didn't like bad publicity, and was certain the yearling (still in Kentucky) was horsehair evidence of some sort of alliance between Lewis and Sinclair. But he didn't know what kind. And didn't know how to address the subject with his son. Lewis was a very grown man. And Mr. Shackleford had come by the horse information by having him spied upon.

The spy, a man he'd never met, and whose name he didn't know, had been employed by his most trusted lawyer for the obvious reason of keeping him at arm's length. The arrangement had been in place for over a year. There had been, and still were, other matters that called for investigation. But on this one, James felt a compulsion to act. And for the first time, he was confronted with the problem of how to best use information he'd obtained surreptitiously on his son.

But, also, information often takes on symbolic meaning. And this colt, who hadn't yet been named, was doing just that. Mr. Shackleford made up a moniker, Burnt Money, while massaging his stump. Then his mind flooded with cascading catastrophes that could be brought on by the shifty ways of his spendthrift, successful son. Mr. Shackleford propelled himself off his bench and started on a brisk walk toward Glendale, trying to relieve his mind.

Hazardous
Business

≡

Two walked the ramp to the platform scanning the planks for anything that might trip Ocher up. The slope ascended forty feet at a forty-five-degree angle. There was a gate on the ground that Two had unlocked, so there wasn't really much chance the ramp had changed in any way since the previous evening. But Two knew she was in a hazardous business, and never skipped her professional routines. Doc Carver had taught her that. He'd attended to every detail. After careful study, had determined that the pool of water should be forty feet long, twenty feet wide, and eleven feet deep. The dimensions were the same at Atlantic City, in Omaha, and out in Seattle. Carver had realized there are few things more dangerous than a large animal fearful of drowning and did everything he could to perfect his tricks. So in the forty years of horse diving before 1926, no horse had ever been injured or killed.

However, several riders had suffered serious injuries. So at the top of the ramp, Two scanned the platform's rails for weaknesses or any breaks in the padding. Then she stepped out into the open and checked the pool, the hooks, and the canvas. The bleachers were already fairly full.

Two saw that out of the sides of her eyes. But she ignored the crowd as usual, so she didn't see the redheaded man in the khaki uniform standing on the ground beside the easternmost bleacher.

Two was wearing sandals that day, so she just kicked them off, and put on her diving socks and shoes without sitting down on the boards. After that, she dropped her sandals and robe through the hatch and watched them hit the washtub. Then she limbered up. She saw Crawford and Ocher appear in the distance. Two kept stretching while they slowly walked toward her, accumulating admirers and followers along the way, but her concentration was focused, as it had to be. So when she went out to wave to the crowd, she was unaware that the redheaded man had moved from near the bleacher to the gate she'd left open, and unaware he'd entered, and walked to beneath the platform. And because the boards were tightly fitted together and the construction solid with no cracks, she didn't know he was peering up.

When she went back into the privacy of the cover over the platform, she did hear Crawford call to someone. But she didn't give that any mind. Everybody who worked in the zoo knew Crawford, and so did many of the visitors. People were always calling to him, and he was always calling back. Two started her visualizing. Hoped she'd get through that completely before Crawford yelled up "Three" to her. And she did. In fact, she'd begun wondering what Crawford was doing by the time she finally heard the signal.

The dive went off perfectly. And since it was the afternoon one, not the last of the day, Two gathered her robe, stuck a sandal in each pocket, and signed autographs, while Crawford took Ocher back to the barn. So they didn't talk, and if they had, Crawford might not have thought to mention that he'd found the college hire under the platform peering into the washtub. It seemed strange, but Jack Older was an employee, and when he'd said he'd been asked to inspect the diving structure from the ground, Crawford hadn't given his reason much thought. His mind had been mostly on Bonita.

Visiting
the
Ill

≡

Though Mr. Shackleford had set off walking toward the zoo, he didn't walk far. At the road just beyond his lawn, a fellow he knew stopped and gave him a lift. Their route down Shackleford Lane passed the Oriental Golf Club and turned south onto a street to the park so new it hadn't been named. Shackleford asked to be let out at a spot near the buffalo pen. He thanked his friend, kept his mind off of Lewis by ruminating on bison near the fence, and wound up, fairly quickly, at the sick hippopotamus's den.

Dinah was out of the water, in the platform's shade near Methuselah. Her eyes were closed, her breathing practically imperceptible. She appeared to be sleeping. Mr. Shackleford focused on an ear. Was it droopy? He tried to recall how hippo ears should appear. His conviction was firm that mule and dog ears provided accurate clues to their health. He pictured his first hound, acquired through his father's death. When healthy, Beau's ears were pink inside; gray or red when he wasn't. James turned over his pet's ear. Saw it clearly. Saw Beau, too. Rummaging, sniffing, and howling.

They all—his mother, his siblings, the slaves, and the livestock— were on a trek through woods, dodging swampy water where they could, fleeing for their lives. But their wagon wheels often stuck in mud and had to be pushed and tugged. Behind them, flames danced on the river. Two steamboats (they learned later) had been lit by the Confederates as a blockade. Fire was also in front of them. They knew at the time those flames were the cotton house, torched by the Federals. They were deep in marshy woods, squeezed by armies burning the world. Not knowing which way to turn.

Beau kept howling. And the Federals were prowling. His mother threatened to shoot his pet. James and his brother, Alex, hid Beau under a quilt on the wagon. The hound toned down, merely whimpered, and didn't get shot. But next, their mother threatened to shoot one of their slaves, who, inopportunely, was gathering a rebellion. He didn't get shot either, or run away. They did, however, lose two goats while fleeing. One to a broken leg, the other probably to a hungry soldier scouting out in the woods. James didn't remember his father clearly enough to mourn his death, but the goats were his friends, and he grieved them long after they were gone.

And he still hated losing animals. Hoped he didn't lose the hippopotamus. But beyond his true affection for the lesser creatures was the matter of competition. Dinah had been purchased from the Overton Park Zoo in Memphis. James knew a lot of the best people in Memphis (and none of the others): bankers, businessmen, and members of the board of that zoo. It was larger than Glendale, and world-renowned for its hippopotamus breeding compound. If he couldn't keep a single hippo alive, he'd look like an incompetent idiot. James couldn't stand even a whiff of idiocy, and he really couldn't stand Memphis. It was a crass, common, mediocre riverboat town. Even if it had been the first refuge his mother had found. He grumbled. Scuffed a pebble with his shoe. Said to Dinah, "Don't dare die on me. We'll figure it out."

James turned, walked a small rise, passed picnic grounds, croquet and tennis courts, sliding boards, swings, and seesaws. He walked over the trolley tracks. The entire terrain was sprinkled with large trees, tall poles of lights, and brightly painted fences, all of which cost a small fortune in upkeep. He marched straight ahead, off the path, through grass, and he kept walking until he reached a log cabin. There, he stopped, turned, and gazed over the park at the casino cupolas, the bird cages, the bandstand, and, far off, the water tank, and the horse diving platform. Miss Two Feathers was out there, waving. He imagined her crowd as large, and imagined, too, attractions long gone. The Flying Jenny, the roller coaster, and the Roulette Wheel, a spinning contraption he'd never taken to. However, for the most part, Mr. Shackleford loved his park and zoo.

And he loved the man in the log cabin, too. The man he was about to disturb. Clive Lovett, the manager of the park and the keeper of the zoo. Clive was currently ill with something more serious than the cover story of a severe cold. In fact, Lovett was so ill that James didn't know if he would answer his knock. He hesitated before he stepped onto the porch. Fidgeted with his cuff, rubbed his stub, and muttered his dismay at the way Lovett insisted upon living — in a log cabin consisting of two ancient rooms, a kitchen and a bathroom added. Not the kind of house the manager ought to inhabit, the kind his salary would buy, his background would predict, or an affable gentleman should maintain to entertain, even as a bachelor.

Lovett was adored by animals, birds, and children. He could, by his touch, calm any frightened creature. And had, by rigorous study, mastered the foods and comforts that kept his tenants easy to manage and, in some cases (those of cranes, bears, and sea lions), eager to entertain. Children saw him as a master of animal tricks and a reliable source of baby chicks, ducklings, and rabbits. Mothers liked Lovett, too, and eagerly pushed their offspring toward him. Thought him kind, gentle, and the perfect model for kiddies who often didn't see daddies except at breakfast and late after work.

As for men, Lovett was respected by all. Nashville, that is, genteel Nashville, the only Nashville James knew (or cared to know), was not an open circle. Preferably, one was descended from the original pioneer stock. Or, like himself, had arrived after the great conflict and helped rebuild the city. Rarely could anyone from afar find acceptance in a single generation. But Lovett had been sponsored by Percy Warner himself, who'd discovered him in Colorado tending an exotic bird collection. Warner, whose father had built Warner Iron, and who'd made his own money in utilities, had bought the birds and moved them to Nashville. He'd moved Lovett, too. And he'd convinced James that the park should take his birds and their keeper and become a zoo.

Lovett wasn't a Coloradoan by birth. He was an Englishman, and Britain still ruled most of the world. The best people in Nashville considered themselves descended from British stock, true or not. When the Great War erupted, Lovett was managing the zoo, tending, by that time, to animals as well as to birds, and running the entire park, not a small operation. He could've shrugged off his patriotic duty. Missed his conscription. Instead, he quit his job, returned to his country, and was shipped from England to the continent. He fought the bloody battle. Twice he went missing in action. Twice he was wounded. And, yet, when the war was over, he returned to the zoo as though he had merely been away on holiday. No mention of what he'd been through.

And that, James knew, was at the root of Clive's illness. Every so often, the congenial, gregarious personality disappeared, and so did Lovett, into his cabin. Not to come out. Not to be disturbed. Until, without a word, he'd reappear in the park. Usually at the bears' den, where, inside the bars, he'd offer the oldest, Zana and Zerle, chewing gum sticks from between his own teeth. Then he'd lure Tom Noddy, the juvenile cinnamon, out of the enclosure with peanuts so children could pet him and, to the delight of both humans and the cub, would walk Tom on a leash through the entire park. A parade of children would follow them. Clive and the little reddish bear were welcome everywhere.

James knew to the marrow in his bones what war does to people. He had lived frightened every day as a child. Been reduced to poverty and near starvation. Ridden his mule past countless stinking bodies, braced himself against the ever-present possibility of robbery, the depravations of desperate people, the brutality of morally righteous victors. He'd hardened to survive. But well over a half century later, he still woke up at night running through woods, pursued by invisible bushwhackers, deserters, and Yankees.

So James had a deep, terrible, and abiding respect for the effects of war. He paid Clive Lovett when he wasn't able to work and averted his eyes to his illness, though he wouldn't tolerate it in others. And he really needed Clive to diagnose the hippopotamus's ailment. He knocked on his door rather loudly. Stood still and listened hard. Heard behind him music, and then sudden wild applause. Probably from the diving event. Also, closer, he heard shouts of children. And piercing shrieks from the peacocks and cranes that roamed the park and occasionally picked fights. James tried to point his ears forward, away from shrieks, shouts, and applause. Toward the wood of the door, to hear a creak, a squeak of a board. He waited, mustache twitching, rubbing his stumpy digit with that same hand's thumb. He stifled the impulse to knock again, backed up, turned, and strode away. Told himself that a man has a right to his privacy. Told himself, too, that Lovett had earned his solitude. But he tried not to imagine what he might've found had the door opened. Clive was usually meticulous in dress, demeanor, and possessions. However, when a bad cold overtook him ... Shackleford shook his head. He'd never been in Lovett's cabin when he was sick, and had shut off the speaker of the single report he'd been given.

Beyond what he considered good business, James didn't tolerate vices. Neither physical, mental, nor moral. He didn't even allow his employees the privilege of smoking. That included on their own time outside of work—at least with his knowledge. He was certain cigarettes dulled ambition and blunted usefulness almost as surely as novels. He tolerated only expensive cigars and exotic-bowled pipes. He occasionally enjoyed the latter himself. Claimed it aided his concentration. When his daughter, Elsie, who was tired of smoking in secret, had challenged him on the difference between his habit and cigarettes, he'd replied, "That just demonstrates how little of the world you've actually observed."

Mr. Shackleford turned his mind back to his children as he walked the path toward the trolley tracks. Elsie was in Monteagle for the summer, taking mountain air with other Nashville widows, matrons, and maidens. Charles was at his home on the Gulf, enjoying the breezes, and providing some relief for his parents. Meredith was, on that particular day, buying a farm in Franklin. With those three out of the scene, James focused again solely on Lewis.

Clive Lovett watched James's back through a wavy window as he walked away. He'd been sober for a day and a half, but was wearing a stubble and was unsure his hand was yet steady enough to shave. He turned from the glass, picked up a teacup from his eating table, walked to the kitchen, and poured cold tea down the drain. Then he turned on the flame under a kettle, and began sweeping the floor to keep from watching the water heat up. When the whistle blew, Clive turned the flame to a flicker, swept a line of dirt into a dustpan, and dumped it into a bin. He used a holey infuser to pinch tea leaves from a tin, placed the metal contraption in a clean cup, and poured water in. After whistling "Hush, Here Comes a Whizzbang" twice over — a length of time he'd discovered was perfect when brewing a solo cup — he removed the infuser and added milk. Comforted by the ritual and song, he carefully trod with the tea to his bedroom. He propped himself up on pillows and took up a volume he'd left off when disturbed by James's knock. Matthew Arnold; his sonnets.

Things
Unseen

===

When Two came in from her dive, the Juggling Juggernauts were huddled on a main parlor sofa with their heads folded over a newspaper. Two walked over and asked, "Whatcha reading?"

"Sister's gone missing." Franny looked up, eyes wide.

"She's drowned." Marty punched the *Tennessean* with her forefinger.

"No, she hasn't. The police are investigating." Franny said that to Marty.

"Let me see." Two reached.

The evangelist, Aimee Semple McPherson, had apparently drowned while swimming at the Santa Monica Beach. However, the police were working the case. After the missing person's report was filed, a detective had seen Sister and another woman headed toward Los Angeles in a car. Two women reported seeing her hand a note to two men at a hotel near the beach. Scattered sources claimed that underworld mobsters had threatened her life over her condemnation of Sunday dancing. A true believer had seen her walking on water. Two finished reading. Said, "How long's she been gone? I didn't even know she was missing."

Franny said, "This is the first we've read of it. This crummy paper never prints anything important. We oughta get a copy of the *Banner*."

Marty said, "Careful, sis. You'll get us fired." The *Nashville Tennessean* was owned and published by Percy Warner's son-in-law, Luke Lea. Copies of it were delivered to the dorm every morning. The paper was in a perpetual war with the afternoon paper, the *Nashville Banner*, which the park didn't subscribe to, but which was often left on benches.

"The furniture dealers are in town," Two said. "That's the big story." They all were well aware of the dealers' convention. Four conventioneers had been removed from the casino for inebriated behavior. Another had fallen into the sea lions' water. Everybody at Glendale was glad the salesmen were leaving that afternoon.

"We saw her in Buffalo, and in Baltimore and Pittsburg," Marty said.

"In Albany, too," added Franny.

"Did ya get healed?" Two'd seen the preacher at the ranch, as a guest of the Millers, watching the show. She'd never attended a revival and didn't intend to go. But she associated Christianity more with thievery than trickery, which was what she assumed the evangelist was up to.

The Montgomery sisters (really the Mondelli sisters) were Catholics-in-hiding on the road. The Ku Klux Klan was persecuting "Pope-lovers" all over the country, and the girls' parents worried about them traveling with their crucifixes and rosary beads. They posed as Episcopalians and, hit or miss on Sundays, attended Presbyterian services in the chapel in Burgess Hall. But they shared with millions of low-church devotees a fascination with the miracles the female fundamentalist evangelist performed. And as entertainers, they were captivated by her showmanship, energy, and ability to cradle audiences of thousands in the palms of her hands. They debated between themselves about how she mesmerized her crowds. Franny thought people felt the spirit of Jesus in her. Marty thought they sensed her sexual, animal attraction. Whichever, the preacher was a national sensation. The most famous woman in America. And one of the few people anywhere at any time who could be called by a single name, Sister, and be universally recognized.

In answer to Two's question, Franny replied, "We weren't sick. But a lot of people were. And she healed them. I swear. In Albany, we watched her do it for four hours. She was still at it when we left."

"Then why'd she quit?" Two plopped down in a chair across from the women.

"We heard she got tired. And thought the healing was detracting from the saving of souls. The body's just a vessel. The important thing's the spirit."

Two went blank-faced. She didn't have any formal religion. Small-pox had wiped out most of the Cherokee shamans in the early 1700s, and whites had systematically assaulted the tribe's spiritual beliefs ever since. Many Cherokees had converted to get along, but Two's family hadn't. They nodded at Christians and tried not to do anything to get their attention.

Two did, however, agree with Franny that the important thing is spirit. She sensed animal spirits, both collectively and individually. But she also felt spirits in creeks, springs, rivers, and rocks. She sensed some places were sources of strength, others were haunted. She also believed in what her grandparents called "witches." Believed they could take on the disguise of either sex, were most often old, but could be younger, were very tricky, and always up to no good. She thought witches could even kill or cause deaths that appeared accidental. She never spoke about animal spirits, place spirits, or witches at Glendale. She understood that whites had opinions about who had souls and who didn't, and that some-times even other people fell into their soulless pigeonhole. She knew, too, that whites took their religion seriously and, if challenged, could turn dangerous. But she'd never completely figured out what might send a white into some sort of Jesus fit. So she just stayed as far away from the subject of religion as she could get.

She was already thinking about changing the subject to something else when Marty zagged in another direction. "She had the largest hands of any woman I've ever seen. If we had hands like that, we'd never drop a plate."

Franny, who'd dropped a plate not two hours in the past, understood Marty's swerve. And she didn't want to go down that path. "Don't say 'had.' I'll believe she's still alive 'til we hear for sure she's not."

Two nodded as she'd done before. But Marty said, "Maybe we should discuss this now." She wasn't talking about Sister. She figured in front of Two the plate-dropping subject had less chance of devolving into a fight.

However, Franny stood, said, "I'm going to the room," and off she went.

Marty raised an eyebrow. "See?"

See? wasn't much of a cue, but sufficed. Two said, "What're ya gonna do?"

"She won't talk. I don't know what to do. Unless maybe you . . ."

That was no surprise. Two breathed in deeply. "I'll try. Sometimes people just suddenly get spooked. Notice the crowd. Or something, I don't know. But can't do their tricks. Start missing their shots, or whatever. When that happens on the ranch, one of the Millers takes ya aside, and gives ya a talking to. Then a little time to adjust your attitude. Sometimes, it works. Sometimes, people pick up their saddle and ride off. But I don't know what's said. It's never happened to anybody I know very well."

"But you'll try?"

"I'll haveta get an opening."

"Can you make it soon?"

"I can't make one. They come or not."

Marty stayed in the parlor, and Two went up to her room and wrote a letter home. When done, she plucked her novel off her desk and plopped down on the end of her bed on a pillow propped against the lid of her trunk. The pages opened to the envelope she'd tucked in there. She read that letter again and then gazed out the window at the tops of distant trees and the roof of Burgess Hall. Two frowned. The buffalo pen was a favorite spot of hers in the zoo. Somebody else seemed to know that, too. A shimmy ran through Two's shoulders. Was she being watched?

Two occasionally felt corralled by admirers. That was part of being a performer and, maybe, her fault as much as theirs. She was, by nature or rearing, restrained. But she liked her fans, and had been raised with an excellent example of how to cope with them. She modeled herself on Will Rogers, a fellow Cherokee and a friend of her family's. Will was celebrated for saying he'd never met a man he didn't like. Two couldn't honestly say that. But she tried hard to be nice to people, and was usually successful.

Two shook off her suspicion and concentrated, instead, on the old buffalo trace mentioned in the letter. Was that true? Was an ancient trail right there under her nose? The idea knocked her pride and made blood rise to her face. Surely she would've noticed it. She'd been taught to read the ground. Was she losing that skill? Her grandparents would frown. Her father would run his tongue around his lower teeth and cock his eyebrow. Two got up, went to the door, and looked at a clock on the wall at the end of the hall. She had time to hunt for the trace. She could also visit Adam.

She was looking for an indentation in the ground. It could run for hundreds of miles or, sometimes, just between a body of water and a salt lick. Two had previously picked up that the site for the settlement that became Nashville was selected, in part, because it was close to a large lick. With that recollection in the front of her mind, she decided the path, if there really was one, would run toward Nashville, rather than east and west. Chambliss was east of the buffalo pen, so Two headed northwest with her eyes to the ground.

And to her surprise, she found a slight indentation rather quickly. It was about four feet wide, and headed through the grass and under graveled paths toward the buffalo enclosure. At first, Two was amazed she'd never noticed it. But, really, it was faint, and if a person wasn't looking for it, or didn't know it was there, it could easily be missed. Strong-Red-Wolf had told the truth, and Two's shoulder blades folded and dropped with that realization. She turned around to see if she was being followed. She saw children, a covey of women, and youngsters running a sack race in the field. But no strange man pretending to be an Indian. Or no strange man at all. And nobody paying her any attention. She turned back around. Took a deep breath. The buffalo's path was plain in the grass and stretched out before her until it crossed a rise. Two's feet tingled all the way up to her thighs. She heard the thunder of ancient hooves pounding the ground. They shook her legs, her backbone, and her ribs. She hopped out of the path, but a drum beat in her chest. She'd go tell Adam. Then she'd go to the barn and tell Crawford.

When Two got to the barn, Crawford was standing outside the doors with a white woman, a young boy, a mare, and a Shetland pony. Two sailed inside, avoiding their eyes, and straight into Ocher's stall. She scratched her horse's cheek and neck while she eavesdropped. Crawford had just shoed the pony. It'd either been bought from the park in the past or won in an Easter egg hunt. The woman was talking about how much her sons loved to ride. Ocher snorted and Two missed Crawford's reply. Then she heard, "Hank, thank you so much. It's so good to see you again. The Squire built all our fences. My father always says he was the best mason in Tennessee."

"Thank you. Daddy was high on Mr. Kirkman. Give him my best. His fences holding up?"

"They'll be here long after you and I are gone. How're your brothers and sisters, and where are they?"

"They're doing well, thank you. Q's in Chicago. Robert and Hattie are in California. Sam's in Indianapolis. Ellen's in New York, and Noel's in Washington, D.C. The other girls are married and settled in Nashville. Josh, Trimble, and I are holding the fort out here in the hills."

"My, that's good to hear. Ellen and I are the same age. We used to play dolls. Please remember me to her and to your mother."

"I certainly will. And you come on back if you have any trouble. You know how to find me."

The woman left and Two came out of the stall. She said, "Who was she?"

"Miz Betsy Kirkman VanLeer. Her father's land is due south of here, on Otter Creek. I used to hunt his part of the creek for ducks as a boy. Whatcha up to?"

Two was curious about the woman. She was high fashion, and upper crust. And she'd called Crawford Hank. But, at the moment, she was more interested in finding out what kind of person might know about the buffalo trace. She told Crawford about it, but not about the note. She asked if the path was common knowledge.

Crawford opened the lid of a large wooden toolbox. Laid in a rasp. "Never heard of it myself. But the buffalo ran through here. Granny White's built on a trace."

"Who's Granny White?"

He shut the lid. "It's a road."

"Where?"

Crawford jerked his head toward the back wall of the barn. "That way. Less than a mile by the crow."

"Ya know anybody who might know about this one?"

"Mama could. I'll ask her."

Satisfied with the answer, Two said, "That woman thinks highly of your family."

Crawford picked a horseshoe up off a bench. "The Kirkmans and VanLeers are nice folks. Their clans are as large as the Shacklefords, and go further back. Real *sure 'nuf* gentry." Crawford chuckled, hung the shoe on a nail, and challenged Two to a game of gin rummy.

She was down twenty-five cents when they stopped to prepare for the show. After it, she changed clothes and met Crawford back at the barn to brush down Ocher for the night. When they left the stall, to pin Crawford's promise in his mind, Two said, "Thanks for asking your mother about that buffalo trail." When he closed the barn door, she said, "That woman called ya Hank."

Crawford tugged on the lock. "That's 'cause I know her from childhood. I just use Crawford for work."

Clive
Emerges

On Saturday morning, Clive Lovett fully drew back his curtains for the first time in days. He squinted with the sight of light and looked down at his shaded porch. A bunny was making a breakfast of a potted geranium. The darn rabbits were everywhere. And Clive loved every one of them. However, he loved his geraniums, too. And they were tender and just broken to bloom. Clive huffed, "Boo!" The rabbit's ears popped up. It froze. Then scampered. Clive stretched and rolled his shoulders. He'd take a walk after breakfast.

The walk for Clive was more than a stroll. It was a reemergence into the world, the comfort of the animals, and the company of humans. He didn't fully understand the bouts that wrestled him to the floor. He'd seen it happen to other men, but never expected it to happen to him. That sort of thing didn't run in his family. As far as he knew. But he'd been orphaned so young he didn't know much generational history. Still, he'd been passed from relative to relative, taken in by quite a few. All were upstanding. None more noticeably given to spirits or ale than the general

British population. Which was quite a lot by American standards. But Clive took cultural differences into his calculations.

However, Matilda, the wife of his mother's first cousin, was prone to taking to bed. Was aroused only by salts, her husband's slaps on the back, and the pleadings of her three boys. Clive had lived with them for a year. And when he returned to England to fight, he served with the oldest of the boys, Millwood Martell. Millwood said that their father had left their mother and she'd died within months. He felt some pity for her, but mostly hostility. However, he was on loving terms with his father, and he invited Clive to come home with him after the war.

However, one morning as they were playing cards in their hole, a shell dropped in and exploded. Clive dived to his right, grabbing Millwood's arm to jerk him away from the blast. But the arm came off his body. Clive was left grasping its hand and lower remains. It was the most intact piece of Millwood left, and it took two other men to grapple it out of Clive's clutches. Another two to hold him to the ground. To keep him from climbing out of the hole to his death.

Clive was numb for a number of days. And was given a couple of buttons from Millwood's uniform. There was a surviving boot, too; but it was given to a soldier who needed it. Clive took one of the two buttons to Millwood's father when he stayed with his first cousin once removed while his own wounds took their time healing. It saddened him to leave when he did, and he promised to come back when he could. He brought the second button with him when he returned to the States. He kept it in a wooden box on his desk with three medals he'd won. He never opened the lid.

When Clive stepped onto his porch and into the world, the bunny was long gone. But the giant trees were still there, as were the flower beds, graveled walks, park sounds, and trolley tracks. A car came through. The conductor threw Clive a wave and a smile. Clive was a person everybody knew. And though mothers trusted their children with him, men took his advice, and women of all ages batted their eyes at him and blushed, he was fairly unsusceptible to human admiration. That had been true even before the Great War. He'd learned in childhood the fragility of personal attachments and had turned his love to animals instead. Their natural life spans were usually shorter than humans', but predictably so. Particularly if they were kindly cared for in a zoo.

Clive was not yet really worried about Dinah. He was accustomed to animals going off their feed, and he figured she'd eat when she got hungry. His real concern was focused on his primates. A small troop of rhesus macaques had been delivered before he fell sick. They were adolescents, and two of them male. Those were prone to fight, even if from the same colony or actual brothers. So Clive headed first toward the monkey enclosure. He was stopped repeatedly by employees and visitors glad to see him, though most didn't know he'd been under the weather. Normally, he was so busy that if he wasn't in one location, it was just naturally assumed he was in another.

When Clive finally arrived at the monkey cages, he found a crowd of flustered women, distressed children, and his college hire, Jack Older, trying, unsuccessfully, to rescue a Teddy bear from the clutches of a simian. Macaques have strong legs and opposable thumbs. These particular ones were so new to the zoo that their naming contest was still running and the suggestions scribbled on paper and stuffed in a box at the entrance to the zoo were not yet sorted through. So the culprit can only be described as the widest-eyed male. He was at the top of a tree, holding the bear by its foot, swinging it around his head. A little girl, the Teddy's mother, was wailing. The macaques were making a similar racket.

Clive conferred with Jack. Communicated a plan. Jack began enticing other monkeys with a banana toward the next cage. Clive knelt to talk to the child. "What's your name?"

"Pam."

"Has your Teddy been kidnapped?"

Pam nodded vigorously. Whimpered and sniffled. Her mother handed her a hankie. Said, "The hairy fiend just grabbed it."

Clive spoke to both. "Monkeys can be pesky. But they get along with bears rather famously. They both like climbing trees. I bet this monkey is just trying to make friends with your Teddy. Showing him the sights. Leave this to me. Will you go visit DuPont, the camel? Check on him? Then come back and report to me if he has plenty to eat. I want to know if he's fat in the belly, or if his ribs are showing. Can you do that? I'll rescue your bear while you're gone."

"You promise?" That was the child. The mother said, "Yes, of course. Good idea. My mother-in-law gave it to her."

Clive rose. "I see. Well, I'll try even harder. DuPont is that way." He pointed. "Come back in a few minutes."

Jack secured the troop in the neighboring cage, and Clive went away. By the time he returned, the wide-eyed macaque had grown bored with the Teddy, had dropped him on the ground, and was plucking the wire between the cages. Clive retrieved the toy, dusted it off, and inspected an ear that was ragged. It was dry. He concluded Pam, not the monkey, had produced that damage. He wondered, not for the first time, why people allowed their children to bring toys to the zoo when there were so many other things for them to do.

With the exception of the birds, the bears, and the sea lions, favorites Clive kept for himself, the zoo's assistant manager, John Murkin, had direct responsibility for the larger animals, unless a problem arose that needed consultation. John, who was completely competent, but older and less gregarious than his boss, had supervised the entire place while Clive was away in the war. He also stepped in when Clive fell sick. By the time they met at the hippo enclosure, John had heard Clive was up and around and was pleased by that. He was worried about his hippopotamus, and for the first time in a fortnight, could go home to his family at a reasonable hour.

The men glanced at each other. Their eyes darted quickly away. Clive was embarrassed by his absence, and John knew what sickened his boss. He'd seen it in others who'd gone off to the war, and felt considerable empathy for it because he, the father of four, had not been called up for the fight. Too, John often enjoyed a brew he made at home in his basement.

But he worried that Shackleford, a Prohibitionist, would fire Clive for his illness someday. That would be an injustice in John's view; and, worse, would leave him in charge of the zoo. John wasn't as ambitious as he'd been when he was younger, and he loved Clive. He wished he could interest him in his eldest daughter, Julia, who was well on her way to being an old maid. He said, "Still just nibbling at her food," referring to Dinah, not Julia, though the same was true of her, too.

"What're we feeding her?"

"Some reeds and hay. But cabbages mostly." He nodded toward a pile of rotting heads. Nearby, Methuselah had a foot on a leaf and was ripping it apart with his mouth.

"You might remove those. They'll ferment."

John nodded. That'd been his intention.

"Other than being off her feed, how do we know when there's something wrong with one of these? I haven't read up on their diseases."

"I'm not sure. I've been thinking about calling Memphis."

Clive pinched the top of his ear. James wouldn't want that. Before buying the hippo, they'd debated for nearly a year. A hippopotamus was quite an investment. Four thousand dollars for this one, and Memphis had given them a deal. Until Methuselah's mate had died, Clive had been dead set against it. He preferred animals that did tricks or that children could touch. But giant tortoises weren't any better. And a new one of those could live well into the twenty-first century. He said, "Have you checked her stool?"

John had been afraid of that. Mucking is how everybody starts in a zoo. He'd been promoted far away from the shit, and had always hated inspecting it. Then, too, Clive would want it checked when wet. Still, John knew the suggestion was good. He said, "Not yet."

"Might want to give it a look. Worms are often a culprit." Clive's mind flew to a forest in France. To men on the ground, naked, dying of dysentery. To their shivering, indignity, and stench. He pinched his nose. Cleared his throat. Said, "Let me know what you find. I'll help, if you like." He winced.

John cleared his throat, too. He was man enough to pick through poo. He would recruit a junior keeper, Randy Hoffer, to go through it, too. It'd be an opportunity to teach Randy something about worms. John said, "That ain't necessary."

"Thanks, mate." Clive put a hand to John's shoulder. Tapped it and withdrew.

Crawford
Confides

〜

Most resident Glendale employees attended Sunday services in the chapel in Burgess Hall, the old college building next to Chambliss. But Two spent those mornings at the stable, often reading a book on a bench outside of Ocher's stall, or sometimes writing a letter. She was bent over the latter when Crawford arrived dressed in his uniform, his hair highly oiled. Two, surprised to see him so early, grinned with her greeting. But Crawford only nodded. He pulled a bucket off a hook, filled it with water, and took it into the stall across from Ocher's. Two'd already watered the horses, but they always appreciated extra attention. Crawford talked to the horse gruffly, came out, filled the bucket again, and took it into another stall. Two was at the end of her letter, but lingered over addressing the envelope. Something was wrong. She didn't want to finish until Crawford was ready to talk.

He came out of the second stall face furrowed. Two stuffed two pieces of paper into the envelope. Crawford drew more water, opened the door of the stall next to Ocher's, and disappeared in. His boots rustled the hay.

He patted the horse so hard it sounded like spanking. When he emerged, he said, "Mama says your buffalo path was the Big South Road. Ran right through the park. Been there since the beginning." He went to the spicket for more water.

Two bit her lip. Crawford was trying to act normal.

He approached Ocher, who was standing at her door, head out, observing the human activity. He gripped her muzzle, shook it in a way she always appreciated, and added, "Said it went to the French Lick from past the Duck River." He entered Ocher's stall.

On the dusty barn floor, Two saw the dip of the buffalo trail and thought about Strong-Red-Wolf. He might not be a crazy person or a threat. He could be an old codger. Somebody interested in history.

Crawford's voice floated over the wall. He was talking to Ocher, and his voice had an edge in it. Ocher snorted and knocked the side of her stall. That jerked Two's attention. She couldn't have Ocher upset for a dive. She said, "Preaching no good this morning?"

Crawford made a noise to Ocher. He said, "Didn't go to church," to Two.

She squinted. "Tie one on last night?"

Crawford came out of the stall, "My cousin was beat to a pulp."

"Beat?"

"Yelp. In Black Bottom."

The black bottom was the new dance. Some nights, Christa Belle Henley, the park's dance instructor, taught its steps to Chambliss residents around the Victrola. But Two saw modern dancing as something for white people and Negros. And she'd never heard of anyone being whipped for it.

Crawford saw her confusion. "He was collecting on insurance policies in a bad part of Nashville. Close to the river. Was beat up, robbed, and left to die in a ditch."

River bottoms in Oklahoma carried the names of families and tribes. Two'd never seen Black Bottom, but did now understand. "Who did it?"

"Don't know. His wallet was empty. His papers strewed around."

Two dented the dust with the heel of her boot. "What about him? He gonna be all right?"

"Still in the hospital."

"What do the police say?"

Crawford's mouth pulled to the right. His eyebrow arched. "They're helpful."

During Two's childhood, murders of Indians for their allotments ran into the hundreds, if not the thousands. Most were covered up as accidents or still unsolved. And at the moment, the Osage were being murdered, one after another, just miles from the 101. On the ranch, the talk about murder was whispered, continual, and bitter. Children were taught to be leery of people like they were taught to be leery of snakes; to distinguish between the poisonous and the helpful before getting close. One of the things Two liked about Glendale was that, to her knowledge, no one had ever been murdered there.

So beat up wasn't that bad. But "they're helpful" meant same thing to her as it did to Crawford. She laid her clipboard and letter on the bench. Stood and ran both hands down the legs of her jeans. "What're ya gonna do?"

"First, my uncle'll buy information."

"From who?"

"A lip-flapper or two."

Investigations worked the same way for Indians. And justice was personally dispensed. Two said, "Will they be hard to find?"

"Don't know. We're not from Black Bottom. Those folks stick together. But he's gonna try. Jimmy's a good man. Just starting out."

Two didn't know what else to say. In her world, actions meant more than words, and confiding was a gift, not a lid pried off a can. She wanted to show her concern, but didn't know how.

Crawford hung his bucket up, lifted a stool off a wall for himself, and nodded for Two to sit on her bench. Black Bottom was a crowded jumble of wood and brick, built on top a pit of mud and floods. White people owned the buildings, bled poor coloreds for rent, and visited only "to collect money or lick chocolate." Two's spine stiffened, but Crawford didn't notice. He went on. Jimmy had a degree in business from Fisk. He didn't need to sell insurance in the slums. Could make more money in nicer parts of town by pulling accounts from the big, white companies that'd cornered the colored insurance market. It was a damn fool thing for him to be going to Black Bottom. But it didn't justify him being nearly whipped to death. Crawford chewed on his lip. He disapproved of colored trash. Hated injustice that poked its head above the usual kind. Wanted to take the revenge himself.

Rooster, Two's brother, always puffed up before swinging. Lefty was cagier. He lowered his head, rubbed his neck, and swung before his victim knew he was mad. Two didn't know which of her brothers Crawford was like, but felt right at home with his attitude.

What she didn't understand was a Negro getting to go to college. She'd never heard of such a thing. And since Crawford was so open, she threw a rope, so to speak. "Was the Squire a white?"

Crawford ran his tongue over his lip before he spoke. "Granddaddy was. Owned a huge plantation." He pointed west. "Hundreds and hundreds of acres. Left it to his kids."

Two squinted.

"Grandma was a slave, but died shortly after the war was over. We've got three pictures of her. She was a beautiful woman, and smart. When the Federals invaded, Grandpa sided with them, and later married a young Irish girl who was keeping his house. But he kept on loving his kids and sent all of them, white and colored, to school. Daddy was educated up north and at Fisk, and he carried on the tradition. One of my brothers runs a school in Washington, D.C. Another is a doctor in California, and my sister out there is married to one. My sisters in Chicago and New York City are married to lawyers. My older brothers are some of the largest landowners around. Jimmy's mother, Auntie Maria, was educated in a music conservatory in New York City. Her husband is a doctor and a professor at Meharry. Smarts-wise, I'm the runt of the litter."

Most men Two knew could build anything, birth anything, and mend anything broke, but they didn't like books. She admired education, but was rather that way herself. So she discounted Crawford's runt comment. Knew his mind was as quick as a whip. And the mixed relationship didn't rattle her a bit. Her family had been mixed even before the Removal. Two saw the calls for racial purity that were floating everywhere in the air as another way for white people to feel important, to take everything they wanted, and to lord themselves over everybody else.

But, mainly, since she thought of Crawford as a friend, she was glad to have a firmer hold on who he was. As that satisfaction was sinking in, she and Crawford were startled by a loud sound. Screams like a couple of brash bobcat meows. A large peahen was standing in the entrance to the barn. She screamed again. One of the horses snorted loud. One knocked the side of a stall. Two said, "There's something wrong with that bird." Crawford looked at his watch. He said, "We better get a jump on."

The
Last
Dive

≡

The afternoon jump began like the others. Two loosened her limbs under the platform's roof. She inspected the pool and found it calm. Inspected the crowd; found it largely consisting of people dressed in their Sunday best. They were moving more carefully than during the week, and Two attributed that, rightly or not, to more starch in their clothes. But she was looking for a particular person, and didn't envision him wearing a stiff collar and cuffs. He'd written in cursive, but she thought he was exaggerating in claiming a degree from a university. Penmanship was taught early, even in country schools. Strong-Red-Wolf was probably a farmer familiar with dirt, how it lies naturally, how it's changed by animals and people. Maybe somebody from near Nashville, who knew where to look, but, maybe, even a Westerner. A cowboy would see a buffalo path. And even though she seriously doubted Strong-Red-Wolf was one, so would an Indian. Two blushed. She'd never confess to missing the buffalo trace. Never write that home in a letter.

She was still scanning the crowd when she saw a dog raise his head, barking. She heard him over the music, and he recalled to her mind the agitated peahen. But she had to focus. She turned her back to the crowd. Pictured an oak, strong, enduring, and rooted in the earth. Pictured the Salt Fork, flowing with grace and power. She conjured up the 101 buffalo herd, moving over the prairie into the sunset. And, finally, she called up the beaver, the persistent, strong swimmer and survivor. She collected her powers and moved to the ledge. She sat waiting, her back against the post, for Crawford and Ocher.

When Crawford shouted up, "Three." Two echoed, "Three." Crawford shouted, "Two . . . one," then rapidly, the planks rumbled and shook. Ocher's head was coming up right at her, eyes wide, ears alert, nostrils flaring, shoulders rippling. Two grabbed Ocher's mane, clutched her harness, and swung her right leg over her back. She rode into the light; stopped abruptly, four feet from the kickoff board and the drop. The crowd clapped. They waved, hollered, and whistled. Two raised her left hand and waved back. Ocher tap-danced the planks. The audience clapped wilder. Two grinned and glanced at the water. She lifted her eyes and waved in a longer, higher arc. Ocher shimmied, pulled her head to the left, and took a step back. Two tightened her knees to her steed. She muttered, "It's fine." She patted Ocher's neck, twined her fingers tight into her mane to straighten her head. But Ocher took another step back.

That gave Two pause. She peered down at the water. It was brown-tinted, smooth on the surface, ordinary. Two looked out at the crowd. They seemed like the same Sunday bunch. Families with children, courting couples, separate clusters of young ladies and men. Well-dressed, happy Nashvillians. God-fearing, fun-loving, in no way suspicious.

Off to the side, that dog was still barking. That was strange. However, animals roamed all over the park. Peafowl, cranes, pheasants, rabbits, and even, occasionally, the cinnamon bear on a leash. Also, people brought their pets with them. Mostly dogs, but, occasionally, ducks. Wild foxes hid in the groves and the gullies, were caught, carted off, and scampered back after dark. So the park was a zoo even beyond the cages, and a dog could be barking because he'd seen a cat or a snake. Two said, "Come on, girl. Don't get chicken on me."

Ocher swung her head side to side like she was saying, "No." But the clapping was dying, and a voice shouted, "Jump!" The crowd took up the word and began a chorus. Soon accompanied by the stomping of feet. Ocher was backing up. The bleachers rumbled. The dog ran off. Two grew embarrassed. She tried to calm Ocher. Decided the dog had spooked her. Ocher backed up again. Two jabbed her heels into her sides and said, "Gitty up!"

Ocher didn't push off the kickoff board as she should've. She fairly leapt into the air, flying, with her head up, parallel to the water. Two saw the sky, the Overton Hills, and Ocher's crown, ears, and mane. Pulled down by gravity, she saw people on bleachers, standing. And water, moving, swirling, whirlpooling. Two panicked. She let go. Flung herself off Ocher, and floated in air. Time slowed in her mind. Images appeared. Her grandmother feeding chickens. Her father rubbing his horse's foreleg. Her mother braiding her sister's hair. All seemed like what they might be really doing. Two somersaulted like she was mastering a new trick.

And Ocher dropped, too. With her head to the right and her left front leg extended, the other three curled. She hit the pool first. Fell into the eye of the swirl. Disappeared. Two hit the water hard on her side. Her breath exploded. She twisted, reaching for Ocher. Kept falling. Gulped in water and started choking.

Swallowed
by
the
Earth

≡

Crawford was on the exit ramp with a towel on his shoulder when the water began swooshing down, down, and away in a vortex. Ocher was in it, belly up, legs thrashing, hooves pawing for purchase. Two was alone in the air, twisting, dropping, gone. Crawford was suspended. Then jerked alert when the crowd started shifting, screaming, jumping off the backs of bleachers, scrambling, and fleeing. Or not. A man rolled on the ground, clutched his ankle, and howled. Crawford's ramp began sliding. Two's robe slid off the rail. Her boots toppled over. Crawford lost his balance, his knee knocked a plank. He laid a palm to the wood. Pushed up. Staggered, steadied, and started to run.

He was hit from the side by someone who said, "Outta my way, nigger." Crawford instinctively shoved back. Tensed every muscle. Expected a fight and wanted one. But the man ran on.

One of the bleachers was sagging. Maybe collapsing. The pool had disappeared. Its planks were exposed. Its canvas ripped open. Below was a hole, a melting away from the day, brown fading to black as night. Crawford remembered caves under the park. A dark, dangerous tangle that the Squire had once whipped him for traveling. He knew what had happened. The water had weighed on a roof, the earth had shifted, the ground had collapsed.

Crawford stood out of measurable time. The sagging, hanging bleacher also stood. People began creeping back to the scene. Bending and kneeling around those who had fallen. There was a scream or two, but much more shouting. And, over a speaker, "Toot, Toot, Tootsie" started playing. Crawford pressed the ground with his soles. Was the earth still moving? He pressed to the right, and to the left. It seemed steady. He stepped closer to the hole, patting with his soles for trembles and shakes. But he was afraid to move nearer. He turned away and climbed the bleacher. Walked it shakily until he got to a better position. He cupped his hands to his eyes to focus his vision and mind, a habit he'd acquired from the Squire.

He saw nothing more than he'd seen before. Ripped canvas and a hole so deep it dissolved into darkness. He moved his cupped hands to his mouth. Yelled, "Two!" into the opening. Listened. Turned slightly. Yelled again. A faint *Two, Two* came back. Could he have imagined that? He did hear a roar for sure. Was that blood rushing through his head? Or underground water? Streams ran all through the caves. Popped out in the springs in the park. Flowed into the creek below the rise that held the zoo.

Crawford was thrust toward action. Someone should alert Lovett and old Shackleford. Get ambulances brought in. Find Two. Which should he do? Lovett lived in the park. He'd hear quickly. He'd call the ambulances. The Shacklefords were farther away. Digesting their Sunday dinner. Generations spilling into rooms and out onto porches. The children playing hide-and-seek, daring each other into the springhouses in the hill below the mansion. Crawford didn't strain to imagine. He'd seen the Shacklefords at play for most of his life.

He decided to leave the job of telling Shackleford to somebody else, both because he didn't want to fool with him and because he knew how to get into the caves. And probably no one else in the park did. He yelled twice again and got no response. He descended the bleacher cautiously and then ran for the barn. He'd saddle his horse and ride down the hill to the creek. Find the tangle of bushes hiding an entrance. His grandfather had once owned that land. His older relatives had worked it as slaves.

For the past many years, the land west of the park had been owned by a white farmer who wasn't particularly successful. Crawford knew him slightly, but didn't respect him, and decided not to bother to ask if he could trespass. The field was used as a pasture, and after crossing a cattle guard, he remounted and trotted to trees lining the creek. He scattered a few cows and slowed his horse to a walk. He tried to recall which stand of growth hid the hole he was searching for. He hadn't been along this stretch of the Brown's Creek west fork for many a year. The tangle had spread, the trees grown taller, and the undergrowth thicker. Crawford's mind shifted to a judgment that had nothing to do with finding Two, and a lot to do with white people who didn't make good use of land.

But that was for only a moment. Crawford was busy listening. At the mouth of the cave, a spring came out of the hill and joined the creek. He should be able to locate the entrance by a change in the sound of the water. But he didn't hear any change, so he dismounted, tied his horse, Bang On, to a scrub, and walked the curve of the growth by foot. "Yes! We Have No Bananas" was playing up the hill. He didn't like the song even when it didn't interfere with his listening. Finally, abruptly, the music stopped. The sound of the creek grew louder. Crawford trekked back south, trying to hear if he'd already passed the entrance. But the babbling was the same closer to the road, so he turned and proceeded north again along the course he'd just trod. Shortly, the babble diminished. Crawford stopped. Turned to the bushes. Found a narrow path that looked worn by animals coming and going. He reminded himself to look for one of those if he ever again had to find a hidden entrance.

Behind the foliage was a bridge of stones that led directly into the side of the hill. Crawford remembered the rocks from childhood; remembered, too, that they were submerged after rains. He gave a prayer of thanksgiving for the dryness of the season. He planted a foot and walked the stones without slipping, even without his boots getting wet. In only four long steps, he was at the cave's entrance.

It was about four feet high. But wider than tall. He bent, cupped his hands around his mouth, and called, "Two." His word echoed. He heard flutters. Bats. He cupped his hands again. Called "Two" again. Heard nothing then. The cave was dim. He wished he'd brought a light. He remembered back years. Inside, the roof was higher, and about twenty feet on was a turn. Another after that. A zigzag. But then the passage widened into a cavern. And unless something had changed since his childhood, that chamber was dry. But was it beneath the water tank? Crawford tried to get his bearings. Where was the tank from the cave's mouth? How far away and in what direction? He turned. To get an answer, he'd have to come back out of the bushes, walk to the center of the pasture, and look up the hill. The diving pool was south of the park's entrance steps, but north of the bear pit. He couldn't see either unless he walked fairly far up the rise in the pasture. But he could see the water tower without going very far, and it was north of the entrance. He could figure it out.

So Crawford was out of the cave, looking toward the park, making those calculations, when he heard from a distance, "Hands up, nigger!"

Crawford tensed. Told himself not to do anything stupid. Slowly raised his arms and turned. "Mr. Karr. How do you do, sir?" He articulated each word with a whiff of space between them.

Karr was holding a pistol. He hadn't expected the colored intruder in his pasture to call him by name. Neither did he expect "How do you do?" He paused. Frowned. But held his gun steady.

"Surely you remember me, sir. I'm Hank Crawford. Josh's little brother. Squire Crawford's son."

Karr raised his eyebrows, but lowered his pistol. Crawford lowered his arms. While the farmer was deciding how to respond, Crawford went on. "There's been a terrible accident in the park. The diving pool collapsed. A young woman and her horse disappeared into the ground. We think they're in the cave. I remembered an entrance" — he turned and pointed — "along in there. I was trying to figure out how far back they could've fallen. Have you ever been in that cave?"

Karr was confused. He'd thought he'd discovered a nigger cow rustler; instead it was one of the Crawfords. On top of that, the accident sounded serious. Also, he'd been asked a question, and even if a colored had been the asker, he was as programmed as most white people to answer. He said, "No. I ain't been in it, myself. Have a grandson that crawled in there. Whupped him fer it."

"The Squire whupped me for the same thing. Your grandson wouldn't happen to be around, would he?"

"Nah. He lives in town." By this time Karr had stuck his gun in the back of the belt and was hoping it wouldn't be remembered. His wife was always on him for being weapon-happy. If he'd accidentally shot one of the Crawfords, there'd be some people who'd be fairly delighted, but a lot more would be fairly mad. The damn mongrels had a lot of protectors, owned a lot of property, and held a lot of notes. In the past, had held his.

Karr was from Illinois originally. He'd been around Nashville for a mere thirty-one years. Not long enough to understand its ways. He'd certainly never completely grasped how a colored family seemed to have so much power, so much land, and so many friends. Clearly, from a whole lot of sin. What he didn't understand at all was how everybody tolerated it. He was from a state that had stayed in the Union, and it didn't even seem right to him. Nevertheless, his better instincts surfaced. He stepped closer to Crawford and said, "If ya need to bring in cars and trucks, I'll herd my cows to the back pasture."

"That'd be mighty helpful, sir. Thank you. I think we will. But I'm just trying now to figure out how to find where she fell. I think it must be right about there." He pointed.

Karr said, "Ya can't go in that cave without a lantern. I got plenty. I'll get them. Go round up some men. I'll move my herd." He became cooperative without even intending.

Organizing
a
Rescue
Attempt

≡

The Shacklefords were much as Crawford had imagined. Children were darting this way and that, ladies were in the garden admiring irises and peonies, and Meredith was practicing his putts in a circle of grass closely mowed for precisely that purpose. But James had Lewis cornered in the library on the pretext of showing him a book on the heraldry of the British nobility. That discussion could quite naturally lead into the subject of lineage, which could easily turn to the subject of racehorses. Lewis might confess to buying the yearling and, in the spill, reveal more of his dealings with Harry Sinclair. James could then instruct his son on the hazards of collaborating with a man who was so clearly ill-bred and, additionally, under serious indictments. That was the plan, and it had morphed to the horses when Adelaide appeared in the door frame and announced, "There's been a terrible bad accident in the park."

James's and Lewis's eyebrows knitted in exactly the same way.

Adelaide went on. "That Indian gal and her horse waz swallow up by the earth."

"That's impossible," James replied.

"I'z jist repeating what I'z told. Tank of water sure swooshed 'em away."

Lewis asked, "Adelaide, are you saying the tank burst?"

"No, sir. I'z saying they waz swallowed by the earth."

James and Lewis exchanged glances. Adelaide maintained that the sure cure for warts was burying knotted strings in dirt. That teeth shouldn't be pulled under certain zodiac signs. And the opinion which annoyed James the most, that pregnant women should never visit the zoo under any condition.

And Adelaide knew that Mr. James didn't believe a thing that didn't come out of his own mouth. However, she had a deep understanding with Mr. Lewis that had blossomed when he was a little boy in trouble with his parents, and that was still blooming fully that day. She wanted to direct her information to him only, and did that a lot, but knew it would be a mistake at the moment. She said, "Don't take it from me. Ask Mr. Shelton. He's here."

"Well, bring him in!" James said, as though the order should've been obeyed before spoken.

But Adelaide was used to outmaneuvering Mr. James. Often at his wife's or son's instigation. She said, "His shoes is dirty. He dudn't want to get mud on yer fine rug. He's on the south porch."

Lewis, nearer the door, left the room first. James not far behind. They found Shelton surrounded by Meredith and the children. He was holding his cap in his hand. Though tanned, his face was as pale as his bald head. His eyes looked particularly bugged. Lewis spoke. "What's happened, Duncan?"

Duncan looked first to Lewis and then to his father. Mr. Shackleford was touchy about Lewis's success. He should address him first. But Lewis had asked the question, and he'd known him since he was a little shaver. Duncan clutched his cap tighter and looked at the sky. "The diving tank gave way. Right in the middle of a dive. The girl, the horse, and the water swooshed into the ground. Some bleachers nearly slid in, but they held."

"Are you saying a sinkhole opened up?" Lewis asked.

Duncan looked at his boots. "Think so. Never happened before. But there're little caves all around. There must be a big one growing somewhere."

"That's preposterous," James said.

Lewis turned to his father. "No, it's not. This is karst topography. Think of the springhouses."

"What about the springhouses?"

"They go so far back in this hill. Ever see any other springhouses that deep? I bet old Norvell had an easy time of it. Probably started digging where there was a cave already."

One of Meredith's children said, "Are we gonna disappear into the ground?"

Another child said, "It's like Alice in Wonderland."

James had had quite enough. "It's not anything like Alice in Wonderland. And Norvell had slaves. He could've had springhouses dug from here to China if he'd wanted."

Both Adelaide and one of Meredith's maids were on the porch. Lewis tried not to glance toward either of them. He said to Duncan, "What's being done?"

"We've closed off that part of the park. But it's Sunday. My crew's off. We've called the fire department. They'll have ropes and ladders."

There was a dither gathering the women in from the garden, deciding who would go to the park, and telling the children who could come and who couldn't. In the end, James; his wife, May; her sister, Maggie; Lewis and his wife, Mary Ann; Meredith; Duncan; and seven of the children made the trip. James was genuinely concerned about his act, the Indian girl, the horse, and, of course, the liability. Fortunately, he'd been in the insurance business for decades and Lewis was buying up insurance companies like he was picking up marbles. Still, James was certain there'd be lawsuits. Everybody was after his money.

When the Shacklefords tumbled out of their cars and raced at different paces up the hill to the tank, they found a scene of confusion. However,

Clive was there. Lewis and James made a beeline for him and crashed his conversation with a khaki-clad man. That employee stepped aside fast, and Clive said without greeting, "Apparently, there's a cave under our feet. We don't know how deep."

"How many people were injured?" James asked.

Clive wiped his hand over his mouth before he spoke. "Fifteen or sixteen have been taken to hospital. But I think only three are seriously harmed. Two broken legs. Maybe a broken shoulder. All the injuries were sustained by jumping and running. Miss Feathers and Ocher are in the pit. Maybe Crawford. Nobody has seen him since it happened."

James heaved for breath and rubbed his stub furiously. He'd lived on this land since 1878, and it'd never trembled beneath him. But his mind raced to the earthquakes of 1811 and '12. To the stories his grandparents and some of his uncles and aunts told. The earth trembled for months, frightening flocks of people living on the edge of civilization into religious conversions. One terrible series of quakes turned the flow of the Mississippi backwards and created Reelfoot Lake. A new Reelfoot could swallow the entire zoo. His home, too. Only the cranes, seals, alligators, and sick hippopotamus would survive.

Lewis said, "Father, are you paying attention?"

James said, "Yes, of course I am."

Lewis thought his father was covering. He was worried about his faculties slipping; hoped that wasn't the case. But if it were, he didn't want it seen, so he phrased his next remark with a hint. "If no one saw Crawford fall directly into the hole, it could be that he's run to get help."

James cleared his throat. Crawford's existence irritated him to no end. But he didn't want him dead. He said, "He probably has. He has a lot of people around here."

Lewis was well aware of his father's feelings toward the entire Crawford clan. He changed the subject. "When's the damn fire department coming?"

James said, "Lewis, it's Sunday."

"They work on Sunday."

"I wasn't talking about when they work." He arched an eyebrow. "Language."

Lewis flushed to his temples. He had brown eyes, but was fair-skinned and, in his thirties, his hair was thinning. He didn't like his emotions revealed on his growing forehead. And he didn't like being corrected. He walked away toward the hole.

Clive said, "They should've been here by now. Maybe there's a fire somewhere. We have ropes and ladders. It's just figuring out how to get down into the hole without it falling in." His mind flashed to a cluster of Tommies shielding their heads with their arms. To a dirt wall collapsing. Men crumpling under its weight. The digging with hands. The three they'd managed to save. The terror and dirt on the faces of the dead. He ran his hand over his glasses.

Crawford arrived before the firemen. He was straddling Bang On and above the Shacklefords. That made them twitchy. James said, "Where have you been?"

Crawford remained in the saddle. "On Granddaddy's old property. There's an entrance down there. I need some men."

Lewis said, "Count me in."

His aunt, Maggie, said, "Count me in, too."

Heads turned in her direction. But nobody contradicted her — ever. One of the most prominent suffragists in the South, Mrs. Alex Shackleford was the new superintendent of the Tennessee Vocational School for Girls, the past president of the Tennessee Federation of Women's Clubs, and the first female automobile dealer in the entire United States. It was she who said, "We should go in through that hole. We'll take my car." She turned, marched off, and was behind a steering wheel before the men could prevent her.

James started to stammer to his wife. But May had followed her sister and was almost instantly spreading her skirts on the car's front passenger's seat. Lewis's wife, Mary Ann, was disappearing into a back door. And because the Shacklefords drove new Buicks, the car didn't need to be cranked. Maggie turned it around, scattering a gaggle of people stand-ing close by. Off the women went down the hill.

There was some clearing of throats, and color arose in every man's face with the exception of Crawford's. But there was no discussion at all of jumping in another car and following. To a man, they considered that unbecoming. It was Clive who said, "It'll take them a while." By the crow, Karr's property wasn't far. But the road had yet to be extended for a direct drive to there from the park.

Crawford said, "The best route is down the bears' hill."

There was a discussion then. Some just to avoid looking like they were taking orders from a Negro. But Crawford considered their negoti-ations a waste of time. He caught Clive's eye. Clive said, "All able-bodied men, down the hill."

Now Crawford was hesitant about what to do. Riding off in front of a collection of walking Shacklefords could arouse resentment. But he couldn't lead them to the entrance by riding behind them. He waited until Lewis turned and shouted, "Crawford, we need you!" Then he banged his heels on his horse's sides and rode past them.

The women got to the field ahead of all of the men except Crawford. But it had been emptied of cows, and he hadn't closed the guard. Mag-gie drove through it, and slowed the car. Crawford dismounted near the brush concealing the cave, and Maggie, May, and Mary Ann folded out of the car six lengths away. By this time in their lives, Maggie and May wore dresses hemmed at the calves, and Mary Ann, Lewis's wife, married but childless, dressed as a fashionable flapper. All three tromped through the pasture, heedless of their stockings, but watching for patties.

Crawford cautioned the women about the water and held bushes aside for them to pass as the men marched their way in the distance. Lewis in the lead. Clive and Duncan together. Bringing up the rear, Mer-edith, old Shackleford, and a troop of children. Crawford looked up the hill to see if Karr was coming with lanterns. No sign of him. But from in-side the thicket, Maggie said, "Mr. Karr, how considerate."

Karr had brought six lanterns, all he could carry without saddling his horse. And he'd lit them already. Sun dappling through the leaves and the shadow of the hillside in front of the cave made them look like decorations for a fete or a festival.

May asked Maggie, "Should we go in or wait for the men?" She was as great a force to be reckoned with as was her sister. Or, really, greater, because her husband was still alive and very, very wealthy. But she still often deferred to her older sister, and Maggie had led the charge.

Maggie looked at the ground. Their stockings were already ruined, and she wasn't particularly concerned for their shoes, as they had plenty to spare. But walking a cave without proper footwear could slow the rescue. She said, "We should probably wait. Lewis will want to lead." She looked to Lewis's wife. Mary Ann pursed her lips and nodded.

In
the
Cave

≡

Karr, good about the lanterns, had forgotten to bring any implements. So had everyone else. The men, in a dry room of the cave with a roof a little higher than their heads, dug with their hands. Scooped dirt, grabbed stones. Bumped into one another and got in each other's way. Then Clive ordered them to form a line to pass the rocks away from the cave-in. They fell silent with the work, and Clive, at the head of the line, was transported in body and mind back to the trenches, to lifting and tossing sandbags, wood, and corpses. He fell to a natural rhythm, to dull, repetitive instinct.

Everyone saw Clive knew what he was doing and mimicked his posture, pace, and attitude. Directly behind Clive was Crawford. He was the strongest and had years of practice lifting stones with his father. He handed rocks to Lewis, who'd scrambled to be ahead of his brother and the rest. Lewis handed the stones to Karr, who was glad not to be taking them directly from Crawford. Behind Karr was Meredith, who was perfectly content to let Lewis lead on this particular task. At the end of the line was Duncan. James stood by him and barked orders about where to pile rocks.

The lanterns flickered against the walls, threw dim light, and the line remained quiet, except for occasional grunting and James's directions. The rock slide hid something more real than their daily lives. Something awful. The presence of death. Beyond the rubble, maybe buried in it, was, most likely, a dead girl and a dead horse. Only Clive understood they were in real danger themselves. The wall formed by the cave-in could tumble down. They could drown under rock. His heart pounded so fiercely that he feared others could hear it. To hide its sound, he began whistling, "It's a Long Way to Tipperary." At first, his shortness of breath expelled the tune in unrecognizable fits. But the effort calmed him. And he was an expert at whistling to birds.

All the men knew the song. Singing still often accompanied work and was considered essential for good times and bonding. Most began humming, as no one could whistle like Clive. However, Crawford had sung heartily all of his life. He started singing the tune, and before the others realized they were following a black man, they were doing that, too.

The singing roused Two to consciousness, but also to complete darkness. She, at first, thought she hadn't opened her eyes, but was wrong about that. However, her sense of smell was intact. She smelled Ocher. Smelled the dirt and the damp. Smelled bat shit, but didn't know it was that. She lay still, smelling, for some time, then began twitching her fingers. Reaching. Finding horsehair. A tail. She clutched it and tried to move her legs. She couldn't. She reached with her right hand. Grasped hair that was shorter. A hide, a curve, a belly. She'd been riding Ocher. They'd been on the platform. Was the song from the speakers? She listened harder. Heard sounds she couldn't place but felt were coming her way.

She yelled. Expelled as much breath as sound. But Clive heard her effort. He shouted, "Quiet." The men froze. Clive yelled, "Two Feathers!" Two yelled louder. The men began passing rocks so fast that one dropped on Meredith's foot. He said, "Damn it. Watch it." Karr grunted. He thought Meredith had fumbled the handoff. Thought, also, that the only people who were more difficult than the Crawfords were the Shack-lefords. But all the men stayed in line and kept passing rocks until they opened a hole in the rubble wide enough for a man to squeeze through.

There was no discussion about who would go. Experience trumped pride. Crawford and Lewis clasped hands to form a step for Clive's foot. Karr pushed on his buttocks until he disappeared and uttered, "Blimey! That hurt." Crawford lifted a lantern to the hole, felt a tug from the other side, and let go. Nobody moved. They listened hard. Heard Clive creeping along and saying, "Hold on, Two. Hold on." They also heard one of the women at the cave's entrance say, "Stop that! Both of you. Go to the car!"

After that, they heard more murmurs from beyond the rumble. Clive asking Two, "Does that hurt?" And, "How 'bout there?" Heard her reply, "Ow! Crap!"

Clive said, "Sorry," and pressed on another spot.

Two said, "Ocher?"

Clive kept methodically squeezing. They'd have to move Two, but that'd have to be done carefully. He'd seen too many men go into shock, even die, as soon as they were hoisted onto stretchers.

Two said, "My horse?"

Clive had already felt Two's left leg, determined it was broken, and had elicited movement and her complaint. Signs her backbone was still intact. His hands were on her right calf. "Does that hurt?"

Two, now more aware, shook her head. But Mr. Lovett hadn't answered her questions, and she was still gripping horsetail. She started crying.

Clive mistook that for a sign of physical pain. He withdrew his hands. Said, "We'll get you out of here." He arose and examined his palms by lantern light. They were bloody. He wiped them on his pants. Then he lifted the lamp from a flat shelf of rock behind Two and swung it toward her face. She was quaking. Apparently going into shock. He said, "Two. You have to try not to move. Your left leg is broken. You must stay still 'til we can get a stretcher in here."

Two whispered, "Where are we?"

Clive held the lantern up. Slowly swung it around. "In a cave."

"Is Ocher dead?"

Two was resting on Ocher's upturned belly. The horse's neck was at an unnatural angle, and Clive had seen hundreds of dead horses. He said, "She's at peace. Don't worry about her."

Two's entire body started shaking harder.

"You must lie perfectly still. You have to stop that." The order was stern.

Two gasped and gasped again. She wanted to stop. Was afraid of hurting herself more, and hated her emotions showing. She called on her elders to help her ribs stop heaving. She saw her maternal grandmother's face. Her paternal grandfather's. Her other grandparents' and her parents'. She saw their eyes unmoving. Their tranquility, holding generations of pain without flinching.

Two's breathing evened out. By then, Clive had set the lantern down by his feet and was unbuttoning his shirt. He removed it, revealing an undershirt that covered his chest and biceps. He grasped his shirt's sleeve in one hand, its body in the other. He ripped the sleeve off. Dropped the rest on Ocher's flank, knelt, and carefully lifted Two's left leg. She stiffened. Said, "Whoa!"

Clive said, "I'm sorry. I have to." He wrapped the sleeve high and tight on her thigh. Wrapped the rest of the shirt below that. He picked up a stone with both hands, placed it beside Two's leg, lifted it gently, and shoved the stone underneath. He said, "This will prevent more blood loss. How do you feel in your head?"

"I don't know."

"Well, usually when people have been injured, they get somewhat light-headed. That's from loss of blood. I can't tell how much you've lost without turning you over. And it doesn't matter. What matters is that you'll be fine. But you must do as I say. You are to lie quietly and not move at all. Any movement will make your blood flow faster. We don't want that. Do you understand?"

"Yes, sir."

"Right-o. Good girl. Do exactly as I say, and we'll get you properly fixed."

Clive stood, picked up his lantern, and moved to the opening. He said, "I'll stay in here with her. We need a stretcher. Has the fire department arrived?"

On the other side of the rubble, the men looked to one another. No one had remembered to tell the fire department to come to Karr's. Lewis said, "Karr, do you have a telephone?" Karr shook his head. Lewis said, "Blast it," though he knew Karr wasn't successful enough to make a phone likely.

Meredith said, "Aunt Maggie can go find one."

Crawford said, "I can ride up the hill faster."

James said, "Fine. Do that."

Clive drew their attention back. "I need our jackets to keep her warm."

The men had taken them off before entering the cave, and Meredith left to collect them. The others discussed whether they should stay in the cavern or not. Karr wanted out. He didn't like his company and hated being underground, though he muttered only the latter. He said he'd go up to the barn and get some spades and a pick. Duncan volunteered to go with him. But James, Lewis, and Meredith, who'd returned with the jackets, wanted to stay close to the action. They swung the lanterns around and saw, nearer the entrance, two flat shelves of rock. Meredith and Lewis took seats. James continued to stand. Lewis said, "Papa, why don't you rest your legs? You've forgotten your cane. It may be a while."

James replied, "Do you know what you're sitting on?"

The Shackleford sons looked down and realized they were sitting on graves. They jumped up in unison. Meredith said, "Oh, my God! I didn't even notice."

James said, "Don't swear."

Lewis said, "Are bodies still in there?"

"The bones are. And usually dirt. The tops are generally quite sturdy."

With the exception of Civil War paraphernalia, Meredith didn't share his father's interest in relics. But he owned Nashville Stockyards. He was quite familiar with bones, and amused at Lewis's naivety. He said, "Shall we take a look?"

James said, "Let it be."

The brows of the Shackleford brothers condensed. James's mustache twitched. He tried not to rub his stub. "This is no time for that. The girl is in danger."

The brothers exchanged glances. Meredith sat back down. Lewis continued standing. Neither challenged their father. And he was glad of it. James had, over the years, slowly come to regret his part in dismantling the Noel Cemetery. It'd been an exciting diversion at the time. Had distracted him from worrisome business transactions and his noisy, growing household. But as he'd approached the twilight of his life, he'd gained a different perspective. The dead should be left to rest in peace. Even the savage dead. Not a conclusion he'd arrived at intellectually. And, if anybody had asked, he wouldn't have been able to pinpoint when his attitude had changed. However, standing there in lantern light and the literal underworld, he recognized the alteration, and felt duty-bound to relay his wisdom to his sons. Besides, he had nothing better to do while they waited. He said, "We gained a lot of knowledge from these graves." He went on to describe grave goods, skulls, and one surprising burial of a man, a woman, three children, and a dog.

Clive had set his lantern on a grave's lid near Two, covered her with the jackets, and reminded her not to move. Told her to close her eyes and rest. He didn't know what was in the box, and didn't realize it was anything other than a cave formation. Neither was Two aware of it, nor of any of the others in the cavern. And all of that was just as well. Clive had had enough death to last him for the rest of his life, and Two tried to keep as distant from death as the earth is from the stars. They both needed to stay calm. But calm was harder for Clive than it was for Two. She was injured and not alert; he was pumped with adrenaline. And, underground, surrounded by earth, the trenches of his past were as present as if he were still in France. After he settled in, dear dead friend after dear dead friend arose before him. They flickered past, shadows on the wall.

Clive began weeping silently, a welcomed release during his days in battle. But he needed to stop before Two heard him, and he began to wish for a bottle of whiskey. The urge for drink grew quickly; it ballooned in his mouth, slid down his throat to almost choking, and spread through his stomach like an oil slick. It ate him from the inside to the out. His hands trembled. He clasped them together, intertwined his fingers, and pressed so hard the blood was cut off and his knuckles turned white. He bit his lower lip to keep it still.

Then Millwood came. He appeared in bright white light seated on a grave across from Clive and behind Two and Ocher. He said, "I've been looking for you. You made it back."

Clive sucked air in sharply. Stopped breathing at all. The lantern light was dim. The light around Millwood more brilliant than bright day, whiter than sunlight. Millwood was fully formed, three-dimensional, and in his uniform. And both of his arms were attached. His helmet sat on the stone beside him. He held a cigarette and wore a familiar amused look on his face. He put his fag to his mouth and took a drag. Clive breathed out. Sniffed. Tried to smell tobacco to prove to himself that Millwood was truly there.

Clive had experience with his mind playing tricks under stress. He couldn't ask Two for confirmation. She'd have to twist her head and shoulders. And if she didn't see Millwood and the light, he'd seem deranged. She'd lose confidence in him and panic. If she did see Millwood, that might panic them both. Clive closed his eyes. He took off his spectacles and pinched his nose. Then he hooked his glasses back over his ears and opened his eyes again. Millwood was still there. Still bathed in bright light.

Millwood grinned. Crushed his butt on a slab, and in a rumbling baritone began,

Bombed last night, and bombed the night before.
Going to get bombed tonight if we never get bombed anymore.
When we're bombed, we're scared as we can be.
Can't stop the bombing from God damned Germany.

He waved a hand. Said, "Together now. '*Bombed last night, and bombed the night before.*'" Clive joined in.

Going to get bombed tonight if we never get bombed anymore.
When we're bombed, we're scared as we can be.
Can't stop the bombing from God damned Germany.

They're over us, they're over us.
One shell hole for the four of us.
Thank your lucky stars there are no more of us.
So one of us can fill it all alone.

Gassed last night and gassed the night before.
Going to get gassed tonight if we never get gassed anymore.
When we're gassed, we're sick as we can be.
For phosgene and mustard gas is much too much for me.

They're killing us, they're killing us.
One respirator for the four of us.
Thank your lucky stars three of us can run.
So one of us can use it all alone.

They stopped. Millwood wiped his mouth with his hand. Said, "Old Barney and Alex are with me. They're fine. Take your time."

Clive wanted to embrace Millwood, but he couldn't move, and if he could've, he couldn't get beyond Two and Ocher. He glanced at Two's face. Her eyes were closed. She was either unconscious or asleep. Clive looked again at Millwood. His cousin was still there, putting on his helmet. He stood and said, "I'll see you later. Do carry on." He turned to his right and melted into stone, taking his light.

Clive stood. Stepped forward. Took a deep breath and wiped his brow with his forearm. Millwood was as real as the dead horse and the woman on its belly. As real as the lantern, as his own hands, as the dank smell of the cavern. He would never see anything like that again. At that very moment, Clive, filled to the brim with wonder, shifted earthquake-like in his entire view of existence. Millwood had survived. He had no doubt. And if Millwood had, then all of the other millions of dead had also survived. They all were still alive. Whole. In their prime. Not blown to bits. Not skeletal from hunger and dysentery. Clive began weeping again. Sobbing. He stepped out of the lantern light, and turned his face to a wall. He muffled his crying in his elbow, unable to stop his tears.

Two hadn't seen Millwood. But she'd been aware of a song and thought she recognized it from somewhere outside the park. And now she heard Mr. Lovett crying. She opened her eyes. He was facing a wall, his back to her, his head in his elbow. She gripped bone and hair. Inched her fingers along Ocher's leg. It was cold, and its chill climbed up her arm. She, too, started weeping. Then she remembered that Mr. Lovett warned her against moving. She tried to stay still. Tried to keep her chest from heaving. Worried about Mr. Lovett to keep her mind away from herself.

Clive finally turned away from the wall, holding his arm to his mouth. He looked off into air. His eyes seemed wide and teary, but steady to Two. She relaxed. Swallowed without gulping. Her heart settled into a normal beat. She kept her fingers curled around Ocher's cold limb. Otherwise, she didn't move, and still watched Mr. Lovett's face. He seemed in a trance.

To
the
Hospital

≋

The arrival of the firemen stirred up lots of good intentions, a whirl of conflicting opinions, and more than a little jostling for pecking order. All of that confusion finally concluded with the firemen opening the hole wide enough to get a stretcher in and out. By that time, Two had been unconscious for a while, and Clive was concerned for her life. He was climbing into the back of the ambulance when one fireman called to another, "Hubbard."

Clive backed out. "No. Protestant. It's closer and better."

The fireman jerked. Shook his head. "Not our practice."

Clive said, "She's not a Negro."

"She's not white." The fireman's chin pulled in; his eyebrows jutted up.

"James!" Clive yelled.

James was explaining the events in the cave to a circle including his wife, daughter-in-law, and various children. He said, "What is it?"

Clive stalked toward him, a determined look on his face. "They want to take her to Hubbard."

James frowned, said, "Well," and stopped.

Lewis glanced up from inspecting his jacket.

May said, "She should be taken to Protestant."

The fireman, close on Clive's heels, was now within conversational distance. "With all due respect, ma'am, if we take her to Protestant, there'll be a good chance we'll just have to turn around and take her to Hubbard. We'll lose time, and maybe her life."

May said, "James, do something."

"What do you recommend?"

"Something." May didn't really know what. The fireman had spoken the truth. Two had lost enough blood to make her pale enough to pass for a white. But Protestant would've dealt with the other cave-in victims, and she was advertised in the paper as the Indian half of the "thrilling," "hair-raising," and "death-defying" high-diving act. As soon as her name was given, they could refuse her treatment. But the Negros' hospital, Hubbard, was farther away and, of course, not as up-to-date.

Lewis said, "I'll go with her. You all go back to the house and call John Freeman." He was president of the Protestant Hospital board.

If the idea hadn't been Lewis's, James might've liked it. He said, "Take her to Hubbard."

May stiffened at the tone of James's voice and recognized the stubborn look on his face. She knew its provocation. She said, "James," in a tenor so disapproving that the heads of every person in the group jerked. Except James's. He stood rigid.

May was not accustomed to disagreeing with her husband in public. And did not consider such behavior polite nor conducive to good marital relations. She had had ten children with the man, and they had buried six of those children together. She loved her spouse, and didn't want to embarrass him in front of his sons, his daughter-in-law, and his grandchildren. She said, "We entertained Will Rogers in our home last November. Had he been injured, would you've sent him to a colored hospital?"

James rubbed his stub. That evening had left him uneasy. Rogers had poked fun at Andrew Jackson, the most famous of all Tennesseans. Still, he'd been so comical it'd been impossible to take offense, and everybody had laughed at the former president's expense. Quite unprecedented in Nashville. And the further James was from the experience, the more certain he'd become that the comic wasn't being comical at all. Was, instead, being subversive. Still, he'd laughed right out loud. And he'd entertain the man again if he ever got the opportunity. He said, "You're quite correct. Lewis, go along. Explain the situation. I'll call John as soon as I return home."

By ten that night, Longview was quiet. Mostly the house was empty, but Adelaide and Jamaica, the cook, were quietly gossiping in the kitchen and James and May were sitting together in her room. Under a bright spot of light cast over her shoulder, May was embroidering a lamb onto a pillowcase for a grandchild. On James's lap lay three folders. Percy Warner and Nashville Railway and Light owned the park and zoo, but James was president of its board, and he owned a lot of Railway and Light's stock and over a million dollars of its bonds via a holding company in New York that he'd set up to avoid paying taxes on the interest. James was certain that he, Percy, Nashville Railway and Light, and everybody involved in the park would be sued at least by one of the accident victims. If not by the entire greedy slew. His frustration of the evening was centered on his inability to contact the attorney he used for liability suits. That lawyer was vacationing in Pass Christian, the same small Mississippi Gulf resort his son retreated to. He could call Charles and order him to track his lawyer down. But that would require a conversation, or maybe two, with Charles. James shifted in his seat again and tried to think of a different avenue.

Embroidery was the way May most often ended her day. The repetition freed her mind from concerns and prepared her for sleep. But James's shuffling of papers was ruining the calming effect, and his more than occasional huffing added irritation. She said, "When does Percy return from England?"

"I can't remember."

"Did you try calling Luke?" Luke Lea was Percy's son-in-law twice over, married to one Warner daughter, then, after her death, to another. He was also a close friend of Lewis's.

James said, "Not yet," tapping his papers to keep from rubbing his stub. May continued her stitching. Beyond the lights over their shoulders, their home was as dark as it was quiet. And the tapping was grating. May said, "I don't guess Clive will call this late."

The tapping stopped. "He called earlier. They set the girl's leg."

"What about the cave?"

"What about it?" James finally laid his folders aside on a table.

"What will be done about it?"

"Percy should decide. If anyone can find him. I don't understand all this running back and forth to Europe people do nowadays. You'd think people would've gotten their fill of that during the war."

"We should think about taking a holiday ourselves."

"You can. I have too much to attend to. Why don't you go to the Broadmoor? Take Elsie." Their surviving daughter was staying in Monteagle until the middle of July, and May already had their trip to Colorado planned for August. She hadn't yet mentioned that to James. She said, "I probably will. Are they at least filling in the hole?"

"Duncan and Buddy are handling that. I wish these things wouldn't always happen on Sunday."

May tried to recall another Sunday mishap. She remembered a body discovered with a cigar wedged in its teeth. The result of a thuggish stabbing in front of the buffalo pen on a Saturday night. A colored affair. But the children had been youngsters then. It was at least twenty years in the past. James must be referring to something else. He didn't just make things up. However, he'd lived a long life and did have a head full of memories. Lately, sometimes he referred to things that had happened decades earlier as though they'd occurred in the last week. May assumed that was a reflection of an accounting of the past. However, she didn't do it herself. Or didn't think she did.

James got up, went through the door to his adjoining room, and came back with a small glass of port. He settled again across from his wife and took a sip she could hear.

She kept her eyes on her stitching. "This will be hard on Clive."

James had been thinking that. Worrying that Clive would take another bad cold. He snorted. May raised her head. James twitched and took another sip. May said, "You'll get caught at that someday."

"Only if there's someone in my wife's bedroom. And if there is, a little medicinal tonic won't be the issue."

They both smiled. They'd been faithful to one another throughout their marriage. And were staunch Prohibitionists. May through sincere commitment, James to set an example. But James didn't harbor a huge taste for liquor. As a young man, he'd seen what it could do to people. He considered drink the scourge of the lower classes. However, he found a nip refreshing to himself now and then. Particularly at the end of a day when he hadn't gotten his way or was weary. But he never indulged in front of other people, and certainly not around Lewis or Meredith, who threw lavish parties where wine and spirits were consumed, often in excess.

May said, "Why don't you check on Clive in the morning."

James understood that was more than a suggestion. However, his and May's minds often ran on parallel rails of the same track, and he'd decided on that course before her prodding. He said he would. And she went back to her stitching and he to his brooding.

As James and May fell into silence, Clive was climbing out of Lewis's automobile at the park's entrance. He bid Lewis good night, and walked up the steps and through the grass, avoiding paths that were bright. Clive didn't want to be seen, stopped for conversation, or answer any questions. He stuck to the shadows until he got to his cabin. He fumbled his key into the slot, opened the door, shut it hard, and turned the lock. For a moment, he rested against the wood. Took deep breaths. Noticed his odor. It was rank. He'd gone to the hospital with his undershirt stained with sweat and smeared with mud. His pants were spotted with blood.

He needed a bath. He felt a pull toward running water and a tub. He thought about a bottle hidden under a plank, but decided to bathe before he wrestled with that.

Clive had grown up fully bathing only on Saturdays. In the trenches, he'd gone for weeks washing from his helmet. His current habit was to bathe every day, but, as he'd never grown accustomed to luxury, using very little water. Violating habit, he filled the tub almost to the brim to cover his whole body. He wanted a deep cleansing, a reward, and, although the thought hadn't consciously formed, a baptism. He applied soap to his arms, legs, trunk, and, finally, to his hair. He enjoyed a vigorous scrubbing with a hearty lather. Then he drained the tub, filled it again, and rinsed. He palpated the scar near his groin with his fingers. Sometimes in his dreams, it opened and his guts spilled out. Even washing aroused that sensation. But the scar was raised no higher than usual. He hoped the one on his back wasn't either. He reached around and ran his fingers over its ridges. Then examined his fingertips for blood. Of course, there wasn't any. The wound had been closed for years. Nevertheless, Clive felt reassured, and afterwards drained the tub yet again and ran in even more water. He settled down with only his head sticking out.

The cabin had electricity. The entire park was an electric wonder. But Clive didn't like seeing himself naked in harsh light that clarified his wounds. His coal oil lamp cast the same light on his bathroom walls that the lamp in the cave had thrown on the rock. And in that yellow, dim glow and soothing water, Clive relived Millwood's visit. It was easy to conjure. Through the entire rescue, the ride in the ambulance, the admission to the hospital, and the wait for the doctor's verdict, Clive had sensed Millwood still with him. His presence, his singing. And he felt Millwood again in the room. As near as the sink and commode.

But that wasn't the half of it. In the hospital waiting room, there'd been an old woman. A living one. Who everyone could see. She was wrinkled, and hunched in a wheelchair. And she was crying and saying again and again, "Don't leave me, don't leave me," to her daughter, who also was entirely alive. And who reassured her repeatedly, she wasn't going anywhere, she would stay right there. Then, the daughter left. The old woman whimpered. Then sobbed. Nurses came over. Comforted her and conferred. Went away and came back. But not with the daughter. She didn't return. Finally, the old woman was wheeled away through a door by a nurse. It was a heart-wrenching scene.

But not as disturbing to Clive as it might have been. Because throughout the pleading, the crying, the nurses' comforting, and the wheeling away, Clive saw a figure beside the old woman. A much younger female, dressed in a long skirt and high-collared blouse, with her hair pulled up and hidden beneath a large hat with a flower on the brim. That woman gave the daughter a what-for that included pointing and the stomping of a foot. Then, after the daughter disappeared, the figure turned to the old woman, rubbed her shoulders, and whispered in her ear. The two looked remarkably similar. Clive had no doubt that one was the other much younger.

Beyond that, he didn't know what to think. As a boy, he'd been taken to church on Sundays by this relative or that, but sitting in the pews with both parents dead, he'd never developed much faith. And the little he had, the Great War had destroyed and had led him to the conviction that humans, on the whole, were not even admirable animals. But the apparitions he'd seen were so clear and so absolutely real that they made the physical reality of the cave, the hospital, and the tub seem insubstantial. Like mere shadows of another, greater reality he'd never suspected. Beyond that, they left him with a feeling he'd not had in the past. One he couldn't describe because mere words weren't adequate. He looked over to the sink. He couldn't quite see Millwood, but he felt him hovering there.

James
Inspects

Though James had promised May he'd check on Clive the first thing in the morning, he still went into his office in Nashville on Mondays. He had a meeting to chair, telephone calls to endure, and, by noon, two unpleasant conversations with people who wanted money he wasn't about to lend them. Around three p.m., his unfulfilled promise to May began to make his back twitch. He truly had been busy. But he'd also been avoiding, dreading what he might find. Clive had just gotten back on his feet. James didn't want him sick again. He had his secretary call for his car. And, although he read a contract during the ride, at the park's entrance he left his briefcase on the back seat beside his hat. He told his valet and driver, Harris, to take the car to the house. He'd ride the trolley home.

He asked a ticket attendant for a progress report on the cave-in and then detoured over to see the collapsed diving tank. He told himself that he wasn't procrastinating on finding Clive; that inspection was his duty, and would give him information to relay to Percy, should he ever return from England. Approaching the site, he saw a fence that wasn't there the day before and Buddy Parrish, the construction boss, barking orders to his crew. Rather than interrupt, James inspected the tower and ramp. Contemplated salvaging the horse diving act. There were other diving horses to be had, and the Indian girl wasn't dead. Maybe she would dive again. The accident would spark more interest, and the fear of another collapse would add to the thrill. But would people be afraid to sit in the bleachers?

James understood that moderate risk increases most people's pleasure. But he'd been exposed to real danger by the time he was ten. Had ridden with Alex through woods filled with newly freed slaves and deserters of both armies. When their mule had broken a leg, he'd worried as much about using a bullet they might need later as he did about the animal's pain and how'd they get home. He'd rammed the barrel of the gun deep into the mule's ear to provoke instant death and to muffle the sound from any humans lurking around.

He was still thinking about shooting his mule when Buddy finished dispensing his orders and walked over. James said, "I assume the horse is still in the cave."

"Yes, sir. No use bringing her out just to bury her again."

Dead horses had been a stubborn societal problem throughout James's entire life. He approved of that decision and skipped over to thinking about asking Buddy if he'd seen Clive. But that could lead to a mention of Clive's illness. It provoked resentment in a minority of Glendale's employees, and James knew that resentment centered on him, not on his general manager. Men who came back from the war disabled were respected. Those who returned whole felt thankful and guilty. Ones who'd never served felt chagrined. However, most men, disabled, whole, veterans, or not, wanted to smoke and drink. James said, "What about rebuilding the tank?"

"That'll take some figuring. I ain't sure the tower will hold."

James raised his hand. He couldn't have foreknowledge of the potential for the tower to collapse. Ignorance was a solid defense. He said, "What should we put here, then?"

"I was thinking we could move Methuselah and Dinah. Or maybe the sea lions. None of them need water eleven feet deep. If not them, maybe

DuPont. He ain't in a good traffic spot. But it's up to Mr. Lovett. With yer approval, of course."

James rubbed his stub. "Have you seen Clive?"

Buddy looked off to the fence. "I been building this all day."

"I see. Well, keep thinking about the alternatives."

Dinah and Methuselah were southeast of the bird cages, near the old concert hill, not anywhere close to the path to Clive's cabin. In the opposite direction, really. But Dinah was ill, and quite an investment. It would be negligent not to check on her. She was insured, of course, but fairly soon somebody from the Memphis zoo would be up to visit or in town for business. James could be asked how the animal was doing. "She's dead" would be a mortifying answer.

He headed toward the pen, wondering what he would find and hoping the hippo would suddenly be perky and sporting a healthy hue. When he neared the enclosure, he saw her submerged; out of the water were only her ears, eyes, and nostrils. Two khaki-clad men were in the cage, near the pen's stairs. The taller employee James didn't recognize. But the shorter looked like Clive from behind. Closer, he confirmed that impression. This time, James didn't wait for the conversation to conclude. He shouted, "Lovett!"

Clive turned, smiled, and exited the pen with the other man following him. He said, "Glad to see you, Mr. Shackleford." He always referred to his friend by his surname in front of employees.

James's smile, though sandwiched between a mustache and beard, was toothy. He couldn't have been more pleased if hundred-dollar bills were sprouting from Clive's ears. He said, "You look tip-top." He cleared his throat. "For what you endured yesterday."

Clive knew James was surprised to find him working. He was surprised himself. But after his bath, he'd felt no yearning to lift the board over his bottle. No desire to alter his mind at all. In fact, the world seemed so entirely different from what he'd ever experienced that he was still filled with awe. Clive smiled. Said, "Hope that was a one-off."

James looked to the other employee. Usually when he approached, crewmen and keepers scurried away. This one had followed Clive and stayed. But he seemed rather nervous. Even partially hidden by glasses, an eye twitch was noticeable. Clive said, "Mr. Shackleford, this is Jack Older. He's a graduate of the University of Tennessee. Majored in anthropology. I've hired him while he sorts out what he wants to do. Anthropology is currently rather hard to pursue." Clive cleared his throat.

"Yes, well, that's nonsense. The whole circus was for publicity. Glad to have you here, son."

Jack put a finger to his eye to calm it. He'd braced for a lecture on the sinfulness of his academic major. He knew Mr. Lovett considered the Scopes trial a disaster, but he'd never spoken with Mr. Shackleford directly, and most people weren't very enlightened.

They talked hippopotamus maladies. Jack had read up. Said hippos were prone to schistosomiasis, as were all animals of African origin. Mr. Shackleford, a breeder of mules, horses, and cattle, also often found worms to be culprits. He said, "Has anybody checked her waste?"

"Murkin has. But hasn't reported the results. He's working in the monkey cages today." That was Clive.

They all looked at Dinah. She was still in the water. Her eyes were closed. James said, "I guess they're all lethargic until they attack."

"That's a relaxed posture. Rather like a cat sleeping in the sun," Clive replied. "Wouldn't have been in there, otherwise."

James understood relaxed postures. People used them too much. Aversion to hard work was the modern malaise. The eventual ruin of civilization. He was ruminating on that, so missed what Jack said. And it may have been that Jack had said it to Clive anyway. James did hear Clive say, "I told Crawford I'd take him to see her."

James said, "See who?"

"The diving girl. Miss Two Feathers."

"How's she doing?"

"I haven't heard anything new."

"When are you going?"

"Probably tomorrow. Visiting hours are in the mornings and afternoons."

"I can get you in anytime."

"Crawford too?"

James blinked. Smoothed his mustache and winced. "Does he need to go?"

"They're friends."

James looked off into the park. He said, "They would be."

Clive looked toward Dinah. The Americans, everywhere he'd lived, not just in the South, had peculiar notions about Negros. But Clive had been around James long enough to understand his were more peculiar than most. Shackleford was not a hateful man. And he considered slavery a terrible mistake. Railed against it on both moral and rational grounds. Told stories of working alongside Negros in his youth. And had for years employed Negros in jobs many people wouldn't let them have. But James also thought white and black people were utterly alien to one another. And sometimes he talked at length of the inherent nobility of the Aryan race. Claimed all progress in history could be attributed to its unique ingenuity. He did seem perplexed when challenged about the pyramids of Egypt. But he claimed that future discoveries would firmly establish those as the remnants of the Greco-Latin branch of the Aryan family.

So James was firmly against miscegenation. And that was his problem with Crawford. Clive didn't know how much white blood Crawford had, but certainly enough to produce light skin and some property. So Clive didn't know how to respond to James. He clasped his hands behind his back and shifted his gaze to a rotten cabbage.

James looked toward Methuselah. He was at the edge of the pond, not far from Dinah's head. It was Jack who said, "I hope Miss Feathers is okay. She had quite a fall. And landed in a cluster of graves."

Clive turned to look squarely at Jack. "How did you come by that?"

Jack blushed. He hadn't been able to think of much else except Two since she'd taken her fall. He'd shadowed Clive all day hoping for information. Just pretending to care about worms and the damn hippopotamus was a Herculean effort. "I heard it somewhere, sir. It's the talk of the park."

Clive frowned. So did James. Neither wanted the discussion of graves to continue. James said, "What time do you want to go to the hospital?"

"I'll need to talk to Crawford. See when he can get away."

"When you decide, if it's out of hours, I'll have someone ring and tell them to let you in."

"Should we go in the front door?"

"What do you mean?"

Clive looked toward the rotten cabbage again. "Will I be able to take Crawford in that door with me?" As long as Clive had lived in Tennessee, he couldn't make sense of the laws and customs around where Negros could or couldn't go. Several years back, he'd given up trying and had asked ever since.

"Take him in with you. I'll make sure they know he's coming. But keep an eye on him. He has a tendency to do whatever he wants." James grunted, ran his hand over his hair, and wished he hadn't left his hat in the car.

Visiting
Two

Clive had bought his automobile when he'd returned to the States from the Great War. But Americans drive on the wrong side of the road. And you can't test for pain by touching a fender, show affection by rubbing a roof, or feel for fever by laying a palm on a hood. Clive drove only on days when he felt a compulsion to get into nature, and then mostly on the rural dirt roads south and west of the park. Besides, Crawford was an expert on all types of machinery, even cars, and Negros chauffeured white people all over town. They got in trouble only for driving themselves.

So Crawford drove them to the Protestant Hospital, a large red brick building with a fleet-of-steps entrance railed by more brick and sandwiched between wings three stories high. They both entered by the front door and were met by a tall, thin woman wearing a nurse's uniform and white cap trimmed in red. Clive harbored a deep fondness for nurses. In various parts of his body, he still felt their tenderness and compassion. In fact, he'd been touched more by nurses than by any other women, so there was an erotic aspect to those memories. But this nurse didn't evoke that. She was lanky, long-nosed, and reminiscent of a crane. However, Clive was also particularly fond of cranes. He'd bred them for years. He smiled. "Sister, I'm Clive Lovett. I presume you know we're here to visit the young woman who works for Mr. Warner and Mr. Shackleford." He pronounced those names like Roosevelt and Wilson, and paused for their effect. He didn't introduce Crawford because he feared the nurse might take offense and wear that look on her face.

But, instead, the nurse was surprised by being called *sister*. She certainly wasn't this Englishman's sibling. And *sister* was a word the coloreds used to show familiarity. She'd been told to let the one with the Englishman in, and had arranged a private room for the meeting so as not to frighten the female patients. But *sister* was a bridge too far. She said, "I am not your sister, Mr. Lovett."

Clive blinked. Turned slightly red. It was Crawford who said, "He didn't mean disrespect." He would've provided an excuse had he had an idea of one.

By then, Clive realized the nature of his mistake. He smiled gently. "I was in hospital during the war. First in France, then in England. At home, we reserve the title Sister for our nurses with the greatest authority. I suppose that's who you are."

Actually it wasn't. The nurse had escaped the confines of a rural life in Covington, Tennessee, by being the brightest in her high school class and a big help in calving. She'd intended to stay in nursing just long enough to help birth a few babies and catch a doctor. But the war broke out, and the doctors went overseas. She stayed in Nashville, grew to enjoy nursing, and lived in the dormitory attached to the hospital. She hadn't broken into management because she was blocked by three males who'd learned their nursing in the army. She lived with her resentment like a cat does with its fur. She said, "I see. Well, different countries have different ways."

Both Lovett and Crawford nodded. Neither took the remark as anything other than what it was, a fact the nurse considered unfortunate.

She added, "I've moved the performer to a private area. Of course, visiting her on the ward is out of the question."

Both men nodded to acknowledge the truth of that statement. They nodded again when she said, "Follow me."

The corridor was dark, empty, and lined with silent radiators and closed doors. Its floor tiles were large squares interspersed with diamonds. Clive and Crawford were aware of the sounds of their steps, but the nurse was listening for hints of happenings beyond the walls. Lights were not out yet. That would happen at nine p.m. As they progressed, she heard talking, coughing, and occasional crying. Nothing unusual. She changed her focus to the steps of the men behind her. The Negro was, probably, only three paces back and, of the two, the more sure-footed. The other's walk was just slightly uneven. Probably due to a war wound. If the Negro attacked her, would the Englishman have enough strength to wrestle him to the floor? She stepped harder to sound strong.

If Crawford had given the nurse any thought, he would've been aware of her fear. As it was, he was thinking about how much nicer the Protestant Hospital was than Hubbard and feeling some resentment. Nor was Clive thinking about the nurse. He was wondering about the abandoned old woman. Hoping her daughter had returned, and wondering how to ask about that. But he didn't have a name and didn't want to describe the scene, so he began searching the air for apparitions. He doubted phantasmagoric appearances were always tied to particular individuals. Certainly in England they seemed to be attached to houses. He turned to look behind him. He didn't see any ghosts. The hall was dark and smelled slightly of ether. The three of them looked to be alone.

Finally, they turned a corner and the nurse opened a door. Two was in a wheelchair in a small room that was otherwise empty, except for a desk and a couple of chairs. Her left leg was in a cast, propped up by an extension, and straight out before her. She wore a dark look on her face.

None of the three said anything directly to one another until after the lanky nurse warned, "We make a practice of not tiring our patients with chatting. You have fifteen minutes." She conspicuously looked at her watch, turned, and shut the door behind her. Clive and Crawford took chairs.

Two had learned to ride when she'd learned to walk. When she fell off horses, she was lifted back on until she was tall enough to climb back up herself. Additionally, she'd seen performers trampled by more than one species of large animal and had, on one occasion, pulled an unconscious man out of the path of a stampede of buffalo. She'd also learned by example to show no emotion in front of whites outside of her family. So she was more surprised than either of her visitors when she burst into tears.

Clive looked at his hands; twisted his fingers. He was used to distressed animals. Could magically soothe them to settling. And in the trenches, he'd cradled more than one dying soldier. But he didn't have extensive experience with girls or women. His shoulders hunched. He receded into his jacket like a turtle into its shell.

Crawford, on the other hand, had spent his entire life surrounded by sisters, aunties, and female cousins. Not to mention his mother. In all of his experience (except in his current courtship), the women of his acquaintance never held back their emotions. In fact, they unloaded feelings and thoughts like they were dumping coal off the back of a truck. He produced a handkerchief from his pocket and extended it to Two.

Clive's eyes widened. He's never seen a Negro do that and wondered what Two would do.

She took the cloth and said, "Thank you." Dabbed her tears. Said, "I'm sorry," and blew her nose.

Crawford said, "How're they treating you?"

Two sniffled. Dabbed again. "I've been mostly knocked out. But I need to get outta here."

"Don't you think it's too soon?" That was Clive.

"They can't do anything else. They've given me crutches." She nodded to a pair lying on top of a radiator.

Clive hadn't anticipated Two would be ready to leave. When he'd been in hospital, it'd been for months. He was almost certain her doctor wouldn't allow her to go, and he said so.

Two replied, "He doesn't need to see me again for three weeks."

Clive pushed his glasses higher up on his nose. He'd need to talk to somebody about where to move her. Or maybe her family could come get her. He asked about that.

Two hesitated. She looked to Crawford. Then she looked at the handkerchief in her hands. "I don't want them to know. Has anybody called them yet?"

"I don't know," Clive said. "But you're poorly. They'll want to tend you. You have a mother, I suppose?"

Two looked to Crawford again. He said, "We could take her back to her dormitory. Is your room on the first floor?"

"No. But there're rooms on that floor. Mrs. Hampton could move me."

Clive understood wanting out of the hospital. Men's wards were no better than barracks. Women's might be, but not greatly, and women needed more privacy. He understood that much. He said, "We'd have to see. I could speak to someone. As you know, there won't be any more diving this year." He winced.

Two dropped her head to hide more tears. Before her operation and after, she'd been mostly unconscious. But when she'd come to, she was in a room that smelled bad and looked white and strange. She'd tried to sit up, but found a strap under her breasts. That panicked her. She gasped for breath. Ran her hands along the leather. Tried to locate a buckle. She'd been doing that when she noticed her cast. She stopped and fell back. A woman in the bed next to her had said, "Ya awake?"

Two replied, "How do I get outta here?"

The woman said, "Was ya really the gal on the diving horse?"

That brought Two spots of awareness. Images like pictures spaced on a wall. Falling through the air. Feeling horsehair. Yellow lantern light in the cave.

When the woman asked the same question again, Two said, "Where are we?"

The woman said, "Protestant."

"What's that?"

"We're in a hospital, girl. The best in the city. Them Catholics don't know how to run a hospital. I went in there once to visit a woman who were hit by a car practically right at my own feet. It were the right thing to do. But I got outta there quick as I could. They got these dying Jesuses all over the walls. Arms spread out. Hardly no clothes on a-tall. That ain't right."

The woman had gone on. But Two hadn't listened. She'd shifted into grieving Ocher. And she'd been deep into that when four nurses came into the room. Two of them rolled the woman away. The other two rolled Two to a long room of women in beds lining the walls. Each had a cast somewhere on her body; some had a limb hanging in a rope-and-sling contraption. The ward was filled with yelling, crying, and complaining. Two couldn't grieve in there. She monitored her surroundings.

She wanted to go home. To see her parents. Be nursed by her grandmothers. But the memory of riding the train with broken ribs tightened her chest and diverted her attention. The pain had been excruciating. If she went again, she'd need to go in a Pullman and have somebody with her. But the Montgomerys were her only real female friends at Glendale, and they had to work. Lefty or Rooster would want to come get her. But horses were their mode of travel, and neither had been out of Oklahoma except over the border to Kansas. Her Uncle Steak had a car. He would do it, and bring her mother and aunt. If the roads were good enough. From the ranch to Tulsa, they were paved. But the roads from Tulsa to Muskogee were mostly mud and ruts. And the ones she saw from train windows everywhere were the same or graveled. A road trip could be harder than a ride on the rails. And Two skipped quickly over the possibility that either of her parents could make one of those. Her father wouldn't know how. Her mother, without the protection of the show, would be treated like a Negro. So Two had concluded rather quickly that her best bet was to stay at Glendale. She blew her nose and firmly stated her wish to her visitors.

Clive assured Two he would speak with Mrs. Hampton. Crawford said he'd visit her every day when she was back in the park. But Two's tears were taxing to the men. They escaped the room as quickly as they could, and flew down the gray-tiled hallway as if a strong, steady wind beat at their backs. They were in the car and on the street before either of them spoke. Clive said, "I think it's best to call her family."

Crawford kept his eyes on the road. "No Miz Hampton?"

Clive looked out a window at a boarding house. A man and a woman were under a light, on the front steps, talking. "I will. I said I would. But her family will want to nurse her."

Crawford stopped at an intersection. Cars rolled east in front of them. He said, "How's that gonna work?"

"What do you mean?"

"Are they driving here? Taking the train? I'm just trying to figure it. Out west is a long way off."

"She got here on a train."

Crawford fell silent. His siblings in Chicago, New York, and California visited each other on trains. But they didn't come south very often. He wondered how dark Two's parents were.

They rode down 21st, out Hillsboro Pike, and toward Franklin Pike on Woodmont in silence. It was obvious to Clive that Crawford considered Two's parents coming to get her was a bad idea. Maybe he knew something of her family situation? Maybe the girl didn't get along with them? Diving on horses to stay away from home? It was impossible to tell without more information, but he wasn't one to pry. He moved his mind to trains. To memories of Victorian stations, coal soot, clacking, and whistles. To the green hillsides and hedges of England.

Visitations

Mrs. Hampton had finished her afternoon inspections and was patting her forehead with her handkerchief when Clive walked into Chambliss. Flushed already, she slipped into a deeper shade of red. But her eyes widened, and so did her lips. Clive Lovett was the most eligible bachelor in her orbit. He had a good job and important connections, and aroused affections in not only women and children, but also in other men. He was a doer of good deeds and frequently featured in the papers. And as far as she'd been able to ferret out, he didn't have any family at all, neither here nor over there. No sisters, mothers, daughters, or, in her calculations, competition for his attention, beyond animals and birds. And he hadn't, to Helen's knowledge, ever been married and wasn't courting any particular lady. But she didn't think he was "one of those." There'd never been a hint of that. She thought he must be shy with women. In need of the right one to bring him out of his shell. Helen usually had to pretend an interest in some sort of loud fowl to attract Clive's notice, so she saw his appearance in Chambliss as a rare opportunity. She fairly gushed, "Clive! How lovely to see you." She tucked her handkerchief into her belt.

Clive had spent his morning with animals. Out of respect for the fairer sex, he'd stopped by his cabin to wash. And, as a bear had slobbered on his shirt and muddied his trousers, he'd changed out of his uniform. After seeing Helen Hampton, he intended to visit with James or, maybe, with May. He hoped for the latter. But that was a step ahead, and he was somewhat aware that the widow Hampton was fond of his presence. He envisioned turning her fondness to his advantage. He thrust his chin. Made his eyes dance.

Helen's eyes danced, too, and so did her hips, just a wiggle. She said, "What brings you to our fair abode?"

"Well, of course, it's always a pleasure to see you, Helen. And I was wondering if we might have a chat." Clive had his hat in his hand. He gestured with that.

Helen turned an even darker shade of crimson. Beneath her corset, possibilities fluttered like moths. She batted her eyelashes a little.

Clive could discern the effect he was having, and didn't want to produce a false impression. He said, "There're vacant rockers on the porch. May I escort you outside? I need your permission for something before I approach Mr. Shackleford."

Helen's face rather fell. She tried picking it up with a smile that was a little less than sincere. "Of course. May I have some refreshments prepared for us? Some lemonade or tea?"

"Hot tea for me. A little milk."

"That's easy. Have a seat. I'll be with you shortly."

They settled with cold tea heated up. Spoke first of the weather, then of the pool's collapse, the panic, and the various reports of injuries. But Helen wanted every detail of Clive's going into the cave and saving the day. The tale was not only thrilling; it provided an opportunity for praise, for admiration, for everything a gentleman longs to hear.

And Clive wasn't immune. The tea was terrible, but that was true all over the States. However, the trellis was twined with clematis vines, and bees and hummingbirds were tending their business. A slight breeze was making its way to the porch, and carrying from Helen a hint of perfume that Clive hadn't previously noticed. He didn't tell her the grimmer details of his cave experience, nor relate a word of his visions, but he did dwell on the sad predicament in which he'd found Miss Feathers. He emphasized her bravery and resilience as he inched up to the topic which propelled his visit. When Helen said, "What will become of her?" she fell directly into his snare.

Clive set his teacup on a little table by his chair. He twisted his head a tad and crinkled his eyes in a way he'd found generally effective. "That is of grave concern to me. I've been hoping you could aid. Helping the girl mend is, naturally, best left in the hands of a lady."

Helen couldn't tell exactly where this was leading. It'd taken an unexpected turn that aroused some suspicion. Still, Clive Lovett looked more attractive by the minute. She put a hand to her bosom. "Me?"

"Yes. If the girl's parents can't, or won't, come get her, she'll need somewhere to stay. I understand she lives in this hall." Clive furrowed his brow like that was a question.

"Yes, she does. She has a room to herself. I thought it was best that way."

"Of course," Clive replied. He wasn't clear about Helen's motivations, but assumed decisions about dormitory housing were as specialized as those concerning the caging of animals. He added, "Would her room be on the ground floor?"

"No. She's on the second. In a corner room that's quite nice. Bigger than ones along the hallway, and closer to the bathroom. I haven't given her any less because of her . . ." Helen didn't know exactly how to end that sentence. She didn't know the English attitude toward Indians, and didn't want to leave the impression that she thought all people from far off were inferior.

Clive wanted to give Helen time to suggest the solution herself. He looked over to his cup. Wished the tea had been better, wished he had something to do with his hands. He looked up and out into the lawn. It was speckled with wildflowers, the grass not as closely cropped as the park's, but dappled by sunny spots interlaced by shadows thrown by branches and trunks.

Clive jerked. A man, nude to the waist and clothed in a wide sash and loincloth, was standing beneath a tree. He wore leather or boots (Clive couldn't tell which) from his feet up to over his knees. He was tattooed, and his head was shaved except for a knot on the top. He was not looking directly toward the porch, more up into the leaves. Clive turned to Helen. Her head was cocked at a girlish angle. She was setting her cup on the table. Clive looked back at the man. Then back to Helen. He said, "What type of tree is that?" He nodded toward the one shading the man; clearly, an American Indian.

"Why, a white oak. They're all over the place. Must have been here since the beginning."

"Is there anything dodgy about it?"

"Dodgy?"

"Pardon. Peculiar. Does it look peculiar to you?"

Helen peered. The tree was tall. So were they all. They'd been there for decades, maybe for centuries. The bark on that one looked a little silvery at a distance. Helen said so, as the tree was otherwise unremarkable.

Clive clasped his hands tightly together. He was afraid they would begin to shake. The Indian was still there. Arms across his chest and paint on his face. Clive said, "I suppose these woods were once home to your Indians?"

They'd been talking about Two. And Helen guessed that, being English, Clive was quite curious about the aboriginal population. She was eager to enlighten him. "Well, they were quite a problem to the original settlers. Murderous and depraved. They didn't actually live here. When the Donelson and Robertson parties arrived, there wasn't a single soul in sight. Then, as soon as they started building their stations, the savages attacked." Helen shook her head.

The earliest whites had been attracted not only by the great salt lick, but also by the abundant game and the easy access to the river. At first, they'd maintained the land was theirs by virtue of the Stanwix Treaty of

1768. Then somebody noticed that particular treaty had been signed by the Iroquois Confederacy in New York, had calculated that New York was a long way off, and finally concluded that these might not be the same savages. They had to change their story; the land had always been unclaimed, was merely a hunting ground for the tribes around. The settlements shouldn't be a concern. The land was empty and free for the taking.

They just flatly refused to recognize they were disrupting the way the Indians fed their families just as surely as if they'd been robbing stores and warehouses in London, Liverpool, or Edinburgh. Or burning crops and stealing sheep in North Carolina, where they'd earlier killed off the residents. So, at first, they felt perplexed. Next they felt frightened. Then, terrified of being attacked. They became convinced they were encircled by barbarians of an inferior race. They called on their Lord. Read their Bible. Prayed, and prayed some more. They taught their children and dogs to kill Indians on sight. Gave thanks to Heaven for their rifles and cannon. Helen didn't say all of that. She didn't even know some of it. And many of those poor, innocent settlers had been killed or scalped, or both.

But Helen had taught Latin at Buford College before she'd married. And afterwards, she and her husband had returned for the pageants. She remembered, quite particularly, an operetta, just over a decade in the past, when the college was at its pinnacle. She said, "Here at Buford, we forgave the Indians. It was quite common for the girls to dress up as Indian maidens. One year for Christmas, nearly the entire student body presented *The Feast of the Red Corn*. It was a marvelous operetta about the Queen of the Tribe, the Spirit of the Wind, and a terrible Sorceress. There was smoke, and incense, and ghosts of dead trees dancing, right over there in Burgess Hall." Helen tilted her head toward the building.

Clive was watching the Indian, who was still peering up into the leaves. But he'd been partially listening. He heard the words *spirit* and *ghosts,* and recognized them as an opportunity. He turned to Helen and opened his mouth to ask if apparitions ever appeared in the vicinity of the college, when she suddenly bolted out of her rocker and said, "I have just the thing. Something you'll find fascinating." She disappeared into the building.

Clive looked back at the oak. The Indian was gone. He arose and stepped to his right to see if the aboriginal had moved behind the tree. He hadn't, apparently. Clive's chest deflated. He rubbed his forehead, then put his hands on the railing. Since Millwood had appeared in the cave, and the other apparition in the hospital, he'd alternated between feeling completely comforted and entirely alarmed. He didn't think the Indian under the oak had anything directly to do with his cousin or the hospital specter. But did conclude that his ability to see him did.

The possibility of existence in another near realm wasn't a new notion to Clive. As a child in England, he'd heard tales of Tutbury and Chillingham castles, renowned for their hauntings. And from the moment he'd arrived in Tennessee, he'd heard Bell Witch stories. That vicious, loquacious apparition had appeared in Robertson County, one just north of Davidson, and had haunted the Bell family for over three years. Had thrown fits, moved objects, and, eventually, caused a death. Had also conversed with hundreds of people, including, apparently, Old Hickory before he was president. But seeing and hearing specters didn't settle easily into Clive's concept of himself as a man of the twentieth century. He was pondering the comfort of singing with Millwood, as opposed to the mayhem the Bell Witch provoked, when Helen returned to the porch carrying a framed photograph. It was as large as a tray, and she'd lifted it off a wall. She said, "Take a gander at that. Buford had an archery club."

The picture was of six girls, one rather chubby, all in long skirts and white blouses. Their hair was gathered into buns on the tops or the backs of their heads. They were holding bows and arrows, drawn ready to shoot. Clive wasn't entirely sure what to say. He didn't know if women shooting arrows was a typical, or a strange, American thing. He'd lived in the country for over fifteen years and learned something new every day. He said, "Let me take that." He settled the frame against the railing. Then he said, "Do you suppose they were good shots?"

Helen sat down in her rocker. "I suspect not. Read the motto at the bottom." It said, *I shot an arrow into the air — It fell to earth I know not where.* She giggled. She wanted Clive to see her as young at heart. She calculated he might be seven or eight years younger than she, and she needed to overcome that impediment.

Clive wasn't sure how he'd wound up gazing at a large photograph when all he'd wanted to do was secure a ground floor room for Two. The visit had turned unpredictable in more than one respect. And he didn't see how he could steer the conversation back in the direction he wanted. His British politeness had him stuck. That happened fairly frequently, and he'd learned to charge on as if he were an American. He sat back down and said, "Perhaps Miss Two Feathers can give lessons to anyone who wants them. That is, if in your kindness, you could arrange things so that she can stay here without having to climb the stairs."

The purpose of Clive's visit suddenly came into Helen's focus. Disappointing, but, nevertheless, an opportunity to do him a favor. "I suppose I could. There're four rooms on the ground floor. All of them singles. Two taken by girls. But it would entail some swapping around. That could take persuasion."

Clive smiled. Tried to make his eyes dance again. Said, "Well, you are a persuasive woman."

Helen fluttered. She held her fingers to the notch at her throat and ducked her head. "I'll see what I can do. When do you expect her to arrive?"

"I don't know for certain. I saw her last night. She wants to be released very badly. But, of course, her physician has the final word. And Mr. Shackleford. Mr. Warner is in Europe."

Helen knew Clive actually worked for Percy Warner. Knew, also, they were close friends. Clive certainly ran in the right circles. Though you'd never know it from watching him toss fish to seals, tease the bears with gum, and hand out rabbits to children. He was an unusual man. Helen wanted to reach out and touch his sleeve. She curled her fingers. Said, "If you'll let me know what the doctor and Mr. Shackleford say, I'll make the arrangements."

· · ·

At Longview, Clive was met by Adelaide, who told him, "Mr. James ain't at home." So he was smiling as she led him to the main living room where May stood over a long table with a clipboard and pencil in hand. After greetings, May waved the pencil over a slew of objects set out and lined up. She said, "These have come from New York. Donated by Mrs. Rollin Grant. She's a dear friend of mine and a great-niece of President Polk."

Clive had been in Tennessee long enough to know that President Polk's widow had, for decades, reigned as the queen of Nashville society, the arbiter of taste, the grantor and withholder of invitations. And he knew that May was the president of the Polk Memorial Association, as well as of other commemorative societies. He respected her work in preserving the past, and thought if women like May had their say, in another eight hundred years, America might have some history. He inspected the items on display. Among them, a silver basket, a gold watch fob, and a small marble foot. The foot didn't entirely look Greek, and Clive knew the Polks didn't have any children. It seemed rather odd. "Was that President Polk's?"

"It was his possession, not his foot. It's General Tom Thumb's."

Clive squinted. May said, "Our ladies are meeting to view the relics before they're exhibited in the War Memorial Museum. I wasn't entirely expecting a foot."

"Not entirely?"

"Not at all."

"Is it some sort of joke?"

"I doubt it. The paperwork says it was a gift from Barnum."

"And President Polk kept it?"

"The president wouldn't have noticed it. He literally worked himself to death. But Mrs. Polk kept everything he was ever given. Polk Place was like a museum. Or, maybe, a mausoleum."

"You were in it?

"Many times. It was the scene of grand occasions. And I had visited as a child during the war. My father was a doctor and had a pass to travel the streets. While we were occupied, he'd often take one of us children with him to give us a place to go."

"That must have been a difficult way to grow up."

"Well, I like to think of it as unusual and instructive. It taught me life isn't for the faint of heart. But I assume you didn't come here to discuss odd antiques or a war." She pointed to a peach-colored chair, one of two separated by a table. "Would you like some refreshment? I can have Adelaide bring in some tea."

Clive declined the tea, and May sat, propped her clipboard against her chair, and stuck the pencil in her hair. "What can I do for you?"

"To come to the point directly, Miss Two Feathers wants out of the hospital. But apparently doesn't want to go home to Oklahoma."

"You've seen her?"

"Yes, last evening. Her leg's in a cast to above her knee. And she's emotional. But, otherwise, tickety-boo."

"You were brave to go in the cave. I'm sure she feels indebted to you."

"I was the logical one." Clive cleared his throat. "I've just spoken with Helen Hampton. She's willing to move Miss Feathers to a room on the ground floor of Chambliss."

"That's settled, then. Do you want me to tell James?"

"If you don't think he'll object."

"Why should he?"

"She won't be working. She'll be taking up space."

"Are there plans to hire another diver?"

"I think it's safe to say we're out of the horse diving business. But she'll be an expense."

May blinked rapidly. One of James's mottos was "Work and save." He was always suspicious of expenditures other than his own. She said, "Well, she's slim. I'm sure she won't eat much. Let her stay as long as she wants. Do you want me to say it was my idea?"

Clive smiled. "It may be best coming from you."

Two
Returns

≡

Two was in a wheelchair on the hospital's front porch with her crutches laid over the arms when Clive's car rolled to a stop. Crawford was driving, and Two assumed Mr. Lovett was in the passenger's seat. But a man she'd never seen before emerged from a back door. He was wearing a park uniform and glasses, was tall and redheaded. Two flapped a fan in front of her face as the men climbed the steps.

Crawford took note of the three white people on the hospital's porch. One had already turned her back to him, but the two others had not. One of those was watching him closely. He said, "Miss Feathers, this is Jack Older. Mr. Lovett sends his apologies. He's giving pony rides to girls from the School for the Blind." To Jack he said, "Mr. Older, should you tell the people inside we're here? Ask if we're to take the chair or just the crutches?"

Two and Jack acknowledged each other. He put a hand to his eye. Said to Crawford, "Did anyone tell you who to tell?"

"Do you know, Miss Feathers? Mr. Lovett says it's been arranged. But we don't want to steal a chair we're not supposed to take."

Two hadn't asked about the chair. She didn't intend to use it. She handed her fan to Crawford. "Just leave it." She clutched her crutches.

Crawford held up the fan. "Hold your horses. We have to make sure they don't think we're stealing you. Not like the old days when people could do what they wanted to." He looked to Jack. Felt the white stranger's stare.

Jack had been raised in a segregated town, hadn't gone to school with Negros, and hadn't met any at the University of Tennessee. He'd taken anthropology courses which divided races into various classifications that were subdivided and debated. He'd accepted Darwin's theory of monogenesis, which maintained that all people presently on earth were descended from the same human stock. But he agreed with others who asserted that over the eons some of that stock had risen and some had fallen. He thought the races were three, Caucasoid, Mongoloid, and Negroid, and that they formed an evolutionary hierarchy with Caucasoid on top, Mongoloid in the middle, and Negroid on the bottom. He was currently debating with himself over the extent of the inferiority of the Mongoloid races (which included American Indians), but he had no doubt about Negroids being inferior. And he knew Crawford couldn't go in the front door alone. He thought about telling him to do that, just to see him squirm and show him his place. But he decided against it because he'd have to locate a white nurse, anyway. He said, "I'll see to it," and put a hand to his eyelid again. Finally being near Two Feathers made his body parts jump.

Next to the grand porch was another entrance for people who had to be carried or rolled. While Crawford waited by the car, Jack, Two, and a male nurse came out that door. By the time they got to Crawford, Two and the nurse, Raymond Jenner, were disagreeing. Two didn't want the chair. Jenner wanted her to take it with her. Told her it takes a lot of strength to carry a cast around on crutches. Said he was speaking from experience. And, besides, her physician, Dr. Kelly, said the chair was necessary, and part of the deal with Mrs. Shackleford. Raymond was used to bullying people; glad illnesses and injuries gave him occasions. Also, he'd visited Glendale Park all of his life and read both the *Tennessean* and the *Banner* every evening. He was puffed up to be lecturing the daring performer who'd taken the dive and survived. At supper, he'd tell the story at his rooming house table. He also knew who the colored man was. He'd tell that, too. Sighting a Crawford out and about was like spotting an ostrich at the ocean.

Two felt insulted that the nurse thought she didn't have enough strength to lug a cast around on crutches. But she wasn't entirely sure he was wrong, and she wasn't a combative person. So Jenner won. But the wheelchair was solid steel and hard rubber. At every angle Jenner and Crawford tried, they couldn't squeeze it into the car. Finally, they stood back and wiped their brows with their handkerchiefs. Agreed they'd done their best. If the chair wouldn't go in, it couldn't go. Jack had stood by and watched. Thought maybe he could get it in, but didn't want to fail in front of Two and, anyway, thought the other two men should be exerting the physical labor. That was clearly part of the male nurse's job, and it grated on him that Crawford had the run of the zoo. Besides, it was hot. Ninety degrees at noon.

Jack didn't like sitting in the front seat with Crawford, but Two needed the back seat to herself. She sat with her left leg extended. But no one had thought to bring a pillow, so the armrest, door handle, and window crank attacked her back. Unable to find a comfortable position, she became nauseated by the ride and the heat. They stopped at a light. Two gulped deep. The windows were down, but the back seat was hot and sticky. Three blocks along, at another light, Two tried to sit upright. She opened the door with a struggle that was partially successful, so she didn't throw up on the floor. That spewed onto the running board.

Crawford eased to the side of the road, and Jack pulled Two's door open completely. Told her to get it all out and held her by the elbow while she did. She kept her head down a couple of minutes after she was through, partially to be sure it was over, partially from embarrassment. Eventually, she pushed herself back into the seat. She sat at an angle, threw an elbow over her face, and wished she had a bandana. Crawford stared straight ahead, willed the traffic out of the way, and willed the car to go faster. Jack Older's mind was glued to Two. He wanted to turn around and talk to her. Wished his handkerchief hadn't been too sweaty to offer. Was more embarrassed about that lapse than concerned about Two's vomiting. But he really rather liked seeing her helpless, taken down a notch.

Clive had told Helen Hampton he'd check on Two after she settled in, and Helen hoped he meant that evening. But by the time supper was over and the evening acts out of the hall, Clive hadn't appeared, and Helen began thinking about wandering over to tell him privately that she'd gotten Two set up on the first floor. She rehearsed a recitation of the effort she'd expended to switch her room with Christa Belle Henley's. The dance instructor occupied a first floor single, like herself; Mrs. Watson, the cook; and Winifred Rose, the games organizer. Neither Christa Belle nor Winifred could get along with the other residents, but Winifred was less irritating, and Helen preferred her to Christa Belle. However, Christa Belle gave her resistance. She accused her of being unfair, and agreed to move only after she visited Two's room and found it was cooler than hers.

Helen had pitched in with Christa Belle and the maids to make the switch and had, consequently, talked to Christa Belle more than she usually did. She spent some time deciding how to paint the dance instructor's personality to Clive in a way that didn't sound catty but still enhanced his view of the trouble she had gone to. She wanted Clive to understand that she was above petty gossip, was emotionally mature. But, then, not too mature. It was hard to tell what men found attractive. Except bosoms. Helen pulled her shoulder blades together, and jutted her bust. Breasts were currently out of fashion. But that fashion would change. It was the fault of mannish women in New York City. Not what men actually preferred.

Helen was still developing her story as she strolled down one of the gravel lanes that crisscrossed Glendale. For late May, the day had been unusually hot, and it hadn't cooled down. Music from both the casino and skating rink filled the air along with the heat. The effect was oppressive, but Helen pushed the competing tunes out of her head and wiped her brow with her hanky. She hoped to find Clive alone on his porch. Wondered if she could muster the courage to emerge from the night and start a conversation.

Clive was home. But Crawford was with him. They were in Clive's drive, next to his car. Helen stopped on the path and looked toward the park. Couples and men in groups were clustered. A pack of boys was running. The lights lent a gauzy hue to the path. Helen realized then she could be recognized if Clive looked up. She stepped off the gravel into a tree's shadow. Laid her hand on the bark and felt her way around to the tree's far side. She looked directly into a playground, metal contraptions, and several whiskey barrels turned on their sides. They were a maze for children. Helen didn't have any of those, but knew they like to crawl, dirty their knees, and get stains on their clothes.

She was contemplating that habit in her nephews, still tucked close to the bark, when Clive looked up. He couldn't see Helen because she was hiding. But due to the lights overhead, he did notice a thickening of the shadow cast by the tree behind which she was tucked. He peered closer. Recalling the Indian, his heart started hammering. With difficulty concentrating, he continued his conversation with Crawford about getting his car washed and waxed. Crawford had cleaned the running board, but the odor still lingered. Clive was used to regurgitation, muck, and all sorts of animal residue; however, the car hadn't been tidied in a while and could use some attention. Crawford had a nephew who was automobile crazy and looking to put change in his pocket.

The shadow moved. But it still seemed insubstantial. Clive's heart thumped harder. He said to Crawford, "Please walk with me over there." He pointed to the tree. He felt more wonderment than fear, and wanted to know if he alone could see the apparitions.

With music converging from two directions, Helen couldn't hear the men coming nearer. She was looking toward the lights of the casino, wondering how many couples were dancing, wishing she were in their midst, swinging her hips, wearing younger, more fashionable clothes. So she was surprised. She gasped, put her palm to her chest. Then to her blush.

Clive said, "Out for a stroll?"

Without an escape, the partial truth would have to do. "I, I . . . wanted to tell you. I situated Miss Two Feathers as you wanted. But then I saw Crawford." Her head tilted in his direction. "I assumed he delivered the news. I was just relaxing. Enjoying the music." Her smile was lopsided. Her hand moved to her hair.

Clive was disappointed Helen wasn't the Indian. And was so accustomed to the music that he no longer heard it. He was about to comment on Two when Crawford said, "I'll drive the car to the barn, Mr. Lovett. Get Billy to spiff her up. Nice to see you again, Miz Hampton." Both replied, "Thank you, Crawford." Clive withdrew the key from his pocket and Crawford departed.

Clive looked around. They were in the shadows and grass. A peculiar location. He could go back to his cabin, but in all politeness, he'd need to extend an invitation, and his front room wasn't entirely shipshape. He said, "Shall we take a bench?"

Helen let go of her breath. "Ah! I really should get back to the women." She frowned. "But the dormitory is so hot. You can tell me how the animals are faring."

They sat with a space of about two feet between them. Clive confided his concerns over the hippopotamus's illness and the monkeys' hostilities. But as worrisome as they were, the Indian on the lawn still engaged his attention. He'd brooded on him since he'd first seen him over at Chambliss. Had concluded that if he existed in the same dimension as Millwood, the main promise of Christianity was an expression of a greater, more fundamental, law of the universe. And he was describing yet another attempt by the dominant macaque to harass the next smaller male like a schoolyard bully when it sprung to his mind that the universality of that law resembled evolution. Particular manifestations were like different species of animals. It was a radical notion. He couldn't blurt it out without seeming crazy. He said instead, "If William Jennings Bryan could've seen my monkeys, he might've rethought his position."

That statement, had Clive examined it, had more than one purpose. First, it involuntarily hinted at his sudden connection between the two large underlying and conflicting ideas — evolution and the survival of the soul — which preoccupied not just the whole state, but most of the literate and semi-literate nation. Secondly, Clive was rather enjoying Helen Hampton's company. But divisions left by the Scopes trial were wide and bottomless. Longstanding friendships had been rent, neighbors had stopped speaking, and marriages had fallen apart. It was a gaping gulf. Before furthering any acquaintance, it was best to determine the other person's position.

And, like everyone else, Helen had an opinion on evolution. Fortunately, though less grounded in science, it was the same as Clive's. She replied, "He made the whole state look like monkeys. I'd love to see the court overturn it."

"If you're serious, I can get us in." That came out so quickly it surprised even Clive.

They both had been facing the casino. Helen pulled back, tucked her chin in, and looked directly at him. On the next Monday and Tuesday, the Tennessee Supreme Court was hearing the appeal of the Scopes ruling. A seat in the courtroom was the hottest ticket in town. Helen was so delighted for an invitation that she didn't at first realize it could also be considered a date. It was like two bright stars had fallen from the sky in tandem, one slightly nearer than the other, and obscuring for an instant the further one's brilliance. Helen said, "I'd love to go," in almost a whisper.

Porch
Conversations

The next morning, Two was perched in a rocker situated in a wedge of shade on Chambliss's ground floor porch. Her left leg was propped on a stool and pillow, plastered from the ball of her foot to above her knee, and hurting. Prescription narcotics had been outlawed three years in the past, and Dr. Kelly had refused to prescribe medicinal alcohol for an Indian. Two couldn't get comfortable sitting up or back, tilted to the left or the right, or with her right leg down or up with her injured one. A *Western Story Magazine* was closed on her lap, and she was distracting herself from her pain by watching a bee buzz from bloom to bloom on the trellis when Christa Belle Henley appeared at her foot.

At only eleven in the morning, Christa Belle was wearing a dress with four layers of fringe. She was also wearing a headband and beads. A costume. Two was completely familiar with them. But Christa Belle wasn't an entertainer. Or Two didn't consider her one.

Christa Belle said, "The breeze in your room is better than mine, I'll say that. But it's not anywhere close to the kitchen. When I get in, I like to snack."

"I'm sorry about that."

"How's yer leg?"

"Fine. Except for the cast."

"Yer lucky they didn't amputate. That happened to a friend of mine. He woke up—" Two held her palm up. Shook her head. Christa Belle stopped. Tucked a curl beneath her headband and patted it. "Okay. So how long do ya haveta wear the cast?" She leaned against the railing. The bee flew away.

"I go back in three weeks. He'll tell me then."

"Well, I know ya don't like to face facts. But in Memphis I taught with a girl who got hit by a car. Snapped her leg just like a green bean." This time, Christa Belle held her palm out. "Now, just listen. They didn't take it off. But she walks on crutches to this day. Ruined her marriage chances. Ya need to prepare."

"Don't ya have anything to do?"

"I got a lesson in a few minutes. I just thought I'd check on ya. People've been worried. That was a terrible fall. How 'bout yer horse? What'd they do with it?"

"She. Ocher was a mare. They left her in there."

"So how bad was it? Were her legs broke? I guess they'd have to be in the fall." Christa Belle pulled the curl back out. Her headband was tight. Her best one was drying.

Two shifted and twitched. Clenched her teeth. Recalled Ocher turning cold beneath her grip, under her back. That brought a chill. Two flexed the muscles in her good thigh and stared toward the trellis of flowers and vines.

Christa Belle watched a pair of novelty girls came out the front door and walk down the steps. Their trays, collapsed and unloaded, were strapped on their backs. She wasn't going to get an answer about the horse out of Two, and she began to feel a little embarrassed. She said, "Everywhere else they sell cigarettes." She adjusted her headband from the back.

Two was still feeling Ocher turn cold. She didn't hear Christa Belle, and hadn't noticed the girls going to work. Christa Belle said, "Cat got ya tongue?" Her embarrassment was turning to irritation. She jerked her headband off, said, "Guess it does. Don't take any wooden nickels." She headed toward the steps thinking, *Some people don't know how to appreciate kindness.* She didn't like Two anyway. No cowgirl had style.

Two's chest had been slowly tightening while talking with Christa Belle. And she was beginning to feel like she was in the grip of a clench, strapped and saddled. Two could sense herself wanting to cry, and was determined not to let that happen in public. She should go back to her room. But it had only a single window that looked out on a woods, an old hen house, a cistern, some overgrown courts, and not much else. Its walls were confining, and she wasn't used to living inside. The porch felt freer and the outdoors more familiar. Two put one hand over her mouth to stuff in her feelings and used the other to slide her magazine under her uninjured leg. She settled further into her chair and concentrated on her breathing until she got control of her emotions. The hospital sedation had faded away, and except for the pain, she was clearheaded. Back to the real world. A new reality. An awful one.

Ocher was dead. And, when her cast came off, she couldn't dive on a different horse. Not that there weren't plenty of others. Or enough for the few who had the courage to plunge into a pool on the back of one. But she'd gotten Ocher killed. Diving on another horse would be the worst kind of betrayal.

Two started her real mourning out there on the porch. Ocher was as good as a human. Or better. All horses were. She'd been rocked to sleep as a baby on her daddy's. Given her gelding when she was five. Grown up riding him. Had grieved for weeks when he died. She didn't want to cry. But, in the end, she just couldn't help it.

For a handkerchief, she had only a blue paisley bandana she used as a headband to keep her hair out of her eyes. She drew it off, unknotted and unfolded it, and dabbed her tears. She blew her nose. She lowered her face toward her lap. Hoped people would think she was nodding off and wouldn't disturb her.

Two had become blank-faced when Franny bent down, her hands on her knees, and said, "Whatcha doing?"

"Sitting."

"You've been crying." Franny knelt, put a hand on Two's good leg. "Are you in pain?"

Two nodded.

"Won't they give you medicine?"

"Dope's not legal except in the hospital."

Franny stood. She'd seen plenty of people in pain. Except for singers, all entertainers got injured. "I can't remember. When you broke your ribs, what did they do?"

"Miz Shackleford's doctor saw me. He bound me up and told me not to cough."

That came back to Franny. She'd sponged Two off before she was taken to the train. She hadn't smelled alcohol. She guessed Two'd just stood it. Anybody who dived on a horse had to have guts. Franny touched her nose. A pain spiked behind her eyes, a body memory from the times the nose had been broken. She dropped her hand to her side. "I'm going to get you some whiskey."

"Whiskey kills Indians."

Franny frowned. "I forgot. The Irish can't handle it either. I'm glad I'm Italian."

"Besides, it's double illegal here."

Franny leaned against a rail and crossed her arms. "Well, if that's what's worrying you, that's less of a problem than you'd suspect."

"It is?"

"I can get you anything you want. How about a little vodka? It doesn't smell on the breath."

"Is it as dangerous as whiskey?"

Franny snorted. "Dangerous isn't the word I'd use. Delightful is more like it."

Two looked out onto the lawn. She knew Indians who could drink. But not many. And none in her family. In her imagination, Dan Christy's crushed face flew up, so crumpled that his eye slid off the side of his cheek. Two shivered. Still . . . she had white blood. She'd been put on the roll as . . . She couldn't remember how much, but not as a fullblood. She asked, "Do ya think it'll dull the pain?"

"Pos-i-tute-ly. You want me to get you some?"

Two looked off into the lawn again. Her mind went to her leg. It felt twice the size of the other. And it throbbed. That wasn't going to stop for a while. Maybe not for days. Her doctor would've prescribed alcohol for a white. "Can ya?"

"Easy-peasy. I got a contact in the band."

Dan's face flew up again. A warning. Two squinted. Maybe drinking liquor wasn't such a great idea. "Is that why ya've been dropping plates?"

Franny's eyes widened. Then she socked her palm with her fist. "That Marty. I'll kill her. What'd she say?"

"Not much. She's just worried. It's how y'all make your living."

Franny turned to the rail. Looked down into clematis webbed into wire. Purple and white flowers spotted the foliage. They smelled slightly of almonds. "No, I'm not drinking and throwing dishes. Though that's not a bad idea." She glanced sideways at Two. "The whole world's changing, Two. When's the last time you saw a duo ride a unicycle? Or anybody swallow fire? How long you think people'll want to see dishes, or bowling pins, or whatever, thrown in the air? Nowadays, people want to go to the movies. See Valentino and Garbo. And, soon, the pictures will talk. When that happens, we're all deep-sixed. And it's not far off."

"You think not?"

"I know not. Just look at this place. The biggest attraction here used to be the Flying Jenny."

"An aeroplane?"

Franny turned to face Two. "No. A merry-go-round. Adults rode it, just like children. Considered it the cat's meow. Now, can you picture that? Going on a date to ride a wooden horse up and down? Finding that romantic?"

Two had kept a lot of company on horses. In fact, the romance she was trying to shake had mostly taken place in the saddle. But that'd been on the crests and in the valleys of the Osage Hills, under a wide sky, crimson sunsets, and an eternity of stars. And the horses were real. Two tried to picture sparking on wooden horses, going up and down in a circle, with artificial lights, music blaring, and other people fouling the air. She shook her head. "So ya're dropping dishes to get out of your act?"

Franny bit her lip. She couldn't say, on any particular day, she'd intentionally dropped a dish. Just that carelessness would bust up the routine without having to confront Marty. It probably wasn't a good plan. But it seemed a way to get it done without having to say to her sister that they needed to find fellows, settle down, and get married. That's what Franny wanted to do. But Marty didn't actually like men. And Franny couldn't say that out loud. Not to Two. Not even to Marty. But she knew. Had for a long while. She said, "Sorta," and feared Two would suggest the most obvious solution.

But Two was thinking about the 101. They had competition from Ringling Bros.–Barnum & Bailey and the American Circus Corporation. Money wasn't flowing in and trickling down as freely as it had in the past. That was probably the reason the Millers leased her to Glendale. She didn't know that for sure — but did know Franny was talking sense. And her mind also floated to marriage. That was the path. Almost every woman walked it. But she'd never make a good farmer's wife. She didn't want to work from before dawn to dark, milk cows, feed chickens, wear dresses splattered with tiny flowers, or cook heavy noon meals and clean up the kitchen. She also didn't want to spit out a child every other spring.

She wanted to keep up her shooting, riding, and diving skills. Maybe go into the movies, like Will Rogers, Hoot Gibson, Buck Jones, and Ken Maynard. True, they were men, and all but one were white, but Hollywood appreciated cowboys and Indians. It promoted a great dream of the West, even better than the dream in real life. Then the fact that movie Indians were almost always shot and killed skidded into Two's mind. That turned her thinking back to getting a husband.

However, she'd been badly burned by the only love she'd ever had.

And she didn't have the faintest idea how to flirt. She could ride a horse standing up. Could rope and brand cattle until sundown, throw tomahawks to hit the mark, and shoot a gun, not as straight as Lillian Smith, but well enough to make a living. However, beyond rough cowboys and playful Indians, neither of which appealed to her, Two found men a mystery. She didn't understand how other women wrapped them up. Except with a lot of deception, and by acting like helpless babies. Two didn't mind deception so much, but pretending incompetence was beneath her dignity.

So both women were lost in similar ruminations, until Franny said, "Look, I gotta get some grub before we go on. You want to come in with me? You can think about the vodka. Tell me later. I can get it easy."

Two looked down at the flowers growing up the web of wire at the side of her chair. Her stomach growled. "Sure. Will ya hand me my crutches?"

Little
Elk

The Indian Clive had seen had been watching Two all morning. And when Christa Belle had stopped by her chair, he'd admired the fringe on her dress, her long legs, and her headband. When she'd headed toward the park, he'd darted over to the path and huffed on her neck. She'd shivered, touched her collar, and thought maybe a strand of a spider's web had dropped from a tree branch. Her reaction made Little Elk smack his lips. His attempts to touch people usually didn't meet with success.

After Christa Belle passed, Little Elk had returned to monitoring Two. He usually kept an eye on her when he didn't have other things to do. Which was most of the time. Little Elk was fond of his tree, the bears' enclosure, and the buffalo's, but he didn't like most of the park and zoo. It was crowded with smelly, noisy white people. Even worse, the animals were in cages. Their spirits were angry, or sad, or both. Every time he visited the bears and the buffalo, he tried to reassure them. Especially the bears, who were the Ani-Tsa-guhi clan of the Cherokee, famous for their benevolence and generosity. He talked with them daily and exchanged friendly growls to keep their spirits up, but he really just wanted to wail. He'd never figured out a way to get the bears out.

He also spent some of his time searching the ground. The white people smoked their tobacco in sticks of white leaves. Sometimes, they threw pieces of those sticks in the gravel, grass, and dirt. Not in many places. But Little Elk knew the most likely. He made rounds every day, and was able to gather bits and pieces and separate the weed from its wrapping. Often he did that under his tree, as he didn't really like following Two through the crowds into buildings.

He hated those, particularly the large ones. When he was a child, the white people had started putting them up everywhere, sure signs they intended to stay. Those, and the palisade they'd built on the bluff. That stockade provoked a lot of hot talk when it was going up, and some negotiating. Elders and mature men had tried to reason with the intruders and thieves. Had clarified that they could share the game, but couldn't stay and couldn't have it all to themselves. Explained that the lick and the land belonged to everyone in common, to the different animals and tribes. Everyone should take a little, but not too much. There would be plenty for all forever, down into the generations to come.

But the white people were too thick to understand that. And no amount of reasoning could get it through their wooden heads. They acted like starved turkeys. Gobbled up everything in sight. Broke ground directly in animals' paths and planted corn. Then they sat out next to the plants with guns to scare game away. And when they hunted, they killed more than they could eat. And more of them kept coming.

Finally, at the time Little Elk was becoming a man, the Muscogee came around. They asked the Cherokees to join them in an attack, and the Cherokees were eager to go. In the dead of the previous winter, the whites had suddenly attacked ten Cherokee towns. They'd burned every house, every basket of corn. Killed men, women, and children indiscriminately. The destruction was complete. The cry for blood consuming.

There were days and nights of smoking and talking together. The Muscogees' plan was to kill the invaders, burn the stockade, and keep new whites away. Forces were gathered from several towns around, and from villages south and east beyond the rivers. Little Elk was hungry to go, and so were his brothers and friends. They were young, impatient to become braves, and hot to avenge the murders, the burnings, the smallpox, and the decimation of game.

Four hundred thick, they approached the stockade and split. One group hid on a hillside in cedars and underbrush, the other in bushes along the bank of a creek's branch. At dawn's first light, three of the branch braves approached the fort and stood in the clearing, beyond the range of the invaders' guns. They fired shots to get the attention of the sentinel. He called the alarm while they retreated to reload. They reappeared to an audience, waved their arms, shouted insults, and made faces. They turned around and lifted their cloths. Slapped their thighs and rears. Pointed to their buttholes and whooped. Then they retreated toward the stream.

The whites went into a frenzy. Yelled at each other about what to do. Finally, galloped out of their gates toward the branch, armed and ready to make rapid work of the Indians. A handful of whom arose from the bushes and mocked them again. The insulted whites dismounted to take straighter aim. Then the rest of the Indians emerged from the bushes and rushed them. The other half of the party attacked from the back. They fought hand to hand, gun to gun, war club to hatchet. Then some of the braves broke ranks to capture rider-less horses, opening a gap in the line. The whites retreated through the hole, dragging their dead and wounded into the station.

It looked like the Indians had won. Then a pack of fifty or more dogs rushed out of the gates like hungry wolves, dripping with saliva, barking, and howling. They furiously attacked many Indians, including Little Elk. They bit throats, legs, feet, arms, chests, and backs. While the whites kept dragging their casualties into the walls, the Indians fought the canine pack, killed some, and ran for cover. The whites called their animals back. Shot Indians from the fort as they made forays for their dead, for their wounded, and for the scalps of fallen, un-rescued whites.

By sunset, the Indians had regrouped. They attacked again. This time, the whites replied with a weapon that Little Elk, severely bitten, still bleeding, and down on the ground, couldn't see, but did hear. It roared like thunder. Rumbled the earth and shook the trees. Filled the air with pieces of metal and the smell of gunpowder. Whatever it was, it was terrible. And could come again. Most of the Muscogee had already retreated. Little Elk's band debated and decided to follow. One of his brothers threw him over his shoulders, and his kin and friends took turns carrying him through woods, all the way to the great buffalo path near the mounds, until he, bit to the bone in the chest, became a deadweight. They bound him with deer hide and rested until light. They left him by a young oak and promised to come back with a horse and a litter.

But they didn't. And Little Elk died in agony under the oak alone. His body was quickly gnawed by wolves, and almost as quickly picked to the bone by vultures. He watched them gorge on it from a branch that was then the highest. Still, he waited in spirit for his kin so he could return with them to see his mother, father, sisters, uncles, grandparents, aunts, and cousins. He didn't give up on his party until an opossum passed where his body had been, sniffed, and went on.

Then, despondent, he left. He went somewhere he'd never been, wandered through strangers, and finally found his brothers and friends. They told him what'd happened after they left him. They'd been killed, all but one. So his death had not been avenged. And that was a serious matter. It disturbed the harmony. But there wasn't anything to be done about it, so he forgave his brothers and friends, and they hunted, gambled, sang, rattled shells, told tales, and smoked. He had a good life after life, but with a snag. Occasionally, he was transported back to his death tree to linger.

The first time that happened, he was stunned. It was so sudden he didn't have his bearings, and he landed in the midst of white men running crisscross in every direction. It was a crisp winter day; the sun was dying, and the men wore heavy, baggy clothes, breathing air he could see. Sudden far noises clapped like thunder and echoed off hills. The odor of gunpowder and smoke swam in the air. Some men pressed their hands to their ears. Others held their own sides, arms, or legs. They were bleeding, bound with rags, filthy, bearded, and haggard. Most carried guns, some carried swords, and they ran by him without turning their heads. But Little Elk understood he couldn't be seen by men or by animals. He had, previously, done all he could to keep the wolves from his body.

Every time the thunder clapped, he clasped his hands to his ears until it stopped calling from hill to hill. It was the same thunder he'd heard after he'd been wounded, and he concluded a battle was not far away and the men were retreating. The whites from the fort must have gotten into a dispute and turned on each other. He stayed close to his tree, glad he couldn't be seen, and praying no one had let the dogs free. When he finally felt confident the hateful creatures weren't on the loose, he slipped over to a man who had fallen. He was bareheaded, bearded, holding his belly in his hands. Blood was crusting on his fingers. He was moaning through cracked lips. Little Elk couldn't tell if the cracks were from thirst or cold weather. He tried asking if he wanted water. The man didn't answer. Little Elk tried blowing hard on his face, a remedy his grandmother used on sick babies. The man's lips continued to move, but his sounds stopped. Soon, Little Elk couldn't tell if he was breathing. He plucked a blade of grass, laid it on the man's upper lip, and waited. The blade didn't tremble. The man stared at the sky. The whites of his eyes were both bloodshot and yellow. Little Elk grimaced, held his nose, and touched the man's face, closing his lids and his jaw.

He wiped his hand off on the grass, and slowly crept toward another man down on the ground. This one, bleeding from the chest, was thrashing around. Little Elk knew his moving would bring on his death. He shouted, "Halt!" in the loudest command he could muster. The man got still. Looked Little Elk straight in the face. Then started trembling all over and gurgling blood. He sat straight up right out of his body. He said, "You're real — and you're dead."

Little Elk had learned his English from his linkster aunt, and had practiced with her husband, a white. He'd said, "Yes. You, too." The man (really just a boy) started crying. Blubbering about being dead and never seeing his parents again. Little Elk tried to console him. Assured him his family would be around later. Urged him to find his friends. The boy asked, "Where?" Little Elk pointed to three other dead bodies. The boy started blubbering again. Little Elk couldn't stand that. He said, "Courage!"

He left the crying man and walked the old buffalo path. He avoided the mounds more out of respect than from the fear he'd felt when he'd been alive. He saw other newly dead bodies. Looked for the men in the air, but didn't see their spirits. When night settled in, he checked the bodies' pockets for tobacco. He found three pouches. These he lifted under the moon. He found other things, too. Salt pork, which he loved to smell, but no longer had any desire to eat. Knives, cups, spoons, and canteens. All metal. His hands went through them and through the guns. He tried and tried again. That irritated him to no end. He couldn't even grab the knives.

But he had flint on him. So he made fire and enjoyed the tobacco. And by morning, there was a great deal to watch. More running and shooting. The soldiers were young. Their clothes were baggy and their faces thin. Not fit warriors. And suffering, it was clear, from the cold. Little Elk blamed their parents for that. They'd been raised inside buildings. Hadn't been properly hardened.

Eventually, more dead men speckled the ground. For a space of time, Little Elk sat in his tree, smoked, and didn't see anyone alive around. So he climbed down and walked between the bodies randomly scattered. He breathed through his mouth, avoiding their odor, and gathered more tobacco and some gunpowder. And, surprisingly, he suddenly was able to lift a spoon. He collected several out of packs and wondered about his new power. Wondered also what he could do with the spoons. He was glad to have them, but still didn't have any desire to eat. When he came upon the mouth of a cave, he stashed the spoons in a hole just outside of the entrance. He smelled traces of bears. Told them to help themselves to the utensils, but didn't linger for fear of underworld spirits grabbing him. By then, he'd decided he'd returned because his murder had not been avenged. He didn't want to get captured by evil spirits or witches and get into a worse position.

He had enough spoons, gunpowder, and tobacco to last quite a while. When he found the next body, he didn't try lifting anything off it. He settled down. He smoked, watched, and waited. Near sunset, three wolves came creeping around. Little Elk hated them more than he hated dead white men. He threw his war stick toward the pack. It hit between two, but they still slinked toward the body.

Then he got an idea. He sprinted upwind from the corpse and wolves. Sprinkled a little gunpowder on a piece of cloth and lit it. The pack stopped in its tracks. Sniffed the air. Looked at each other, turned their ears, and milled around. He sprinkled more gunpowder. Lit another piece of cloth. The wolves circled each other again. Little Elk laughed. Recited a formula designed to confuse game. Whooped when the pack left.

The sun set and rose two times. Then men came. Many of them wore boxy blue hats, shiny objects on their coats, and cloths over their mouths. They kicked the bodies. Stripped them of guns, cups, foot coverings, plates, belts, everything Little Elk hadn't been able to take. They threw all of that into tubs on a wagon drawn by boney mules. Some of the men were darker than others, and Little Elk recognized them as slaves. The white men ordered the slaves around and showed them where to drag the bodies, which was to the buffalo path. It was a forearm deep, and saved the first forearm of digging. But the ground was hard-packed from buffalo hooves, and Little Elk thought they would have done better digging by a creek. But he also knew there was no use trying to talk to any of those people.

He did try to beckon the men to a body they'd missed. But they didn't notice him. And then Little Elk realized they couldn't smell very well. He shook his head at his own stupidity. If the invaders could smell, they'd realize they stank and would bathe every day. He thought back to conversations he'd had when he was alive. It was common knowledge that the whites were easy to track because their odor was so rank. Everyone always wondered how they were successful hunters. Their smell alone should have spooked game far beyond the horizon.

After the slaves had dug the holes two more forearms deep, the dead were dumped in and covered with dirt. The cart was pulled off by the boney mules, and the living men left. Little Elk went back to protecting the overlooked body from wolves. He did that until the buzzards came. Unlike his feelings for dogs and wolves, he had some affection for buzzards. The Great Buzzard had made the mountains and valleys of the Cherokees' home by flapping his wings. He figured these buzzards had to eat like everyone else.

The next time he came back, two large carts were in the buffalo path, a short walk from where the dead had been buried, but not far from his tree. Four tethered mules were grazing long grass. Bugs were buzzing, butterflies diving and skirting, birds harassing each other in full-throated song. Only the four men with shovels seemed disgruntled. Little Elk moved upwind to avoid their stink, and crept in closer.

The men were dressed too heavy for their work. That was almost always true of the whites, so it didn't surprise Little Elk a bit. One called out to the others. They all set aside their shovels and picks and walked to the shade of a tree that was growing from a shelf of rock sprouting a spring. They dipped their bandanas in the water and wiped off their sweat. But they drank their water out of canteens. Little Elk found that a little odd, but whites were a peculiar tribe. He chose a shady spot not far away, and settled in to watch and to listen to what they were saying.

The shelf of rock seemed to be a retreat the men had used before, maybe every day. Beside their canteens, their outer shirts were spread on the rocks, and sitting close by was a box, from which they pulled boiled eggs, tomatoes, peaches, and bread. Little Elk rarely felt any hunger, but his stomach muscles contracted. If the whites left any scraps, he'd steal some food, and maybe eat. Or at least try.

After the men ate, they washed their hands off in the spring, wiped their arms and bodies again to cool, and then from a clay bowl picked out pipes. Little Elk's eyes grew wide. He smiled. The men packed in tobacco, lit up, and smoked. Little Elk moved slightly downwind. He could stand their stink mixed with the smell of tobacco. He sat again, this time on a flat rock in the shade, not far from one of the mules. He inhaled deeply and felt better with the first whiff of smoke.

After their smoking, the men went back to work, and Little Elk sauntered over to their retreat. He picked up a crust of bread and put it in his pouch. But he was really after their tobacco, and one of the pipes seemed like it would look good in his hand. He stashed an entire tobacco pouch in his belt and tried to pick up the pipe. His fingers went through it. He tried again. Wondered why he could pick up the bread and tobacco, but not the pipe. He spit, turned his back to the men and the mules, and walked through trees, over to the cave where he'd hidden the spoons. They were still there, but his hands went through them, too. He hit his palm with his fist. Scuffed up a little dirt with his foot. Then he climbed to rocks above the cave's mouth and sat down to figure the puzzle out.

He always found tobacco cleared his head, corrected his thoughts, and gave him new ones, so he chewed some while watching the birds, thinking about the spoons, and contemplating the cave. It would still be a good home for bears. He wondered if they would ever return. He retrieved a childhood fantasy in which he ran off and lived with bears. Then he realized his thoughts had wandered. He really wanted to know why he could pick up some things and not others. He got up and walked down again to the hole in the rock. Tried to pull a spoon out. This time, it came. He held it up. Inspected it like it was a perfectly formed ear of green corn, ready to eat from the field. He put it in his mouth. Felt it with his tongue. It was real and he was moving it around. And he could do it now, but not before. What was the difference? The corners of Little Elk's mouth turned up. He had used tobacco.

The men came again the next day. And Little Elk, who didn't have much to do except to figure out how to get enough strength to avenge his death, settled in to watch them in the same shady place he'd sat before. The insects were busy, but the sun still on the rise, when the men stopped digging and bent over stones and started pulling and tugging.

Little Elk recognized then that they were tearing apart one of the boxes that the dead people were in. He had seen some of those exposed when he was alive, and he suddenly realized he should've understood what the men were up to the day before. Little Elk had heard of people robbing graves, but it was shocking to see, and he stood up and let out a piercing war cry. He beat his chest. Jumped up and down. Screamed again. The men stopped. Looked up and around. Said things to each other that Little Elk couldn't hear. Then two of them grabbed a stone, one that was on the side of a box, and pushed it down to the ground. They got on their knees. Another man handed them small scoops and they began throwing dirt.

Little Elk's face turned to a scowl. He was so mad he forgot about their stink and approached them. Dirt flew straight though him. While he was fingering his thighs for holes made by the soil, one of the men pulled out a skull. Little Elk jumped back. His eyes grew to the size of walnuts. The man passed the skull to one of the others, and that man passed it to another. The fourth man looked at it, spread his legs, swung his arm back, and threw it at the trunk of a tree. The cracking sound it caused made Little Elk's muscles contract. The skull flew into pieces.

Little Elk ran to get away from the evil. And away from the skull's first soul, which lodged in the head, could be brought back to avenge such an act. Away, also, from the skull's clan that could — should — rise up and wreak revenge. He didn't want to get mixed up in that. He ran all the way to his tree, scaled it, and sat on the limb that had become his favorite. He tried gripping the bough tightly and hardening his muscles. He breathed in and out in a practiced, deliberate way. His back was to the destructive men, his face toward a catalpa. It was older than his tree, and its leaves were larger. He wondered if he should switch to it. Bigger leaves would provide him more cover in case disturbed spirits were swarming around.

But the tree had a limb that bent to the ground and grew into the dirt.

That provided two paths of approach into its branches, and Little Elk, though a spirit himself, didn't know if other spirits could fly around or were tethered to the earth as he seemed to be and needed to climb into trees. It was all so confusing. But he did suddenly recall that evil spirits and witches often take the form of birds. So he might be better off in no tree at all. He tried to think of where to go. Decided the bear cave was a better bet. He'd never felt any spirits near, bears were his cousins, and his spoons were there. That made the cave feel almost like home. He climbed down and ran to the cave in a jog, careful not to even look in the direction of the men who were still working and digging, doing things no one should be doing.

Little Elk didn't go inside the cave for fear of underworld spirits, but he'd hung around the outside for a moon and a half when, one morning, a wagon, four men, and two mules appeared some distance away. A shovel handle was sticking up and the men were dressed in the same heavy clothes as before, but Little Elk thought they were different diggers. He jumped to the ground from a rock, landed on a knee, dusted off, and sprinted in their direction. He didn't have to go far, but by the time he was there, the wagon had stopped. The men were out, walking back and forth, studying a mound, and conferring. Eventually, they spread out and started digging.

By this time, Little Elk was completely convinced he couldn't live in the Nightland peacefully until his death was avenged and had decided that he'd been sent back to stop the desecration of the graves. He'd even made forays away from his cave to find other spirits to help him. He'd envisioned an attack that would force the grave robbers back and give him a chance to kill one of them to avenge his death. And he had found three other spirts, two men and a woman, all sitting by different springs. They were round-faced people, unfortunately not Cherokee, and the backs of their heads were flat. Each time he'd tried to communicate with one of them, they stared straight through him. He decided they were even less solid than he. That if living people were earth, he was water, and these strange round-faced, flat-headed people were wind.

The wagon was followed by others and by carts, horses, and men. They were digging in the mounds, throwing dirt, dismantling the graves, stacking bones, and taking the dead peoples' possessions away. Little Elk tried everything he knew to stop them. And had a small amount of luck that unfortunately twisted around on him. The men had tobacco. Smoked it properly in pipes. Those they set down when they returned to their work. So Little Elk scooped out their tobacco when they were bent over digging. When they broke to smoke, their bowls were empty. Even a couple of their pipes were missing. They quickly accused each other of stealing. Got into discussions, arguments, and a few fistfights. Some men began to say the bodies didn't appreciate smoking. Most of those didn't return to the work. And the smoking among the others dwindled. They all agreed the bodies didn't like the use of tobacco. This was at the same time they were plucking pipes out of the graves at a rate Little Elk found quite alarming. The men didn't know how to think. That didn't surprise him. They were digging up dead people.

The dwindled tobacco use was not to Little Elk's advantage. And he kicked himself over it again and again. Tobacco made him strong. Helped him actually pick things up and move them around. Touch people and scare them. Say something and, occasionally, be heard. So the loss of the tobacco was real. And Little Elk grieved it. Then he spoke to himself sternly about being a man, and settled down to watch the destroyers every day. He became used to their ways and to their ignorance. But never to their smell. He always sat upwind.

When he came back the next time, the graves were all gone. Replaced by loud music, big buildings, awful lights, and crowds of people milling around. Little Elk was shocked into complete stillness at first. He stayed close to his tree. Near it, two huge buildings had been built. People, mostly women, went in and out of them all of the time. At first, he thought they were giant huts for their unclean cycle of the moon. But the longer he hung around, the less convinced he became of that. The same women went in and out every day. Never returned to their villages or houses. So he decided that one of the buildings was a living house and the other was a council house.

And while he'd been away, the catalpa tree had been struck by lightning and cut off at the top. The limb that had grown into the ground was untouched, but the trunk was hollowed out. The tree had turned very strange and, Little Elk felt sure, very powerful. He was thankful he hadn't decided to adopt it as his home. Even touching a lightning-struck tree had its dangers. He decided to permanently move over to the cave, and when he mustered up his courage to walk through the people to it, he discovered bears were living there. That delighted him. He made new friends instantly. Particularly with a little bear who was reddish in color and playful. But the bears were behind bars. He could drop into their lair from the rocks, and he did to visit, but he didn't want to live in a cage. That offended everything in his being. It offended him on the bears' behalf, too. He immediately put his mind to possible ways to free them.

He slowly explored the rest of the area, mostly at night when the people weren't around, the terrible lights had been dimmed, and there were finally shadows. The buffalo path was completely filled in with dirt and grass, but he did discover there were actual buffalo around. They, too, were in a pen. He visited them every day and enjoyed their time together. Although, their spirits weren't happy, so he also felt sad for them. But he considered buffalo quite dangerous. And, really, when they're out and about, they have to be respected. Also, if they weren't penned up, the white people would kill them. So, as bad as it was, the fence was the best solution for the buffalo, and Little Elk tried to lift their spirits by dancing, singing, and beating his chest.

One day when he was describing a ball-game victory to the buffalo, a woman came around. She didn't smell like the others; in fact, she smelled like a Cherokee. She was too covered with clothes for the weather, but her skin was dark, her hair was black, and she was taller than most other females around. On top of that, she talked to the buffalo like they were people. Little Elk was surprised, and wondered if the woman was a captive. If so, she seemed peaceful, and he knew more than one captive who'd happily lived in his village into old age without attempting to escape back to their families and houses. He assumed it could work the same way if the whites captured a Cherokee. It was, theoretically, possible.

Little Elk immediately took up following the woman, who was, of course, Two Feathers. He discovered on the very first day that she lived in the big building in front of his tree. He also discovered she dived on a horse from a cliff made of wood, and so was very, very brave. But, of course, she would be. She was a Cherokee. So Little Elk fell into a general feeling of happiness. Nothing just terrible was going on, and the female, the bears, and the buffalo were there for company. It seemed like he could let his guard down.

Visiting
Chambliss

Clive's time in the cave with Two had bound him to her, so he felt guilty for not bringing her home to the park himself. He knew what it was like to be injured. Would've gone batty without the kindness of volunteers who sat by his hospital beds, read to him, conversed, and brought new socks and the occasional apple. He wanted to make up for his lapse, and was thinking about how to do that when, at the monkey cages, he found Jack, tight-jawed, squinty, and gripping a ring-tailed lemur in his arms. The lemur was wearing an indignant look on his face, and his tail was waving over Jack's shoulder like a flag at a parade.

"Top of the morning, Mickey," Clive said to the lemur. To Jack, he arched an eyebrow.

"The punks have been at it again." Jack was referring to Mickey and Harold, a rhesus. "Mickey waved his tail close to the wire, and Harold grabbed it. Mickey howled like the hounds of Hades. You would've thought it was the end of the world."

"I wouldn't want my tail squeezed, either." Clive scratched Mickey under the chin. The lemur turned his head, closed his eyes, and sighed. Clive said to Jack, "He stays frustrated about his tail not working."

"His tail works just fine. He slapped me in the face with it."

"Have you had to bathe?"

"No, sir. Why do you ask?"

"I had his glands removed. Lemurs emit an odor from the ones on their rumps. They rub it on their tails to scare their enemies. The smell is as bad as a skunk's. Mickey doesn't understand why his tail doesn't put Harold off."

Jack sniffed. Mickey smelled bold, but not gagging. Jack said, "Should we reinforce the fence?"

"Is there a break?"

"I haven't found one. But Harold's been screaming a lot."

Clive held his arms out. Mickey climbed into them. "Check again. They've been fighting for years, It's the most intense dislike I've ever seen in animals not of the same species." He scratched Mickey's chest. "It's Harold's fault, isn't it, Mickey?" The lemur licked Clive's ear. Clive tickled his tummy.

There was other work to be done with the monkeys, including taking them out of their cages to be petted by children. Clive knew John was at the hippopotamus pen, so he stayed and helped, and it was almost an hour before he locked the last gate and he and Jack began walking the path to the bears. Clive exchanged greetings with nearly everyone who passed, but in a quiet moment said, "I'd like to call on Miss Two Feathers this evening. Care to come?"

Jack's left eye began to twitch. His heart started thumping. "Yes, sir. I would. Should we take flowers?"

Clive hadn't expected Jack's eagerness. He'd just been looking for a buffer in case he ran into Helen. Since their conversation, she'd dominated his thoughts. He didn't want to look like he was visiting Chambliss to see her again so soon. That would leave the wrong impression. Or, perhaps, the correct one. Clive didn't know.

• • •

After supper, the two men arrived at Chambliss dressed in their street clothes, Jack was carrying some stalky irises, and his eyelid was fairly stable. Helen wasn't at her desk at the door. Clive peeked into smaller parlors as they walked the hall to the large east one that housed a piano, sofas, and clusters of soft and hard chairs. Helen wasn't anywhere to be seen, and neither were many residents, as the park's attractions were still going strong. However, one couple was in a corner, whispering, shrugging, and shifting positions. Clive and Jack looked to a row of three wingbacked chairs, all facing far open windows. Next to one, the stems and tips of crutches protruded.

Two was in the center chair, her cast propped on a footstool, her issue of *Western Story* tucked between her thigh and the upholstery. She was playing a kind of solitaire that passes cards from one hand to the other without needing a surface to lay them down on. She looked up at the men. A card fell to the floor.

Jack said, "Let me get that," as he stooped.

Two had slept in most of the morning, occupied a porch rocker for most of the afternoon, eaten supper with the others, but had been left on her own after the rest rushed out to their evening work. She'd taken a chair facing a window in hopes of a breeze and because the room had been too empty to bear. Her only entertainment except solitaire had been eavesdropping on the spatting couple. (The man had shown up late. The woman, the games organizer, didn't believe his excuse.) Two was grateful for company. She greeted the men warmly.

Clive smiled with his "Good to see you," but clasped his hands behind his back, as he considered touchy greetings suggestive of French and Italian hysteria, and, at the time, extending one's hand first to a lady just wasn't done. However, Jack brushed Two's palm when he returned her card.

A shimmy ran through her arm, into her body and good leg. She flushed to the top of her head. Said, "Sorry about the upchuck."

Jack replied, "Happens to me all the time. DuPont got me last week."

"Is he sick?"

"No, just off his feed. Or being unruly." Jack hadn't intended to get in a conversation about camels and vomit. He touched his eye and looked to Clive.

Clive said, "DuPont has a weak stomach. May we take seats? Please tell us how you are."

Jack held out the flowers. The park was filled with PLEASE DON'T PICK THE FLOWERS signs. He'd plucked them from behind a building where no one could see him. "These might cheer you up," he said. They'd cheered him. He enjoyed breaking rules.

Two hoped Jack and Mr. Lovett couldn't see her blush. She mumbled, "Thank you," and added, "There's usually a vase around here."

Jack left to search. And Clive started with, "Please tell me how you feel. Less poorly, I hope."

Two tapped her cast with the deck. Chewed her lower lip. Said, "I miss Ocher."

Clive's legs were crossed, his hands clasped over a knee. He also grieved Ocher's loss. He felt upset every time an animal died at the zoo. He did better with the small ones, like the rabbits, who multiplied in a blink and lived longer in the park than they did in the wild. But a horse was a different matter. Fearing losing control of his emotions, he focused on his thumbs. "She was a brave one."

"Ya think she suffered?"

Clive looked squarely at Two. "Not a-tall. Her neck was broken in the fall. I'm sure it killed her instantly. She was true to you to the end. Saved your life." He glanced to a window. "That's the wonderful thing about horses, they're loyal. Better than most people in that regard." He sighed.

"I made her jump when she didn't want to. Now she's dead and I'm alive."

Too many men had died beside Clive. No reassurance could fill the space a body had taken before it was hit and rained down in bits. He didn't have an answer to *Why not me?* He looked back at his thumbs, but Millwood rose up in his chest and comforted him instantly. He looked at Two. "I've read that your people believe in spirits. Would that be true for you?"

It was an unexpected question. But Clive could do no wrong in Two's eyes. "Yes. But I'm a Cherokee. We're not like whites. We're not organized in religion."

"Didn't Christians convert you?"

Two smiled for the first time since her accident. "They sure tried. But it didn't take with my folks. We saw them for what they are." Now she looked out the window. She'd said too much.

However, Clive had a grasp of British and European history that encompassed several centuries of religious persecution, mostly by Christians of other Christians. He was saying, "Believe it or not, I understand that," just as Jack reappeared with the irises stuck in a red vase. He held them out for Two to admire.

"They're super," she said. "And so's the vase. Red's my favorite color."

Jack set the flowers on a table next to her chair. They all chatted for a while. The conversation was light and carried by Clive's affable skills. But he thought that the younger people might enjoy each other more if left to their own devices and that he might possibly bump into Helen if he wandered out through the hall and onto the porch. He told Two he'd be back to see her in a couple of days and took his leave.

Jack said, "If you're tired, I can go, too."

"I haven't done anything but rest all day."

"Would you like something to drink? A Coca-Cola, maybe? A lemonade?"

"Ya might have to go all the way to the park to get those. There should be fresh buttermilk in the icebox."

Jack stood and held up a finger. "Point the way."

"I better go with ya. After hours, the women invade the kitchen in their nightgowns." Two reached for her crutches, rose, and led Jack to a room that was, at the moment, quite empty. He secured their glasses and milk, and they made their way back to their chairs. The spatting couple was long gone, and no one else had arrived. That suited Jack's intentions completely, and he could be charming when he wanted. He'd practiced that sort of deception all of his life. And Two wasn't immune to him. They chatted about the animals, about what college was like, and about the 101. Jack wanted to reel her in slowly, and Two, who had been bored all day, liked that he had an education and was tall. But, later, when he offered to carry her flowers to her room, she demurred. Her bed was unmade, her clothes scattered around, and the Montgomerys would be in from their performance. She said one of them would do that, walked Jack to the front porch, and watched him fade into the dark between the hall lights and the one shining at the trolley station.

Cheering
Two
Up

≡

Two awoke the next morning damp from the heat and with her leg throbbing all the way from her pelvis to her exposed toes. She shifted around and sat up on the side of her bed. She reached for the bandana on her bedpost and used it to wipe her face and her neck. She tried to move her cast into a position that lessened the pain. She didn't succeed, but managed to stand, sponge off over a bowl on her dresser, clothe herself, and get to breakfast, all without increasing her ache. There, the other women's chatter distracted her. But after they left, she was alone with an empty plate, a cup of tepid coffee, and a sharp pain on the underside of her thigh. By the time she'd moved a chair to where she wanted it on the porch and had propped her leg on a little table, she was exhausted. She fanned herself for a while, listened to insects, and watched a butterfly. Then she nodded off.

Little Elk had returned to his tree from visiting the bears in time to see Two fall asleep on the porch. He was elated to see her. He'd missed her so much that he'd eventually visited the diving arena. There he'd discovered some of the bleachers were gone and the hole was filled in. The diving tower was still standing, but, by itself, it looked like a giant, dead tree. He'd assumed Two had left for another place, and his heart had sunk to his feet and stayed on the ground. He'd really been moping around.

So he trotted over to the big building with his heart back in his chest, thumping hard into his throat. He stopped at the clematis trellis and looked up lovingly at Two's face. She was paler than usual. It was clear she'd been sick. But she didn't have any pockmarks. Little Elk shivered. The pox was a terrible curse. His elders told about it coming again and again ever since the whites had moved in. And the ones who'd built on the bluff had brought it with them on the river. His own sister had died, one of his aunts, and three of his cousins. Many of the sick had drowned themselves. Some had slit their own throats. Others lived on recovered, their faces like cobs shorn of corn. Little Elk was relieved when he first got to the Nightland and found those who'd died with red sores or scars on their faces were smooth, dark, and beautiful again. Still, just the thought of the pox and its deaths could make him furious. He fought back his emotions to keep them from ruining his happiness over the woman's return.

He glimpsed the white log around the female's leg. It was harder to see than her face because it was mostly hidden by flowers and foliage. But Little Elk knew what it was. Grandmothers made those out of straw and mud. The woman had broken her bones, probably in a fall. Little Elk was wondering how bad it hurt when Two woke up. He decided he'd stay where he was. She probably couldn't see him, but she might recognize his odor. He fancied he smelled fairly enticing.

And Two did smell something. Bologna frying. She glanced at the shadow on the planks. It was almost time to go in and eat. She drew a bandana from her pocket, wiped her brow, folded the cloth, and wrapped it around her forehead. Then before she could move, a bee landed on her exposed big toe. She sat still and, while waiting for it to go, recalled the night before. Jack had caught a moth and had killed it by rubbing its wings together between his thumbs. He'd also related a childhood memory of blowing up anthills with firecrackers, and had told her honey is regurgitated by bees. Two saw insects more as companions than enemies, but understood whites didn't tolerate them well, and also didn't think Jack was right about the bees. She'd never heard that before, and thought she probably knew more about bees than he. But he'd seemed sincere and had no real reason to lie. Men lied about other women, drinking, gambling, and stealing. Not about honeybees. Two asked the bee on her toe, "Do ya throw up honey?"

Little Elk thought she was talking to him. The paint on his cheeks crinkled with a grin. "Ka! It is me! Little Elk!" He poked his chest. "I here for you!" The bee flew away. But then, a man came up beside him, brushing his arm. Little Elk jumped. Pulled his scalping knife from his sash and drew his elbow back. He jabbed forward, punctured the man below the ribs, and jerked his blade up.

Crawford scratched his side. He assumed he'd been bitten by a sweat bee. He said, "Hey, Two."

Two saw Crawford's head through the clematis. She grinned. "I'm sure glad to see ya. Where've ya been?"

Little Elk's eyes narrowed. He tested the edge of his knife with his thumb. It was dull. He growled, spit on Crawford's back, and stalked off.

Crawford felt tickled by a trickle of sweat. He patted his shirt. "Working. The Modern Woodmen get here today. They're giving a car away. We had to set it up on a platform outside the casino. Got her done, so thought I'd slip over. How's the leg?"

"It hurts. And I'm dying of boredom. Come on up here and play cards with me."

They generally played on a wooden board set on a crate in the barn, a penny a point. They did that several times a week and were evenly matched. But Crawford said, "I didn't bring the cards."

Two reached into a bag where she'd stuffed her possessions. She held up her deck of Bicycles.

Crawford looked off to the woods back of the dorm. "We don't have our box."

"There's a table over there." Two nodded to one about twenty feet away.

"Folks might think I'm goofing off."

"Mr. Lovett won't care. And he won't be around. He came last night."

"How's he doing?"

"He's fine. I can hardly see ya through the vines. Come on up here."

"Folks'll think we're keeping company." Crawford shook his head. "And you know how crazy white people can be."

The races mixed a lot more on the ranch than they did off of it. But Two did know how crazy white people could be. She said, "There's an old bench behind the hall. We could use it. Nobody goes back there."

"That'd look like we're carrying on under the trees."

Two sighed. "I thought ya came to cheer me up."

"I did. But people get beat up. And worse, if you know what I mean."

She did, of course. Their friendship had bloomed in the barn and was mostly confined to its shady inside. Together in the park, they kept a horse between them so it was clear they were working. Two said, "I need to get to the barn. I'm going loco here."

Crawford looked down at the vines growing out of the earth. He wished they'd gotten the wheelchair in the car. He said, "What you need is a buggy."

Two tried to picture that. On the 101, buggies were used to drive visitors who wanted to see how Indians live out to the Poncas' village. She'd never ridden in one.

Crawford said, "I might can cobble together a ride from an old bench."

"Whaddya mean?"

"Before your time, there was a merry-go-round here. Mostly had horses on it. And a goat and a unicorn. But it also had a bench. Ladies and mammies used it for watching children. I might can convert that bench into a contraption to get you around. Lord knows we've got enough Shetlands to pull you. Lovett told me you're not going home."

"Not if I can help it. I haven't told my folks."

Crawford wasn't surprised about that. But knew Two'd go stir-crazy cooped up. He said, "The Flying Jenny is in pieces in crates in a barn. I can probably locate that bench."

Two wasn't sure about the bench-buggy idea and couldn't quite picture it. But she did need off the porch, and a rig might work. She said, "Ya'd put wheels on it?"

"Sure. Probably four. I can't recollect its exact size. There's a legless man in downtown Nashville. Don't know if you've ever seen him. He gets around in a little wagon with wheels drawn by a big black dog. Everybody calls him Harmonica. Makes his living playing for nickels and dimes. It'd be sorta like that, only bigger. Harmonica rides real close to the ground."

That picture didn't appeal to Two. But she couldn't tolerate porch sitting much longer. She said, "Let me think on it."

However, Crawford felt like he had a good idea. And his hands twitched to build. Also, he harbored an old yearning for those carousel horses. They'd been brightly painted every color of the rainbow. He particularly recalled a yellow-tailed, white palomino whose saddle was blue. He'd wanted to ride that horse so badly as a child that he'd stayed away from the merry-go-round.

Crawford said, "I'll try to round that bench up," before they bid farewell and Two went inside to eat bologna.

When Two came back out to the porch, she got some help moving her chair to follow the shade. But then the other women went back to work. She looked out at the trees, fanned herself, listened to distant park music, and watched the trolley when it passed. She couldn't see the Cherokee sharpening his knife against a stone, even though he sat cross-legged in the grass close to the clematis. Her idleness gave her time to feel her pain, to mourn, and to think. And as the afternoon wore on, sweat inside her cast tickled her leg and set her teeth on edge. Her mood got worse. She was used to being a star attraction. She didn't think she could ride through the park on a jerry-rigged contraption. Also didn't think she could sit on the porch for three more weeks. And she couldn't go home.

Two wished Mr. Lovett would come again. And wished Jack Older would, too. He'd said he would. But he hadn't said when. She mulled over the night again. He had thick red hair. That was unusual, but not unattractive. His glasses masked a tic in his eyelid. But he was tall and muscular, and he had an education. Two wished she had more school- ing. Decided she should read some real books while she was laid up. She didn't know where to start, but there were leather-bound volumes in the parlors and Jack had graduated college. She could get his advice.

But, really, she was off men. And she'd go on home when she could. There weren't many places outside of Oklahoma where an Indian could work. She could get a job in Tulsa, Muskogee, or Claremore. But doing what? She was a roundup star, nothing else. She'd ride the circuit. That'd be her career. But what if Franny was right? What if their whole way of life was fading fast? She could star in Westerns. She mulled that possi- bility again. However, Helen Gibson had done that, and she was now touring with Ringling.

Two looked off into the future. It looked blank and white. The pain in her leg felt red, and she felt like a big purple bruise all over. Her disposi- tion had turned to black when Franny climbed the front steps and called, "What's up, Pocahontas?"

"Me thinking about taking scalps. Yours first."

"Ouch! Let's make peace. I got no pipe, but look in here." By then Franny was next to Two. She spread the flaps of a bag. In it were a pair of gloves and a bottle.

Two said, "Is that the medicine?"

"You betcha."

Two reached for it. Franny moved the bag. "Not here. We'll get caught. It's illegal, remember?"

"Not for medicinal purposes."

"But I'm not a doctor. We need to take it to your room."

Crawford's
Problems

≈

Crawford had hung around the park since childhood. When the zoo started up, Clive gave him nickel and dime jobs from the change in his pocket and, before going overseas for the war, he put him on salary. Crawford was so good with the horses that if one became sick, he slept in its stall. He was also so clever with machines that he could tell exactly how one was in trouble by listening to its sound before it broke down. He'd slept next to those, too. That kind of work ethic resulted in Clive never supervising Crawford, leaving him free to do what was needed. So Crawford went straight from his conversation with Two to a box of keys in a small office in the main barn. Then he hiked to the south end of the park where the carousel horses were stored in a big red barn that housed not only the remains of the Flying Jenny, but also the roller coaster skeleton and cars. Additionally in there were six boxes of human skeletons from Indian graves that had been dismantled as the zoo had expanded.

The roller coaster cars were heavy metal carriages, so Crawford was interested only in the wooden bench. As the rusty door hinges screeched, he winced, then tried to picture where the bench had been stored. He'd helped with the dismantling and crating. Crawford walked about forty feet down a dim lane stacked high with crates, thinking the Flying Jenny had been stored on his right, near the east corner. He heard something rustle and scratch. He stopped. It didn't sound like a human being. It could be a ghost. Skeletons were in there. Crawford breathed in deeply. Made fists. Those skeletons had probably turned to dust. Surely ghosts didn't linger for hundreds of years. That noise was made by an animal. A possum, or rats. Maybe bats. Crawford looked up and saw the outline of the rafters. There was nothing above him but beams. Nothing would attack him from the air, but it still felt creepy in there.

The rafters reminded him of the ropes and pulleys they'd used in stacking the boxes. If the bench was high up, he'd have a hard time getting it down. If it was in a bottom crate, he'd have a hard time freeing it up. He turned around, glad to have a need to leave before he came back with help. He walked toward the door, searching for markings on the crates. Found only numbers. Then he recalled the contents had been logged.

When he got to the door, he listened for sounds. Heard a peacock screech in the distance. Heard the monkeys. Nothing from inside the barn. He breathed out deeply, felt a little relieved, and applied his mind to where that log might be and to the rigging he'd need to extract the bench when he returned with a torch and some help. After solving those problems, his mind turned to the woman he was courting, Bonita Boydstun. And once on Bonita, it stayed there.

Bonita lived with her parents, siblings, and that printing equipment in a house on Market Street in downtown Nashville, three blocks north of the courthouse. Her paternal grandfather had been born a slave in Mississippi, owned by a family named Clark. He'd followed the Clark men into war, helped bury three of them, and returned home with the youngest. After Emancipation, he dropped his owners' last name and took up Boydstun as part of his new identity. A white girl taught him to read, and eventually he went to Bishop College. Leaving there, he became a leader in the Central Baptist Association of Texas and in the movement to free Negro churches from the grip of Northern white denominations. After that, he established the National Baptist Publishing Board and moved to Nashville, attracted by its Negro colleges and publishing industry. With money from mortgaging his wife's property in Texas, and with the help of a white friend (the president of the Baptist Sunday School Board), he began publishing leaflets and picture lesson cards for Negro churches all over the nation.

Naturally, Negro congregations liked seeing Negro children in pictures. Richard Boydstun built up quite a business. When he passed, he left his son, H.A., a publishing company, a newspaper, a bank, and his manufacturing concerns (mostly furniture, church bells, and dark-skinned dolls). H.A. (really Howard Allen) was as smart as his father. And he possessed a personality that made most people, both black and white, want to associate with him. All of which is to say that Bonita's father was used to achievement and was a force to be reckoned with.

So Crawford's courting was unfortunately confined to the parlor. That parlor resembled others in substantial homes of successful people of the time. It had two sofas, a couple of stuffed chairs, tables, lamps with tasseled shades, and pictures on the walls, mostly of dim scenic vistas. The only exception to those were portraits of Bonita's grandparents over the north-wall sofa. Richard in a high starched collar, cutaway coat, and bow tie. His wife, Harriett, in a ruffled collar with bird-capped hat tipped on her head. Crawford didn't much like courting below the formal couple. And he didn't like courting in the parlor. But he liked Bonita so much that he'd do just about anything to stay on the good side of her father, who was also an acquaintance of his mother, aunties, uncles, and older sisters and brothers.

That's not to say that the Crawfords and Boydstuns were close. They had their differences. The Crawfords came to the area directly after the Revolutionary War. The Boydstuns, by Nashville's standards, had just barely arrived. But they were educated, citified, and dignified, and were committed to furthering the race. The Crawfords had just as much schooling, but the ones who'd stayed in the area cherished their rural roots. And, as importantly, had alliances with powerful whites that went back for generations and that included kinship bonds that were quietly acknowledged by members of both races. Crawford hoped he didn't look under the white heel or countrified in Bonita's eyes, and when he called on her, he dressed to the nines, even though his neck was usually raw from his collar until the next Tuesday.

He was twenty-four, and she only nineteen. Five years was an acceptable gap; many couples had much wider between them. But she, a freshman at Fisk, had been protected all of her life, and she still lived at home. Her parents didn't mind her keeping company, but H.A. was aware Crawford had a reputation as a breaker of hearts and suspected his intentions might be fleeting and dangerous.

Thus, the couple hadn't left the parlor for their first five dates. But Crawford had tracked animals since childhood, and knew all catching involves patience. He could bide his time to win his prize, and did so that night by telling Bonita every detail of Two's fall, rescue, hospitalization, and current predicament.

Unfortunately, H.A. was in the room, too, sitting across from the couple on a horsehair sofa with a clipboard on his knee and a pencil in his hand. This was not, from Crawford's point of view, an ideal situation. But H.A. was also the owner and editor of the *Globe,* Nashville's foremost Negro newspaper, and Crawford did have inside information that cast himself in a rather heroic light. He took full advantage of that by delving into those details.

H.A., always a busy man, left after he obtained particulars of the accident, rescue, and injuries that the white newspapers hadn't already published. And Crawford and Bonita started discussing Two's problem with transportation. He'd shared his plan of using the old carousel bench to build her a ride, and had moved to describing the barn full of crates, when Bonita interrupted him: "I might not be comfortable on that bench." She said that quite firmly, but batted her eyelashes.

Crawford pulled his chin into his collar, looked directly at her, and arched an eyebrow.

"A lady doesn't ride around on a bench."

"Two's not a lady. She's an Indian."

"Indians don't ride on benches. They ride on horses or in canoes."

"Well, true. But there's not a river in the park. And she can't get on a horse."

"Did you ask her what she thought?"

Crawford felt ruffled by his idea falling flat. But he tried to remember. Maybe he had asked? Or maybe he hadn't? He couldn't quite pull that up. He told Bonita he'd told Two about Harmonica.

Bonita rolled her eyes. "If I were a betting person, which I am not, I would bet that chandelier" — she pointed up — "that Miss Two Feathers will never ride on your bench. You better come up with another solution."

Crawford covered his mouth with his palm. Looked at his glass of ice tea. Wondered, just for a moment, why he wasn't spending Friday night in a juke joint like a normal man. He cut his eyes over to Bonita. She was lovely. Her complexion was darker than his, but her hair was marcelled and her dress scoop-collared. She was twisting slim fingers around two strands of long beads. Crawford wanted to gently put his hand over hers, draw her to him by the beads, and kiss her in a way she'd never forget. Then he heard a noise. Her mother saying something to a child. Crawford blinked. He tried to get his mind back on whatever they'd been saying.

But Bonita read his face. She reached up and pulled his earlobe. "A penny for your thoughts."

Crawford took a deep breath. Smiled, tilted his head, and said, "They aren't entirely proper."

Bonita held her beads up close to her mouth, rubbed them ever so slightly. "Do tell. No, don't. I might be shocked."

"Could we just go out onto the porch? It's hot in here."

"We could. But people are always walking up and down the street and stopping to talk."

"How about the ice cream parlor? Would your father allow that?"

"Mother might. Let me ask her."

But just as Bonita was rising, H.A. appeared again. He said, "Hank, I forgot to ask after your cousin Jimmy."

There hadn't been any progress on finding who'd attacked and robbed Jimmy. But there had been on convincing him to change his insurance-selling territory from Nashville to Davidson County. He worked for a start-up Negro-owned company that was trying to compete with National Life and Life and Casualty, two enormous corporations that had sewn up all the dark-skinned business in Nashville. National Life and Life and Casualty hired only white salesmen; so unless their potential Negro customers lived in known ghettos in town, they didn't have any idea where to find them. Both of Jimmy's parents were descended from Davidson County slave owners, and between them knew the location of every Negro general store in every wide spot in every county road for miles around. They also knew all the people who owned those stores and bought from them and knew, too, who their ancestors were for a couple of generations before the Civil War. The only obstacle was Jimmy's dignity. He didn't much like the idea of sitting in a rocking chair next to old checkers players while waiting for prospective customers to arrive in search of chewing tobacco, fishhooks, and flour.

However, H.A. agreed with Jimmy's parents, Maria and Henry, that Jimmy was a lot safer in the country than in town. He also thought the young man wouldn't be damaged by getting closer to his roots, and would be serving the race by selling insurance to folks who didn't have another way to get it. Crawford felt like he'd scored a few points by telling that story, and after that discussion said, "Bonita and I were thinking of cooling off with some ice cream. Might I bring some back for the family?"

H.A. could recognize a bribe as clearly as Old Hickory's face on the ten-dollar bill. But it was still unusually hot, and he had a wife and three younger children who would appreciate cooling off. However, the thought of Crawford walking dark streets with his daughter raised his temperature a notch. On the other hand, ice cream was a melting commodity. Once bought, it'd have to be hurried home. And it was already nine o'clock. H.A. said, "My wife needs to get the younger children to bed. Could you make it quick?"

So Crawford and Bonita escaped. Not for long, but it was their first private outing, and on the way home, Crawford made the most of it by licking a dab of vanilla off of Bonita's face. That led to a kiss that Crawford contemplated for the entire trolley ride back to Glendale. He also thought about it riding his horse along the dark, wooded path from the park to his home.

Vodka
Night

≋

Supper was over, Marty and Franny were in the casino throwing dishes, and most other resident entertainers and employees were also out working their jobs. Mrs. Hampton was on the front porch, chatting with a friend who'd come in from Nashville and joined her for supper. Two went to the bathroom, sponged off, and changed into her nightgown. When she returned to her room, she locked the door and wedged her desk chair under the knob. She sat down on her bed, twisted the cap off Franny's bottle, and sniffed. It didn't smell like anything in particular, but her nostrils burned, and she jerked back a bit. She pulled her chin in and decided to dilute the contents.

She struggled into her robe and down to the kitchen, thankful it was now accessible to her room without going through a public hallway. She didn't find what she wanted in the icebox, and had moved to the cabinets when another girl came in. Two asked her where they kept the soft drinks. The girl, Sandra, whose specialty was party decorations, opened a cabinet door, and said, "What's yer poison?"

Two picked Orange Crush, thinking it might go better with vodka than Coca-Cola or ginger ale. Sandra got her some ice, and Two talked with her for a few minutes to be polite and because she was lonely. But her leg throbbed, and when Sandra asked if she wanted to play duets, she turned her down, not only because of her pain but because she had no idea how to play a piano. So Sandra carried Two's glass to her room and left her there with it.

Two dispensed with the chair against the door. Mrs. Hampton's room was just one over, but she had company and it was too hot for her to come inside until she was ready to sleep. Sandra had set her soft drink on her bedside table, so Two laid her crutches on the floor, picked up the bottle, and settled against her pillow to brace for an instant reaction. She didn't pour much vodka in. She stirred with her finger and put it in her mouth. It tasted bitter. She sipped from the glass and swallowed. That burned. She waited, holding the glass against her forehead, enjoying its chill and trying to sense if the throbs were weaker or farther apart. She took another sip. That one burned, too. But not as bad, and she liked Orange Crush. She drank some more. Pressed the glass to one cheek, then to the other, figuring then it might take minutes for the effect to get from her throat, through her stomach and intestines, and out into her leg. She'd cut open and gutted hundreds of animals and fish. She knew insides curl around and that it takes a while for food and water to go down. Two recalled her Uncle Dub's hog-killing parties. One fall while gutting, someone found a bone that was big enough to cause conversation about what the hog had been up to. There were some theories that weren't too polite, lots of laughter, and some stories about what other Indians eat. The bone, having provoked so much enjoyment, was set aside to be polished. At the next hog-killing, it was dangling on a piece of string and her little cousin was using it as a teething ring.

The homeyness of hog killing made Two lonesome and teary-eyed. If she stayed in her room, she'd dissolve into full-out crying. She poured in a little more vodka and downed the rest of her drink. Grabbed her crutches and struggled up. Her leg did feel less achy. She hid her bottle in her trunk, dressed again, and went to the porch. There she found her favorite chair surprisingly empty. Mrs. Hampton, who she'd temporarily forgotten, was nowhere to be seen. But her rocker had been moved closer to the main door than she liked, and she was afraid she'd lose her balance if she tried tugging it back to her spot. So she sat down, propped the heel of her broken leg up on a rail, and hoped a herd of people wouldn't tromp past. The trolley approached and stopped at the station. Three people got on, but no one got off. Two settled deeper into her seat. Her broken leg felt almost, but not quite, like the other one.

Two wished her own family used liquor so she'd know what to expect. Her father hadn't taken a drink since she was little. Her parents had fought a lot then. But that'd been long in the past, and she hadn't really known until later that her mother, grandmothers, and grandfathers had put an end to the whiskey. They were united against firewater for Indians. Considered it as tricky as Christians. So Two began to feel guilty for trying the vodka. Got so out of sorts with herself that when Christa Belle Henley came up the walk, she was thankful to see her. She called out, "How's it going, Christa Belle?"

Christa Belle settled against a rail, pulled off a shoe, and rubbed her toes. "It's the last night of the Retail Grocers. The Nashvillians have gone. Just the hicks left. This one appleknocker weighed three hundred pounds. Guess who he wanted to dance with?"

"He could dance?"

"He wanted a feel."

Two raised an eyebrow.

Christa Belle pulled off the other shoe. Massaged those toes. "I didn't give it to him. Told him my time was up after the first dance. If they want that sort of thing, they oughta go into Nashville."

"Nashville's wild?"

"I guess. I don't really know. Nashvillians keep to themselves. I'm from Memphis. I came for a dance contest and liked it here in the park.

Don't know why. There's more dancing at home." Christa Belle fanned her face with a hand.

"Ya going back?"

"Not for a while. How 'bout ya?" Christa Belle glanced at Two's cast.

"I'm gonna stick it out. Riding a train'll hurt."

"Who's paying yer room and board?"

"It's part of my contract."

"Your contract's deep-sixed."

Two jerked. "Ya know that for sure?"

"I don't know anything for sure. But why wouldn't it be? They pay ya to dive on a horse. And yer horse is deep-sixed."

Two's breath caught in her chest. Ocher appeared in her mind. Followed by a piece of paper she imagined to be her contract. She hadn't considered it. She didn't know much about legal matters. They were between George Miller and Mr. Shackleford. Or Mr. Shackleford's friend, Mr. Warner. She really didn't know which.

On the 101, when people couldn't work, some left and were never heard from again. Others the Millers took care of. Assigned easier jobs. Or if they were old, just let them sit. But the outside world didn't operate like that. If people couldn't work, they were taken in by relatives or died. Two winced at the thought of that.

Christa Belle saw she'd lost Two's attention. She guessed she shouldn't have mentioned the horse. Said, "My dogs are killing me." She rubbed an arch.

Two focused on Christa Belle's foot and felt some sympathy. "Do ya take anything for the pain?"

"Normally, a little vinegar and salt."

"Do ya drink it?"

Christa Belle stopped rubbing. That was an odd question. But Two was an odd person. She picked up her shoes. "I soak my dogs in it. That's what I'm gonna do now. It'd be easier if my room weren't all the way on the second floor, away from the kitchen. Don't take any wooden nickels."

Two returned to worrying about her contract. She was still doing that when Marty and Franny got in. They sat down, talked about their night, asked about Two's, and chewed over the possibilities for how her deal could play out. They'd been negotiating and signing their own contracts since Marty had reached twenty-one. They understood clauses that covered the inability to work. They agreed Two had reason to worry. Decided they'd all worry better with a little refreshment of a medicinal nature. They did that in Two's room. The sisters didn't leave until Two nodded into oblivion.

Two
and
the
Buffalo

$$\equiv$$

Two woke up slowly, hot, heavy, and dull. Her head hurt. She was sweaty
all over, and the leg in her cast itched. She rubbed her palm, a distraction
she'd discovered that would take her mind off an itch. Then she thought
about Christa Belle, who had her two windows and the breeze that blew
through them. That helped dull her itch, but didn't help her mood. She
pulled herself upright and sat on the edge of the bed. She tilted, stabi-
lized, and reached for a crutch. She dressed in slow motion.

After bacon, eggs, juice, and coffee, the ache in her head dissipated.
But the pain in her leg started up again and so did her worries. She settled on a sofa in a small Chambliss parlor, propped her cast on a stool,
and brooded again over her predicament and future. Both were dark. She
didn't even really have a tribe.

In exchange for their home in the east, the Government had given
the Cherokees land in Indian Territory for "as long as grass grows and
water flows." They'd promised their chief they could control it. Promised
to keep the whites out. But like all other treaties, that one was broken.
And when Two was a little girl, the Cherokee Nation had been divided

into pieces and distributed to individuals as personal allotments. She'd been in front of the Dawes Commission herself, standing silently with her mother, grandparents, and siblings. Looking at her bare feet and listening to her father name his parents, who were standing right there, as clear as cattle, and who'd already said their own names and birthplaces. He'd also named her mother's place of birth, her parents' (standing there, too), all the children's names, and their birthdates. She still recalled the sweating, bearded man in a full suit of clothes who'd asked the questions. He reeked like a deer dead for a week.

Her father soon sold their allotments to a man prospecting for oil. He, at least, had gotten some money. They knew people who had been locked up and kept drunk until they signed their land over. And hundreds more had their allotments taken by whites, who went before judges to be declared Indian guardians and who pocketed the money made off crops, cattle, trees, and oil. Some Indians had even been killed outright and their allotments stolen by whites who pretended to be Indians when they weren't kin to anybody at all and when everybody could see plain as day their true color. Two'd heard those stories continually growing up.

To lift her mood, she decided to walk over to see Adam. She took the trek across the park, resting on benches when the pain of swinging her cast made her arms tremble. And the effort lifted her spirits a little. Saturday was the park's busiest day. There were lots of people to watch, and she'd made that her habit long before Glendale. The visitors to the 101 dressed in heavy clothes, even in the summer. They were wrinkly and pale and, often, too loud. It was like they'd never before felt freedom and didn't know how to act. The ones at Glendale were more restrained. They had a good time, but, except for the conventioneers, usually within limits. Most were polite. Subtle in their actions. Happy in their play. Two liked that.

But she was grateful for where she was from. The land of the 101 took several days to ride. Out on the range at night, the stars of the Milky Way were magnificent. Closer to home, there were fires to gather around in the evenings, animals to befriend, and all the good food you could eat. But while it was wonderful, the ranch hadn't prepared her for anywhere else. *If* an Indian could be prepared, a question Two mulled resting on benches during breaks in her journey.

It boiled down to being herself and also making her way in a world built by whites. It would be difficult to do, but, really, she didn't have any other options. And, when she performed, she made whites admire her. She knew she was prideful, but she liked that — although her grand-mothers' glances, stances, and nods said they considered it a failing they hoped would fall away with age. She got their message. But the attention was intoxicating. And so was the danger. She liked walking on a plane a few inches above everyone else. She often carried herself that way, using an attitude she'd learned from more experienced entertainers. But she sure couldn't pull it off on crutches.

Her pride hurt as much as her leg. And by the time she'd made it to the buffalo pen, she was glum again, consumed by pain, and sticky with sweat. She sat down on a bench under a tree near the fence, untied her bandana, and wiped her cheeks and her neck. She looked for Adam. He was on the other side of the pen, also under a tree, and down on the ground. His head was turned her way, but he probably couldn't see her. She called, "Haba, haba." Adam kept chewing, but his horns seemed to move. Two flexed her shoulders, trying to feel if there was a breeze at her back that would carry her odor. She thought maybe there was. Her blouse was stuck to her. A trickle of sweat tickled the leg in her cast. She retied her bandana around her head and tried rubbing her palm to dis-tract from the tickle. That didn't work. She looked around for a stick. She wasn't supposed to scratch in the cast. That could set up an infection. She should endure it. But a stick was just out of reach. She was debating on picking it up, when a voice said, "Hello, Two."

Jack had a wide grin. A lock of red hair that had escaped his hat curled over his forehead. Dark patches of sweat circled his uniform arm-pits, but Two didn't mind those a bit. She smiled for the first time that day. Forgot about her tickle. Noticed that his eye wasn't twitching.

They talked about buffalo. Two told Jack she knew Adam person-ally. Told him about Buffalo Bill, about the 101, and the large herd there, following their instincts, enjoying the range, safe from extinction. And bathed in Jack's attention, Two started feeling like herself again. She didn't care that the sun was getting hotter by the minute.

And Jack felt electric. He'd been on his way to fill the buffalo's troughs when he'd spied Two under the tree and detoured. It wasn't an opportunity he'd expected, and he was determined to make the best of it. He suggested they visit the concession stand. He offered to buy ice cream.

"Aren't you working?" Two asked.

"I am. But I've already watered the buffalo. Their troughs are full. I have to check on the hippopotamus next. The concession stand is on the way." He smiled. Both of them knew the concession stand wasn't between them and the hippo den. And Jack didn't care if Dinah or the buffalo, either one, lived or died. He was on the path to getting what he wanted, which was . . . He couldn't say exactly. But it had to do with sex with Two. Having her at his disposal. Keeping her as his own. His only pleasures came from feeling in control and pulling things over on people. He liked lording over animals. And sex with an inferior race didn't put him off at all. That was a well-known Southern custom. In years past, it would've been a right; there were people like Crawford all over the South. Jack hadn't thought through how his own children might be considered if he mated with Two. He hadn't thought about marriage. He didn't know if marrying an Indian was legal. Marrying a Negro sure wasn't. But there were different rules for different people.

As for Two, some company and ice cream seemed more important than a sick hippopotamus. So they were making their way slowly to the concessions when Jack said, "I have a confession."

Two, watching where she was placing her crutches, didn't look up. "It'd better be bad."

"It's a little embarrassing." Jack's eye started twitching.

Two stopped. They were on a walkway between rows of bird cages several stories high. Not a place Two felt comfortable. But it was the shortest route to the ice cream, and she hadn't wanted to suggest another without a good explanation. A group of children were close on one side, a couple of mothers on the other. Two said, "Maybe it should wait until we get our ice cream." She swung forward, eager to get away from the bird cages and hoping Jack wasn't going to say anything strange.

Jack bought cones and carried them to a more isolated bench in the shade with its back to the foxes' cage. They licked and began to cool down. Then Jack took his cap off and put up a finger to calm his eye. He said, "I've always wanted to know an Indian."

Two captured a drip sliding down her cone. She'd heard that before. Found it peculiar, but no longer surprising.

Jack gazed at the casino; at its wide porch, red cupolas, and billboards. He wanted to impress Two. "Are you aware that the park, particularly from the casino, to the buffalo pen, to the area below the creek, for as far as we can see, and even farther, used to be a cemetery?"

Two squinted, inspecting the top of her cone for where she might next lick. "With dead people?"

"Yep. Mostly in mounds. Over four thousand graves. But the really interesting thing is that the people were buried in limestone slab boxes. That's unique. You don't find that anywhere except in middle Tennessee."

Two lowered her cone and grew still. She pictured mounds covering the ground like giant, rounding waves coming into a beach. She imagined them being there, maybe under her feet. Holding layers and layers of ancestors, elders, and ancient ones. Trapped somehow in rocks or stones. That picture was harder to imagine. "You better not tell me any more." She held up a palm.

"Just a little. I wrote you notes about the buffalo path. Signed them Strong-Red-Wolf. I've imagined myself being an Indian since I was a little boy. I'm fascinated with the cemetery. That's why I got a job here. And you're the only other Indian around. I figured you'd like it, too."

Two felt like she'd been stung by a bee she hadn't seen. Stunned, she tossed her cone to the ground. "Well, I don't like it. Please don't say another word." She reached for her crutches. Fumbled them into place and stood. She tilted at first a little to the left, but then straightened up.

Jack flashed red from his collar to his forehead. He didn't rise before he said, "But they were Indian graves." His eye flickered like a moth's wing.

"Yes, I'm sure they were. I'd bet my life on that." Two lurched on her crutches. Said, "Don't follow me. Stay away."

Little Elk heard all of this. Before Jack had approached, he'd been blowing on Two to cool her down. He'd stepped off far enough to avoid the white man's smell, but stayed near enough to eavesdrop. When Two and Jack left the buffalo pen for the shadier part of the park, he followed them as far as the bird cages. He detoured around those to avoid enemy spirits and picked them up again as they settled on the bench. He sat down in the grass and folded his legs.

Little Elk was as surprised as Two was by what Jack said. By the fact that the white even knew about the graves. Every time Little Elk returned to his friends in the Nightland, there were different ones of them. They were going back down; becoming flesh and blood again, and then coming back up. But he'd never seen any of them around Two or the animals. Or not any he'd recognized. And he wondered if this man, who called himself by an Indian name, was actually a brother of his? Or a friend? Little Elk hadn't anticipated this development. It grabbed his attention, and it made him wonder if finding Strong-Red-Wolf was the reason he'd landed back at his tree. As Two hurried off, he took a long look at the man's head. It was round. His hair was red and curly, rather ugly. Little Elk put one hand on the hilt of his knife and the other on his chin.

By the time Two was on the sidewalk to Chambliss, she was soaked in sweat, and so flushed with exertion that Helen Hampton, on the porch, fan in hand, jumped up and lurched to meet her. She said, "My goodness, child. You shouldn't be out walking." She reached out to touch Two's shoulder, but retracted her hand before making contact.

Two said, "I can make it." She tightened her grip on her crutches and swung on.

Helen didn't know how to help. She would just stay by the girl's side in case she fell.

Two's arms and hands trembled with each lift of her cast up the steps. When she reached the porch, she collapsed into Helen's chair and her crutches fell in a clatter. She put her hands to her face. Her headband was wet. She tried to stop shaking.

Helen saw Two could easily faint from exertion. She said, "I'll get you some ice. Wait here." She rushed off, not realizing that "wait here" was an unnecessary order.

When Helen returned, Two's head was still against the pillow on the back of the rocker. Her eyes were closed. Her bandana in her lap. Helen pressed an ice-filled sugar sack to her forehead. She said, "If you can't hold this, I can."

Two put her hand to the sack. "I've got it. Thank ya so much."

Helen stood still for a moment to be sure Two could handle the ice pack. Then she dragged the closest chair over. She sat in a nervous dither, but also in silence. She leaned forward, wondering what Two would do next.

Two felt Helen's gaze. She normally wouldn't like that, but she also was worried about what she'd do next. And Mrs. Hampton's perfume was having a reviving effect. She concentrated on controlling her breathing like she had when she'd first started diving. She grew calmer slowly. But she kept the sugar sack ice pack pressed to her forehead.

Helen noticed Two's breath get steady. She said, "You've overdone it."

"Yes."

"You just can't go out into the park on those crutches in heat like this. It's hard to bear, even up here on the porch without a cast."

"I know."

"You need to stay here. It's the coolest location. When supper's served, I'll bring it to you. You know how hot the dining hall gets when they've been cooking."

"I think I'd rather go to my room."

Helen could understand that. The girl needed to lie down. She got up, reached for Two's crutches, and stood them up. "All right. I'll trade you these for the sack of ice. We'll get you settled."

"Could I have an Orange Crush? I need something wet."

"Certainly. There should be some in the kitchen. Let me get you to your room first."

Helen brought an opened chilled bottle, but no ice. As soon as she retreated, Two extracted the ice from the sugar sack into a glass she had in her room. She poured Orange Crush and vodka over the cubes.

Crawford
Has
a
Date

≋

That night, Crawford went courting carrying a bouquet of dainty blue violets from his mother's flower bed that, because of her age, he tended himself. During his ride into town, he endured some ribbing from a friend. But they were alone in the back of the trolley, and the friend was also riding in to court with half of a pecan pie, so the ribbing was mutual and mild. And the flowers, when delivered to Bonita, had a positive effect. Even better, her parents were entertaining and their front parlor was filling up with guests. Crawford and Bonita were freed to go out on their own.

They went over to Fisk, to a practice concert given by the Jubilee Singers. While looking for seats, they saw Crawford's Aunt Maria and Uncle Henry, and accepted an invitation to sit with them. After the concert, they went with Bonita's friends to the college's commissary. Over sodas, they talked about the Scopes appeal scheduled for Monday and Tuesday. The discussion caused a dispute between two vocal males in the group. Crawford and Bonita didn't enter in. Both were worried that the other was on the opposite (wrong) side of the question, and neither had the desire to let an issue beyond their control interfere with urges and hopes that were, in large part, biological, and building blocks, acknowledged or not, of natural selection.

They walked back to the trolley holding hands and caught a car filled only with Negros. Their stop was a mere two blocks from Bonita's house, so they were walking particularly slowly when Bonita asked, "What did you come up with to transport your Indian?"

Crawford's mind was below his belt. At first, he didn't catch Bonita's drift. "What Indian?"

"Miss Two Feathers, silly."

"Oh, Two!" Crawford raised his thoughts. He'd spent his day helping Buddy Parrish and Duncan Shelton determine what kind of enclosure should be built over the filled-in diving pool. They worried any new digging would give way, and their concern had taken them back to the cavern. This time, with lamps. But fifteen feet in, rotting horse smell slapped them. They turned back fast, retreated past the creek, and agreed to tell Clive that another pool over the cave, no matter how shallow, was risky. Crawford didn't want to tell Bonita about the decaying horse smell. He said, "Nothing yet."

"I've been thinking. If you could find a wheelchair, Daddy's automobile is open-topped."

Crawford instantly saw himself behind the wheel of H.A.'s touring car, Bonita by his side. They were a handsome couple. Turning the heads of people on the street. The vision didn't include a wheelchair in the back seat. But it didn't entirely preclude it either. He said, "Hum. I suspect that would do. If I could find a chair somewhere. Know anybody with one?"

"My Auntie Lula. But she needs it right now. Could you ask your uncle?"

"My uncles don't use wheelchairs."

"Your Uncle Henry." Maria's husband was the first Negro doctor at Meharry.

Crawford started to say, "I wish you'd thought of that while we were with them." But he hadn't thought of it at all, and that sounded accusatory. He said, "I'll ask him at church in the morning."

The couple walked on hand in hand in the silence that often engulfs the romantically inclined before they've poured out their hearts and proclaimed their intentions. Into that silence, thoughts intruded. Crawford's were entirely of a sexual nature. But Bonita's were of a more practical nature. Her father had made it clear that any man worth her hand had better be a professional and a Baptist. So Hank's job was a problem. And she didn't understand that any more than her father did. Even the Crawford women had educations and professions. But it seemed all Hank wanted to do was hang around that park, mess with animals, and fix equipment. She assumed he was collecting rent like the rest of his family, and wondered if that money could've hampered his ambition.

She hadn't decided how to test that theory, so her mind momentarily moved to the other problem, religion. The Crawfords were Methodists. But that wasn't like they were Catholics, and Bonita figured that with a little effort she could get Hank converted. She wished she hadn't boxed herself out of inviting him to services by bringing up the wheelchair. That was a mistake. However, the conversation did rather indicate Hank didn't harbor intentions toward the Indian woman, and Bonita felt some relief about that and intended to ensure they didn't arise in the future. She wasn't jealous by nature; but, like all Nashvillians, was aware that Glendale Park was the scene of many romantic adventures. And Miss Two Feathers was, from newspaper reports and pictures, an exotic, beautiful woman who was willing to take risks.

Crawford and Bonita slowed their gait even more the closer they came to her house. Other people were on the sidewalk, but so few cars were on the street that older boys were throwing a football across two pools of light cast by streetlamps. Separate groups of women and men were seated on steps. There was really no privacy. And if Crawford didn't at least get a kiss, he wasn't sure he'd be able to sleep. He spied an alley between two houses. Suddenly he pulled on Bonita's hand and, rather quickly, led her into the shadows. She said, "Hank! What're we doing?"

He kissed her. He kissed her deeper. Longer. And with passion and tenderness. Bonita shouldn't have been letting him do that, particularly practically on the street, but she couldn't help herself. In fact, she became rather weak in the knees, and needed to lean even closer to Hank to hold herself steady. She felt something hard in the front of his pants, to the side of his buttons. She knew what it was from conversations at college. But she'd never felt it herself, and it seemed appealing. She pressed against it.

When Crawford felt that, his mind went haywire. His fingers fumbled with his buttons, and he got three undone. Slid his suspenders off his shoulders, swooped a hand to the front of Bonita's dress, and cupped the mound of her body below her waist. That's when a little rationality invaded Bonita's mind. She said, "Hank, we can't." She gasped.

Crawford said, "Just put your hand on me. Please." He sounded pleading, desperate. He pulled Bonita's hand into his pants and guided it. He nearly went to his knees from the pleasure. His heart beat so rapidly it felt like a drum. But Bonita felt fear. She had never touched a man in that place, and she wasn't sure of the exact nature of what she had in her hand. Was it a bone? Was it a muscle? Was it gristle? It was unlike anything she'd ever held. And holding it had an effect on Hank she'd never seen. It was like she suddenly had complete control over him. He was reduced to whimpering and whining. Bonita was savoring that marvelous effect when she heard her father say, "What's going on here?"

Jack's
Pickle

≡

Jack had been agitated since Two had bolted from the bench and their conversation. His impulse had been to grab her, or trip her and throw her on the ground. He'd actually dropped his cone, sprung up, and lurched in her direction. But he was stopped by three adolescent boys who crossed his path. He'd pinched his nose under his glasses. Held the corner of his eye to keep it from twitching. He felt so enraged that he trembled. He realized he was out in public and needed to do something to settle himself. Go water the buffalo. Or over to the hippopotamus enclosure. If he went to the hippo, he'd have to lure her into a cage under the platform and shovel shit into a wheelbarrow. Nasty, smelly work, and out in the hot sun. The buffalo were probably thirsty. And they were close to the Oriental Golf Club Trolley Station.

Jack fled to the buffalo. Finally filled their troughs. But from there, he abandoned his job, caught the trolley, and rode home to a small apartment on a street near Woodmont Boulevard. He soaked in his tub to cool himself down, and listened to the radio while he prepared and ate his supper. If the Cardinals and Reds game had been a night one, he might've been able to get his focus off of Two. But they'd played during the day, so even cooled down and filled up, his mind was stuck. He couldn't get it off Two, what she might be up to, what she might do.

When the sky grew dark, he walked back to the trolley line, hopped on the Glendale car, and got off at the park's entrance. He wandered to kill time. Shot several rounds at the shooting gallery, watched the skaters, and felt his mood go down and down. Finally, as the crowds were thinning, he boarded the trolley and disembarked at the dormitory. He crossed the lawn in the shadows until he got to the lightning-struck tree with the damaged top. He climbed up and straddled the limb bridge. Two's light was out. She could be asleep. Her leg might have sent her to bed. But it was before her usual time. She was probably in one of the parlors, talking while her friends wound down. Jack tried to wait patiently and still, like he imagined a savage would stalk prey. But he was still agitated. He extracted a roll-up from a box in his pocket and lit it. The tobacco calmed the twitch in his eye as he waited.

Little Elk was fascinated by the trolley. He called it "rattling buffalo" and hated to miss one rolling into the station. He'd recognized Jack when his feet hit the ground, and was surprised because earlier he'd followed him as far as the golf club station and seen him leave. But he'd also previously seen him climb the tree and perch like a buzzard. And he'd seen him smoke. He knew he'd throw away some tobacco. So he'd followed Jack, not bothering to hide in the grass or behind a tree because he couldn't be seen. A constant frustration. Usually. But sometimes it worked to his advantage.

Before the dogs got him, Little Elk had been an enthusiastic young man. He was attractive to women. But he'd needed some scalps, success in battle, and a new, prestigious name before he could settle down and provide for a family. However, he'd been killed before attaining his manhood, and sent off to the spirit world with only his own scalp and a name that was childish. There, in the in-between, the energy between his legs dwindled to an occasional hiccough. That mortified him all the way to his topknot.

But he still understood the motivations of carnal men. He'd figured Strong-Red-Wolf spied on women because he couldn't whittle a straight arrow, didn't have enough air to send a dart through a blowgun, and was probably too slow to steal a horse. Little Elk wanted to knock him from the limb just for fun. But in his current insubstantial state, he couldn't swing that. He spit. The lightning-struck tree was terrible luck even when that toad wasn't squatting in it. Little Elk hunkered down away from its trunks. He watched and waited for Jack to drop some tobacco.

Soon, a light came on in Two's room. A female appeared in the window. Jack flicked his butt to the ground. Little Elk scampered to it. Pinched the fire out and scampered back away from the tree. There was hardly any leaf left. Little Elk was disappointed. Then Jack pulled another cigarette from his pack, lit it, and leaned forward. Little Elk dropped the burnt tobacco into his pouch. They both watched a woman pull a dress off over her head. They saw her camisole, garter belt, and panties. Saw her sit down on the bed.

Little Elk knew that wasn't Two. He recognized the female he'd huffed at before. He looked up at the man on the limb, who said, "Damn," pulled in, and exhaled more smoke. Little Elk decided to risk getting nearer. He moved to the smoke and caught all he could until Jack rubbed the butt on the tree and threw it to the ground. Little Elk dove for the remnant. The fire was crushed, but the stub longer than the first. He held it under his nose. Tobacco didn't smell like it used to, but it was still delicious.

Little Elk pinched the burnt part. Pulled the wrapping leaf away, and cradled the little bits of tobacco in his palm. He sniffed some more and crumpled to the earth with relief. He crossed his legs and sniffed again. His respite bordered on homesickness. He missed his parents, grandparents, his mother's brothers, his own, his sister, and cousins. His whole clan. The next sniff almost brought them to him. They were all there, just barely out of his reach. He lapsed into a daze. Forgot about the evil tree, about the weak man in it, and the woman in the window. That is, until the limb above started moving. Little Elk looked up. The man was doing something peculiar. Was he climbing down? No. Getting ready to fall? No. Rocking back and forth? Yes. Little Elk's brow furrowed. Then his eyes widened. He recognized the movement. But in a tree? And while spying? How disgusting! Little Elk pinched the precious fragments of leaves into a firm little wad and popped the ball of tobacco into his mouth. He rose, curled his upper lip, and marched back over to his oak.

The next day, Jack went looking for Clive. Neither of them usually worked on Sundays, but Jack knew his boss was taking Monday and Tuesday off for the Scopes hearing, and he couldn't wait until Wednesday to talk. He came to the park out of uniform and went to Clive's cabin. When his knock wasn't answered, he feared Clive was entertaining visitors to the park, something he did when the guests were old friends or important. He stepped off the porch and headed toward the bear pit, hoping Clive was just out playing tricks.

And he did find Clive there in the den, teasing Zerle with a stick of gum between his teeth just out of the big bear's reach. Jack felt relief. It was better than Clive engaging with human beings. This would come to an end. But Jack had seen the trick before, and it made him jumpy. Bears still roamed the Smoky Mountains where he'd grown up. He'd looked for their claw marks on trees, and, when old enough, hunted them himself. Bears were a dangerous species, and if every last one of them died, in Jack's opinion, the world would be a better place.

Clive was famous for his chewing gum trick, and a large silent crowd was gathered around. The custom was to remain quiet and still until Clive let the bear take the gum, and then to clap wildly. Jack was as still as everyone else. But he did wonder how people got into thinking that practically kissing a bear was a good idea. And, finally, when Zerle took the gum and the crowd erupted, Jack was glad it was done. Clive would repeat the game with Zana, if he hadn't done that earlier, or take Tom Noddy out and about so children could pet him. He'd have a lot of conversations, but eventually he'd be free.

And when Clive finally extracted himself from the last admiring mother and child, Jack fell in with him on the path toward the casino. He started the conversation with the subject of the weather as he'd discovered that Mr. Lovett, or perhaps all English people, liked having that exchange before any other. They agreed it was hot. Also, humid. And unlikely to change. Then Clive said, "Is this not your day off?"

"It is, sir. But I'm in a pickle. I need some advice." Jack didn't calm his eye. He wanted Mr. Lovett to see he was upset.

Clive stopped in the path and looked at Jack's face. "You don't say?" He thought about Jack's work with the animals. The young man was quite knowledgeable. Always researching anything he didn't understand.

"I've, uh, I've . . ." Jack looked around. An older girl and a herd of six children were bearing down on them. They both stepped aside to let them pass. Then Clive said, "Let's get something wet and sit under a tree."

Clive chose a bench with a view of the bandstand. A musician was setting up cymbals and drums, but the crowd hadn't started gathering. After a sip of lemonade, Clive said, "Might as well get it off your chest. It can't be entirely bad." He had, by then, intuited the problem was of a personal nature, nothing to do with the animals. He was relieved about that.

"I've developed an affection."

Clive sipped.

"For a female person."

He sipped again.

"And, uh, she got mad at me and ran away."

Clive frowned. "You don't say."

"I do say. It's Two Feathers."

Jack told Clive about telling Two about the cemetery and the buffalo path. About her dropping her cone, telling him not to follow, and hurrying off. He left out a few details. He didn't say he'd discovered another girl was in her room. Or that he was afraid Two had left the park for good. And he didn't mention he'd written her notes using his Indian name.

By the time he finished, they both were crunching ice. Except for that sound, they were silent. Clive wondered why Jack had come to him, a bachelor, instead of a friend. He must have some. But he didn't dwell on that long, because many people confided in him. And he had, some time ago, decided it was because he was English and not from Nashville. Nashvillians' tangled connections went so far back that one couldn't really discern if the person one was speaking with wasn't actually the first cousin twice removed of the one under discussion.

However, Jack was from East Tennessee, and Two was unlikely to be related, even distantly, to anyone around. She was more likely related to the people whose graves had been destroyed and who'd lived on the land before Europeans had come. When Clive spoke, he did so recalling the Indian he'd seen under the tree. "Perhaps Miss Feathers was alarmed by the idea of graves being desecrated. Maybe she feels like the spirits of her people, or at least of people like her, were disturbed." The wound on Clive's back contracted. He laid a palm on it.

"I've thought about that. But science benefitted. Vanderbilt, Harvard, and the Peabody Museum. The knowledge they got was invaluable."

Clive believed in science. He used it every day and couldn't manage his zoo without it. And, certainly, he didn't approve of the anti-evolution fools who'd made Tennessee the laughingstock of the nation. He hoped they'd get their comeuppance starting the next day. On the other hand, he'd seen Millwood, the apparition in the hospital, and that Indian under the tree just as clearly as he was seeing the man setting up the drums and the cymbals. Even more clearly, really. The drummer looked imaginary by comparison.

And since seeing the Indian under the tree, he'd seen yet another one in the park. A woman sitting on a rock at the opening of one of the springs. Her hair was pulled back in a knot on the nape of her neck, she was unclothed above her waist, and was weaving a basket, but not intent on her work. She frequently looked up, apparently to watch the visitors. Clive had observed the woman for what seemed like a long time. Until their eyes met. Then the woman set her basket aside, arose, and disappeared into the spring's source. Clive had seen her so clearly that he'd hurried over. But as he got closer, the basket also went away.

He felt like he could hear his heart beating. He tried to quieten it by speaking. "I've seen some of the grave goods over the years. At the State Fair and in private collections. A complex culture, evidently."

"Oh, yes. They traded all over. Up and down the continent. Even into Mexico and up to the Great Lakes. And it wasn't a subsistence culture. They had leisure time. Had tradesmen, artisans, and medicine men. Or, more likely, medicine women. They had an earth mother religion. And they believed in underwater spirits and in reincarnation."

"I see." Clive frowned. He really did see. Or he had seen. He looked far away.

Jack said, "Interesting, isn't it?"

"Yes, yes, of course. Reincarnation? You don't say?"

"Evidently. I'm not sure how they reached that conclusion. My interest was more focused on bones."

Clive looked into the distance again. He was half expecting to see the woman or the brave sitting on another bench. He saw park visitors, ladies and girls in summer dresses, men in straw hats. No Indians. Clive took in a deep breath and expelled it slowly. The visions had opened another world to him. They were changing the way he looked at the one he was presently in. And they were beginning to seem more real to him than the trees, paths, music, and even the animals of Glendale.

Jack said, "But we were talking about Two Feathers."

"Hum. Yes, of course. I was just thinking . . . about what to do. It seems Miss Two Feathers' knickers are in a knot. But females, of course, are hard to fathom, even on good days. They're always doing the unexpected. And it may be that mentioning graves to her is worse than mentioning them to somebody else. Since they're Indian graves, she understandably might take it rather personally."

"They weren't her people's graves."

"Do you know that?"

"Yes, she's a Cherokee. The people buried here aren't her ancestors."

"I thought it was the Cherokees who terrorized the early Nashville settlers? That's what everybody claims. Their great-great somebody was scalped outside of some station. I've never really understood what a station was. They didn't have trains."

"A station was a fort. Sometimes a group of houses or outbuildings, usually behind a palisade."

"You'd think they'd just say so. *Fort* is a perfectly good English word. Comes from the Latin."

Jack didn't want to talk etymology. And he was beginning to feel he'd gone to the wrong person for advice when Clive said, "Look, I'm going to Chambliss in the morning. I'll go over early and visit Two. I need to see her anyway. I'll try to get the lay of the land."

Jack sighed deeply. That was what he wanted. But he was so afraid that Two had run away from Glendale that he wanted Mr. Lovett to go immediately. He looked into the bottom of his cup. Didn't see any way to force that. The drummer hit a cymbal. Jack jumped. His whole body twitched. He'd just have to spend a miserable night. Or maybe he'd make another run for artifacts.

Vodka
and
Fried
Chicken

≡

Every Sunday morning, Helen Hampton and most female employees housed by the park attended services in Burgess Hall. The preacher was Presbyterian, usually one of the assistants at the Glen Leven Church, which held the Shacklefords' memberships. It was an hour Helen enjoyed. And often when the sermon wasn't entirely to her liking, she studied the hats, backs, and shoulders of the other attendees and mused on fashion. She didn't want to dress too old to catch a man. But neither did she want to dress too young. She was pursuing the sweet middle spot, and the services provided an occasion for calculation. Her religious views had long been set, and they didn't need improving.

So the Montgomerys knew Helen wasn't in Chambliss when Franny knocked on the door and Marty said, "Two, are you in there? Open up." Both cocked their ears, held their breaths, and listened. They heard a sound. Some movement. Neither could tell its nature. Marty tried the knob. The door was locked. She knocked again. "Open up, Two. We know you're in there." They listened hard. Franny heard breathing. Marty's. She huffed, touched her sister's arm, and jerked her head toward the main hall. She said to the door, "We're going away now. We'll be back later."

In the hall, Franny stopped under an oil painting by a former Buford College student. Those were all over the walls, in both the hallways and parlors. This one was of a ship tossed by a stormy sea. A face in a cloud was blowing on the water. Franny said, "Let's try the window. It'll be open."

Outside, the sisters stopped on the porch at the southwest corner of the building. They whispered about which window was most likely Two's. They settled on the third one down and crept to it. The founders of the college, Eb and Elizabeth Buford (but particularly Elizabeth), had believed in promoting health by avoiding flies and mosquitoes, so Chambliss had screens on its windows. Franny slid up to the third one, and Marty ducked under it and rose up. In a unison honed by their act, they folded in toward the screen.

They could see Two's legs on her bed, but not her head. On the floor was a wastepaper basket and a magazine. Franny didn't believe for a moment that Two was sleeping, but said, "Wake up, Two!"

Two's good leg moved. She said, "Go away."

"Open this screen, Two." That was Marty.

Two wasn't sure she could get to the window. She'd been sick in her wastepaper basket. After that, she'd slept. Quite soundly, for the first time since her accident. But if she moved, would she throw up again? She slowly arose on an elbow, squinted toward the window, and said, "Why don't ya use the door?"

Franny looked at Marty. Marty said, "We tried that. You wouldn't answer."

"I thought it was Miz Hampton."

Both jugglers knew that was a lie. But neither called it. Franny said, "Will you open it if we come around?"

Two's head hit the pillow. "Yeah, sure."

• • •

Marty procured a glass of water from the kitchen before coming to the room, and she handed it to Two. Two returned it empty. She said, "My leg didn't hurt for a while."

Franny said, "You're overdoing it. You wanta drink just enough to make the pain go away."

"How do ya calculate that?"

"When Marty breaks my nose, I drink 'til it starts feeling numb."

"I don't break your nose. You break it yourself by not being fast enough." Marty wiggled her own with her fingers. It'd been broken twice.

Two rolled her eyes. Who broke whose nose was a familiar topic. She said, "Somebody hand me my crutches. I need to go to the bathroom."

Marty did that, and Franny picked up the wastepaper can. She'd put the magazine over it when they'd first entered the room and she kept it in place. She went to empty it outside, and Marty went with Two to the bathroom, carrying her pail and some clothes. The sisters had Two dressed, fed, and on the front porch by the time their dormitory mother returned from church.

Mrs. Hampton said, "We missed you at services." She was addressing only Franny and Marty. She had no hope for Two converting.

Marty said, "We've been doing our Christian duty by visiting the sick."

Mrs. Hampton felt the prick. But it was small, and the Montgomerys were, she thought, good Episcopalians. She'd leave who would go up or down to God in His wisdom. She said to Two, "How's your leg this morning?"

"Fine, thank ya."

"Doesn't hurt?"

"It's better than it was."

"That's good. You'll make progress every day. Soon be fit as a fiddle. Dinner's in fifteen minutes." She proceeded into the hall.

Franny said, "Let's go for hot dogs."

Marty enjoyed Sunday dinners in Chambliss. The meat was always fried chicken, a food she'd never tasted until they'd toured the South and one she couldn't get enough of. She said, "That's a good idea. But I want to swipe some chicken for later on. Anybody want a thigh or a breast?" She rose from a step. Two asked for a thigh, Franny for a breast. Marty disappeared into the hall to procure those pieces and two for herself.

After hot dogs, popcorn, and lemonade, the sisters left Two in the dressing room and went onstage to throw dishes. By the time they returned, Two was weary from chatting with the singing act, but still on the sofa with her leg propped up. She looked glum, but neither Montgomery noticed because Franny had dropped a dish and both were making a show of not speaking.

Marty said to Two, "Tell the other half of our act that I'm taking a walk."

Franny said, "Tell Marty she can walk all the way to Nashville for all I care."

Two said, "I'm gonna go see Crawford."

Two found the smell of horses, a standoffish cat, and hot, stuffy air in the barn. But not Crawford. She eased down onto the underside of an overturned wheelbarrow and settled her leg on the slope. But resting on tin, her rear end soon started hurting, and it hurt, too, to be so near Ocher's stall. She struggled up and swung to a bench outside next to the door. She figured Crawford was detained by a windy sermon, but would soon be around. Most of the horses were pastured, but he enjoyed spending time in the barn, and they both liked playing gin rummy.

While waiting, Two looked at the trees and blocked out the sounds of the park. However, Jack's facts pushed their way into her mind. More than four thousand graves. Two was shocked that anybody would disturb a single grave, let alone so many. She couldn't swallow the disrespect, couldn't even get it through her lips, into her mouth. It was just crazy, crazy behavior. And sickening.

But she didn't think they were Cherokee graves. She'd never heard of her people building mounds, and was sure they'd never pen their dead up in stones. But they had lived in Tennessee. Been killed, run out, and cheated. Elders who'd walked the Trail as little children told stories of cold and snow, of bleeding, bare feet, of few clothes, few blankets, and lots of spoiled meat. Their grandmothers, grandfathers, parents, and siblings had been buried in shallow graves along the way. Two hoped those hadn't been destroyed by crazy white people.

But she'd gained strength from those stories. They were instruction to children about the toughness and the endurance of the Cherokee people. And education about the greed and deception of whites. Two, unable to bear picturing the destroyed graves, homed in on those lessons. But she also reminded herself that she liked white people. Or liked individual white people. Liked Franny and Marty. Liked Mr. Lovett. Liked even the Miller brothers. But she thought white people, in general, were dishonest, ruthless, and greedy. Wondered if that was caused by them being poor or caused by them being rich. Concluded it could be both, and due, underneath, not to their race, but to their love of owning things. She worried about being proud of her scarves. Wondered if loving scarves could turn her toward evil.

Two's thoughts traveled up and down those paths, all over the place. And the shadow of the barn was long before she resigned herself to the reality that Crawford wouldn't show. She began to feel foolish. With Ocher dead and the diving stopped, there was no reason for him to come to the park on Sunday. Except friendship, and he probably had plenty of pals. A mockingbird landed on a nearby branch. It squawked and squawked. Two felt like it was talking to her, mocking her. Her whole life had changed. And she'd spent a long afternoon at the barn for nothing. Just being stupid and pitiful. Dumb and lonely. She felt hungry for fried chicken and vodka.

Crawford's
Sunday

≡

Crawford had built his house on the side of a hill off Hillsboro Pike, southwest of Glendale Park. West, beyond trees, was the two-story frame house he'd been raised in. His mother, his brother Josh, and Josh's wife and younger children currently occupied it. Josh was a farmer, a builder of stone fences, and a holder of mortgages, cut in the mold of their father. His wife was his second, twenty years younger and a good fit for the family. Squarely downhill was their brother Trimble's house, his outbuildings, and barns. Trimble was a farmer, holder of mortgages, and a mule man. He also was married and the father of many. From Crawford's front porch, all of the land he could see (if it weren't for the trees) had been, or still was, owned by his family. The voices of his nieces and nephews playing after Sunday dinner bounced off the back of the big house and the hill.

Crawford hadn't gone to church, or to dinner, and hoped his family thought he'd ridden over to the park. He didn't want to visit. Least of all with his mother, sisters, and sisters-in-law. Avoiding the gathering, he'd settled on his back porch, a screened rectangle that gave him a view of the hill above his house, its peaceful trees, hanging vines, and sprinkles of wildflowers and weeds. His dog was curled in a dust hole so close to the foundation that Crawford couldn't see him. His horse, secured by a long rope to a sapling, was munching grass.

Crawford was whittling, a habit he'd taken up while being punished as a child and had continued as an adult when his mind needed clearing or his time needed killing. He'd developed real skill, and was sculpting a whistle when his front door was rapped. He didn't get up, but did look at his horse. He should've hidden Bang On in the mule pack in Trimble's pasture downhill. Knock, knock came again. Crawford kept whittling. He paused when Josh called his name, and he listened to him walk through the house.

"So here you are," Josh said through the screen door. He opened it and took a seat in another chair. "Mama sent me."

"Tell her I'm under the weather."

Josh looked out at Bang On and up the hill at the foliage. Neither brother said a word. Crawford whittled. Josh opened his right palm and started picking at his calluses. Finally Crawford said, "I got female trouble."

"That's a natural thing." Josh flicked a piece of skin.

The dog moved to a cool, flat stone under a tree, flopped on his side, and stretched. Crawford added, "Been courting Bonita Boydstun. H.A. caught us in an unfortunate position."

Josh rubbed his palms together. Then he picked up a duck Hank had recently completed. Too small to be a decoy, it was purely ornamental. Josh sometimes sold those for Hank when he peddled excess vegetables on the side of the road in Hillsboro. The ducks brought in eight or ten dollars apiece. Good money for what they were, but not a living. He guessed Hank whittled for the same reason he raised corn, tomatoes, cucumbers, and okra. To create something new out of nothing.

"H.A. threw a fit. Not like Daddy. No yelling. More of a clenched-teeth type of fit. We had a man-to-man."

"And?"

A blue jay squawked. Both men looked to see where it was. Josh said, "You need to whittle a slingshot."

"Mr. Boydstun doesn't think I'm making enough of myself. Wants me to go back to school. Get a degree. And if I'm serious about his daughter, come work for him in printing and publishing. Oh, and become a Baptist."

Josh set the duck back on a rail that circled the porch screen. He picked up a bird with a long neck. "What's this?"

"A crane. They're all over the park."

"What'd Bonita say?"

"She went up to her room crying. I didn't see her before I left. In fact, I'm not to see her again until I reform my ways."

Josh rubbed the bird's neck with his thumb. "Well, ya should be able to get around that if ya wanta."

"Probably. But the Boydstuns aren't going away."

"No, that's the Lord's truth." Josh sighed. He rubbed the crane's breast.

The Boydstuns and Crawfords had known each other for three decades. Some of them went to college together at Roger Williams, and they were allies against whites whenever necessary. They also had financial dealings, as H.A. was president of Citizens, the largest Negro bank around. But the families had never married into each other. There was that rural-city divide, as well as the Methodist-Baptist one. Also in the background not spoken was the fact that both clans tended, at times, to look down on the other. In addition to being newcomers to middle Tennessee, the Boydstuns were somewhat darker in shade. The Crawfords generally married light-skinned people who were descended from masters, and whose lineage from both races they could recite backwards for several generations.

In Boydstuns' estimations, the Crawfords, as a family, didn't do enough for the race. And, while most had higher educations, a few were content to be land owners and farmers. That choice, from the Boydstuns'

point of view, could be the residue of a slave mentality, a serious problem. The Crawfords were more aware of the Boydstuns' attitudes than
the Boydstuns were of theirs, but the Crawfords, generally, didn't care.

However, Hank Crawford suddenly did care. And he'd spent his day
trying to untangle the unspoken web of attitudes that divided the families. He'd also spent the day trying to get over the humiliation of being
caught with Bonita's hand in his pants. Every time he pictured that, his
pelvis squirmed, but his heart sank.

"Whatcha gonna do?" Josh asked.

Hank took a strong stroke with his knife. A long, curled piece of
wood fell to the planks. "I have no idea."

"Well, ya know what Daddy would say: Wait and something'll
change."

"H.A. won't change."

Josh looked through the screen. Bang On seemed to be dozing.
"Would going back to school and working for him be so bad?"

"I didn't like school." Hank flicked a chip of wood off his knife.

"I getcha there." Josh could feel school in his flanks. Hard wood when
he wanted to be outside, wanted to work with his hands, wanted to make
something grow. The blue jay squawked again. "It's not like ya can't read
and write. You don't need to go back to school just to print Sunday school
material."

"I don't know exactly what he had in mind. He was highly agitated."

A smile crept to Josh's lips. He set the crane on the shelf while trying
to keep his mouth from widening into a grin. "What kind of compromis-
ing position were you in?"

Hank laid his knife and wood on a table beside his chair. Took a long
sigh. "Not what you think. Unfortunately, just a hand in the wrong place."

"Yours or hers?"

Crawford blushed. "Hers."

Josh grinned. Looked off at Bang On again. Tried to imagine the situation. Couldn't quite bring up enough detail. Said, "Where were you?"

"In the fucking alley."

Josh burst out laughing. Bang On woke up. The blue jay flew away. When Josh got his mirth under control, he said, "No shit?"

Hank was chuckling, too. His mood was considerably improved. "Yeah. We went to a concert. Her parents were entertaining. We just slipped into the dark where we could."

"My, my," Josh said. The picture was in his head. His wife kept him satisfied, but he wasn't dead. "Did she like it?"

"I think so. But she's innocent. Young."

"How young?" Josh was several years older than Hank. He knew H.A.'s family, but couldn't keep his children straight.

"Nineteen."

"She's a grown woman."

"They treat her like she's a piece of porcelain."

"She'll buck 'em soon. Remember Q's temper?" Quentina was their sister. She'd had a stormy relationship with their parents.

"Yeah. Particularly the night she threw that vase."

"Mama sure had a go-to-pieces. I thought she was gonna roll on the floor."

"I reckon that was her favorite urn."

Both men chuckled again. Q had grown up to be the most proper of the clan. She was married to a lawyer in Chicago. Enjoyed giving etiquette tips to her brothers and fashion advice to her sisters.

Josh squeezed his little brother's shoulder. "Come on over to the house. Trimble's churned ice cream. Laced it with chocolate. It'll be pretty damn good."

The Most Marvelous Proceeding

True to his word, Monday morning Clive arrived early at Chambliss Hall to speak with Two before leaving with Helen. But a blond woman told him Two hadn't yet made it to breakfast. Said since she'd broken her leg, she hadn't always eaten with the rest of them. She'd be glad to deliver a message, but first had to run over to Burgess to set up for a meeting of an Eastern Star committee.

Clive was looking around for an alternative messenger when Helen arrived. He didn't want to start their day by asking her about another woman. He wished Helen the top of the morning, remarked on a break in the heat, and waved his hat toward the door. They walked to the trolley station, extending their weather conversation. Due to a cool front moving through, the temperature was quite pleasant, nearly fifteen degrees below the day before.

The trolley was empty, but filled as it traveled toward Nashville. They disembarked at the Transfer Station, so close to the state capitol building, their destination, that they climbed that hill by foot. The sidewalk was crowded with people heading in the same direction. It was such a throng that many had to walk in the street. Honking horns interrupted a great deal of excited conversation.

There were only a few hundred seats in the supreme courtroom. But Clive had tickets. An usher handed them fans and led them to a bench eleven rows back from the tables provided for lawyers. Helen clucked her gratitude, and Clive felt rather pleased by the position he'd secured. He'd never been in the room before and hadn't known in advance how good his tickets were. They and others nodded to acquaintances and exchanged good-to-see-yous across the room. Really, everyone was carefully noting who'd managed to get in and feeling glad to be included in the select few. Nashville was still quite a small town, at least in regards as to who could get tickets. The regular, plain people took up posts outside the windows.

The state capitol, a Greek Revival building, was considered by many (not just Tennesseans) to be the most beautiful structure erected for its purpose in the entire forty-eight states. It'd been electrified years before. But as the heat was likely to rise during the day, the courtroom lights were off, and with people clustered at the windows, the room was dim. But Chief Justice Green had prohibited the use of flashbulbs and motion picture cameras. He was determined not to repeat the circus in Dayton the previous summer.

The proceedings progressed with decorum until Ed Seay delivered the last speech. Though a judge himself, Seay launched into a fire and brimstone sermon outlining evolution's threat to the very foundations of Western civilization. Then he attacked the opposing lawyers, Arthur Garfield Hayes, who'd already quietly spoken about legal issues, and Clarence Darrow, who'd not yet said a word. After an hour and forty minutes of tirade, Judge Green banged a gavel, shutting Seay down and raising mixed emotions in the crowd. Seay's oratory had been the most exciting of the day. And some felt his attack on the opposing lawyers for previously defending Communists and anarchists was something that needed to be said. Others were merely glad for the excitement. A third group thought Seay was a raving maniac, and typical of the general blathering incoherence of the anti-evolutionists.

When the drama was over in the late afternoon, Clive suggested to Helen they take tea in Nashville. They walked to the Hermitage Hotel only to find long lines at the dining room's entrance, on the stairs to the mezzanine, and on the ones to the basement's vaulted rathskeller. Fortunately, Maggie Caldwell spied them at a distance and sent a mutual friend over to fetch them. They wedged in with her group in a dining room corner. It was a tight squeeze with two extra chairs brought in from back rooms, but Clive knew everyone there and Helen was thrilled to be with them. The tea lasted three rounds of nibbles into the early evening. Most of the defense team was housed at the Hermitage, and Maggie's set, like everyone else, hoped for a closer glimpse of the famous Mr. Darrow.

However, the famous Mr. Darrow needed to prepare for his speech the next day. He slipped into the hotel through a back entrance and went to his room unseen by anyone other than the bellman he'd paid. Eventually, the crowd gave up and thinned out, and Maggie offered Clive and Helen a lift home in her Buick. She dropped them off at the park's entrance.

Clive contemplated talking with Two that evening. But he was emotionally drained, and needed to shine his shoes and get some sleep. He left Helen at the front door of the hall, and she was in such an elated mood that she fairly flew into the parlor, where Two was trapped by Christa Belle Henley. She interrupted, "Guess what I did today!"

Christa Belle said, "Ya went to the hearing."

"How did you know?"

"Everybody knows. Ya were gone with Mr. Lovett all day. And while the cat's away . . ." She stopped midsentence, tilted her head, and smiled in a sly way.

"Did something happen?"

"I really can't say."

"But you just did say."

"No, ma'am. Just reciting one of my mama's favorite maxims. We've all been quiet as little mice here." Christa Belle smiled again and raised both of her eyebrows.

Two knew Christa Belle was just trying to spoil Miz Hampton's day. She said, "Did ya learn anything?"

"I'm so glad you asked. It was just the most marvelous proceeding." Helen plopped down in a chair across from Two and began talking about the speeches. Christa Belle quickly left with the excuse of needing to soak her feet, but Two was still caged. However, she didn't mind. The Scopes trial had set the entire country ablaze, even breaching the fences of the 101. And like Mr. Lovett and Mrs. Hampton, Two thought the verdict had been idiotic. Humans and animals are kin. Only a stooge could miss that. So Helen poured her story out to a sympathetic ear, and reveled in the most wonderful day she'd experienced since her husband had died and left her behind. An hour later, when they headed to their rooms, Two asked Helen if she'd help her by carrying an Orange Crush and some ice. Helen eagerly agreed. She felt sorry for Two, and her connection to Clive made her even more appealing.

Monkey
Business

Jack hadn't learned that his boss had taken Mrs. Hampton to the hearing until the late afternoon. His mind had wandered through the romantic implications as he was watering DuPont, the camel. He'd decided Lovett must be a breast man. Tried to picture him cupping Mrs. Hampton's. Sucking her nipples. But there his imagination fizzled out. The woman didn't have any modern appeal. But then Mr. Lovett was British. They were notorious for old-fashioned taste. Mrs. Hampton was probably his cup of tea. Jack chuckled and turned his mind to his own problems. By the time he reached the buffalo lot, he was wondering, had Lovett spoken with Two as promised? Gleaned anything? Made any progress?

Jack hung around the zoo after his hours were through, waiting for his boss's return. He watched Clive and Helen disembark from a beautiful new Buick. But when they walked toward Chambliss, Jack balked. People were still out and about. He couldn't lurk around until Lovett left the dormitory and "accidentally" run into him at that time of night. He started to formulate a new plan. The hearing would run two days. Surely if Lovett took Mrs. Hampton to the first one, he'd take her to the second.

The tickets were probably sold in pairs. And the next day was the big one. Likely, they'd both be gone again. But, maybe still, he could get some information.

The next morning before the zoo opened to the public, Jack visited the monkey cages. He picked up Mickey the lemur, stuffed him inside a carrier, and draped it with cloth. He carried the carrier to the back of the park, circled behind the barns, and crept through the woods behind the old college halls. Between the trees and Chambliss were weedy croquet and tennis courts and a covered cistern. Back of the hall was an old, dilapidated hen house. Jack stayed away from the hennery, as it was near trees, and he imagined Mickey could pick up a chicken odor and get agitated. He needed to release the lemur in a location that would make him run into the dormitory, rather than up into branches. Jack couldn't think of a way to accomplish that without being seen and got worried that Mickey, who'd been cooperative so far, would start to scream.

Jack turned back, proceeded the way he'd come, but avoided the barns; by that time the zoo was open, and he worried that Crawford might see him. He spied a boy of about twelve near the alligator pit. He was alone and wearing long pants with his shirttail hanging out in the back. He looked like the type that could enjoy some mischief. Jack approached him. Said, "Care to make fifty cents?"

The boy had jug ears, a ring around his collar, and a smudge on his cheek. He said, "Depends."

Jack lifted the cover on Mickey's carrier. "I've got this monkey here. He likes the girls, if ya know what I mean."

The boy snickered.

Jack set the carrier on the ground. Brought Mickey out, cuddled him in the crook of his arm, and tickled his tummy. "He's real friendly, see. Little kids pet him all the time. He just doesn't like other monkeys. Wanta hold him?"

"Sure." The boy reached out. Mickey scampered onto his shoulder and then onto his back. The boy folded over double and swatted. He gritted his teeth. Said, "Git him off me."

Jack grabbed Mickey with an arm under his stomach. "He can see you're afraid. It makes him nervous."

The boy straightened up. "He makes me nervous, mister. Why ya walking around with a monkey?" He used both hands adjusting his shirt.

"I work here, see." He pointed to *Glendale Zoo* embroidered over his pocket. "Look, I just wanta play a joke on a girl I'm courting. I need some help. Do you think you could take this monkey into the women's dormitory, just open the cage, and run?" He pulled at the corner of his eye to keep it from twitching.

The boy smiled. "Ya're joking me, right?"

"No. Dead serious. I just wanta see the gals get excited."

"Fifty cents?"

"Yeah."

"Make it a dollar."

"That's some serious money."

"Up to ya. I'm guessing, if I get caught ya'll want me to keep my kisser shut. Think of the extra fifty cents as insurance."

The boy's name was Ken. He followed Jack back to the woods behind the tennis courts. Jack took Mickey out of the carrier and wrapped him in the cloth. He held him securely and told Ken to hold him that way until he released him.

Ken said, "Where d'ya want me to let him go?"

"That building there." He nodded toward Chambliss. "If the women are still eating, do it in the dining hall. If not, look for the largest parlor."

"Where will ya be?"

"I'll be around. Don't worry. You just run. Hightail it as fast as ya can. Get lost in the park."

"What if I get caught?"

Jack bit his bottom lip. He'd sized the boy up as one who could sprint. He said, "Are ya slow or something?"

"No, mister, I ain't slow. But somebody might see me carrying this monkey and ask me some questions."

"If anybody does, just set Mickey free and hightail it. They'll be more concerned about him than about you."

Ken saw the wisdom of that. And found the whole idea fun. Jack handed Mickey to Ken, reminded him again to keep him wrapped tight until the right time, and then to run like the dickens.

Ken said, "What about my dough? I ain't doing it until I get paid."

Jack said, "Oh, yeah. I should've given ya that first. He stuck his hand in his front pocket and drew out a small wad of bills wrapped in a rubber band. A five was on the outside, but the rest were ones. He pulled a bill out and stuffed it in Ken's top pocket. "Go to it. Let's have us some fun."

Jack waited until Ken disappeared around the corner of the hall, then hurried to the hennery. He'd figured out that Two had been moved from the second floor to the first because of her leg. He just needed to know which room. Mickey would soon cause such a stir he could enter the hall and snoop all around the first floor. There couldn't be that many sleeping rooms on it, and he could identify Two's by her diving shoes. If he got caught, he could say he was looking for the escaped lemur. If he ran into Mickey before he accomplished his goal, he could say he needed to check the other rooms to be sure Mickey hadn't brought along a pal. Spout some hogwash about lemurs running in pairs but being afraid to climb stairs.

Ken had calmed his fear of Mickey. And the lemur was too interested in the scenery to pay attention to him. Ken held Mickey tight and secure, except for his tail. Too large to be confined by the cloth, it tickled Ken on the back of a thigh and made him wiggle as he walked. But otherwise their trip to the building and up the steps of Chambliss was smooth. The front porch was empty. Also the front hall. Two women descending the stairs were in deep conversation, not paying attention to the kid with the bundle.

The dining hall door was open, the long tables visible, residents lingering at three of them over their coffee. Ken slipped in the door, ducked down, wiggled between chairs to beneath a tablecloth, and unwrapped

Mickey. The lemur sat on his haunches. Clutched his tail in both hands and bared his teeth. Ken whispered, "Go on, pal. Give 'em a scare." He poked Mickey in the side with his thumb.

Mickey screeched. Leapt from under the table. Scampered on two legs toward a cluster of women. Cups overturned. So did chairs. The women spread like billiard balls broken by a professional. But fear, confusion, and yelling did not deter Mickey once he spied a banana. He jumped on a table and grabbed it. Unpeeled the fruit. Dropped the peel. Ate the banana in only two bites.

Ken slid out from his hiding place, keeping his eyes on Mickey. He stood up, took a step, and collided with a gaggle of women. He pushed through them. But one yelled, "Stop him," just as Two neared the door. She held out a crutch. Ken ran into it and fell. His nose hit the floor. He yelled. Started scrambling up. But Two stuck the tip of a crutch between his shoulder blades and pushed down hard. Ken's nose hit the floor once more. He yelled again. Two said, "Move and I'll shoot ya dead." She shoved the tip of the crutch deeper into Ken's back.

Marty was in the gaggle of women and saw what Two was doing. She whipped the belt of her dressing gown out of its loops. Said, "Kid, get your hands behind your back."

Ken said, "She's gonna shoot me."

Two said, "I sure as hell will. Do as she says."

Marty tied Ken's hands tight with her belt. Two told him, "I am gonna take this gun off ya in a minute. But if ya turn around, I'm gonna shoot ya between the eyes. Can ya keep me from doing that?"

"Yes, ma'am. But I think my nose is broke."

"That's too damn bad. Marty, let's use that closet there." Two nodded toward one under the stairway. To Ken she said, "Now, remember, one look at me and I'll kill ya."

Marty opened the closet. It was lined with linen. Two said, "He'll need help getting up. I can't do it holding this gun."

Marty took Ken by the elbow. Said, "Kid, don't get us both shot. Keep your eyes on the closet.

Ken whimpered, "I'm bleeding."

Marty said, "Believe me, broken noses heal. Get in there. Don't turn around."

Two and another woman leaned against the door until Marty secured a key from a maid and told her to call the zoo. Then they joined the crowd watching Mickey eat all the visible fruit, slurp cereal from three different bowls, knock everything over he could, and then swing from the chandelier. After that, he urinated in random directions. That's when one of the women had the presence of mind to slam the dining room doors.

Mickey had certainly been heard, but not actually seen for a while when John Murkin arrived. He'd been apprised of the situation by the maid and came carrying a cage. He briefly listened to several women before he slipped through the dining room door. Mickey was glad to see him. Came running and leapt into his arms. John said, "What the hell ya been doing?" He surveyed the room. "Never mind. Ya've left yer evidence behind."

Back in the hallway, John held Mickey securely and listened to stories of what was damaged and in what order. He said, "My, my," several times, and finally, "How'd he get in here?"

Marty said, "We've got the other culprit locked in the linen closet."

John said, "Ya do?"

Marty said, "You want us to let him out?"

"Is he a monkey?"

"A human one." That was Two.

One of the women said, "Humans aren't monkeys," but neither John nor Two paid her any attention.

John said, "A man?"

"A boy," said Marty. "I think his nose is broke."

"Will he run if we let him out?"

"He might, but he needs tending to."

John was surrounded only by women. And his arms were filled with the lemur. He said, "We need to call security."

Two was seated on a sofa next to a phone. She picked up the receiver and said, "What do I dial?"

"Just O for operator. Tell her to get security over here fast. If one of you gals will pick up this cage," he nodded, "I'll take Mickey to the porch and put him in it. I wanta be here when security questions the boy."

Security was Leo Orr, a six-foot-three-inch amateur boxer who chewed bubble gum to keep from smoking at work. Leo didn't carry a gun because Mr. Warner thought it looked bad and because, at his size, he didn't need one. But he did carry a billy stick on his belt and brass knuckles in his right front pocket. When he entered Chambliss, the women who hadn't left for work were still there. Two was on the sofa drinking coffee. Marty was beside her doing the same. Franny had taken Helen's chair behind the desk at the door. The rest of the women, some of whom had run to their rooms to change clothes, were spread out on the steps to the second floor. John, who'd been given the key to the closet but still leaned against its door, gave Orr most of the story. He deferred to Two and Marty to describe the capture. Marty did most of the talking, but Orr asked Two, "Ya didn't actually have a gun, didja?" He'd parked his gum in his cheek.

Two did have a pistol in her trunk. She hesitated. "I used a crutch. He was too scared to tell the difference."

Marty added, "She talked like she had a gun. She's an Indian."

Orr's brow furrowed. "Great act. Sorry 'bout yer horse. That were a shame." Two looked into her coffee, and Orr turned toward the closet door. Loudly he said, "If yer ready to talk, I'll let ya out."

"I'll tell ya ever'thing ya wanta know" sounded muffled. John offered the key to Orr, but Orr said, "You do it." He pulled his stick from his belt and raised it.

John opened the door slowly. Ken was in front of the linen with his hands still tied behind his back and a track of blood running from his nose over his chin and down his neck. Bright splotches of red dotted his shirt. Leo said, "Git out here."

Ken emerged, and a maid said, "Ya better not have bled on the linen."

Leo said, "Ya wanta explain the monkey?"

"Can ya untie me?"

"I'll lock ya up if ya don't tell me the truth in a minute." Leo lifted his wrist, looked at his watch, and blew a bubble.

"A man made me do it. He gave me a buck. Said it'd be fun."

Leo grabbed his bubble with his tongue. He said, "What kinda man?"

Ken nodded toward John. "Waz wearing a uniform like his. I figured he worked here. Knew what he waz doing."

John's eyes widened. "He had on a Glendale uniform?"

"Yes, sir. Like yers."

"What'd he look like?"

"Almost tall as him." He jerked his head toward Orr. "Wore glasses. Can somebody please untie me? I ain't gonna run."

Leo did that and asked, "What color hair?"

"Red." Ken twisted his wrists.

John's eyebrows went up. Orr said, "What else?"

"His eye were twitchy. Like he had something in it he couldn't get out." John said, "I know him."

Two said, "I do, too." Her chest tightened.

The grown men turned toward Two, and Ken said, "Are ya who he's courting?"

"Whaddya mean by that?" John said.

"He said he wanted to play a joke on a girl he waz courting. I don't know nothing more about it. I just met the guy. I wish I never had."

John asked Two, "Are ya keeping time with Jack Older?"

Two sat up like in the saddle. "Not in a million years."

"But ya know him?"

"Yeah. He came with Crawford to get me out of the hospital. And we've visited a couple of times. But I told him to stay away from me."

Leo said, "And why would that be?"

Two looked at the floor. Light coming in the door and windows fell in rectangles. Nobody spoke. Finally, John, who knew Two somewhat and assumed Indians didn't always act like regular people, said, "It don't matter. He'll be history when I get to him."

Jack
Flees

$$\equiv$$

By the time Jack was history, he was too agitated to wait at the park's entrance for the trolley. He marched the tracks by the creek below the buffalo's hill to the golf club's station. He looked at his watch while he caught his breath. Either the trolley was late or he'd missed an earlier one. The clubhouse was directly across the tracks and not far away. Jack was fairly certain that they sold cigarettes in there and that members brought guests. If anybody asked, he could say he'd been invited and was waiting on his friend to arrive. He looked down at the *Glendale Zoo* embroidered on his shirt. John had told him to return the uniform in the mail. Hell would freeze over first, and he could make use of the clothing. Murkin, the S.O.B., was a member, but clearly not playing golf.

Jack left his lunchbox on the porch, went inside, and purchased a package of cigarettes in a room with a sign over the door saying THE NINETEENTH HOLE. He told the man at the counter he was looking for his boss, John Murkin, and asked if he'd seen him. The employee hadn't, but said he was welcome to wait. Jack set himself up in a rocker on the screened-in front porch of the Oriental Golf Club, ate boiled eggs he'd brought in his pail, smoked cigarettes, and fumed.

His eyelid furiously flickered. Murkin had fired him outright. Didn't even wait for Lovett to return. Said it was for the abuse of an animal and the destruction of property. But Mickey hadn't been abused. He'd had a grand time. Jack pressed fingertips to his eyelid. Murkin might have had a point about the destruction of property. But he didn't do it and he couldn't've stopped it. He was searching the sleeping rooms on the first floor, finding the one with the diving shoes. After that, he'd slipped out of Two's window onto the porch and melted into the woods. He had, just on impulse, taken her kerchief, a red paisley bandana. He plucked it out of his pocket and held it to his nose. He drew a deeper breath. It smelled like her. He stuffed it back in his pocket and shifted in his seat. He was getting a hard-on.

Little Elk had been following Strong-Red-Wolf since he'd seen him creeping around in the woods behind the big buildings. And he'd followed him to the alligator pit, and seen him recruit the boy. He'd tracked them and the little ringed-tail person on their trek back through the trees. He so hated big buildings that he hadn't gone in with the others. He'd waited on the cistern, wondering if Strong-Red-Wolf's eye would jump less if he smoked more. He retagged him Pale Jump, snorted in mockery, and wished his brothers were around to laugh at the name.

When Pale Jump came out of the building through a window and alone, Little Elk was startled. He trailed him through the woods until he stopped at the edge of a meadow, looked around, pulled a tobacco stick from his pocket, and struck a fire stick against bark. Little Elk crept stealthily until he reached Pale Jump's side. Every time the white man exhaled, Little Elk inhaled. He did that five or six times. The tobacco was delightful. It filled Little Elk with a feeling of power and gave him a sensation that he was about to appear. That he could be seen if Pale Jump would just look sideways. And Jack did jerk. Shook his shoulders and frowned. Then he dropped his cigarette to the ground and crushed it under his boot. He picked up the butt, deposited it in his pocket, and continued walking.

Little Elk wanted to scream. He jumped up and down. Turned a full circle. Pulled his war stick from his sash and threw it into a tree. Jack looked back. But Little Elk didn't see him. His eye was on his stick. It'd stuck in the trunk. That was an astonishing thing. He'd gained some power. From the tobacco. He had to get more.

He dislodged his stick and continued tracking. First to the alligator pit, then to the bears' den. But when Pale Jump entered a building with another man, Little Elk waited outside again. When Pale Jump came out nearly running, Little Elk saw distress written all over his face. Thought he would surely light up. But, no. He fled through the park's entrance, all the way down the hill, past the site of many old mounds, to the place the rattling buffalo stopped. Surely, he would smoke there. Just to appease the spirits he'd offended. Little Elk shivered. He hated walking through graves, even if they had been leveled to the ground. The other souls, the wind people, were still around. They'd never communicated, but it was clear to him that they were the ancient people of the mounds. He didn't want to disrespect their lives or their families. Again, he wished his brothers were with him.

When Pale Jump climbed a rise to another big building, Little Elk followed. He settled under a tree where he could monitor both the entrance and the rattling buffalo. The trolley came quickly, as intriguing as ever. And shortly thereafter, Pale Jump reappeared on a porch, sat down, and lit up. Little Elk rose carefully, moved to the edge of the veranda, and rested his arms on stones that extended beyond the screening. He drew in as much smoke as he could, and was feeling its power in his chest when Pale Jump took a kerchief from his pocket and sniffed it. Little Elk straightened up. Stiffened. Recognized the cloth. Thought, like a scalp, it was a token of victory. And an attempt to distress the Cherokee woman's soul.

Little Elk jutted his chin. Withdrew his war stick from his sash. He would kill Pale Jump, even if he had to go in the door. He crept up the steps and pushed on the frame of the screen. The wood moved a little. The wire shook. But the door didn't budge. He remembered then, some doors open by pulling. He gripped the handle. It didn't move like he wanted. There had to be a trick to it. He was still fiddling with the handle when the door swung open from the other side.

Little Elk stumbled back. Pale Jump hurried away from the building and scurried up the hill behind it. Little Elk followed, stopped, spread his legs for balance, raised his war club, and threw it. It went right through Jack's back. Jack stopped and turned. His eyes were so wide they seemed bigger than his glasses. He swung his lunch box like a weapon. Little Elk raised both fists in the air. Screamed like a wild turkey. Pale Jump looked to the sky. Looked to the right and to the left. Shook his shoulders and head. Clutched his box to his chest, spun away, and rushed on.

Rebalancing

When the excitement subsided, Two had gone to her room. She'd intended to fully dress, leave quickly, and find Crawford. She'd gotten fairly
far into that plan when she discovered that her bandana wasn't on her
bedpost. She searched her bag of dirty clothes. Came up with the blue
one she'd blown her nose on. She looked back at the bedpost to be certain
her eyes hadn't tricked her. The bandana still wasn't there. She swung
to the bed, tried to fish under it with a crutch. Couldn't reach far. She
backed up to where she could see underneath. On the floor were only
dust and a rubber band. Two's breathing stopped. Her fingers tingled.
She gripped her crutches tighter and breathed in deeply. She'd already
pulled on her camisole, so she balanced a shoulder against the wall and
stuck her hand inside it. She unpinned a little cloth purse that kept her
valuables close to her breast. She pulled out the key to her trunk.

Two dropped one crutch to get into position to unlock the trunk and
lift the top. She did that without losing balance, and then grabbed her
crutch from the floor and used it to wiggle her chair close to the trunk.
She sat down with a huff and started shuffling through her possessions.

Costumes, extra clothes, her sewing kit, a coat, purses, scarves, and pictures. They all were there, and so was her vodka, her pistol and ammunition, her throwing knife, and writing equipment. She leaned back and sighed. She trusted the other residents and the maids and never even pinned on her little cloth purse until she dressed. But her bandana hadn't been mislaid. And she was fairly certain who'd taken it.

Two sat as still as a bird watched by a cat. She pictured Jack. Then she picked up her gun, a four-barrel derringer she kept only for self-defense. She pressed a button under the receiver, and slid forward the barrels. The chambers were loaded as usual, but checking was her safety routine. She slid the barrels back into place, stood, and slipped the gun into her pocket. She was wearing a costume skirt she'd made herself with a smaller pocket, just for a gun, tucked inside a larger one. Two suddenly felt thankful for the cast that had forced her out of her jeans.

She found Crawford in the barn, on a bench, repairing a bridle. From the door, she could tell by the tension in his legs and the way he was twisting his tool that he was either having to force the leather or was angry about something. She called, "Whatcha' doin'?"

Crawford had been worrying on his life all morning. He was glad for a break. He said, "Look who's up and running."

Two took big swings across the barn floor as Crawford vacated his bench for her and took a stool for a seat. He said, "What's the news in your part of the world?"

Two started with the lemur, moved to tricking the boy into thinking she had a gun, and, finally, to his confession. Crawford said, "Jack Older. Well, well, well." He recalled Jack peering into the washtub under the diving tower. He was thinking about telling that when Two said, "He's got a dark side. I think he stole one of my bandanas."

Crawford nodded.

"I think the lemur was a decoy to distract attention while he searched my room."

Everybody who worked at the park was familiar with pickpockets' decoys. A lemur as a partner was a spin on the old organ grinder setup. Crawford hadn't figured Older as sharp enough for that. He grinned.

"It's not funny." Two tapped him with the tip of her crutch. Then she smiled, too. "I guess it is funny. Sorta. Ya should've seen the dining room. He not only wrecked it, he peed all over it.

"No shit!"

"No, there wasn't any of that." Two was still smiling. "But that's a miracle. And beside the point. Jack said some weird things to me."

"What kind of weird things?"

"Well, for one, he thinks he's an Indian."

Crawford again debated telling Two about finding Older under the diving platform. But that would touch on Ocher's death, and his heart, as well as Two's, still hurt over that. He said, "He's sweet on ya. And he's a sap."

"Maybe. But he sends me notes signed 'Strong-Red-Wolf.'"

The sun was passing to the side of the barn. The patch of light at the entrance was growing smaller by the minute. Crawford tried to imagine why any white man would think he wasn't white. Negros passed. A couple in his own family. But there was good reason for that. And Jack Older was clearly a white man, not even a dark one at that. He said, "That is strange."

Two felt relieved. "Back home, some city folks who come to the 101 and have never even been on a horse before take to the life, and don't want to leave. I've known a dozen who didn't go back to their families. They stay around the ranch, live in the bunkhouses. Or in the village for married families and guests. That happens. But none of them think they're Indians."

Crawford could feature the 101 being the same kind of haven for white people as California and the North were for his kin. He said, "Well, some people want to pass. But white people never want to be anything but white. They've got all the advantages."

"Some of those slickers ride the range with my father. A couple come around to the house to talk at night. They think their city lives were mistakes. Like they started out in the wrong life or wrong body."

"Lots of people want an escape. Freedom is a powerful thing."

"I know. I can't stand being cooped up. But Jack seemed like he was talking about something different. And he said something else. "Did ya know this park's built on a burial ground?"

Crawford put his palms to his thighs and stood. He stepped to a wall and hung the bridle he'd been fixing on a hook with some others. While he had his back to Two, he said, "Yeah, I've heard that."

"Jack said they were Indian graves. Over four thousand. What happened to 'em?"

The larger part of the Noel Cemetery had been dismantled and looted before Crawford was born. But, naturally, Negros did much of the hardest and dirtiest work. He'd heard stories of taking sledgehammers to skeletons. Of breaking them apart. Stacking rib cages together. Skulls together. Leg bones and arm bones piled head high. Hauled off in wagons to be crushed for fertilizer. But he also knew from his own experience that many of the graves scattered in groves and caves had been missed. And he flashed on the ones in the cave where Two and Ocher fell. He didn't know if she'd seen any of them. He pursed his lips and shivered.

Two saw Crawford's shirt move when his back twitched. Took it for words held in. But she was accustomed to waiting. Crawford lifted a bitless bridle off a hook. Then he lifted another. He said, "Well, that graveyard's a long story. And the Shacklefords are having a kid's birthday party this afternoon. I gotta take some Shetlands up there for the children to ride."

Two didn't move or speak. Crawford lifted another hackamore off a hook. He finally turned. Two was looking toward the open door. Her face was blank. Crawford was familiar with blank faces. They were for dealing with white people. He said, "Look, people do things they shouldn't. It's in the past. We can't do anything about the past. We have to live in the here and now."

Two had heard that all her life. That looking back was poison to Indians. And she wasn't surprised Crawford felt the same way. But she was trapped at Glendale until her leg healed, and there were things she wanted to know. Still looking out the door, she said, "Ya know, the Poncas believe some of their spirits come back to live other lives."

"That's not in the Bible."

"The Poncas don't read the Bible."

Crawford also looked out the open door. He knew people who believed in spirits. Mostly in evil ones. But old folks who'd been field slaves believed all sorts of crazy things.

Two turned and said, "Look, he thinks he's an Indian. Says he's thought it all his life. What if? Well, you know. What if he's a dead Indian come back to life?" She really wanted to say, *What if he's a witch?* But Two'd never heard talk about witches off the ranch or by anybody other than Indians. She'd read that white people thought witches were old women. She had no idea what Negros thought about them, and hesitated to broach the subject. She said instead, "I guess they really were Indian graves, right?"

Crawford huffed. "You think white people are gonna be destroying their own graves?"

"What tribe were they?"

"I don't know. Some forgotten race of folks. Not kin to you, not kin to me, not kin to white people."

"Did they just die out?"

Crawford shifted the bridles to his shoulder. "I don't rightly know. Daddy said they were long ago people. Said the mounds and graves were here when his grandpappy came from Virginia. That's all I can really say for sure. I don't want to mislead you, and I gotta get the Shetlands up to the Shacklefords.'"

Returning to her room, Two discovered her screen was unhooked. She recognized the window had been Jack's bolt hole and felt stupid for not noticing it earlier. She secured the latch and then again searched through her belongings. Nothing else seemed to be missing. And for several minutes after the effort, Two sat on the edge of her bed, holding her bottle of vodka in both hands, rubbing its glass with her thumbs. It was still half full, and her mouth felt its pull. It'd been a hard day. A sip would settle her nerves. She slid her tongue over her bottom lip. She untwisted the top. Bent her elbow and slowly lifted the bottle to her mouth. Then she stopped. She lowered her arm. It was midafternoon. If she got drunk, she'd get caught. And probably sent home. Besides, she couldn't let her guard down or get in a helpless position. Jack would be back.

Two set the bottle on her bedside table. Rose with one crutch, pulled the hook back out of its eye, and opened the screen. She picked up the vodka, bent out the window, and poured a little at a time, aiming to get it to dribble into a crack between planks. As the liquid flowed, she prayed for the strength of her elders to come and fill her up. She heard her grandparents' voices, her mother's, her father's. *Crazywater is the poison of the whites. They use it to take your land, your family, your life.*

After the bottle was empty, Two's eyes rose to the cistern, the hen house, the croquet and tennis courts, and Burgess Hall. She had much the same view from the back window of her upstairs room, except the cistern, hen house, and courts were closer from the first floor. She decided to go out and look for Jack's tracks.

She easily found the ones leading from the porch beneath her window. Then, near the tennis court, she found a smaller set running toward the hall. Those were the boy's, and he must've been carrying the lemur. She looked for Jack's tracks near the cistern. Didn't find any, but found some around the hen house, heading toward the hall. She envisioned the route Jack had taken into the building without having to walk it. She rested for a moment with a hand on a plank of the hennery, then swung around the side of the building to the padlocked door. She tugged on the lock and it didn't give, but the wooden latch of the chicken flap was twisted up and the little door slightly open. Squirrels, chipmunks, maybe foxes, probably went in for shelter and back out for adventures. Two peered through one of the dirty windows. The sun on the far wall lit up the nests and roosts. The musty residue of chicken shit clung to the building. The smell was so unexpected and familiar that it threw Two back to the 101. A lump arose in her throat. Homesickness followed. She slumped on her crutches and rested her forehead against the wood. She wanted her mother, her aunt, her brothers. Especially her brothers. They'd beat the tar out of Jack.

Then she heard: "We need a good smudging." Two jerked. Lifted a palm to the wood and said, "Grandma?" She held her breath, listening. Heard a noise behind her and turned. She saw buildings, the courts, the trees, and the cistern. A squirrel; no, two, three of those. She heard faint park music. But the voice had been near, real, and so clear she was certain whose it was. She looked again in the window. The interior was dim. The wood gray, stained by the years, and unpainted. Two touched the glass. Got grime on her fingers. Her grandmother wasn't in there. Was she in her own head? The voice hadn't sounded like that. It'd sounded all around. And Two felt a driving compulsion to do as she'd been directed.

She looked to the woods. She needed cedar, sourwood, sage, pine, sweetgrass, and tobacco. She was surrounded by maple, oak, and hickory. But down a slight hill was a willow and some sort of evergreen. Two swung off in that direction. It wasn't a short walk in a cast on crutches, but she had plenty of new energy. She found two old pine cones and a small, dead branch of cedar. She stuffed them in a pocket. Walking back, she broke off hickory bark already semi-dislodged from a tree. She put that in the pocket with her pistol. By then she was breathy from exertion, and she swung slowly back toward Chambliss, her arms a little wobbly. On the way, she figured on how to get some tobacco.

She paid Franny twenty cents for a pack of Chesterfields and asked her to buy her another when she next went to Nashville. Franny said, "A drink does taste better with a smoke. But don't set the building on fire." She was joking and serious both.

Two begged dried sage from Mrs. Watson, the cook, and took a salad plate from a counter. She retreated to her room winded, rested on her bed, and felt a little defeated over how weak she'd become. But she also felt her grandmother's urging. She soon sat up, hid her gun under her pillow, and stirred with her fingers three cigarettes of tobacco, cedar leaves, pine cone scales, chips of bark, and sage, all in the little plate. She pulled a match from a book with a rider and bronc on the cover and lit the concoction. When she was sure it'd stay lit, she stood and held the plate toward the window. Jack had been there last, and she could smudge it without walking. Afterwards, she smudged her little table and bed. She set the plate down. Carrying embers on crutches would be tricky. It'd be easier if she went counterclockwise, but that was in the wrong direction. Two bit her under-lip. Spirits could be kind and forgiving. The same couldn't be said of fire. She set the dish on the window ledge, readjusted her crutches, and slid it to the seat of a chair. She hopped, picked the plate up again, and waved it in the air. She set it down on the desk, and moved over there. She dipped into the smoke to smudge herself. Did that twice more. Then she repositioned, and moved the plate over to her dresser. She opened and smudged every drawer.

But she had to get to the other side of the room to smudge the clothes on the pegs, the closet, another chair, and the trunk. However, she'd gained some confidence with practice. She tilted back a little on her crutches, tilted forward, and hopped. The top of the trunk was curved, but the bedpost was flat on top. And it was where Jack had lifted her bandana. She set the plate down there, rested, and then opened her trunk. She waved the plate all around and over its contents. Then she tackled the chair, closet, and remaining clothes. When she was through, she eased into the chair, set the plate on the floor, and watched the smoke waft through the air.

Two fell asleep sitting up, and quickly into dreaming she was riding Ocher. They were traveling through a tall woods of cedar and pine. Their path was soft needles, faintly worn, but unfamiliar. The light was diffused except for full, well-defined shafts occasionally breaking through. A slash or an X marked a trunk here and there. As she rode farther, she became surer. She was riding well. Her own horse was alive and warm beneath her. Her destination, though unknown, was within her endurance.

Two awoke slowly, ruminated on her dream at length, and felt in harmony. The world was in balance. She was aligned with the spirits of earth, air, and water, with those of the animals, and trees, and humans around her. She looked down at the cast on her leg. Even it was as it should be. She'd been captured and imprisoned by plaster. But restraint had come to teach her a lesson. She felt pure and ready to learn. Two sat in her feelings, breathed them in, and breathed them out. Strengthened her will and her body.

Harmony
and
Disharmony

≈

On the second day of the hearing, the crowd again overflowed the courtroom into the hall and watched from the windows. There were only three speeches, the first two fiery, the last, Darrow's, a patient, logical appeal to reason, freedom of thought, and the progress of science, bolstered by references to Socrates and the Greek ideals embodied in the very building which provided them shelter. The audience found all three speakers so moving that spontaneous applause repeatedly plundered Chief Justice Green's attempted decorum. And afterwards, for a second time, Clive and Helen joined Maggie for tea at the Hermitage Hotel. The group at the table relived the best of the rhetoric, guffawed at the ignorance of the general population, and guessed what the ruling would be in the fall.

It was, to Helen and Clive both, a most successful excursion, and one they were still relishing when Maggie let them out of her car. But they grew silent as they walked through the park. Perhaps they were enjoying an intimacy prevented by the throngs of the day? Perhaps they were wondering how to conclude the outing? Perhaps considering what's next? The evening concert was playing. People were scattered on benches. Others skating in the rink. The moths were clustered around lights on tall poles, and the mosquitoes were shooed by a breeze. The temperature remained pleasant.

Then they came face-to-face with Christa Belle Henley walking in the opposite direction. She said, "Turns out 'while the cat's away' may be the truest words ever spoken." She looked directly at Helen and smiled.

Helen said, "I beg your pardon?"

"Y'all missed all the fun." Christa Belle looked at Clive. "Hi, Mr. Lovett."

Clive returned the greeting. He couldn't remember the young woman's name. But he'd seen her around and thought she was an entertainer.

Helen said, "What fun, Christa Belle?"

Christa Belle glanced up at the lights. "The lemur swinging from the chandelier and the capture of the boy. I think they've just about got the dining hall cleaned up. But I ate a hot dog for dinner. I don't really know."

Clive had stiffened at the word *lemur*. And he was growing red in the face. He said, "Our lemur? Mickey?"

"I guess. Are there other lemurs around?"

"My dining room?" Helen said.

Christa Belle nodded vigorously. Her eyes and smile widened.

Helen put her hand to her breasts. "Tell me everything you know."

Christa Belle shook her head. "I'd love to. But hear that?" She pointed toward the bandstand. "One more song, and I go on. I gotta run."

Clive and Helen both fairly sputtered. She said, "Oh my, my, this sounds bad," and he said, "Somebody's been up to no good." They headed straight toward Chambliss.

Two was still in a smooth mood when Clive and Helen arrived at the porch in a dither. They hurried inside to inspect the dining room, but quickly came out to get Two's account. She told them of Mickey's shenanigans, the boy, Jack and his motives, and the actions of Murkin and Orr. They moved to what Clive would do if Jack returned to the zoo, even to visit. They had quite a chew. And when Clive and Helen left, Two remained on the porch, excited by the talk, but still feeling in harmony. She watched moths circle a light and wondered if she was hearing cicadas.

Little Elk was hunkered next to the clematis, alert, safeguarding Two. He felt certain Pale Jump would be led back by the cloth he had stolen. Knew that's how the whites work. Take a little, then take a lot. He huffed in disgust, but giggled as he inhaled his next breath. The story of the ring-tailed person was comical. He appreciated the joke and wished he hadn't missed the fun and confusion. Maybe Pale Jump wasn't all bad?

No, no! He was! Little Elk frowned. He'd gotten distracted for a moment. Pale Jump was evil. Maybe even a witch. He needed to do something about him. What? Maybe kill him. Send him to his next world. Force him to wander in the Nightland or go back across the waters. Little Elk swatted at a moth. He didn't faze that little nuisance; he wouldn't be able to dispatch the big one. He needed more tobacco to get enough strength to break through and strangle Pale Jump. Or club him. Or scalp him first, then put a foot to his neck. He wasn't certain of the best method of dispatch. Probably clubbing or strangling. Scalping would release Pale Jump's first soul in a flash. They'd both be in the spirit world, face-to-face. That could lead to a fight. And Pale Jump, newly freed, would be stronger than he. But clubbing or strangling would keep his first soul trapped in his body for a time. He could lift Pale Jump's tobacco, smoke it, and be strong enough to win the fight when he took his scalp.

Turtles
and
Hippos

On Wednesday afternoon, Two set up on the porch to write to her mother. She didn't mention her fall, her cast, or Ocher's death. She wrote about the weather and the lemur in the dining room. No details about Jack. But lots about how she'd tripped the boy and tricked him into thinking she had a gun. Toward the end of the letter, she asked for news of her family, particularly about her grandmother, who'd spoken so clearly it was as if she'd left this world for the next. Two knew her folks would call her if there'd been a death. She wasn't really worried about that, and couldn't actually imagine her grandmother dying; she worked every day, had no aches or pains, and laughed with her head thrown back. But she didn't often give advice. And when she did, she delivered it in the form of a story or a memory. So the instruction at the hen house was unusual in more than one way, and Two still found it unsettling. She wondered if her grandmother was aware she'd come to her. Two'd never before given much thought to how spirits work.

She finished addressing the envelope as Duncan Shelton came up the walk. He was in uniform, his Glendale cap in his hand, and small beads of sweat on his bald head. He smiled before he got to the porch. Said, "Mighty fine day." He rubbed his palm over his pate and wiped the moisture off on his pants.

Two smiled back and commented on the weather. She assumed Mr. Shelton would pass her and go into the hall, but he stopped close to her chair. He said, "Them turtles have come."

"From the 101?"

"Yelp. Arrived last night, boxed up. About four hundred. 'Fore we let 'em lose, I was wondering if ya'd take a gander. Be sure we got the right sort. If they're the wrong ones and scatter, we'll have a heck of a time rounding 'em up."

Two squinted. The 101 didn't sell more than one kind of turtle. But she needed somewhere to go and something to do. "Just let me drop this in the basket." She held the envelope up.

The turtles were on the back of a truck, in open-sided crates, five wooden floors high. They were huddled together, and a few had died. Two couldn't stand to see them caged, and quickly confirmed they were the right kind. A couple of workmen started unloading the boxes, carrying each crate between them, and setting it down inside the new fencing around the grove. Two recalled there was a grave in there, but only one, not four thousand, and she was more worried about the turtles than it.

When all the crates were on the ground, one of the men crowbarred a side off of each one. Then he, his buddy, Duncan, and Two watched the animals figure out what to do. Turtles close to the openings and not burdened by others on their backs waddled out first. Others tumbled off each other. One fell on its back, and Duncan, who was inside the fencing, set it upright. He pulled a rag out of his back pocket and wiped his hand. "They need a bath. There's turtle do-do all over 'em."

Since Two had last seen the grove, wire had been nailed into its wooden fencing and washtubs laid in holes and filled with water and logs. Logs were also stacked in a formation that resembled a fort children might build. The trees and bushes of the grove weren't noticeably changed, but inside, according to Duncan, the mouth of the cave had been covered with wire secured by blocks. He hadn't mentioned the stone box.

Two poked the fencing with the tip of a crutch. "A turtle can get through this."

Duncan fingered his goiter. "Ya sure?"

"Yelp. They can see through it."

"How well do turtles see?"

"I don't know. A few feet, at least. And they can smell and dig. Turtles will dig under a fence like this. Burrowing's their nature."

Duncan had really recruited Two to get her approval of the pen. And he didn't doubt she knew what she was talking about. He wasn't surprised they'd gotten it wrong, but he wasn't happy. They'd need to do something quickly. But Buddy Parrish was busy building a new enclosure for DuPont over the collapsed diving pool and still had to take down the tower and remove some of the bleachers. He said, "What's the best way to keep 'em in?"

"Here, I don't know, exactly. We use a natural break in the earth. Lower ground under a cliff. Sort of a bowl. They've got water, sun, and shade. Rocks that are too high to climb." Two bit her lower lip. Occasionally, a weak animal, a calf or a deer, wandered into the rocks below the cliff and couldn't escape. They died and became food for the turtles there. Two shook that picture from her head. The land in the park was nothing like the land in the West. As soon as the turtles came to their senses, they'd escape. A smile crept onto Two's face.

Duncan said, "What's funny?"

"Just thinking about turtles all over the place."

"Should we crate 'em back up until we figure it out?"

"Ya could dig a shallow trench. Lay concrete blocks along the edge outside the fence." She pointed with her crutch again. "That should work."

Duncan was relieved to hear that. And Buddy should be able spare a man or two to get it done. Maybe even to paint them green. He said, "That's the plan, then. Ya want a lift back to yer dorm?"

"That'll probably be out of your way. Where're ya going?"

"To see Buddy Parrish."

Two knew Mr. Parrish had been overseeing the filling in of her pool and demolition of her tower. She didn't want to get anywhere near there. But she didn't want to go back to Chambliss. She said, "Can ya take me up the hill? Drop me off at the hippo's pen?"

When the truck stopped at the hippo compound, John Murkin and a junior keeper, Randy Hoffer, were up on the platform. Dinah was in the water, her head and back out, her eyes closed. Methuselah was in the filter's shade, east of where the men were pitching cabbages to the ground. Two opened the door, gripped the roof of the cab, and balanced her right foot on the running board. Duncan came around the front of the truck saying, "Whoa, let me help ya."

John disappeared from the platform, and was with Two by the time she reached the dirt bank around the pen. He said, "I took care of that dang idiot. Told him not to step foot in the park again."

John's cap was in his hand, his face tanned and creased from the sun. His forehead was light, his hair still brown, receding, and a little wet with sweat. Two figured he was the right age to have daughters at home. She said, "Thank ya."

John had mulled Jack's actions. Older had seemed a good hire. More educated than most Glendale employees. Polite, almost refined. Claimed his father was a doctor. But a bad apple if there ever was one. John didn't understand that. Said, "He just better not try to come back."

Two was worried about that. He had her bandana. She tugged on the one she was wearing. "He took a piece of clothing from my room."

John shook his head and started turning red. "That ain't right. You call me or Orr if ya even see him from a distance."

"I'll keep an eye out for him and sure do that. But let's hope for the best. How's Dinah?"

Firing someone always upset John, and firing Older had done so particularly. But he'd probably stole the girl's panties. If he did that to one of his daughters, he'd break his neck. Not being able to say that, John grunted. Said, "She'll be better soon. Got worms. They hatch in the water, and she drinks it before it goes through the filter. We're having to drain every day, scrub the concrete with vinegar, and fill up with new water. It takes time and money, but it's better than losing a hippo."

"Has Methuselah got 'em, too?" He was munching grass.

"I didn't check his . . ." John hesitated before ending with, "You know." He added, "If he does, fresh water'll work for him, too."

A hose was in the water, but the pond wasn't completely full. Two asked, "Where's the drained water going?"

"Out the filter's pipe and into the field on the far side of the platform. Ya can't see the flags from here, but we've roped the field off. It's soggy."

Two doubted a rope and flags would keep children, or even adults, out of anywhere, but sogginess would. She felt relieved they'd found a solution, but wished Dinah had more water to rest in, and felt she shouldn't be at Glendale to have that problem in the first place. She knew the behemoth had been born in Memphis, not captured in the wild. But Two didn't think Dinah belonged in Memphis, either. She wasn't just caged; she was completely disconnected and out of place.

Dinah's eyes opened slowly, and Two suddenly felt a deeper connection to her. They both were away from their families, their tribes, and their land. For lack of friends, they were filling in with a tortoise, a buffalo, and a few bears. Two was accustomed to animal friends, but they didn't make up for the loss of a whole herd, family, or tribe. Dinah's eyes seemed sad. Two felt the animal's loneliness, and her heart fell to the ground. She knew large, foreign beasts were in zoos in part because they were being hunted to extinction in Africa. Her own tribe had been hunted, too, and would vanish with the passing of her generation. Their government was already abolished; they didn't even have a chief. And her children wouldn't be Cherokees; born after the allotment rolls were closed, they'd be white people by law. Like her profession, her tribe, her people, her history, were fading and narrowing to nothing. Tears formed in Two's gray eyes.

And through their watery distortion, a vision came: Dinah dead, lying on her side. Her mouth slack, her long teeth exposed, her tongue hanging out. An owl flying over her body. Two blinked. Wiped her tears with her hand. The vision went. But Two was as certain of what she'd seen as she was of the platform, the concrete sides of the pool, and the cabbages on the ground. She tightened her grip on her crutches. "What if draining the water doesn't work?"

John pulled an earlobe. "I'm not worried 'bout that. We just gotta break the worms' cycle. It's pretty dang hard to kill a hippo."

Two
Goes
Visiting

≈

The next morning, Two was sitting on the porch, still and alert like her elders, when over the lawn Crawford appeared in a cart, driving a Shetland pony. Two jumped up fast and knocked her crutches off the table they were resting against. They fell to the planks with a clatter, and she balanced against the rail and clapped her hands. Crawford grinned ear to ear. He pulled up to the trellis and said, "Wanta take her for a ride?"

Two grabbed her crutches and descended the steps so fast she nearly fell. By then, Crawford was on the far side of the pony, adjusting its harness. Two threw her crutches down and pulled herself into the seat. She said, "I thought ya'd forgot."

"Nope. Couldn't find the Flying Jenny's bench. Then Bonita told me it was a stupid idea."

"She said that?"

"Sorta."

"Where'd ya get this?"

"Remember I took Shetlands up to Longview for the birthday party?

When I got back, a friend of mine who used to work here was at the barn wanting to jack jaw about the good old days. He asked why I hadn't taken the cart for the kids. I didn't know anything about a cart. He said there used to be one here. Used it for years. I figured if it was still in existence, it'd be in Shackleford's old carriage house. Next day, I called Adelaide. She knows when everybody blows their noses up there. She asked Miz May if you could use it. And here we are. I had to spend an afternoon cleaning her up, softening the leather."

"Crawford, you're the best friend a gal could ever have. I'll never be able to repay ya."

"Take her for a ride."

"What's her name?"

"Gay."

"She seems even-tempered."

"She's put up with a whole lotta children."

"Come with me."

"Can't do that. White folks'll have a go-to-pieces."

"It's none of their damn business."

"They'll make it their business. Then we'll be in heap big trouble, as your people say. Hold on, let me get your crutches. You just can't leave them on the ground. Another cripple'll come around and steal 'em."

The bears were closer to Chambliss than the buffalo. And Two had missed Tom Noddy, and wanted to see him, in particular. She'd had many discussions with Tom about them being kin, teased him about streaking his cheeks with war paint, told him stories about the great white bear chief, and about people living with bears and growing hair. But a crowd was around the bears' fence; she couldn't get close to Tom, and lost hope for a confidential conversation. She turned the cart, and drove on a wide gravel path skirting the bird cages, but still through the zoo's heart toward the hippo pen. There was no shade there, and not many people. She drove up to the dirt bank, as close to Dinah as she could get, and looked her in the right eye. The hippo was wide awake and pink on the neck and ear. She opened her mouth wide and showed her teeth. Two took that as a yawn and said, "You wanta nap, Dinah?"

Dinah blinked.

Two looked over her right shoulder. No one was close or coming her way. She turned back. "I hope you're better. I'm Two Feathers, your friend. People come look at me, too. Say strange things. We need to stick together."

Dinah blinked again.

Two continued. "I wish ya had a hippo friend. But ya've got Methuselah and me. He's a pretty good turtle. Old. But old is better. We wanta be alert and live long lives. Get to be elders. You keep . . ." Two stopped there. Dinah was turning. Two'd seen the unfortunate way hippos eliminate and was very close to the edge of the bank. She jerked the reins. Said, "I'll see ya later." To Gay, she said, "Let's visit Adam."

The big old buffalo was standing under a tree, chewing his cud, and flicking flies with his tail. Two called, "Haba, haba." Adam lifted his head. Then he leisurely left the shade and came right up to the fence beside Two. He saw her as clearly with his left eye as she saw him with both of hers. She said, "I've missed ya, partner. I'm sorry I've been away. I broke a leg." She tapped her cast.

Adam shimmied a horsefly off his back, but Two felt certain he was listening. "Ocher and I fell from the sky into the underworld." Two looked into the clouds. "She saved my life. I'll never forget her. I can't replace her ever." She looked back at Adam. Wondered if he missed Buffalo Bill. If he even knew Mr. Cody was dead. At least she knew Ocher was; she couldn't make a mistake about that. She looked around again, and then the tears came. Her chest suddenly heaved. She put a hand on her ribs to settle them down. Then she untied her bandana, wiped her eyes, and blew her nose. When she got that done and felt her voice would come out steady, she said, "Ocher's running with the horses in the upper world. I'll see her again, somewhere. A white man rescued me. They took me to an infirmary and wrapped my leg.

"But that's not what ya need to know. The thing is, Adam, there's another white man around here. He visits this pasture. He knows a lot about buffalo, and ya need to watch out for him. He could be a witch. He carried this destructive . . ." She searched for an explanation Adam would understand and continued with, "Little human being into a building. While the little human was tearing things up, the white man stole my bandana." She held her dirty one up to Adam. "I don't know what to do about him. But I think he'll be back. Maybe around here. Keep an eye out. We gotta fight him together. I need your strength."

Adam snorted. He shook his shaggy head. He liked this human. Her smell recalled others from the past. His muscles were slack, his heart lonely, and his power gone, but he was still a buffalo. He dreamed of his family grazing on a hillside under a wide sky. He took a bite of grass.

Two felt an urge to get out of the cart and touch Adam's tangles of hair. But she was unsure of her pony. She hadn't driven her enough to know if she'd take off on her own. She said, "I'll be back tomorrow, Adam. I love ya."

When Two drove into the horse barn, Crawford was reading a manual. He got up from his bench and said, "Let me help you." He took her crutches first, then gripped Two at the waist and settled her on the ground gently. He started unbuckling the harness from a shaft.

"If I get out of the cart in the park, will Gay move?"

"I doubt it. She's been here longer than me. And is used to children." Crawford moved to the other shaft. Started unbuckling its harness.

Two sat down on the bench. "Whatcha been reading?"

"A manual on car repair. I've got less to do now that . . ." Crawford put a knee to the ground.

Two looked toward the barn door. The sun was on the west side of the building. The light sliced at the entrance, but lit the higher limbs of the trees. Crawford was sweet not to finish his sentence. She said, "Thank Bonita for me. Bumping around on a merry-go-round bench would've busted my butt."

Crawford moved Gay away from the cart. Kept unbuckling her harness. Two kept looking out the door. A breeze had suddenly come up and the light had dimmed. Wind began whistling through the boards. Crawford kept unbuckling. Soon he lifted the harness off Gay and laid it on the floor of the cart. He gripped Gay's mane and led her into a stall. Said, "I'll bring ya some oats."

After he fetched the oats, Crawford grabbed the cart by the shafts, backed it out of the barn, turned it around, and pushed it back in. He picked a stool off a wall, turned it over, and sat about four feet from Two's cast. He said, "You're a woman."

Two chuckled.

"You think I've made enough of myself?"

Two had no idea where Crawford was going. But she habitually followed the water to its source. "Depends on where ya wanta go."

Crawford looked down at his hands. They were large, calloused, and strong-nailed. "I'm thinking about getting hitched."

"To Bonita?"

He nodded.

"Does she think you've made enough of yourself?"

"I don't know. Her father doesn't think so."

Two looked out the barn door. Wind was whipping branches. They'd be trapped in by rain. That was a good thing. Better than being trapped in Chambliss. "Why don't ya ask her?"

"I'm not supposed to see her."

Crawford told Two most of the story. By the time he finished, rain was beating on the tin roof and branches were dancing beyond the doorway. The two of them were speaking louder over the din. Two said, "Does it really matter if you're a Methodist or a Baptist? Is there a difference?"

Crawford's eyes widened. "Oh, yeah. A big one. For instance, for baptizing, the Methodists sprinkle and the Baptists dunk."

Two looked up to the trusses. She was sure that meant something to somebody. And she had, from a distance, seen people baptized in the Salt Fork River. They'd worn white gowns, and she'd heard the singing from the crest of a hill. She looked at Crawford again. "What else?"

"Well, the Baptists believe when you're saved, it's once and for all. But we believe you can fall from grace."

Two looked up again. She focused her eyes on a sparrow's nest wedged between a beam and a joist. There were babies in it. She thought about falling.

"And Baptists won't let you take communion unless you've been baptized. That's dunked, not sprinkled."

Two looked back down again. "You've gone through this sprinkling thing?"

"When I was a baby."

"Okay. Can't ya just get dunked?"

"I could. But I've already been baptized. Once you're baptized, you're in."

"In what?"

"In the . . . Well, I'm not sure. In the Methodist church."

"But she wants ya in the Baptist church."

"I don't know what she wants. Her daddy wants me in the Baptist church."

Two looked at the barn floor. Her bare heel had made cup-shaped dents in the dust. Christianity had never made any sense to her. And didn't seem worth the effort people put into it. However, she did understand the problems of marrying out of your tribe. She could marry a Creek if she wanted. A white, a Chickasaw, a Seminole, or a Choctaw. But there'd be considerable grunting and grumbling about marrying a Wild Indian. And the Osage were completely below the horizon, no matter how much money they had. Two wasn't one to displease her family, and didn't approve of bucking elders in general. But matters of the heart were a little different. To be happy, people should make their own choices. She said, "I'd ask Bonita how she feels about the situation."

"Can't." Crawford shook his head. "I haven't proclaimed my intentions."

Proclaiming intentions was so old-fashioned that Two nearly laughed. People didn't talk that way on the ranch, and certainly not in Chambliss. She raised her eyebrows and smiled. "What d'ya think her intentions are?"

"She likes me." Crawford paused and added, "I'm pretty sure." He hadn't mentioned the particulars of the alley situation, and hoped Two wouldn't ask how he came to his conclusion. However, that's what she did next.

Crawford looked out the door. The storm had settled into a rain. He looked at the dust. "She's pretty buttoned up. But I've made some headway."

Two blushed. Her mind flew to the botanist. An ache caused her legs to spasm. She lifted the encased one with both hands and set it closer to the other one. She took a deep breath. "I see. Well, she's either loose, or likes ya a lot. Which is it?"

Crawford shook his head fairly fast. "Oh, she's a lady."

Two grinned. Like all Cherokees, she took a deep interest in romance. And she thought Crawford and Bonita probably would make a good pair. "Then I wouldn't worry too much 'bout the tribe thing. Unless they've got some sort of rules 'bout not letting Methodists in. The Poncas took Joe Miller into their tribe. They call him Waka-huda nuga-ski, 'Big White Chief.'" He dresses up like them. War paint and all. Sometimes people can belong to two different tribes, and have more than one spirit."

That reassured Crawford some. But he wasn't sure H.A. was wrong about him not making enough of his life. He'd had every advantage imaginable for a man of his race. Yet his reading was mechanics manuals, his time spent mostly with animals. He hadn't had enough to do since the cave-in, and he felt restless. Still, the idea of being cooped up inside a building, running presses, or overseeing the printing of Sunday school materials seemed like a slow, sure death. He said, "Maybe I should ask for more responsibility around here."

Two recognized Crawford had jumped back to earlier in the conversation. "What can ya do that ya aren't doing already?"

"That's a problem for sure. I do the horse work, and as much of the mechanical work as we have the tools for. But I can't supervise white men, and I'm not picking up a shovel for anybody except my mother."

Two didn't have an answer. She didn't have an answer for her future either. She said, "My generation, we go out and grab things. But my elders sit and watch, see what comes along."

Crawford picked up a chip of wood and threw it.

Two ran a finger over the lip of her cast. "This leg has given me time to just be. To go back to tradition. If ya sit real still, the world will come to ya. A path will open up."

Crawford threw another chip. Shook his head. Said, "No disrespect, but how's that worked out for your folks? Haven't most of them been slaughtered?"

Two reached for a crutch. Poked him with the tip. "We'll come back. We're just waiting. You can't see us, but we're everywhere." Then blood came up into Two's face. She didn't know why she said that. It wasn't the way she usually talked, or thought. Maybe it came from sitting, watching, and waiting. She wasn't going to pull it back. She used one of her father's sayings: "Mark my words."

Broken
Barriers

$\equiv$

Little Elk, perched on a beam in the barn, had listened to Crawford describing his problems with romance. He liked the black man; assumed he was a slave, but saw him as an ally, and powerful enough to get his woman. But when the talk turned to religion and work, Little Elk's mind wandered. He eyed the sparrow's nest, wondered how many fledglings it held, and mulled his own problems with women. He didn't have any get up and go under his cloth and hoped he wouldn't be floppy forever. He was determined to get back to earth-life somehow, and wanted more sexual success when he did.

Little Elk dipped into self-pity. He would've taken scalps, achieved his status, and won a wife or two, if the dogs hadn't gotten him. His hatred for canines was one of the strongest emotions he felt. When he saw a dog in the park, he yelled so sharply that most of them could hear him, and they became sniffy, jumpy, and yappy. They got scolded by their people, and got their ropes jerked. That pleased Little Elk. When he succeeded, his smile grew wide, he held his sides, and he laughed.

He was daydreaming about getting dogs in trouble when Two left the barn. He joined her, a few lengths behind on the path. The rain had stopped, though that didn't bother him one way or the other. Neither did heat or cold. He was so well hardened, weather hadn't troubled him even when he was alive. He just wished he could break through to someone other than dogs. Make himself felt and known. Feel less lonely.

He'd enjoyed the company of other men who'd come to the porch and smoked after Pale Jump had run up the hill. He'd inhaled when they'd exhaled, and gained enough strength to steal their tobacco stick stubs. He'd separated the burnt and unburnt weed, and had smoked the unburnt in the pipe he kept in his leather pouch. That was the first time he'd smoked much since the grave robbers had been around, and the tobacco gave him hope and strength enough to scour for more. It was easiest to find over at the porch with the netting. But he couldn't guard the woman over there, so he found himself running from the park to the porch two or three times a day. That was fine with him. When he'd been more substantial, running had been one of his favorite activities.

Little Elk had smoked before he'd gotten to the barn, and was, for a change, not feeling as light as a feather. Could he make the woman see him? She was off the pebbled paths, swinging through grass, headed like an arrow toward her sleeping building. Could he get her attention before she got there? He pictured the big tree with two trunks, damaged in its top by lightning. It was on her course and had strong magic. It was frightening, but he'd been near it again and again, and nothing bad had happened to him. He thought being a spirit must give him protection.

The catalpa's head had been sawed in a smooth plane above the large limb that ran twisted and horizontal for several feet and then branched down and grew into the ground. The original trunk was so hollow its hole was large enough for children to step inside and hide. In the years before the lightning strike, Little Elk had occasionally rested in that space. But after the strike and the top had been sawed off, the tree was more frightening than attractive. Besides, it was farther from the rattling buffalo than his oak, so not as entertaining. However, it stood straight in the woman's path. Little Elk ran to it and settled on the horizontal limb with his legs dangling.

By the time Two approached, Little Elk had a plan. He howled like a wolf, an animal he didn't like, but one that sure raised a ruckus. And Two stopped. Looked around and behind her. Little Elk howled again. Two looked up at the wide bridge made by the branch.

There was no wolf up there. But she'd heard the call. And she recognized it'd come like her grandmother's voice. That made sense in some way, as lightning-struck trees had more power than others. She swung over to the hole in the trunk. Peered in there. Poked the space with a crutch. Found nothing. She lifted a hand, almost placed it on the bark. But she hesitated, a little afraid to touch. So she just listened with all her might. She heard the call again. Her heart leapt into her throat. She took a deep breath. Her strength grew. She placed a palm on the trunk. Asked the tree for its power.

Two was a member of the Wolf Clan. The clans had been abolished a hundred years in the past, but the knowledge hadn't been completely forgotten. Her maternal grandmother considered membership information as essential as knowing who your third cousins are. And Two believed wolves (considered nuisances by the Millers) were really protectors. Especially for the women in her family. So she took in the wolf howl with more meaning than Little Elk intended.

However, when he saw the effect his howling was having, he howled even louder. He was delighted to have broken through. Communicated. Touched a living human being. A Cherokee. He stood up on the limb to take more power into his lungs, to expel more sound. And when he did, he lost his balance. He swayed, flapped his arms, toppled off backwards, and hit the ground. That stunned him. But hurt only his pride, as he was already dead and too insubstantial for pain. He jumped up and checked his pouch to be sure his pipe hadn't broken. It hadn't. And he was so close to Two that, with a few steps, he could reach out and touch her. He even felt a little stir beneath his loincloth. That thrilled him. But he was afraid he'd frighten the woman, and he didn't want to do that. So he just looked closely and deeply at Two. And, of course, Two was extremely attractive. And Little Elk had been deprived for a century and a half. So love struck him like lightning.

Two was struck, also. But not by love. She couldn't even see Little Elk. But in the last three days, her maternal grandmother had spoken to her, she'd had a clear vision of Dinah's death, and now the lightning-hit tree and the wolf spirit were sending her strength. She realized something unusual and important was happening. It gave her hope and also aroused powerful emotions. Two started crying again. Got a little wobbly. She had to keep both hands tight on her grips, so she couldn't blow her nose. Her face melted into a ruddy mess as she hopped off toward Chambliss, short of breath. She stopped at the dormitory steps and leaned on the newel post while she pulled off her bandana, wiped her tears, and blew her nose.

Helen Hampton saw that and assumed Two was in physical pain. She rushed down the steps. "What can I do to help?"

"I'm okay. Thank ya."

"You must be worn out. Does your leg hurt?"

"Yes. It's killing me."

"Let me help you. We'll get you settled on the porch. I'll bring you dinner. We're having succotash and fried fish. How does that sound?"

"Really good. Thank ya."

Helen had never touched an Indian before, but she put an arm around Two's shoulders. She felt tender toward the girl. Maternal. Almost loving. She was surprised by that, but found it both odd and natural.

A
New
Routine

$$\equiv$$

The next few days began the height of the Glendale season. Weekday crowds blew up like balloons, children multiplied like mosquitos, and vacationers drove new automobiles into Nashville and arrived on the trolley like an invasion of locusts. If Ocher had been alive, Two would've been diving three times a day, and the other entertainers were hoofing hard, singing continually, and, in the case of the Montgomerys, throwing even more dishes, bowling pins, and hoops. In spite of the increased activity, Clive and Helen were able to spend most evenings together on one or the other of their porches. Chambliss's residents and other park employees became aware of their romance, gossiped about it, and watched with titillation and approval. Mrs. Hampton seemed easier, livelier, and younger. Mr. Lovett had extra pep in his step. When together, they attracted people wherever they sat. They were in danger only of being worn down by conversation, congeniality, and company.

When alone, Clive told Helen more about himself than he'd told anyone since the trenches. He didn't, however, tell her about singing with Millwood in the cave, or that he was seeing apparitions. Occasionally, the faint ones sitting near springs in the park, seemingly just watching the visitors. More often, a distinct Indian near Two, both when she sat with them on the porch and while she was riding in the cart in the park. He found that Indian fascinating, but no longer unusual. However, he was quite certain that Helen couldn't see him. He remembered that she'd called the Indians who'd attacked the stations murderous, depraved savages. She'd find a nearly naked brave with a topknot, tattooed skin, and a painted face quite alarming.

Clive was the opposite of alarmed. Since Millwood's visit, he'd felt contentment like never before. Not in childhood while his parents were alive, not in his first work with birds in Colorado, not as he built the zoo from an aviary to a multitude of exotic animals. His happy peace helped him open his heart to Helen, like he'd opened it before only to animals. However, he still felt protective of the wounds on his body. He knew they were red, ragged, and ugly. Surely off-putting to women; now, specifically, to Helen. So he remained private in that respect. But his loneliness had abated. And he hadn't a single urge to partake of a drink any stronger than a good cup of tea. Which he was teaching Helen to make properly.

As for Crawford, he brought Gay and the cart around to Two the first thing in the mornings. They met behind the dormitory, at the cistern near the hen house and talked with Gay between them, like they had with Ocher. Crawford was still wrestling with what to do about his work, but he didn't share that with Two because he didn't want her to think he was about to bolt for another job, or leave her while she was bunged up. But he did rely on her advice for dealing with Bonita. He declared his intentions to H.A. and then, after another lecture and some rule setting, declared them to Bonita. She declared hers. They started talking hopes and dreams. Unfortunately, their talk was still usually whispered in the Boydstuns' parlor. But twice they'd met on the Fisk campus, once for an art show and once for a concert. They were making progress, and so far H.A. had been stern, but polite.

Two drove her cart around to the animals and communed with them daily. She always visited Tom Noddy first before the crowds came. Tom had been brought to the zoo as an infant, while he was still bottle-fed, and Two and he had bonded the previous year with her using peanuts as glue. The little, roly-poly red bear loved the nuts, and Two had imagined he also particularly appreciated her scent. It was sweet, different from the perfumed odor of whites.

Two was familiar with Cherokee lore that bears were a lost clan of the tribe, driven into the forest by famine. They were cousins and kin, who hid wounded warriors retreating from battles. They were especially revered for their generosity, and never killed unless absolutely necessary. Two knew the Glendale bears were purchased from breeding programs, and brought to the zoo by train from faraway cities. But she liked to think of them as her extended family, and she often imagined the mountains their mutual ancestors had roamed as smoky, silent, and green; really, home. She felt the bears had walked a Trail of their own. Felt, also, they'd like to walk it again, right back to the mountains they ought to be living in.

Though they were old friends, the first morning Two arrived at the bears' den in her cart, Tom Noddy wouldn't come near her. She'd discovered early that spring that he enjoyed biscuits as well as peanuts, and loved cinnamon buns more than anything. The biscuits were served every breakfast, the buns only twice a week. That morning, she had a biscuit and held it up high for him to see. But Tom tilted his head, looked puzzled, and then went over to the pen's bathtub and stuck a paw in. Two decided he was afraid of the cast. She returned to the cart, reached to the floor, and grabbed a bag of peanuts she'd bought for the monkeys. She pitched a peanut toward Tom. That caught his attention and distracted him from the tub. He snatched it up and ate it. She pitched the next one closer to her. By the fifth one, Tom had overcome his fear, and she fed him as usual. There weren't yet many people around, so Two told Tom her leg was broken in a fall and she'd have to wear the white pipe for a few weeks. She didn't tell him about Ocher's death, as she didn't want to distress him.

Two generally stayed with Tom, sharing ancient or newly made-up bear stories, until the crowds started arriving. Then she'd climb back in her cart and head for the hippo enclosure. She wanted daily reassurance that Dinah was still living. Often she found her reddish, awake, and out of her pool; once, nudging Methuselah with her nose. The change of water seemed to be working, and Two began to think her vision was wrong. Still, her predicament and Dinah's were similar. And she couldn't imagine a remedy for that. She began trying to make real friends with the hippo. Asking Dinah to tell her what she wanted, figured it wasn't chewing gum, buns, or peanuts.

Unfortunately, Dinah couldn't tell Two what she wanted. She wasn't dumb, just mostly instinctual. That instinct should've been honed by her mother and her herd. But Dinah hadn't seen her mother in an eon, and her herd in Memphis had been divided. She'd seen and smelled a few other hippos, but had never had the comfort of contact or the instruction of the group moving together or lolling in a river. Dinah didn't know what she'd missed. She felt dull most of the time and, lately, hadn't even roused when balls of food were thrown near her. She'd taken to staying in the water at night, which was not, even with her dim awareness, right. So her days and nights were getting confused, and she felt out of sorts. She was on land in the sunshine, and doing the only thing she found comforting, standing close to the other living creature in her enclosure.

But Two figured it was just a matter of time, and of finding the right channel, before she and the mammal connected. And once, upon Two's approach, Dinah did lift her head, pound the ground walking over, and stop close to the block-and-dirt wall next to the cart. Two thought maybe Dinah was beginning to recognize her. She spoke to her like she spoke to horses, bears, and buffalo. She wondered what the giant animal knew and didn't know. Wondered if she could see in color. If she wanted out. Or was afraid of freedom. She imagined what a hippo on the loose would do. Probably a great deal of damage.

Two also visited Mickey and the monkeys. Looking back, she thoroughly enjoyed Mickey's destruction of the dining hall, and the monkeys reminded her of home. The Millers owned a show ape, Bozo, who Mr. Lovett had seen at the Scopes trial the previous year. One evening on the porch, he described Bozo shaking hands with William Jennings Bryan. Two'd been in Oklahoma nursing her broken ribs by then, but knew Zack Miller had taken the gorilla to Tennessee to get a prank picture. When Bryan died a week after the trial, the Millers sent out a press release expressing deep regret for Zack's joke and promising not to use the picture for promotion. Two told the group Mr. Miller had sincerely felt awful, and also shared with them a few of his other pranks. As Two rarely spoke about her famous employers, she held her audience as well as when she was performing. And talking about home made her feel like the ranch wasn't on a distant planet, but near enough to Glendale that Mr. Lovett, Miz Hampton, Marty, Franny, and Sandra, the party planner, knew something about its wonders.

The days were growing hotter. But the heat and sun reminded Two of home, and hot in Nashville wasn't really hot in Oklahoma. Nevertheless, while visiting the buffalo, she parked under a tree to keep Gay cooler, and eased out of the cart to sit on a shady bench close to the buffalo's fence. On most days, Adam came over. Occasionally, two or three of his friends came with him. They stood by the railing, swatted flies with their tails, and snorted.

Two'd never been inactive in her life. Forced into it, she recognized that the world inside her and the world unseen were every bit as engaging as the world she'd always inhabited. She practiced the stillness of her grandmothers, her grandfathers, her parents, uncles, and aunts. They all were gregarious people; socializing while they were busy with animals, sewing, shelling, or repairing. But when alone, and seen from a distance, they were often immobile. Two'd grown up wondering what they were doing. Now she knew. They were listening and being. Seeing the unseen and the fleeting.

Practicing that, Two felt greater harmony with animals. Could sense the spirits of the springs that bubbled up from the earth. Sense the trees moving together as a herd. She also began drawing more strength from her elders. And from those who'd come even before them. Those who had survived the Trail, and those who had died on it. And one day, it came to her that if there'd been a gigantic cemetery of unknown Indians on this very land, there'd also been an entire city. No sane Indians buried their loved ones far from where they were living. Death didn't break ties of kinship and affection. There was no far-off heaven, no void, certainly no hell. The dead were immediate, close to the living.

These meditations drew Two away from her worries about her future and more fully into the present. She recalled her grandmother's *we need a good smudging*. Began also to ponder the problem of witches. That problem was not new to Two. Everybody on the 101, even the white people, felt sure the ranch was haunted. Some said the ghosts were spirits of cowboys the Millers had killed for revenge or convenience. Others thought they were spirits of Indians murdered for allotments. There were all sorts of theories, but the general agreement among the tribes was that many of the ghosts, but not all, were witches. And Two had begun feeling a presence near her. Had sensed it for several days. Sometimes she thought it was helpful; sometimes she thought it might be a witch.

One day at the buffalo pen, when she was wondering if she should smudge again, she heard "Are you that Indian girl?"

Two looked up to her left. Three young women as real as herself were there, stair-stepped in height and wearing a family resemblance. Two didn't know which had spoken. She hesitated. The one on the far right filled the space. "You are, aren't you?"

"Guilty as charged."

"The one who fell in the cave?" the middle girl said.

Two nodded. The same girl said, "Our paper said your horse was killed. I'm sorry."

"Thank you."

The one on the left said, "You're just like Persephone. That's wonderful."

Two smiled.

The middle one said, "Did you go to school?"

Two nodded.

"I bet you didn't study Greek mythology." That was the middle one again. "We didn't ourselves, 'til we got to Ward-Belmont."

The one on the right said, "We didn't study Greek mythology, Debbie. We studied comparative literature." She flipped her hair with her hand. Long for the era, it fell to her shoulders.

"That's what I meant, Shirley. Don't be a drip."

The girl on the left addressed Two, "Do you like the buffalos?"

Before Two answered, Debbie said, "Of course she does. They're both on the nickel."

Shirley said, "She might not. Not all Indians are alike." To Two she said, "Do you?"

"Yelp," said Two.

Shirley said, "They're almost all dead. That's a shame."

Two breathed in deeply.

The hair of the girl on the left was blonder than that of the others. She was also red in the face, apparently hotter. She pulled at her collar. Flapped a hand as a fan. "I don't see how they stand this heat with all that fur."

Two looked toward Adam and the other buffalo at the fence. They'd shed their winter coats. The hair that remained was clumpy and shaggy. Summer wasn't their most attractive season.

Debbie said, "Would you like your picture taken?"

Two was still looking toward the buffalo. If she didn't move, the girls might leave out of boredom. But she was a performer. These were fans. Sort of. While she was thinking about a picture being taken in her cast, Debbie went on. "We're sisters. Donna, Debbie, and Shirley. Our father works for the *Banner*. Very high up. We could tell him you're still here. He might send a reporter to interview you."

Two looked toward the stacks of hay. The *Banner* was the enemy paper. But she did like publicity. Or had. She looked at Debbie. "There's not much to say."

Donna said, "Well, you're like Persephone. There's that."

Two ran a hand down the tail of her bandana headband. She wanted away from the sisters. But walking was a task, and a picture in the paper might not be so bad. She shrugged. "Sure, okay. If he's interested."

Death
Visits

≡

Two waited for Crawford sitting on the cistern, as close to uncaged nature as was possible without wandering into the woods. She usually arrived a few minutes before he came and spent her time watching squirrels, studying the damaged catalpa, or just enjoying the presence of her maternal grandmother, who she could feel attached to the hen house in an unseen, spiritual way. The rising sun was concealed by Chambliss, so she measured time by the retreat of the building's shadow. It was cut in half the second time she looked. Crawford was oddly tardy. She grabbed her crutches and turned toward the path he would travel, hoping to glimpse him. When she got bored standing, she swung over to the catalpa and studied its branches and twisted bridge. She looked inside the hollow trunk. Put her hand on the bark and wiped her palm off on her skirt. Gave up, a little worried, and swung back toward the hall.

As she reached the steps, Christa Belle Henley rushed out the door in silk pajamas. She said, "Come on. We don't want to miss this." She swished past as Two called, "Ya're not dressed!"

Christa Belle halted. Turned. "I'm covered. They look like a costume. Come on." She beckoned with her arm. "We wanta see this."

"See what?"

"The hippopotamus is dead."

"Dinah?"

"Yeah, come on. We'll talk as we walk."

Two flashed hot. When she caught up with Christa Belle and could speak, she said, "What happened to her?"

"That's the question. Just dead as a doorknob in her pool."

"She was getting better."

"Was she sick?"

"Only with worms. But they were going away."

"How do ya know all that?"

"Mr. Murkin told me. He's Mr. Lovett's assistant."

"Do ya think he and Miz Hampton are barneymugging?"

"I don't know what that is."

"Ya know, doing it."

"That's none of our business. When did Dinah die?"

"Sometime in the night. We heard it right after breakfast. Ya would've too if ya weren't out meeting your jigaboo."

Two stopped. "Don't call him that."

Christa Belle stopped, too. "It's better than some things I could call him. We call 'em niggers in Memphis."

"Why don't ya just call him Crawford? That's his name."

"Don't be so touchy. I didn't mean anything. Come on. I wanta see this hippo. I've never seen a dead one before."

"You go on. I'll catch up."

Christa Belle put a fist on a hip. "Look. I didn't mean to hurt yer feelings. I know he's just bringing ya your cart. But he's probably sweet on ya. Yer both dark."

"He's engaged."

"He is?"

"Yes. And can't people just be friends?"

"I suppose they can. But ya know how colored men are. They just wanta stick their big dicks in ya."

Two swung her left crutch. Whacked Christa Belle in the ribs and knocked her off the path, down into the grass. She jabbed her right crutch into Christa Belle's stomach. Then she placed her cast on her shoulder, moved her right crutch to the grass, and pressed the tip of her left crutch into the notch of Christa Belle's neck. She said, "Move and I'll crush your windpipe."

Christa Belle went rigid. Croaked out, "Have ya lost yer mind?"

"I'm telling ya. Don't move. Listen up. Crawford's my friend. He's a human being, like you. Only better. He's kind to me and minds his own business. What do ya call me behind my back? A savage or an injun?"

"Let me up," Christa Belle whispered.

A man behind Two said, "Ya gals in a fight?"

Two took the tip of her crutch off Christa Belle's neck, but didn't move her eyes or her cast. She said, "She tried to trip me."

"Oh. Ya shouldn't do that." He was speaking to Christa Belle.

Two said, "Just leave us alone. I've got this."

The man was in the park to organize a Knights of Khorassan outing for underprivileged children. He didn't want to get into a fight between two women. He said, "The hippopotamus is dead. Ya oughta come see it," and left.

Two said, "Lesson learned?"

"Yeah. Get your foot off my shoulder. Ya're hurting me."

Two removed her cast. Christa Belle sat up and rubbed her collarbone. "You're damn dangerous with those crutches. Wherecha learn that?"

"I've swung ropes since I was four."

Christa Belle got up and fingered her throat for damage. "Well, people are talking. Ya oughta know. 'Specially since the lynching."

"What lynching?"

"The one on Tuesday."

"Where?"

"North of here. A little town on the border with Kentucky."

"Why would anybody do that?"

"People do it all the time. Do ya want to stand here and jabber, or go see the dead hippo?"

"I'll come in a minute."

Two swung over to a bench and sat down. Her stomach was queasy. Dinah was dead. Could Crawford be, too? She imagined him swinging from a tree just for bringing her Gay and the cart. For talking at the cistern. For playing gin rummy. Negros were lynched for standing up for themselves. For not saying "yes sir." For touching a white woman. For any excuse whatsoever. Newspaper pictures of Tulsa's race riot flew into Two's mind. It was only five years in the past and not far from the ranch. Blocks of Negro homes and businesses burned to the ground, turned into piles of smoldering rubble. People slaughtered like deer on the run. And no telling how many. That death count was like the count of allotment murders. Far under the actual amount. Two knew that as well as she knew her own fingers and thumbs. Knew dark deaths didn't matter. White people always lied about the numbers. Had done it forever.

Two felt surrounded by hidden deaths. She looked out at the park. She saw the casino's cupolas clearly. Knew the shooting gallery, concert pavilion, skating rink, and bird cages were just beyond the trees. All so peaceful. So entertaining. Built on top of desecrated Indian graves. Four thousand. Maybe even more. Wiped out of memory. Completely erased. Hidden by a park built solely for the purpose of white people having fun.

A heave arose in Two's throat and chest. Saliva flooded her mouth. She lowered her head to between her legs. She aimed her vomit away from her cast, and after she stopped, stayed bent over waiting for more. Finally, she swiped a piece of food off her cast with her thumb and slowly looked up. People had to have seen her, but nobody had stopped. Everybody was rushing toward the hippo enclosure. Two undid her bandana, wiped her face and mouth, and spit into the cloth. Then she pulled herself up, planted the tips of her crutches, and swung down the path.

The crowd at the enclosure was quiet and three people deep; from

Two's perspective, only backs, hats, and heads. A man on the platform was looking down into the pen. The sun was hazy and dim; the air heavy with silence, as the music had yet to begin. Two started out going right, but remembered the soggy overflow field, so turned left and swung around the circle to the back of the platform's stairs. A locked gate blocked them, but Crawford was sitting three steps up with his back to the pen. Two yelled at him. He met her, saying, "Sorry. I was recruited soon as I got in." He'd unlocked and swung open the gate.

"I'm just glad to see ya."

"You know I wouldn't abandon you for no reason."

"I know." She wouldn't mention the lynching. "I wanta see Dinah. Can we go up?"

"If ya can handle the steps. I better not help you."

Two changed her mind. "I heard about the lynching."

Crawford stepped aside. "I think he was a no-account. Murdered his wife. But that shit needs to stop. Pardon my French."

"Shit, French is all we speak on the 101. I can manage these better with one crutch and the rail. Will ya bring my other crutch up?"

"Glad to. Just don't fall. I'll have to let ya break your neck if ya do."

The man on the platform was aiming down with a camera, snapping away. Though Two liked being photographed, she felt he shouldn't be taking pictures of Dinah. She recalled her mother's Pawnee friend who didn't want her picture taken at all. Ever. Believed the box trapped spirits and stole them away to be converted to Christianity. Two considered that nonsense. Felt Dinah's spirit was too large to be trapped in a black box that folded up. And she probably wouldn't make a good convert. Two chuckled silently, but realized she was distracting herself because she wasn't ready to move forward and look down. Wasn't ready to see her friend dead. Crawford had climbed up. He held her crutch by the tip and poked it toward her. She took it. The photographer kept snapping pictures. He lifted his angle and focused on the crowd.

Crawford said, "Old Shackleford isn't gonna like this a bit."

"I hate it. She seemed to be getting better."

"She was, according to Murkin."

"What happened?"

"Nobody knows. Found dead early this morning. You wanta take a look?"

"Not really. I don't like this kind of thing. But I guess I'm up here now. Come with me."

"I'll be right over there." Crawford jerked his head left.

Two gripped her crutches tightly and swung forward. She forced herself to look down. Dinah was on her side in the water. Her mouth wide, teeth showing, eye open. Two shuddered. She quickly looked away to Methuselah. He was at the edge of the pen, as far away from the water as possible. His head, tail, and legs were in his shell. Two felt he was frightened. She wished he could tell her what happened. She glanced back at Dinah to look for blood in the water. But the water was the color of concrete, not pink. Dinah hadn't been wounded. But what could've killed her? Two was thinking on that, looking into the sky at one of the cupolas, when the photographer intruded, "Are ya the horse diving gal?"

She glanced over. "Yeah, I am."

"My boss told me to talk to ya, too. But I haveta get these pictures developed by deadline. Ya gonna be around the next few days?"

"Sure. Got nowhere to go."

Dinner
at
Longview

≡

Clive and John, both wearing seersucker suits and holding straw hats, went to the side porch closest to the drive and the park. When Adelaide opened the door, they each said, "Evening, Adelaide." Adelaide said, "Mr. Lovett, Mr. Murkin. Mr. James and Miz May are sitting on the front porch."

Clive said, "We can just walk around. Thank you kindly, Adelaide."

"Will ya be wanting ice tea, or hot?"

"Iced for me."

John said, "Yes, ice for me, too." He started off on the gravel path to the front of the house and Clive followed. They were grim-faced like doctors come to deliver bad news.

James and May were seated in cushioned wicker chairs in the shade on the north end of a wide porch. Two empty identical chairs were opposite them, and the swing beside James was also empty. After greetings, Clive and John took the chairs, May laid her clipboard on a table, and James stuck a folder in his briefcase and snapped the lid shut.

Adelaide came through the screen door, balancing a tray holding a pitcher, glasses, and lemon wedges. Clive wished he'd remembered to tell her he wanted his tea unsweetened. He said, "John took a stool over to Vanderbilt. I have a mate who's a biology professor. He had three different students examine samples. They found no sign of worms, so we've excluded schistosomiasis. We weren't able to draw blood. That's difficult to do from a dead animal unless it's refrigerated. Which, of course, she wasn't. And hippopotamus skin is thick, even in the mouth. She could've had a heart attack, I suppose. But she was young. Only six."

"How long do they live?" May asked.

"Usually thirty-five to forty years. But then Caliph, the Central Park hippo, was exhibited alive for only thirty years before he died."

"Oh, yes, I've seen him. Quite odd. That isn't normal taxidermy. How do they do that?"

"With plaster. And cutting the animal's skin and sewing it back together. It's quite a chore."

"We're off the subject here," James interjected. "What did they find?" He looked over the top of his spectacles.

Clive leaned back against a cushion. Sipped tea. Tried not to wince. "Absolutely nothing so far. And I don't know that we will."

James looked to John. "Is that your opinion, too? You haven't said anything."

John took in a gulp of air, but remained leaning forward in his chair. "Yes, sir. We could do an autopsy. But she's a large animal. And it's hot. We've already got a problem with the odor."

James leaned back in his seat and looked over the heads of his guests. He saw dead bodies stacked on a riverbank. He smelled their stench and rubbed his stub.

May realized James was seeing something that would keep him awake. She said to John, "What can you do about that?"

John looked to Clive. Clive said, "We'd like to bury her as promptly as possible. Perhaps directly there in her pit. Moving a hippopotamus carcass is quite a task. Buddy could dig a new hole. But dragging her through the park would be a big job, and we'd have to do it at night to keep people from peering. Probably the best thing is cover her over right where she is. Move Methuselah to the sea lions."

May said, "That sounds reasonable to me. What do you think, James?"

James was remembering a body he'd seen half in and half out of a swamp near the Mississippi. He said, "Cover her quickly."

May said, "It'll be a shame not to know what happened to her."

"I agree," said Clive.

James's mind suddenly returned to the porch. "I've been going over the insurance. We can get three thousand dollars for her. But Memphis is going to find out." He tapped his teeth together. Wished he could bite off somebody's head.

John left to join his family, but Clive stayed for supper. Dinah's death reaching the prying ears of people in Memphis dominated much of the talk. When May couldn't stand it any longer, she changed the subject to the Battle of Nashville Memorial. As president of the Ladies Battle-field Association, she'd been trying to get the memorial built since 1913, which seemed to her (and to many) like a lifetime. Innumerable ben-efits, pageants, performances, and balls had been given to raise money for a park and a statue. May had organized most of them and had hosted a slew at Longview. A plot of land less than a mile up the pike was set aside for the park and accessible by the Franklin interurban.

But the Great War had interrupted the endeavor. After which, there'd been years of decision-making, falling-outs, and making-ups while vari-ous stakeholders argued about expanding the memorial to also honor the fallen of that war. That question had been settled. It would not.

On most days, the memorial made May want to throw good china against the wall. However, the statue commemorating the battle had re-cently been shipped from Italy to Baltimore. She was thrilled about that, and shared the news with Clive. She said also, "We'll be giving a dinner for Giuseppe on July the tenth. You'll receive your invitation in a couple of days." Giuseppe Moretti, the statue's sculptor, was world famous, and a favorite of both Clive's and May's.

Clive said, "I wouldn't miss it."

"You may bring a guest." May smiled. The several worlds of the park overlapped only somewhat. But Clive was fully imbedded in the Shacklefords' arena, and Helen, as the widow of a doctor, could get through the gate. Word of a possible romance had come to May through Maggie on the evening of the first day of the Scopes hearing. May knew Clive would return a card naming a guest if he were bringing one, but was holding a figurative finger aloft for which way the wind was blowing. It was a lot better than talking about a dead hippopotamus, insurance money, or nosy people in Memphis. And May had long hoped to see Clive married.

Clive looked at his water goblet. Though they were publicly courting, he hadn't discussed Helen with anyone. He didn't really have anyone to discuss her with. But May had been his true friend, and she, a female old enough to be his mother, might provide insights he didn't have. He said, "Well, since you bring it up, I might ask Helen Hampton. She and I get on."

"You do? Tell us about that." May's eyes widened a little. Her head tilted into a listening position. But before Clive could answer, James said, "If you'll excuse me, I need to call Lewis on his baseball matter." He laid his napkin beside his plate.

"What're you going to tell him, dear? If you don't mind me asking." To Clive, May said, "Lewis wants to buy the Vols."

James scooted his chair back. "I'm going to tell him it's a damn foolish idea."

"Is it?" May wanted specific information. James, of late, had seemed particularly angry at Lewis.

"Yes, of course it is. There's no money to be made in baseball. He wants to buy that team just for the publicity."

"Aren't they at the top of the league?"

"That makes no difference. It's still a losing proposition. You agree, don't you, Clive?"

"I know nothing about baseball."

"But you know Lewis."

Clive blotted his mouth with his napkin. He, too, knew James was angry with Lewis. And had been for a while. But he didn't know why. Usually, James was angry with Charles for not making even the pretense of work. But Charles was in Mississippi. Maybe that gave James's ire a different rivulet. Clive said, "He seems to have the Midas touch."

James cleared his throat. "*Seems* is the operative word there."

"You think he doesn't, darling?" May didn't really know the answer. James was secretive about Lewis. Just that past Saturday night, during a toast to his father, Lewis had announced to them and to others that he'd bought a racehorse and named it Mr. James. That type of thing usually pleased her husband, but it hadn't that night, and he'd left the dinner party abruptly, and had been in bed when she'd arrived home. Since then, he'd avoided all conversation about Lewis, until that evening. So May had been looking for an opening to get more information about Lewis's dealings and James's anger with him. Clive's presence provided the ideal opportunity.

James smoothed his mustache to keep from rubbing his stub. He was even more furious with his son than he had been before. The announcement of the naming of the horse had aborted his plans for warning Lewis to stay away from Sinclair; now he couldn't do it without seeming ungrateful. Lewis had boxed him in in a way that seemed almost deliberate. But to his knowledge, May didn't know who Lewis had bought the horse from, and if she found out, it would distress her. He said, "I think Lewis likes to make a big show. Someday that's going to be his downfall."

"So you think he wants to buy the Vols just for show?"

"I certainly do. It's just like the racehorse. Who makes money in racehorses?"

"People in Kentucky?"

"We aren't in Kentucky, May. Racing isn't even legal here. And you can't make money in things you can't tend to." He picked up a knife, held the handle to the table, and fought an urge to bang it.

Clive didn't want the dinner to end unpleasantly. He took an extended sip of water and tried to think of something distracting to say.

May said, "What're you going to tell him?"

"I'm going to tell him his proposed business partners are just using him."

May put her hand to her locket. "Is that true?"

"Of course it is. One's an editor, and the other's a writer. How much money do you think they have between them? Who do you think'll foot the bills?"

"I haven't thought about it at all. I hardly know anything about it. What do you think, Clive?"

Clive wasn't inexperienced in being invited into his friends' spats. And not only the Shacklefords'. He had concluded married people considered that one of the primary utilities of an unmarried man. "I think James is probably right. Writing isn't a lucrative business. Publishing can be. But only with big operations. What's the chap edit?"

"The *Southern Lumberman*."

May said, "What's that?"

"That's exactly my point. It's a trade magazine. It's probably losing money as we speak." James stood up. Finally gave in to rubbing his stub. "I'm going to give Lewis a piece of my mind." He turned to go.

May said, "Remember he's grown, dear." But that was to James's back, and he didn't turn around. She raised both eyebrows to Clive. Said, "Let's have dessert."

The dessert was strawberry pie. A gift from Maggie's garden and the last of the season. Clive was half into his slice when May said, "We were speaking of Mrs. Hampton. You'll bring her?"

Clive had been hoping talk would twist again in that direction. "Yes, if you don't mind."

Maggie was always telling May she needed to socialize with a wider circle of people. And Maggie already approved of Mrs. Hampton. "Of course I don't mind. I understand her husband was a physician."

"Yes. He died from the influenza. Caught it treating his patients."

"I remember that now. They lived in Franklin?"

"Yes. She's from there. I don't know about him."

"Any children?"

"No, unfortunately. Or, perhaps, fortunately. From a courting perspective." Clive smiled.

"So you're courting her?"

Clive had asked for hot tea with his pie. He lifted the cup to his lips, drank, and applied his napkin before saying, "I took her to the hearing, as I suspect you know. And we've spent some evenings together. I rather fancy her. I've been searching for somewhere to take her beyond the park."

"I see. Yes, that's a problem at the moment." Summer was the low season in Nashville. The plain people flocked to parks such as Glendale. But many of the elites fled to their homes elsewhere, mostly in the mountains. Men who stayed behind for business played golf and tennis. Women swam and rode horses. The anemic summer social season had been on May's mind as she'd tried to fill her party for Giuseppe. She said, "Does she like to motor around?"

"I hadn't thought of motoring. That's a good idea. We could picnic."

"Yes. Or take her in to the library. There's currently an exhibit of Tennessee artists there."

Clive cut into the thickest part of his crust. The library was on Polk. The streets around it were busy. He envisioned having a wreck. "I might need some practice for that. It's hard to put in the time to stay proficient."

"Well, I suppose if it's important, you'll find the time." May smiled.

Clive wiggled a smidge in his seat. "I've asked Crawford to drive Helen and Miss Feathers to see her doctor tomorrow. I suppose I could do that myself."

"Sounds like a good opportunity. How's Miss Feathers doing?"

"Actually, quite well. Considering what she's been through, better than one would expect. Of course, she's amazingly athletic. I hope her doctor lets her out of her cast."

"Will she go home then? Or has someone come up with plans for her here?"

Clive applied his napkin again. Tilted his head. "That's still a problem. I know she'll stay through the turtle derby. She's the only person around who has any experience in racing them. After that, I can't say. Evidently, besides diving, she has other skills. She's been a competitive calf roper. Also, she says she can ride standing up. Or could, before she broke her leg. And she's thrown hatchets. Tomahawks, I believe they're called. She's also a sharpshooter."

"How do you know all of that?"

Clive had finished both his pie and his tea. And May was resting an arm on the table. Clive did the same and cleared his throat. "She and I have, well, become rather close." He lifted a hand. "Nothing improper, of course. It's that, well, since our time in the cave . . ."

"That's understandable. I would expect nothing less. You saved the girl's life. I believe the Chinese think that links people together forever. The rescuer becomes responsible for the person he saved. That part never made sense to me, but no doubt it creates a covenant."

"Yes, quite. And the time I spent in that cave will be with me for the rest of my life. It's changed me in ways that are hard to put into words."

"Oh? Please try. I'm interested in things beyond committee work and giving parties."

The light in the room had grown dim with the onset of evening, and Adelaide, familiar with her employers' penchant for private conversations after dinner, had not been in to switch on the lamps. However, there were candles on the table, and a box of matches. Clive picked up the box, and said, "Do you mind?" He gestured to a candleholder.

"Of course not. Or would you rather lamplight?" May looked around.

"No, don't bother. Candles always feel more comfortable to me." He struck a match and lit a wick. He laid the burnt stick on top of the box and leaned in, placing both forearms on the table. He said, "You and I, May . . ." He hesitated. Glanced up at the flame. "We've lost so many of those we love. Lost them too soon, and in terrible ways. That haunts me. It did as a lad, and has even more since the war. I imagine you might feel the same way."

May was never far from grief. Her busy schedule and charitable endeavors were, in part, attempts to keep it at bay. She bit her bottom lip and nodded.

Clive looked at his hands. "I've had problems with that. As I suspect you know. But something happened in that cave that brought me relief. That caused me to think we haven't lost our loved ones for good. Just temporarily." He glanced up at May.

Her eyes glistened. She nodded again.

"I was orphaned, you know. My mother died during childbirth, along with the baby. Shortly thereafter, my father succumbed to scarlet fever. I was handed from one relative to another. Some of them were better than others, but all were kind in their way, trying to help me. I grew close to the boys of one particular family. The sons of my mother's first cousin. And, later on, I served with one of them in the war. We were together for months, mostly in the trenches. Then the inevitable happened. One of us was killed.

"I took it rather hard. And, of course, so many others were slaughtered. I know you felt the horror over here. But it was right in our faces in Europe. And in England. I've never been able to come to terms with that. With the waste. The millions of premature deaths. The horrible disfigurements. It turned me away from God. Certainly away from religion. I came to believe that life is meaningless, except, perhaps, for the kindness we show to animals and one another. Otherwise, we flicker and die, like the flame on this candle. But when I was in that cave, May, Millwood, that cousin of mine who was killed, he came to me. He was as clear to me as you are. Clearer. And he stayed. I know it sounds bonkers, but we sang together."

"Sang?"

"Yes. A war song. One we sang all the time in the trenches. 'Bombed Last Night.' You're familiar with it?

"Yes. It became quite popular over here, too. Grim, but darkly humorous."

"That it is. But we sang it quite a bit. Millwood and I particularly liked it. It fit our range. So it was natural for him to come back singing it." Clive took his arms off the table. He leaned back and shook his head. "I must sound daft."

"No, no, not at all. I've buried six children. If I didn't believe in an afterlife, I would've drowned myself in the creek long ago. Besides, there's a ghost in this house."

The room was dark, but the candle illuminated both sides of May's face. Plump with age, it was barely wrinkled. A tear fell from her left eye. Unwiped, it ran down her cheek. Clive said, "One of your children?"

"No. Though you would think. Our little girls died in this house. So did William. And we held Shirley's, James Jr.'s, and Danny's services here. I sometimes feel this is a palace of death." She looked up and around. She wiped the tear with her fingertips.

Clive's natural impulse was to comfort. "But, surely, it's a palace of life, also."

"Yes. I try to make it so. The living must go on."

Clive clasped his hands between his knees. "So, if you don't mind me asking, who's the spirit?"

"I'll tell you. But first, excuse me for a moment." May got up from the table. She walked through the dark, stopped in the door frame, closed the door, and turned back. When she sat back down, she struck another match and lit the second candle. She said, "It's just as well this conversation is private. James is haunted enough as it is."

"Does he know about the spirit?"

"I don't think so. I used to ask him if he, you know, heard it, or saw it. But he never wanted to talk about it if he did. So I gave that up long ago."

"If it's not a loved one, do you know who it is?"

"It's a he. A soldier. A Confederate one."

"And you've seen him?"

"Oh, yes. But usually I just hear him. He wears boots. They make noise."

"Why is he here?"

"I don't know for sure. This house was General Hood's headquarters. There were soldiers all over it. Also all over the grounds. Camping for about two weeks before the battle. Building trenches and breastworks. Cutting down every tree on the place, except the hickories. They were spared for their nuts and, probably, because they're so hard to fell. Then the war went through here. The lines moved back and forth. No telling how many were killed."

"But there's only one spirit?"

"As far as I know. And for a while he gave me fits over the monument."

"How so?"

"Well, you know, most of the monuments going up commemorate the Confederate dead. The generals, mostly, not the soldiers. But ours honors the dead soldiers of both armies. That's made a lot of people unhappy, including the ghost."

"He blames you for it?"

"I am to blame for it. Giuseppe and myself. He brings a European perspective. A "long view," so to speak. And I agree. Nashville was an occupied city for three years. My father doctored the wounded and sick of both armies. I eventually came to know, at least as well as a child can, some of the Northern soldiers. They were kind to me. And they suffered. Just like our men and boys."

Clive picked up the matchbox. It was silver. Engraved on the top. He slid the lid open and deposited the two burnt matches inside. He pinched it closed and tapped the end on the table. Lightly, he tapped again. "Your ghost, is he attached particularly to you? Or to the house?"

"I've wondered about that. I think he's attached to the house. But I also think he's attached to me, especially. Though, one of our little granddaughters, Edith, can apparently see him. She's asked me on two occasions who that soldier man is. But you'd think Adelaide would notice him, and I don't believe she has."

"Have you asked her?"

May chuckled. "No. I can't afford to lose her, and she'd be out of here in a flash. There are plenty of people who'd hire her. I've already lost two friends over that. You can't have friends who'll come into your house and steal your help."

Clive laid the box on the table. Said, "No, I would think not. That'd be worse than stealing the silver."

May nodded. And because the subject had turned a shade lighter, she ran a thumb over her plate, picked up a few crumbs, and put them to her tongue. She said, "We couldn't have this discussion in public. But I do understand your cousin's effect on you. Rest assured of that. I find my soldier quite comforting at times. Especially when James is twisted in knots. Or Charles is particularly irritating. Or Lewis, or Meredith. Sometimes my soldier seems like my only friend in the house."

Clive felt the conversation had crossed a bridge. Had moved from the tentative and abnormal to the understood and taken for granted. He said, "Miss Feathers has a ghost attached to her. I don't believe she can see him, but he's very clear to me. And he's been around frequently lately."

May's eyes widened. "Is that so? What does he look like?"

"He's an Indian fellow. Not our Indians. Yours. He's rather bare on the chest, except for tattoos. Those are also on his arms and legs. He has a cloth and sash covering his necessary parts. And paint on his face. He frowns a lot."

"Perhaps he's upset about something?"

"That may be. He guards Two like her life is in danger."

"It has been."

"True. But he wasn't in the cave. Or maybe he was, and I couldn't see him. I don't know. I've thought about mentioning him to her, but that takes some gumption, and I don't want to cause her alarm."

"You'll be with her tomorrow?"

"Yes. But so will Helen. And I'm quite sure I don't want Helen to know I see ghosts."

May lifted an eyebrow and smiled. "I thoroughly understand that."

In
the
Big
Building

≡

Little Elk was frowning as he watched Clive usher Two and Helen into his automobile. He saw cars as boats on wheels. Recognized their handiness for getting around, but wasn't about to get in one himself. And he felt alarmed that Two was being taken off by white people. Would she be safe? And would she come back? If she didn't, the light would go out of his day. His heart had become strongly tethered. Not so much that he wanted Two to join him. But strong enough that he did, increasingly, stay by her side. And adding to his attachment was the fact that she had, on several occasions, used tobacco. Once she'd smoked it sitting with friends on the porch planks below her window. More often, she mixed the leaf with other plants and bark and smudged her room.

The aroma made Little Elk heartsick for his old life, but the strength it gave him outweighed that disadvantage. After whiffing the magical concoction, he could blow on Two's ear and make her rub it. He could touch her arm and make her scratch. And if he could smoke enough, he thought he could make her see him. That was his constant desire.

After Two and the white people rode off in the boat, Little Elk walked to the back side of the building and looked in Two's window. Her belongings seemed in place. The clothes she wore most were hanging on knobs. Her trunk was still at the foot of her bed, her comb and brush on her big chest, her bound talking leaves on her table. Little Elk breathed in relief. Two would return. Probably before the sun set. However, for now, she was gone. And that presented a chance to get her tobacco. Little Elk had discovered he could melt through wires over at the big porch where people carried skinny ball sticks in big quivers. He should be able to melt through Two's screens if he chewed a little tobacco for strength.

He did that. And her room was magical. Little Elk touched everything. Tried out the bed. Found it too soft. Opened the book. Saw the talking leaves. Felt their power. Wanted to take them with him. But he couldn't read, and never stole more than he needed. He got off the bed, and tried the trunk. The lid wouldn't budge. He sat back on his heels. Licked his lips. Licked them again. He didn't want to risk trying to melt through the box and being successful. He could get trapped inside. So he didn't know what to do. He grunted.

Then he remembered the needle he carried to repair his moccasins. He pulled his pouch to the front of his body. Carefully stuck his fingers in and pulled out a sliver of bone. He held it up to inspect. He hadn't used that needle in forever, as now his moccasins never wore out, snagged, or ripped. The bone was still pointed, and the lock resembled the mouth of a fish. He'd wiggled loose many a hook. The trick was in the wrist. And it didn't take long.

He lifted the lid carefully, holding it in place until he was certain it wouldn't drop. Then he fingered through warily, trying not to leave a trace. He found Two's pistol and sat back on his heels. It was different from any he'd seen. A little scary. He carefully set it back down. He found her tobacco pouch. Painted on its front was a rearing red horse. Was it the horse Two had dived on? He rubbed his thumb over the picture. He wouldn't take the pouch away from her. And he would leave her some tobacco. He untied his own pouch, pinched leaves into it, dropping a few to the floor. He retrieved all he saw, replaced Two's pouch, and closed the trunk's lid. He applied his needle again until he heard the lock turn. Feeling confident from accomplishing his mission, he went back out through the building. The walls felt tight, but held pretty pictures. He stopped to inspect many. But when he got to the photograph of the white women drawing the bows, he laughed out loud. He hadn't meant to do that, and he looked around quickly. The women walking past didn't seemed to have heard him.

What
Would
Kill
a
Hippo?

While Two was with Dr. Kelly, Clive and Helen ate fried fish, green beans, cornbread, and banana pudding in the hospital's cafeteria. They lingered over the pudding. Talked about how "pudding" means a certain type of after-dinner sweet in America but all desserts in England. And, quite naturally, since they were already discussing the far side of the Atlantic, Clive asked Helen if she might be available for the Shacklefords' party for Giuseppe Moretti.

Helen's heart fluttered. Her nostrils flared to take in more air. She'd grown to believe dreams coming true were rare. Yet, right there in a cafeteria smelling strongly of fried fish and vaguely of ether, hers were materializing. She said without coquettishness or hesitation, "Yes! I would. How delightful." Then she began worrying about what she would wear.

Clive was relieved the invitation had been so easily accepted. He'd assumed it would be, but felt fidgety from lack of practice and awkward enough that he veered quickly to the subject of Dinah. That jerked Helen's mind off of her wardrobe. They talked about the dead hippopotamus until a woman brought a box of food to take to Two.

Dr. Kelly had replaced Two's cast with a shorter one that was a little lighter and that freed her knee. But until the plaster dried completely, she had to be careful. When she got back to Chambliss, she was tired, it had begun to rain, and the porches were wet. She went to bed early. Dreamed of giant tortoises with their heads and feet pulled into their shells. Dreamed of Dinah still living. Woke the next morning yearning to visit the hippopotamus enclosure.

She went to the bathroom, dressed, and joined the women in the dining hall for breakfast. Back in her room, she turned quickly to her bed, drew the cover up, pinned her pouch to her camisole, and turned to the bedpost to grab her bandana. Then she noticed two bits of tobacco on the floor. They were merely flecks. Flakes. Notches. Signs. Her hand dropped to her crutch's grip. She stopped breathing. Started to bend. Tilted forward awkwardly and straightened up quick. She patted her cast to be sure she hadn't damaged it.

Two could see well enough to shoot a row of pennies off a wall at thirty paces without missing a single Lincoln's head. She didn't have any doubt about what she was seeing, or what the bits signified. She looked to her dresser. Her bathroom pail was where she'd left it before breakfast. Her hairbrush and comb were still to the right of her mirror, her tin of vanishing cream to the left. The mirror, itself, was tilted on its stand at its usual angle. A postcard picture of 101 cowgirls was propped against it. She looked toward her nightstand. The book she'd borrowed from one of the parlors was next to her lamp. Also a pencil, a small pad of paper, used chewing gum in a wrapper, and a glass of water Mrs. Hampton had brought her after she'd gotten in bed. She looked to the hooks on the wall. Her clothes seemed untouched, her skirts the same, her jeans where they'd hung since she'd broken her leg, her belt with the big buckle still there, the blouse she'd worn to the hospital beside it. Two swung to her closet and opened the door. Her footwear was on the floor, her helmet on the shelf, a few clothes and her swimming costume strung from hangers. All just as she'd left them.

She closed the closet door and swung to the dresser. She looked again at her vanishing cream, postcard, hairbrush, and comb. She backed up, balanced, and opened the top drawer. Her underwear was stacked as usual. Her everyday scarves folded in neat squares and shingled on top of each other in a rainbow of colors. She touched one, thinking of the stolen bandana. Whoever had been in her room may not have been Jack, but it wasn't a woman looking for clothes.

Two swung to her trunk and withdrew its key from the pouch pinned in her blouse. She had a hard time with the lock, lost her balance, steadied herself, and lifted the lid. She looked first at her best scarves. Some were the most valuable pieces of clothing she owned. Unique, and fashionable east of the Mississippi. But they all were still there, and looked untouched. She found her traveling pistol, its gun belt and holster, her ammunition, knife, clothes, sewing kit, box of letters, writing pad, pencils, stamps, pictures, and tobacco. She squeezed the pouch. It was flatter than she recalled. By a good bit. She bounced it in her palm. It was also lighter. But who would steal her tobacco? Chambliss's secret smokers preferred packaged cigarettes. No self-respecting flapper would smoke roll-ups, chew, or dip.

Two stuffed the pouch in her pocket, closed the lid, and locked the trunk. She was running late to meet Crawford. She snatched her bandana from the bedpost and stuffed it in her waistband. She'd fold it into a headband when she got to the cistern.

Little Elk had been waiting by the hen house for Crawford to bring the little horse and cart. Two's tobacco had made him stronger than he'd been in a while, and he yearned to be seen. While Two worked with her scarf, he scuffed his moccasins against the ground, trying to make some sound. Two didn't look up and around, except toward the path from the barn. And while Little Elk was searching the ground for an acorn to throw, Crawford came up the trail on his horse, leading the Shetland and cart. Little Elk felt a slight prick of jealousy. He crossed his arms, spread his stance, and listened to Two tell Crawford about her missing tobacco. Little Elk hit himself in the forehead. He felt blood rush to his face. He couldn't even steal tobacco without getting caught. He was worse than a child. His parents would ridicule him if they were around. Which they were not. For once he was glad about that. He slowly crept closer to the cart and the conversation. When Two and Crawford parted, he hopped on the back of the pony to hitch a ride to wherever Two was going.

That was the hippopotamus enclosure. But it looked entirely different. There were no people around. The scaffolding was down and stacked on the ground. The filter removed and the big turtle gone. A mound of dirt covered the pond and extended over the blocks. In its center was a single sapling. The only familiar marker was the light pole, now towering over the piles of wood. Two shifted her cast and squirmed. She'd imagined the destruction of her own scaffolding. The filling in of her pool. Now seeing Dinah's, she felt even closer to her. Tears arose. She untied her bandana. Used it to dab her eyes and, finally, to blow her nose. Little Elk wanted to comfort her, but didn't know how. He'd hopped to the ground, so he rubbed Gay's muzzle and distracted himself with the horse.

Two quit crying and settled into staring at the mound of dirt, still dark and damp from the rain. Dinah had seemed to be recovering. She was healthier and more active. But then she'd died, young and suddenly. Why? What would kill an animal that size? A large-caliber gun? Yes. But that shot would've been heard. And killing a hippo would take more than one bullet. Officially, except for the night watchman's, the only firearms in the park were the shooting gallery's BB guns. Those made puffy little noises and were fired close to the casino and bandstand. Not loud enough to even bother the bears. And BBs couldn't kill a hippopotamus. Besides, according to Mr. Lovett, Dinah hadn't been shot.

Two's eyes shifted to the sapling. It should grow as big as the pig-hanging tree in her Uncle Dub's yard. They killed their pigs with knives to their jugulars. That took roping, tying, and, generally, two people, though a hog properly tied could be killed by one. Two had done that alone during wild boar chases. But Dinah was the size of several hogs. She possibly could be roped from the platform, but at Glendale nobody besides herself had enough skill to do that. And a roped hippo would pose a beehive of problems. Getting a knife through the hide would be tough, even if Dinah was securely tied down by cords and stakes in the ground. And, really, there hadn't been a wound of any kind. No blood in the water.

Two glanced over at the electric pole. On the range, there was nothing more dangerous than a thunderstorm. Cattle spooked by thunder and rain would trample men, horses, bushes, and calves. Cowboys died in those stampedes. And lightning was even more hazardous. It zagged from horizon to horizon, plunged in bolts to the earth. Horses were freakishly susceptible to dying by it, and it could kill cattle without direct hits. Any strike to water they touched executed them instantly. Two'd seen the carcasses of cattle — seven or eight — that had died together one stormy night. They lay on their sides in a shallow pond, just like Dinah.

Two was studying the light pole when a flatbed truck rumbled over a gravel path toward her. Buddy Parrish was driving. Duncan Shelton riding shotgun. Three park employees stood in the bed, holding on to the sides. The truck pulled up at the lumber piles and the men poured out. Two tapped Gay on the rump and drove over. Buddy was giving orders. Duncan examining the new tree, patting the ground with his foot. When he was done, he walked to the pony cart and said, "We just 'bout got her cleaned up."

"Is Dinah in her pond?" Two knew the answer. She wanted conversation.

"Yelp. Easiest thing to do. The mound'll sink. We'll plant grass on it. She'll be fine. Grow that tree up fast."

"Will the concrete be a problem?"

"It'll break down. We put some . . ." Duncan hesitated. They'd filled the pond with manure to nourish the tree and to break the concrete down. He finished his sentence with "chemicals in there to help."

"Any idea what killed her?"

Duncan shook his head and slumped. For all the problems they caused, he still loved the animals. "Beats me."

"Was there a storm that night?"

Duncan looked to the sky. "Not that I recollect."

Two nodded toward the pole. She was closer to it than before. Noticed the electrical box at its base. "Ya ever seen an animal killed by lightning?"

"Can't say as I have. Seen 'em choke to death." Duncan's mouth twitched.

"Electricity in water kills animals fast. Even big ones. The little ones, say, calves, look burnt on the outside. Sorta seared and shriveled like bacon. But I've seen horses and steers electrocuted where ya couldn't tell what'd happened if ya didn't know there'd been a storm."

Duncan looked toward the pole. Rubbed his chin. Was silent for a while. Then he said, "I don't see no way that could happen. We got electricity all over this place. Never lost an animal to it before."

"Is there any way to get electricity from that box or from any of the lines into the water?"

"None of the lines fell. There weren't nothing in the water 'cept her."

"Methuselah wasn't in it?"

"Nope. He were on land when I got here. Wouldn't come out of his shell. But I asked Hoffer about him, and he said he'd poked a stick up toward a foot, and it moved. So I paid him no mind. We all just tried to figure out what happened to Dinah."

Two shifted her cast. Gay flicked her tail. Duncan said, "I'll mention it to Clive."

After that, Two bought a hot dog with relish and a bottle of lemonade. She drove to the buffalo enclosure and popped the top off the bottle using the lip on the rim of the cart. The people she'd passed on the way were still walking away. No one was coming. She set her drink on the seat, cupped her hands to her mouth, and called, "Haba-haba." Adam raised his head. Two called again, picked up her drink, and settled into her lunch. Adam started sauntering over. As Two watched him approach, she envisioned storms she'd seen on the ranch; their magnificence, their terror, the death they often left in their wake.

Adam was scratching his hide on a nearby fencepost when Two finished eating. She asked how he was doing, if he'd noticed anything odd going on, anybody strange hanging around. He closed his eyes listening to her voice, felt her nearness and warmth. Then she suddenly said, "Somebody killed Dinah, the hippo. Ya gotta be careful. They're using lightning in water."

The horseflies were bad that day. Adam flicked his tail. Went back to scratching. Two held her empty bottle to the back of her neck, trying to cool it. She hoped Adam had gotten her message. She couldn't bear to lose him. That would be much worse than losing Dinah. She thought on how hard it is to communicate with animals who know more than they pretend to, but do what they please. She fell into imagining she'd set Adam and his friends free. They'd all run away from Nashville on the Big South Road. Two didn't know what was to the south, except Atlanta, and she didn't have any idea how far away that was. She envisioned prairie flowers, wide plains, and big sky. Adam envisioned the same. Little Elk didn't join their vision. He was intent on killing the horseflies. He grabbed at one and then at another. Most escaped his clutch, but one he caught and pinched particularly hard fell to the ground. Little Elk sat down next to it and Adam. He inspected the fly with a great deal of satisfaction. Adam sniffed and snorted, but didn't bother to move. He was used to that human.

Crawford was off for the afternoon, so Two returned Gay to the barn, unhooked her poles, undid her tack, and managed to hang that up on a wall. She couldn't handle buckets of feed and water without spilling, so she led Gay to the pasture, left her there, and swung toward the casino. She found the Montgomerys in the dressing room and chatted with them until the sisters went on. Then she swung over to the shooting gallery. She stood around and watched until she was challenged by three flirty men who paid the fee for her to shoot with them. She missed every duck, rabbit, and eagle. Then she was offered another dime from a freckled, bespectacled young man eager to please. She bet a nickel of it by challenging a fellow wearing a checkered flat cap who had beaten the others as well as her. By the time she was done with him, she'd shaken her worries and replaced them with some fun, nine one-dollar bills, and some quarters.

A
Notable
Date

Clive wasn't a Shriner, so couldn't be a member of the Oriental Golf Club. But he frequently golfed over there, and on Saturday morning played in a foursome with his chum "Dad" Jones, the club's pro. Dad mentioned a dance and dinner that evening, and Clive expressed an interest and snagged an invitation for himself and a guest. That fed his need to see Helen again, and to take her somewhere entertaining outside of the park. If she could go.

Which, of course, she could. On a hastily arranged date, they ate at one of several long tables set up on the club's lawn. Afterwards, they went in to dance. On fast numbers, Clive watched from the side, as those were new, evolving, and madly American. Too, he harbored an irrational fear of bursting stiches that he hadn't needed to hold his wounds together for years. But he was too generous to be jealous, and he didn't mind other gents asking Helen for the pleasure. She was a snappy dancer, and in spite of her foundations, certain parts of her anatomy bounced in a rhythm Clive found rather captivating. For slow songs, like "All Alone" and "Always," he kept her to himself.

The dance was over at midnight. They drove back to the park on a dark, roundabout route that involved Shackleford Lane, Franklin Pike, and a dirt road. Clive parked in a garage close to the horse barn and debated moving in for a kiss. He and Helen had previously engaged in some meeting of lips, but not often, as their courting had been in the park, and the opportunities there were rare, and the possibilities for interruptions almost unlimited. But Clive decided musty planks and old license plates nailed to boards didn't provide a romantic enough environment for an encounter. He wished for moonlight over the cliffs of Dover, for a canopy of stars over the moors of Yorkshire, for the shadow of the steeple of the Salisbury Cathedral.

So he engaged the parking brake, went around the boot of the car, and opened the door for Helen. He took her hand and told her to watch her step. He didn't let go, and they held hands while they walked the park's back paths toward Chambliss. The lights on the poles were distant and dimmed, the trail shadowed and dark. Clive had refused alcoholic refreshments at the party, and Helen, not actually a strict Prohibitionist, had followed his lead. So they both were entirely sober, at least in the sense of spirits and beer.

However, they were giddy in the enjoyment of each other's company. And they had to stick together to keep from falling. Clive moved closer and slipped his arm around Helen's waist to assure her balance. And, then, suddenly a rustle in the foliage forced them to huddle together. The noise was fleeting, but did come from an unknown source, so it was natural that they hesitated to part. And with "Always" still wafting through their hearts, it was even more natural that Clive put his lips to Helen's and that she removed her hat.

That's really all it took. Helen was, underneath, as full-blooded as she was full-bosomed. Her mouth was hungry for Clive's, and she had spent considerable time imagining more extensive involvement than they had yet managed. She dropped her hat and handbag to the path, and rather quickly, lips and hands moved, soft became hard, and hard became soft.

There was a great deal of heaving. A strap was slipped off a shoulder, a hand slipped in, a breast cupped, and a nipple fondled. Helen had enjoyed lustful relations while married, and afterwards had lived like a nun. She reached her climax without her corset being breached.

But the equivalent didn't happen for Clive. As much as he desired Helen, he worried she would touch one of his scars or, worse, see one, and feel repulsion. He pulled his palm off of her breast, his pelvis away from her dress. He gasped for breath. Said, "We've gotten rather out of hand. I'm sorry."

Helen was familiar enough with the English to know that they apologize as a matter of habit. She wanted to make sure Clive was merely doing that and wasn't actually sorry in the least. She put a hand on his crotch.

He groaned. Went weak in the knees in a flash. He didn't push her arm away, but did moan, "Please don't."

She rubbed up and down. Used her other hand to drop one of his suspenders, then began working on his buttons. He moved her fingers away from those, so she switched hands, used the left to massage his member and the other to drop his other suspender. After that, Clive gave in, and undid his buttons himself. His trousers slid to his hips, and because he wore smalls in summer, suddenly his primary private part was exposed to what little moonlight was shining.

One of Clive's wounds was high on a thigh near his groin, the other snaked around his side from his back to his belly. Both were still covered by clothing and hidden from light, out of sight. But Clive, even excited, couldn't bear having either of them touched or seen. Afraid Helen's fingers or palms would find his ridges and snarls, he stiffened all over his body. Helen sensed that. And she wasn't about to let Clive go unsatisfied. She used a trick she'd learned in her marriage. Bent down on one knee, balanced herself with a hand to Clive's thigh, and applied her mouth to his swollen appendage.

Clive's head filled with heat, and his mind fled to a far-off region he couldn't have named if he tried. His willpower followed. He gasped for breath, groaned, and began to weep. But Helen continued to apply her particular magic, and before long, an eruption took place. It was accompanied by a cry like a small animal's. After that, Clive lifted Helen to a standing position, kissed her on the mouth, and for the first time in his life tasted his own secretion. Its saltiness surprised him. But that was a minor shock compared to the previous one, and it didn't inhibit their kissing.

Two
Tells
Her
Theory

———

In church the next morning, Helen sent up a prayer of thanksgiving and promptly nodded off. She was awakened by the congregation rising to sing, and remained alert for the rest of the service. She'd wanted to spend the night with Clive, but he'd nixed that, out of, he'd said, a concern for her reputation. He was, of course, correct — she hadn't been quite rational — but there seemed to be more to his hesitancy. And slowly, as the service progressed, that niggled at her mind, even though it had nothing to do with the sermon, which was on . . . Well, she couldn't say.

Upon leaving Burgess Hall, Helen felt an urge to turn left to Clive's cabin. But that might be a strategic mistake. Clive's reluctance could be nothing more than his British reserve. And it could be that he was telling the truth. People did do that, and a true gentleman would protect her reputation. Still, she sensed there was something more. Something she couldn't quite put her finger on. But she had no doubt she would in the fullness of time, so she joined the residents for dinner in Chambliss, and shelved the problem in the back of her mind.

Sunday was a workday for the entertainers, so the gathering was small, and by the time Helen had finished her cobbler, Two was the only other person left at her table. A maternal feeling for Two was blooming in Helen's heart. And since Two ate with utensils, used her napkin like other women, and didn't gulp her liquids, Helen had begun to forget she was an Indian. Until Two said, "Looks like to me Dinah was murdered."

Helen laid her spoon on a saucer. "Murdered? What makes you think that?"

"I've seen animals killed by lightning. And I can't dive into a pool if a storm's coming up." Two looked to her own spoon. "Couldn't, that is. Anyway, water and electricity don't mix. And an electric shock wouldn't show on a hide as thick as a hippo's. Also, I had a vision of her death."

"A vision?"

"Yeah." Two licked her bottom lip. "Visions aren't unusual where I come from. Neither is murder. All you need to kill an animal as big as Dinah is electricity, water, and a copper wire."

Helen pushed her cobbler's plate away. "Why would anybody want to kill a hippopotamus?"

Two turned her palm up. "That's a good question. I don't know. Insurance, maybe?"

Helen's brow furrowed. She cleared her throat. "Mr. Shackleford, or his son, either one, holds the insurance. They'd just be moving money from one pot to the other. Besides, they have so much they can buy a whole herd of hippos if they want them."

"Then it's somebody else. I'm going over to the enclosure and take another look. Wanta come?"

Helen had never before received an invitation from Two. That softened her heart toward her even more. And she admired the gumption Two had displayed since her fall, and was beginning to understand that she was smart as well as athletic. She was worried for Two's future and for how she'd turn out. Helen understood life can suddenly change for the worse. She knew all about making hard adjustments, and she saw many of those in Two's future. Also, Two's theory could be a way to see Clive.

He hadn't mentioned Dinah's death at the party, but no doubt it was still on his mind. She said, "Have you told Mr. Lovett?"

"I told Mr. Shelton that Dinah could've been killed by electricity. But I didn't realize it had to be murder until I was talking with Adam."

"Adam?"

Two blushed. A stupid mistake. Talking to a buffalo sounded too Indian. However, Mr. Lovett talked to animals all the time. And it was clear that he and Miz Hampton were smitten. "The big buffalo. I know him from Oklahoma. The Millers boarded him for Mr. Cody. We visit a lot."

Two and Helen passed Sunday picnickers, a potato sack race, and a rope pull on their way to the mound over Dinah. The sky was overcast, but the humidity high. By the time they arrived, both were beaded with sweat. Helen patted her face with her hankie. Two used her bandana. When she was through, she folded it, and trying to tie it around her forehead, dropped a crutch. Helen picked it up and handed it to her. Two said, "Let's look at the electrical setup."

The box at the base of the pole was gray, about four feet high, a foot thick, and two and a half feet wide. A line ran into its back, and its door was padlocked. Two looked from the box to the mound and from the box to where the platform had been. She did that more than once. Found it hard to envision how anyone could rig an electrocution. She said, "They'd have to open the box, tie a copper wire in there, and string it into the water."

"Wouldn't they get killed doing that?"

"There's a lever inside to turn off the current."

"How do you know that?" Electricity was a mystery to Helen.

"The 101's filled with electricity. Just like here. We have our own power plant."

Helen tried to envision that. She'd always thought of the 101 as prairie grass, buffalo, and tipis.

Two said, "He either had to snake the wire through the fence under the platform or throw it over the dirt barrier. Or, maybe, take it up the platform and throw it down from there. But the stairs had a gate. And it would've been locked to keep the visitors out. I saw that lock the other day."

"That's a lot of copper wire," Helen said. "Is it expensive?"

Two shook her head. "I don't know. But that'd be two locks to pick." She bit her bottom lip. Maybe she was wrong. It'd take a lot of wire either route. And why would anyone kill Dinah?

When Two and Helen returned to Chambliss, Clive and another man were sitting in rockers on the porch near the front door. They stood for the women. Clive and Helen grinned in ways that looked goofy on respectable people, but Two didn't notice because she was trying to recall where she'd seen the other fellow. In the park for certain; not at the shooting gallery, but somewhere else, and recently. He said, "Miss Two Feathers, I'm Edgar Maxwell from the *Banner*. I wonder if ya would be so kind as to give me an interview?"

He was the newspaper photographer. And she was sweaty and not dressed in her best. She looked for his camera. It sat on the boards next to his hat. She said, "I guess. Could I refresh?"

"Take your time. Mr. Lovett and I've been catching up."

When Two returned, the three were sipping lemonade and swapping hippopotamus death theories. Helen poured Two a drink, and Two told Clive and Edgar stories of electrocutions on the range, adding one which she hadn't told Helen and that produced a full pond of dead fish and three or four snakes with their bellies turned up and fried. The subject moved to the price of copper wire. Edgar supplied that answer — neither cheap nor pricey, and easy to obtain. Then Clive said, "This is all speculation. I trust you won't put it in the paper."

Edgar hesitated. He hadn't been taking notes, but the bones of an article were assembling in his mind. On the other hand, there wasn't much to go on, and a hippopotamus murder was unlikely to the point of preposterous. He said, "Nothing really to write up. But if ya do find the cause, will ya tell me before the *Tennessean*?"

Clive knew Luke Lea well. They were friends, and he couldn't be a turncoat to his employer's son-in-law. But he thought, regardless of their speculations, Dinah had most likely died of natural causes. He said, "If we have a murdered hippo, you'll be the first to know."

Soon afterwards, Clive and Helen left on a stroll, and Two and Maxwell moved to more secluded chairs on the northeast side of the porch. Two had improved her looks by toweling her hair, flipping it forward and back, applying rouge, changing her blouse, and donning a silk scarf. She gave a lot of interviews, always dressed for the camera, and was happy to be moving away from the subject of death.

Maxwell started by asking how she came to take up diving, what Doc Carver was really like, and how horses are trained to dive into water. All routine questions, all practiced answers. Two was careful only when she responded to a question about liking the park. The *Banner* had never gone after Glendale. But the newspaper feud was hot, and with a tiny spark, could spread like fire through dry woods. Two said she enjoyed working at Glendale. Said it was "magical" and "entertaining." "The best place near Nashville for all-around fun." That was the routine storyline on the park, and it was certainly true for the visitors.

Then Maxwell asked, "What do ya remember about falling into the cave?"

A turn to a more serious topic came in every good interview. Two had expected it in some form, but hadn't anticipated exactly which. She took a long sip of lemonade. Blotted her mouth with a napkin, and said, "It was quick."

"What was it like in there?"

Two set her glass on a table between the chairs. "Didn't Mr. Lovett tell you?"

"No. The story is yours."

"He was the hero."

"We ran something about him when it happened. I wanta get your point of view. And your plans."

"My main plan is to get out of this cast." She lifted her leg with both hands and moved it about an inch to the left.

"What then?"

"I plan to keep performing. I've fallen off more horses than most people have petted dogs." Two's fingers moved to her scarf. She fingered the knot.

"More diving?" Maxwell looked up from taking notes.

"Probably not."

"Ya know for sure?"

Two's voice pitched higher. "I've never lost a horse before. In fact, in the several decades of diving, Ocher's the only horse that's ever been killed. She'd be hard to replace."

"But there are other diving horses."

"Sure."

Maxwell scratched his cheek with his eraser. "Feel guilty?" he asked.

"I didn't open the earth up," Two said quickly. She'd seen plenty of performers lose control of interviews. Reporters always went for that, and she didn't want to fall into Maxwell's trap. But she hadn't talked much about losing Ocher, and the bottled-up words spilled out. "No performer wants her horse killed. They're people. Not just part of an act. It's like losing a sister."

"A sister?"

Two paused. She wished she hadn't said that. It wasn't accurate. She'd been closer to Ocher than to either of her sisters, and the loyalty was different. She said, "Ya have a dog?"

Maxwell nodded.

"Like him?"

"The best birder I've ever had."

"Ya hunt ever' day?"

Maxwell shook his head. "Wish I could."

"I rode Ocher every day. She did things for me that few horses can do. Barely ever balked. Just dove. Kicked me once, but by accident. A person gets a horse like that once in a lifetime. Maybe twice, if you're lucky. A horse like Ocher's more like a husband than a sister. A good husband. Not a jerk."

Maxwell felt blood rush toward his lap. He shifted in his seat. Two was damn attractive. And tears were coming up in her eyes. He wanted to brush them away. Instead, he said, "Tell me more about that."

Two put a knuckle to her tears. Tilted her head up. Spoke with more force. "There's not any more to say. I'll get back on a horse as soon as I'm released for riding. I've been getting back on horses all my life. My daddy's a cowboy. I fell off my first horse when I was three. He lifted me back on. Said he wouldn't lift me off 'til I stopped crying. By then, I didn't want to get off. We just rode on."

"Your parents let a three-year-old ride?"

"I could walk. Why wouldn't I ride?" Two sounded a little offended, but felt back in control.

Maxwell recognized that. But liked the new open path. "Your daddy a real cowboy?"

"Yeah. And so are my grandfathers."

"Your folks really Indians? Or is Two Feathers a stage name?"

"Both. We're really Indians, and Two Feathers is a stage name."

"What's your real name?"

"I don't want that published."

"I won't publish it. I'm just curious."

Two looked sideways at Maxwell. He was a dirty blond. Clean-shaven, with lines between his cheeks and his nose, but maybe not as old as she'd first reckoned. His fingers were long and thin for a man, and not tobacco-stained. She said, "Why aren't you in church with your family this morning?"

"I don't go to church as regular as most. The newspaper business doesn't keep normal hours."

"What about your three daughters? Ya don't set an example?"

Maxwell's chin touched his collar. He squinted. "I don't have three daughters. At least, I hope I don't."

"Oh. I thought . . ." Two waved a hand.

"Thought what?"

"I ran into three girls a few days ago. They said their father would have his newspaper do a story."

Maxwell laughed. "Those were probably the Cain sisters. Do I look elderly enough to have produced three daughters that old?"

Two couldn't really tell how old white people were. "I guess not."

"Guess not? I'm thirty."

"Oh." Blood rushed to Two's neck. She added, "I'm sorry."

Beyond the porch railing, Little Elk had listened to all the talking, and kept his eye on Two to be sure the white man didn't do anything to her. But his mind lingered on the first part of the conversation. It didn't make complete sense. He'd grown accustomed to the wires on the poles in the park. Figured out they had something to do with the awful lights, but didn't understand how they worked. However, he did understand large animals could be killed by lightning; he'd seen that. He always stayed far away from water when the thunder boys were out and about. And it didn't seem implausible to him that someone would kill a large animal for no reason at all. White people did that all the time. And though he hadn't seen him recently, he was pretty sure who the culprit was. He quickly formed a resolve to find that redheaded, twitchy, dirty-as-a-snake Pale Jump, and grow strong enough to kill him. Little Elk fingered his pouch and felt the power of his stolen tobacco. He also felt sure that he knew the reason he'd returned this time. To kill the murderous night-going witch. To save the woman and animals. His chest puffed up, and his eyes and lips went to slits.

Visits

Maxwell's article about Two in the next afternoon's paper was flattering, and accompanied by a picture taken against the porch railing that, at her request, didn't include her cast. Paired with those was another piece announcing the preliminary trials for the big turtle race, instructions for turtle purchases, and turtle racing rules, those gotten from Two, as nobody else yet knew what they were. Two spent the evening in a circle of attention, more comfortable in her skin than she'd been since her fall. She went to bed feeling like herself again, and dreamed of a new act on horseback, shooting glass balls thrown by the Montgomery sisters riding horses of their own. It was an old routine, performed long before Two's birth by Lillian Smith, Buffalo Bill, and Annie Oakley. But it was new to Two, and in her dream at the end of the act, Annie herself hung a medal and a ribbon around her neck. Two awoke feeling like she'd been blessed by Little Sure Shot. And that blessing wasn't dissipated by breakfast, two cups of coffee, and the awake awareness that neither of the Montgomerys had ever been on a horse.

When she met Crawford at the cistern, he was also chirpingly cheerful. Really, for the second day in a row. On Sunday, he and Bonita had taken in a baseball game at Greenwood Park. It'd been an unchaperoned outing, as the other Boydstuns had Sunday dinner with friends, and those lingered into the late afternoons. He'd also seen Two's write-up, had cut it out, and asked her to autograph her picture for Bonita's little sister. He was charming the entire Boydstun family.

When Two started out on her visiting rounds, she purchased a sack of peanuts to feed to Tom Noddy. But, not being able to shake Dinah's death out of her mind, she first headed Gay to the mound over the dead hippo. She sat in the cart pondering her theory until she heard the giggles of a gaggle of women swinging picnic baskets between them. She was recognized, and signed a few stray pieces of paper they scrambled up for autographs. They were part of an Eastern Star chapter in Nashville, at the park for a convention, contests, and conviviality. Two wished the women luck in their afternoon games and races, then turned toward the bears' enclosure.

There, she found Clive in the first stages of the chewing gum trick. Zana was on her hind feet, cupping her left paw toward her body as though she were beckoning him in for a cup of tea. Clive was holding a green-and-white-striped Juicy Fruit package high in the air, rubbing his chin with his own hand, pretending he couldn't decide whether he should open it or not. This display of paws on both of their parts continued until the crowd grew to about fifty. At which point Clive tore open the pack and, with a flourish, pulled out a stick of gum sealed in white paper. He slipped the pack in his pocket and held the stick conspicuously in the air. He waved it under his nose, sniffed loudly, lifted and lowered his shoulders, and sighed, Chaplinesque, as though he were dying of pleasure. Zana tapped her claws together and grunted encouragement for her keeper to unwrap the gum.

The crowd stayed silent, but during the pantomime, Tom Noddy waddled up behind Clive and gently nipped at his trousers. Clive turned and said, "Tom, you naughty boy! Do you want gum, too?"

Tom shook his head. Clive said, "Of course not. It's always peanuts for you."

But even though Two had exactly what Tom liked, the Indian act feeding peanuts to the juvenile cinnamon bear would distract from the main attraction. Two was too respectful of other performers to do that. And knew she should've come earlier, and she would come back first thing in the morning. She turned her cart away, went back to the concession stand, bought a hot dog and lemonade, and ate with Adam.

Little Elk rode on Gay's back through Two's travels. While she communed with Adam, he leaned against a wheel, sharpening his knife on the whetstone he carried and preparing for his confrontation with the witch when he eventually found him. He didn't have enough tobacco to try to appear, but he enjoyed being with his friends. Visiting seemed like old times to him. The buffalo smell, the grass, the sunshine, protecting the female. His world was in harmony, for a change. He was so content he didn't mind that he was neither here nor there, but caught in between. He had a purpose and some companionship. He could've enjoyed the visit forever, but Two told Adam they'd see each other again, gathered her reins, and said to Gay, "To the barn."

Little Elk knew Two would visit with the black man and probably play a game. He trusted Crawford to protect her, and the buffalo enclosure was close to the Oriental Golf Club. Instead of hopping on Gay's back, he took off toward the club in search of tobacco. He'd been visiting there twice a day, and had recently discovered how to open the porch door. By the time the sun dipped in the west, the ashtrays were always filled with butts and, occasionally, entire packages of tobacco sticks were left unattended. Little Elk didn't know his stealing those was causing a commotion among the club's members. Even one fistfight, as it didn't occur to anyone that the thief was a spirit. But if Little Elk had known the hubbub he was creating, it would've filled him with pleasure.

He was back guarding Two that evening when Edgar Maxwell climbed the steps of Chambliss and walked over to her and Helen; when he took a seat next to Two; commented on the weather and complimented Helen on how well she ran the hall; when Helen complimented Edgar on his article; when he said he had a good subject, cut his eyes at Two, cocked his chin, and grinned. Little Elk suddenly discerned the white man's intentions. The no-good, foul-smelling, invading, low-down skunk. Little Elk growled. Then pulled his pipe out of his pouch, stuffed it with tobacco, and walked around the front of the hall over to the lightning-struck tree. He slipped inside its hollow trunk and used a match he'd lifted at the club. He puffed and puffed. Thought about the skunk. Asked lightning for strength. Prayed to the thunder boys. Looked at his arm. Saw his leather bracelet quite clearly. But he could always see himself. That didn't mean anyone else could.

However, Little Elk felt visible. Not invincible, but certainly solid. He thought there was a good chance he could be seen and scare the white skunk off the porch and away from Two Feathers. He arose from the hollow and jerked his war club out of his belt. He intended only to raise it, not strike; still, he tested its tip with his finger. The bone was still sharp. The weapon had been made by his grandfather. Little Elk gave thanks to his elder for it, said a prayer, and went off around the back of the hall so as to approach from the least traveled side of the building.

When he got to the east side of the porch, the Englishman had joined the group. He was Two Feathers' friend, and in Little Elk's parents' time, the British had been the Cherokees' staunch allies. Little Elk didn't want to scare him. But the skunk's chair was pulled even closer to Two's, and that was maddening. Little Elk scowled. They all were talking and laughing. Little Elk backed away from the building and out into the open space of the lawn.

He jumped up, down, and spun around. He swung his war stick. Made terrible frowns. Stopped only to piercingly scream. And when he did that, the people on the porch stopped talking. They all looked toward him. The Englishman rose. Pointed in his direction. Two stood, too. The skunk and the older woman rose, also. Those two squinted and shook their heads, but Two's eyes grew wide. She grabbed the Englishman's arm and said something in his ear. She looked out again at the lawn. She nodded.

Little Elk became quite still. Finally, he'd been seen. Relief flooded his body. He began weeping. He let his tears flow freely until they clouded his vision so he couldn't see Two clearly. He brushed the water from his eyes with his knuckles. Stood proud. Raised his war stick high. Held his other fist against his chest. Sang to the sky.

Later, Two had trouble falling asleep. The Indian had been so unexpected, so startling, and so real. Wide awake in her bed, she brought up and examined ghost stories she'd heard. Stories about dead 101 cowboys, old Indian spirits, and newly murdered Osage seeking revenge. Also, stories about witches. Two wished she knew how witches worked. As a child when asking, she'd been ignored. But never told they weren't real. She recalled frequent smudgings. And Wild Indians dancing for cleansing, wearing masks, and calling spirits. Her mind, wrestling with images, was blown around. She began spinning. Her grandmother's hand touched her arm. Her palm stilled Two's motion. She breathed more regularly, and felt anchored as securely as a tent tethered to the ground by strong poles, ropes, and stakes.

Two thought more about who she'd seen on the lawn. A bare-chested Indian, wearing moccasins to over his knees, a cloth and a sash, but no leggings, no hunting shirt. But definitely tattoos, a topknot and feather, and ears stretched slightly in the ancient tradition. His face was painted for war. She tried, but couldn't recall the colors. Maybe she hadn't caught them in the dusky light. But she could recall a war club. She'd seen him hold it to the sky. She'd heard his cry.

And Clive had seen him, too. He'd nodded in response to her question, had quietly said, "Yes," and had asked the others if they saw a man in the distance that looked like an Indian. They hadn't. So Clive had told Helen and Edgar he must be mistaken. That must be a deer out there. They all sat back down. So did the Indian. He'd hunkered and stared.

Helen said there hadn't been any Indians living in the vicinity since the mysterious race disappeared. The land wasn't inhabited when the pioneers settled there.

Two was acquainted with that lie. She knew that unless there was an actual roundhouse, wigwam, tipi, or longhouse sitting on an exact spot, whites considered all land unpeopled and free for the stealing. And although it was the sorest of subjects, Two had decided not to debate that with Miz Hampton. The ignorance was too useful to whites and too deep to overcome. And she didn't want to start a fight. Miz Hampton had been kind. Besides, Two was so taken with the Indian on the lawn that she couldn't waste the time.

The talk among the others on the porch had moved to deer. How thick they were in the woods. How often they grazed in the park in early morning mist. Particularly in winter when the zoo was closed up and the caged animals were sheltered in the casino, barns, and animal house. The Indian had kept his eyes on Two. And she'd tried to keep hers on him, even though Edgar was vying for her attention. Finally, it became too hard to attend to both men, and she'd excused herself, blaming weariness due to her leg. When she left the porch, she nodded to the Indian. He lifted his chin to her.

At
the
Bears'
Den

During the week, the last trolley of the evening between the Oriental Golf Club and the park's entrance was often empty. So Jack, who didn't want to be remembered, took the next to the last one, which always had riders. Earlier, he'd gone out of his way to buy peanuts at the downtown Transfer Station for the same reason. When he disembarked at the park, he pulled his cap as far down over his face as he could without exposing too much red hair on the back of his head. His satchel was secured under his left arm by a strap across his body. It was heavy, but not enough to slow him down. He skirted the congestion and glare of the main entrance by melting into the woods rimming the hill above the creek. He stayed in the trees until the park's lights were dimmed. Then he made his way to the bears' den by the moon's shine and the big bulbs atop the electrical poles that were made even hazier by swarming moths.

He was twining copper wire inside the electrical box when Tom Noddy smelled the peanuts. He waddled to the bars and grumbled. Jack was startled, turned, and said, "Shhhhh." Tom lowered his voice to a whine. Jack said, "Okay. Here." He opened the bag, stepped to the iron ribs of the cage, and threw a few nuts over Tom's head. That distracted the little bear until Jack could finish in the box, straighten the wire, and feed it through the bars.

Tom, roly-poly and still growing, was always hungry. Always happy to see the creatures that carried the food. He wanted more peanuts. He stood on his hind feet, held on to a bar with a paw, and tilted his head. Jack threw more nuts to Tom's right, so he'd have to move over to get them. Then he set the sack down, pulled in his stomach, and slipped through the bars into the cage. Though the bears knew him, he didn't want to spend much time in the den. Any of them could get cranky fast, and Zana, like Tom, was awake and roaming. Jack picked up the wire, took three long strides to the bathtub, and stuck the line's end in the water. He was afraid it would plop out when Tom climbed in, so he laid in a little more. Then he realized a bear could knock the line out just by walking, so he looked around. He saw a small log. He pulled the wire out of the tub, laid the log on top of it, and bent the copper wire to climb up the side of the enamel and over into the water. He stood back and assessed his work. He wanted to use his flashlight, but didn't feel he could risk it. Tom nipped at his pants. Jack said, "Hold your horses."

Jack slipped back through the bars, went to the electrical box, flipped the lever, and wiped it off with a rag. He picked up his sack of peanuts, returned to the cage, and gave one to Tom. Tom wanted another. Jack supplied it. Then he said, "Can you fetch?" He threw a peanut toward the tub. Tom turned, snatched it off the ground, and turned around for another. Jack threw that one a little closer to the tub. Tom gobbled it. The third peanut hit the water. Tom looked toward Jack. Took a step in his direction. Jack said, "Catch!" He threw a peanut that hit Tom's snout. Tom batted the air. Jack threw another peanut that hit in the water. Tom looked to the peanut on the ground, to Jack, and then to the tub. Jack threw another one in. It sounded like a little fish gulping. Tom put his front paws and a hind leg on the rim of the tub. When his nose hit the water, his body went rigid.

• • •

Little Elk sniffed and caught an odor from his distant past that was faint, but so novel he recognized it instantly. Burnt bear. He knew the direction without sniffing twice. Then he heard a howl. He recognized Zana's voice, but had never heard her use that particular growl. However, in his last lifetime he'd certainly heard it from bears, and he recognized it as a yell of extreme distress. Little Elk jerked into motion. He ran over the rattling buffalo tracks, past the bandstand and casino, and down the slope toward the bear pit. His moccasins hit cement. He fled down the path that curved around the cave. He saw Pale Jump hunched over his bag.

Little Elk stopped so fast that he tilted forward and then backwards. Zana was still howling. Flailing her arms. The other bears were standing up at the bars, pacing, and roaring. They were making quite a racket. Pale Jump rose and said something harsh to the bears, trying to hush them. Little Elk jerked his war stick out of his belt. He planted his feet wide to steady himself and said a prayer as he lifted his arm. He threw with the precision of eons of practice.

Jack felt the deer antler strike just below his left clavicle. He dropped the wire, fell to his knees, and clutched his chest. He thought he'd accidentally electrocuted himself. He groaned and moaned. He tried hard not to yell. He twisted, jerked, and crumpled on down to the ground, pulled his knees up to his stomach, clutched his chest with his hands, and clenched his teeth. The pain shot all the way to the base of his spine. Little Elk closed in and kicked him in the rear. Jack screamed, and his hands flew from his chest to his buttocks, giving Little Elk a chance to grab his war stick without a struggle. He raised it again, and he lowered it fast into Jack's chest. Jack's body lurched, twisted, lurched again, then suddenly stiffened. He cried out softly. He slowly unfurled and relaxed.

Little Elk pressed a foot into Jack's groin. He tugged his stick out of his chest. Touched the tip of the antler to see if it was damaged. He thanked his grandfather for picking a strong buck. Then he thanked the deer spirit. He slipped his weapon back in his belt, and turned to Jack's bag. He rummaged though it until he found tobacco sticks and matches.

Then he sat down, howled with the bears, and smoked to gather his strength while Pale Jump's first soul remained trapped in his head.

Little Elk fiddled with the wire just to see what it would do. He decided it was like sinew. It could be very handy. He drew his knife out to cut a piece off, but stopped. That could dull his blade, and he had more work to do. He'd better get to it. He stood. Spread his legs and grabbed Jack's hair in the front. Then he stopped again. The bears were growling so loudly they could wake the night watchman up. Little Elk didn't want to kill anyone he didn't have to and he didn't want to be interrupted.

He slung the bag over his shoulder, turned his back to Jack's body, and lifted his legs by his ankles. He dragged Jack behind him as he headed toward the woods. As soon as he was sure the body was concealed by trees, he dropped Jack's legs and slung the satchel off his shoulder. He moved to Jack's head, lifted it by the hair, and made his cut left to right. He placed a foot on Jack's shoulder, gritted his teeth, and ripped. Then he turned and sprinted out of the trees. When he got to the edge of the woods, he tore a branch off a pine and swished it along the ground as he made his way back to the den. Then he dropped the branch, lifted the scalp high over his head, and waved it for the bears to see. By then, his tobacco was wearing off. He was getting weaker by the minute and less able to maintain his grip on the material world.

It
Gets
Worse

≋

Upon waking, Two's mind went immediately to the Indian on the lawn. In fact, he'd been in her dreams, and her waking just extended her nighttime visions of him. She felt the Indian had come for her, and she wanted to see him again. To find out who he was and what he had to say. She knew from his clothing, or lack thereof, that he was a pre-Removal Cherokee. But she didn't think he was a witch. He seemed too earnest and friendly. Although she reminded herself that witches come in disguise. She could need to smudge. Take a precaution that wouldn't offend a friendly spirit, but would shoo away an evil one. She was thinking about gathering bark and twigs when a knock came on the door. Franny's voice floated though, "You awake, Two?"

"Yeah. Come on in."

Franny stopped at the end of Two's bed and rested a hand on the post. "Sleep well?"

Two had propped herself up on her elbows. "Once I got there. What's up?"

"Mr. Orr's here to see you."

"Who's he?"

"Remember the lemur? He's the big security guy."

"What's he want?"

"I'm not sure. He and Mrs. Hampton are in the west front parlor with the door closed. And Mr. Lovett arrived while Mrs. Hampton was telling me to get you."

"Something's happened."

"Yeah. I don't know what. But they're all acting weird. As soon as they tell you, I want to hear."

When Clive opened the parlor door, his eyes were strangely wide. Two interpreted that as a sign to be wary. She greeted and was greeted. Took a seat next to Helen and rested her crutches against the side of the sofa. Leo Orr was standing, but Clive sat, too. He leaned forward in his chair and rested his forearms on his thighs. "Two. I have some bad news. Tom Noddy has died."

"Died?"

"Yes. In the bear tub."

"But he wasn't three years old."

"Yes, I know. But, nevertheless, he's dead and in water."

Helen said, "I've told Mr. Orr your theory about Dinah."

Two's lip trembled. But her gray eyes were steady. "There's a murderer loose. Electrocuting our animals. He'll kill 'em all if he's not caught."

Clive sat up straight, ran a palm over his mouth, and then said, "That may very well be the case. But there's something else."

"If ya don't mind, sir. I'll take it from here." Orr was at the window across from Two, holding a burlap sack. He added, "Miz Hampton, ya might wanta leave."

Helen rose slightly, then eased back down, hoping Orr hadn't noticed her motion. "I was married to a physician. You'd be surprised at what I've seen." She sounded slightly offended.

"I respect that, ma'am," Orr replied. "But it ain't pretty." He'd been so repulsed he couldn't chew his gum.

"I'll leave if I need too." Helen jutted her chin.

"If ya say so." Orr shook his head and stuck his hand in the sack. "When we found this, first we thought it were part of Tom Noddy's hide." He drew out red hair and skin crusted with blood. "But it ain't exactly the right color."

Two had never seen a fresh scalp, but she instantly knew what it was. And who it belonged to. She said, "Did ya find his body?"

"No, we been looking. Thought maybe ya'd have an idea."

Two blinked rapidly and twitched. "Why would ya think that?"

Orr dropped Jack's scalp back in the sack. "Well, yer the only Indian in these parts."

Two was so shocked her breath was knocked. When she caught it again, she grabbed her crutches, stood, and swung them in place. When she steadied, she said directly to Orr, "Have you lost your mind?"

Clive had risen with Two. "He doesn't think you killed Older, Two. It's just that it appears to be his hair. And he has a history of bothering you. Helen and I've told Mr. Orr we were on the porch together last night. That you were exhausted and went in and straight to bed."

"Not to mention that she's on crutches," Helen said. "Although I have mentioned it, I think now, twice." She frowned at Orr.

"Even if I wasn't on crutches, I wouldn't be scalping anyone. I'd shoot 'em at a distance."

"Shoot 'em?" Orr's eyebrows lifted.

"Yeah. Shooting is one of the things I do for a living."

"Hum," Orr said. "Well, we don't know he weren't shot. We don't have a body."

"You don't have a body!" Two's eyes were egg-wide. "So, let me get this straight. You think I slipped out of my room, shot Jack Older, scalped him, and hid his body? On crutches? Really?"

Orr frowned. "No, I actually don't. I jist don't know what to think. And yer the only person around here who knows about scalping."

"I don't know a thing about scalping. Though I'm tempted to learn." Two twisted toward the door and took a giant step.

Clive said, "Two, please stay. Mr. Orr didn't mean to insult you. We have a dead hippopotamus and a dead bear. Now we have a scalp and probably a dead man somewhere. It's a distressing situation. Tell us, you do agree that's Jack Older's hair, right?"

Two had turned back around. She huffed, paused, bit her bottom lip. "It appears to be. But I didn't kill him. And I don't even know if he's actually dead. People can survive scalping."

Helen said, "That's true. There were one or two famous cases right downtown."

"When was that?" Orr asked.

"Back in . . . Never mind. It doesn't matter. It was a long time ago."

Clive said, "Leo, Miss Feathers has answered your questions. Please go back and join the search. Ensure nobody tells anybody anything. We can't have a rumor of a murder when we don't even have a body. I'll tell Mr. Shackleford. Call up to his house if you find anything. But don't let on 'til I'm on the phone."

Orr held the sack out. "Ya want the evidence?"

Clive shook his head and waved a hand. "You keep that. I can't imagine he'll want to see it."

Clive wanted to speak with Two privately. But Helen remained after Leo left, and there wasn't a way forward. So he called Longview, was told that James had left for work, but that May could talk to him. That suited Clive, and he spoke with her briefly. Then he told Two that Crawford was busy with the search, but if she wanted to walk the park, to tell Helen where she was going, and he'd locate her later. He bid them goodbye and hurried for the trolley as showers started.

May had alerted Adelaide about the need for tea and shortbreads, and by the time she and Clive entered James's study, a silver pot, the necessary equipment, and warm cookies (or biscuits) were on a tray on James's desk. May had chosen his study to ensure privacy, and she was curious and uneasy. As soon as she closed the door, she said, "You said there's a problem in the park." She pointed to the tray.

"I'm afraid so." Clive secured a cup between his thumb and forefinger. "Thank you."

She poured his tea, and set the plate of goodies on a table between chairs in front of the desk. "Have a shortbread and tell me."

"Thank you. They look delicious." Clive poured his own milk in and stirred. He waited until May was seated, and said, "Unfortunately, we've lost Tom Noddy." He took the other chair.

"The juvenile bear?"

"Yes. The little red one."

May picked her cup up, but didn't drink. "He was quite an attraction. How?"

"Apparently, he was electrocuted. John found him in the bears' bathing tub early this morning."

"Electrocuted?" May winced. "Fried?"

"Probably not fried. But stunned into a heart attack. I haven't seen his body."

"How do you know he was electrocuted?"

"Miss Two Feathers figured it out."

"She saw his body?"

"No. Let me back up. Two has seen cattle that were electrocuted during storms. Out on the range. And you remember Dinah died for no apparent reason. She was also in water."

"But she'd been sick."

"Only with worms. And we had those on the run. Otherwise, she was a young, healthy animal. And she up and died suddenly. Two became suspicious. I don't know why. But she communicated that suspicion to others, and they to me. The important point is that Dinah died in water and there was an electrical box nearby."

"So somebody killed her?"

"I believe so. Then, this morning, Tom turns up dead. Again, a young, healthy animal dead in water. An electrical box nearby."

"How would that be done?"

"Probably with copper wire. It's easy to string, and it's a brilliant conductor. Remember Topsy, the elephant?"

"Who could forget that? But wasn't she also poisoned?"

"I don't know. I was still living in England at the time. But it was the electricity that did her in. I've seen the film of her death. It's perfectly horrid." They were talking about a female elephant killed on Coney Island in 1903.

May had also seen the film. Everybody had. She said, "Oh, dear. Then the other animals aren't safe. We need to call James immediately."

"There's more."

May set her cup down. Looked at a shortbread and decided against it. "Go on. Tell me."

"Well, as I said, John found Tom's body. He found something else, too. Outside the enclosure. Really, rather close to the electrical box, he found, ah . . ." Clive winced. He looked down at the plate of biscuits, then up to the ceiling. "I don't know exactly how to put this."

"It can't be that bad."

"It is, rather."

May clasped her hands. "Clive, nothing you can say will be unbearable to me."

Clive looked back at May. She'd suffered. That was why he felt a connection to her. "John found a scalp. It was red. With blood, of course; but also, the hair was red. He thought it was part of Tom Noddy's hide and went back into the enclosure to check. He tried turning Tom in the tub, but he couldn't manage it. A dead bear, even a small one, weighs quite a lot. And the other bears were extremely agitated. He had to get out. But in doing that, John recognized that the hair of the scalp wasn't exactly the same color of red as Tom's coat. And that it wasn't the hair of a bear."

"I see. That's remarkable." May looked at the veins on the backs of her hands. Looked up. "Where was the body?"

"Hum. Well, that's another problem. Duncan and Leo Orr are in charge of the search. But, so far, we haven't found a body."

"But you will. Have you called the police?"

Clive winced. Picked up a biscuit, but didn't lift it to his lips. "Not yet. One wouldn't call the police over a dead bear." He settled the biscuit back on the plate.

May looked up at shelves of books. Their spines were dark and perfectly aligned. James wouldn't take the news well. There hadn't been a murder in the park since . . . when was it? James Jr., William, and Shirley were still alive. Before 1908. Probably 1907. Before Clive's time. She looked back at him. "The last murder here was a sordid affair. A man shot another one over a woman. It happened near the trolley tracks. But they took him to the skating rink and laid him out there. Trying to save his life under better lights, I guess. His blood discolored the planks."

Clive looked at his biscuit again.

"I don't know why I said that. The stains weren't important. I just recall them. And the ruckus they caused. For the first couple of days there was a lot of screaming at the rink. Then when new planks were laid, they weren't the same color as the old ones. And people got into shoving each other over them. Caused falls and scraped knees. The whole section had to be redone." She held a palm in the air, "Sorry. I did it again." The palm went to her hair. "What're you going to do? James, you know, wouldn't want the police."

"They may not be necessary. I'm not entirely sure we'll find a body."

"You think someone survived a scalping?"

"Helen and Two say that's possible. But, no, I don't."

"What do you think, then?"

Clive got up and set his cup on the tray. He walked behind the desk to a painting of a white house with six columns and a wide porch with four rockers on it. On each side were trellises twined with vines. In the front was a large tree with low branches dripping with moss. Clive knew the painting was a representation of the home James had lived in as a small child. Done by an artist who'd never seen it, as the house had been razed and no pictures had survived. James and Alex, his brother, had directed the artist with only their memories. Clive thought about how most things are lost to time. Unless somehow, someway, they're resurrected by somebody.

He turned. "The ghost here in Longview. Is he capable of mischief?"

"Mischief? You mean like the Bell Witch?"

"Yes, exactly."

"No. That witch drove nearly all of Robertson County crazy. And she poisoned John Bell and ruined Betsy Bell's engagement. My ghost, other than when he was angry over the monument, has usually been quite docile. I believe he's lonely. Wants to go on. Or come back. Whichever. He wants companionship, I think."

"Remember I told you I've seen a ghost guarding Two? Well, last night he appeared so substantially on the lawn that she finally saw him. But Helen and a newspaper fellow, Edgar Maxwell, from the *Banner*, were there also, and they couldn't see him."

May tucked a strand of hair under a comb. Patted it in place. She cleared her throat. "That's fortunate. The *Banner* will do anything to discredit us all. But how do you know Miss Feathers saw him?"

"She whispered to me, 'You see him.' I then asked the others. They hadn't seen a thing. So I told them I must have seen a fawn on the lawn."

"That was clever thinking. But what does it have to do with the scalp?"

Clive came out from behind the desk, picked up a biscuit, and bit into it. He sat down again in his chair, chewing and trying to figure what phrasing to use.

May interjected into the quiet. "You think the Indian spirit scalped and, presumably, killed someone, don't you?"

"Rather specifically, I think he scalped and killed a man named Jack Older."

May's chin receded into her neck. "Why?"

"To protect the animals, probably. Jack worked for me. He seemed like an upright fellow. Degree from U.T. I thought he was a good hire.

Much more educated than most. But he let our lemur, Mickey, loose in Chambliss Hall, and John had to fire him."

May picked up a shortbread. Dipped it into her tea. "Why would he let a lemur loose in a dormitory?" She bit her cookie.

"Probably to get Two Feathers' attention. It caused quite the ruckus."

May chewed slowly and swallowed. Said, "I can imagine that."

"Jack is a redhead. Or was."

"And, apparently, sweet on Miss Feathers?"

"Apparently."

"Well, the Bell Witch killed John Bell as certainly as we're sitting here. And she had quite strong opinions on romance. What should we do?"

"I don't know. We may not find a body. If we do, I presume we should call the police."

May winced. "Let me think about that." She laid her cookie remnant on a plate. Rose and went to the window. The showers had stopped and the sun was peeking through. Clive picked up his teacup and sipped. Poured more tea and milk for himself. Finally, May turned from the window. She said, "I don't pretend to have the same kind of experiences you did in the trenches. I try not to even imagine them. But I was raised in an occupied city during a war. As a mere child, I heard men screaming in hospital beds. Saw the dead stacked on carts and dumped in mass graves. Over at Fort Negley, there are about eight hundred dead emancipated slaves. The Federals worked them to death and then tossed their bodies into ditches and covered them up. They hoped everyone would forget, and many people have. There're also bodies in cellars all over town because it was too dangerous to leave our homes to bury our loved ones in cemeteries.

"If Mr. Older really was killed by an Indian ghost, nobody will believe that in this day and age. The investigation would go on and on. It'd be a cloud over Glendale, the park, and the zoo. We both know automobiles and moving pictures are eating into attendance. An unsolved murder could finish Glendale off. And that would be a shame. It's given so much pleasure to so many people for so long. It's truly a magical place. It has been for generations. If the body is found, Clive, I think it should be disposed of quietly. That's certainly been done before. It was almost a habit during the war."

"I see." Clive felt relieved. "Do you have any idea how to do that?"

May moved to the table. Picked up the remains of her shortbread. "No, frankly, I don't. But I'm fairly confident you can figure it out. I'm sure you have memories, yourself. I probably shouldn't know anything about it. And neither should James. He has enough on his mind worrying about Lewis." She set her cookie back down.

Clive wasn't happy about his charge. But he recognized that May was right about the effects an unsolved murder could have on the zoo, and recognized, too, that she was displaying confidence in him, not shirking responsibility. He said, "I'll think on it. We don't have the body yet. Maybe we never will."

Crawford
Investigates

≈

Crawford had been assigned the area below the bears' enclosure because he was the only man with his own horse, and because Duncan thought the murderer might've concealed the body in the cave. Crawford appreciated the mission. He wanted to return to the entrance again. Wanted to know if the smell had gone away. He went after the showers and closed the cattle guard, balancing if he should ride up to the farmhouse for permission to search or just hope not to get caught. The latter could conceivably get him shot. But mentioning a body was risky, and it rankled him to ask Karr's consent to ride in what he considered his own family's pasture. Also, Karr had turned cooperative the day Two had fallen into the cave and this time would recognize him. So Crawford swung a leg over Bang On and rode straight toward the creek.

He tied Bang On to a limb and walked to the underbrush. The creek was loud, probably some higher from the showers. When he found the stones to the entrance, he rolled up his pants, took off his brogans and socks, and carried them over, trying to grip the rocks with his toes. Safely across, he sat down on stones that had been moved to rescue Two, rolled down his khakis, dressed his feet, and sniffed. Damp, maybe mold, but no dead horse odor. Crawford ducked inside the mouth. Smelled more damp, dirt, and limestone. Stopped sniffing and started examining the ground as far as the light from the entrance permitted. No fresh tracks. No dragging marks. He walked back out and looked at the foliage. He should've inspected it before he'd gone in. But there were no traces of his own entry, so it probably didn't matter.

He found a narrow animal path that headed up toward the point below the bears' enclosure. He pushed limbs and leaves aside, stopped every few feet, and looked up. The body might've been rolled down the hill. Left to rot. If so, the odor wouldn't fly straight up. It would skim along the side of the hill with the wind. Dissipate before it reached the golf course. Or, if the breeze should turn a bit, before it reached the Bible school to the northwest.

Crawford was slowly fighting his way through the underbrush, holding back limbs and vines, feeling thankful the rain hadn't penetrated much, and looking around and up, when he saw above him on the hillside something unnatural and brown on the ground. He couldn't tell what it was. And he was figuring the best route to it when Bang On neighed. He neighed again. Crawford slipped his pocket knife out, opened it, and stuck it in his back pocket, tip down. He carefully descended the hill toward his horse.

Before he broke through the growth, he saw Karr next to Bang On. He watched the farmer study his horse. Prop his rifle against the tree, untie him, pick his gun back up, and start up the hill toward his house and barn, leading Bang On behind him. Crawford didn't want to startle Karr. And he didn't think the farmer was quite dumb enough to think he could get away with stealing his horse. He'd investigate the brown thing overhead before dealing with him. When Karr was out of hearing range, he began climbing again.

The unnatural brown thing was Jack's satchel. Crawford didn't approach it immediately because about four feet above it was Jack's body, legs splayed and arms askew. Crawford crept to it until he could see the whole thing. Jack's face was contorted, but worse, the top of his head was still bloody in spite of the showers. Crawford's breath became shallow. He bent over with his hands on his thighs. He huffed and huffed. When his breathing returned to normal, he looked to his side to avoid the bloody pate, uneven face, and spidery body. He focused on the satchel. He lurched to it, grabbed, and walked back toward the creek. After a few feet, he leaned against a tree, took some breaths, and started searching the bag.

The copper wire was rolled, except for an end sticking up. Next to it was a rag. Past it, deeper in, were wire clippers, a ring of keys, and a roll of tape. Crawford studied the keys. They were newly made. He wondered if Older had had them made before he was fired, or afterwards. He decided before, and that Older had probably been creeping around the park for a while, maybe planning his attacks. Or, maybe, not. He looked up the hill, toward the body. That might be something he'd never know. He looked back toward the pasture below and stood for a while, concocting a story for Karr. When he thought he had a believable one, he wound his way through the growth to a spot near the mouth of the cave. He descended from there.

He was smiling when Karr opened his cooling porch door. He said, "Good to see you, Mr. Karr. I believe you have my horse."

"That yours?"

"Yes, sir. Mr. Lovett sent me down to the cave. They're worried up there in the park about another break in the ground if they build over that spot. Thought it'd might be a good idea to look at the roof from down here."

"Find anything?"

"No, sir. Couldn't get past the rubble. Dead horse smell's gone, though. Nature takes her course." Crawford smiled more. Nodded his head to confirm all was right with the world.

Karr had recognized Bang On as soon as he'd gotten within twenty feet of the horse. And he wasn't reckoning on doing Crawford any harm. He just wanted to know what was going on. He said, "What's in that bag of yers?"

"Oh, just some tools, sir. I didn't know what I'd have to do in that cave."

That didn't seem exactly right to Karr. But it could be. Everybody knew Crawford could build or fix anything. He said, "Yer horse is in the lot behind the barn. My property line is thirty feet below the crest of the hill. The hillside and creek are mine."

"Yes, sir. I remember that well. I tagged along one day when Daddy and Mr. Shackleford walked it."

Karr rubbed a hand over his mouth.

From a distance, Crawford saw Clive, Shelton, and Orr on the front porch of Clive's cabin. Duncan and Leo were propped against rails, their backs to the park. Clive was leaning with a palm on the door frame. Crawford could tell they were conferring. Shelton had given him his assignment, so, technically, he needed to report to him. But he didn't have qualms about reporting to all three, and felt some pride about finding the body and pulling one over on Karr. He dismounted with a genuine smile on his face, not at all like the one he'd used on the farmer.

Clive intuited the smile's meaning. He held up his palm as Crawford got to the steps. "Crawford. I'll come to you in the barn."

Crawford's lips straightened. Duncan and Leo had turned around. Leo blew a bubble. Duncan said, "I assigned him to look in the cave for the body."

"Oh, I know. Crawford told me. But I pulled him off. We've got a Shetland I'm afraid we're going to have to put down. She's twisted her leg. It's infected and getting worse. She's in a lot of pain. If you'll go on to the barn, Crawford, I'll be there shortly. If we have to, we'll do the dirty deed together."

Crawford's face went blank, except for a smile at the corners of his mouth he just couldn't conceal. He said, "Yes sir," and walked off leading Bang On by the reins.

Where
to
Put
Him?

Clive startled Two. She was on the bench beneath the tree at the buffalo enclosure, thinking deeply and trying to get through to Adam. But she was so glad to see Clive that she scooted over and patted the wood. He sat down and took her hand. Side by side, from a distance they looked like a courting couple, except that they eyed Adam, not one another. And Adam eyed them back. He liked them both, but had never seen them together.

Clive spoke. "Do you think your native spirits are capable of murder?"

"I haven't really thought about it much before. But I know a lot of people who do."

"What kind of people?"

"Mostly Osage and Pawnee. But Cherokee fullbloods still believe in night-goers, particularly in Raven-Mocker. He's the strongest killer witch. But my family, we're mixed and modern Indians. We farm, ranch, and earn livings. Have a lot of white ways. I doubt Raven-Mocker even exists."

"But you saw that Indian on the lawn?"

"Yeah, I did. Just as clearly as we see Adam now."

"How do you explain that?"

Two disengaged her hand to pass her palm over her mouth. "I can't. But my Papaw, my mother's father, can. He says spirits with unfinished business hang around. And that the whole earth is filled with spirits people used to see, talk to, and deal with. That Adam has a spirit. And is part of the larger buffalo spirit. That every cave, spring, and river has a spirit. And are part of their greater spirits. That the whites' religion is one of their greatest evils because it drives all the spirits from the earth into the sky. It makes everything feel dead, when it's really very much alive."

"Where does he suppose people go when they die?"

"I think he'd say to different places. Some to what white people think Indians call 'the happy hunting ground.' But others come back as babies. And some split off into more than one soul. Of the ones who hang around, he'd say most are witches. I guess that's what we saw." Two touched her bandana. "He seemed real friendly to me. But deceit is a witch's basic nature. Or so I've heard. I don't really know. It seems like, maybe, this spirit was trying to help the animals. Maybe even me. I haven't got it all worked out yet."

Clive clasped his hands together between his knees. "I was orphaned as a lad. Passed around relatives. Never stayed very long and was mostly alone. But when I returned for the war, I fought with one of my cousins. A chap named Millwood. Millwood and I lived between walls of dirt, side by side, for weeks at a time. That changes relationships, as you can imagine. I came to love Millwood as a brother, as a father and a mother. Then one day . . ." Clive tightened his fingers and clamped his teeth together. The muscles flexed in his jaw.

Two put a hand on his arm. "What happened after that?"

Clive shook his head. "I couldn't put it behind me. Had some terrible times. Took to the bottle. But while you were delirious in the cave, Millwood came 'round. He kept me company. We sang." Clive glanced in Two's direction. "You weren't in any shape to see or hear Millwood, were you?"

Two lifted her leg and moved her cast. "I remember singing. A song, I think, from the war."

Clive's chest rose and fell with relief. Tears formed in his eyes. He removed his handkerchief from his pocket and blew his nose. He folded it and returned it to a different pocket. "Yes, it is a war song. One that was quite popular on the lines and at home." He put an arm around Two's shoulder, squeezed her arm, and let go. "I hope we'll speak of this again at another time. But today, I'm afraid we have a problem."

"Yes, a scalp is a problem."

"A bigger problem than that. I believe Crawford has found the body. And I don't know how we're going to explain it. Or, really, if we should."

Adam snorted. Both Two and Clive looked his way. The buffalo's eye was directly on them. Clive said, "Is he trying to give us advice?"

"Probably."

"What sort would it be?"

"To hide the body."

"You're sure?"

"I'm only about eighty percent sure that's Adam's opinion. But me, I'm one hundred percent sure. Everybody in the park would be a suspect. We'd never be able to explain that an Indian spirit killed someone." Two paused and then added, "It won't be the first body somebody's hidden." She was thinking about the disappeared cowboys of the 101. About the corpse of an Osage woman found in a ravine.

Clive thought Two sounded amazingly like May. But he couldn't share that. He said, "Orr already has the scalp."

Two sighed and came back to the conversation. "Remember, people survive scalpings."

"All of you seem to think that."

"It's true. People do. Almost nobody died of scalping. They just wished they had. Or were killed and then scalped."

"Crawford is waiting for me. I'd like for us to talk to him together. But we need to get to him before he tells anybody. Can you walk quickly? Help me figure out what to say?"

The barn was a long way from the buffalo pen. By the time Two and Clive got as far as the casino, her arms were shaking with effort. She said, "You go on. I won't be a minute." She swung toward a bench circling a tree trunk close to a sulphur fountain. She sat down hard and breathed in deep. Clive took his handkerchief out and wiped his brow. He said, "Stay here. I'll send a child to run for Crawford, and we'll meet you at my cabin."

"We still don't know what to tell him."

Clive looked right and left before he said, "We'll have to improvise."

Two got to Clive's cabin shortly after he did. Crawford was walking another path within sight. They clustered behind a locked door in Clive's main room, but kept the windows open for the breeze. Two sat, but Crawford stood close to a window where he could monitor the porch. He spoke first. "There's a body about thirty yards below the bear enclosure, but above the creek. It's outside the park's boundary. On land that's now Karr's."

"It's Older, right?" That was Clive.

"I think so. It's scalped. I couldn't get past that. But it's got long arms and legs. And this is his satchel." He nodded toward the floor. "I've got what he used to murder the animals. Let me show you." He picked up the bag, slid leather from buckles, and opened the top flap. Both Two and Clive looked in. Clive said, "Just as suspected." He backed away. The tea-kettle whistled. "Milk and sugar?"

"Sugar," said Crawford. "No tea for me," said Two, "but thank ya."

While Clive was in the kitchen, Two looked around the room. Crawford kept his eyes on the porch. Clive returned with a tray holding a pot, two cups, a small pitcher, a sugar bowl, and spoons. He set the tray down. Said, "It still needs a bit of a brew. Won't be long."

Crawford said, "Is it Orr we should call? Or the Davidson County police?"

Clive said, "Technically, we should call the police. But I have a few reservations." He put a palm to the pot, removed the lid, and poured. He said, "Sugar's there. You can add your own. Hard to get that right."

Crawford put a spoonful of sugar in his tea and stirred. He lifted the tea to his lips, sipped, and swallowed before he said, "But Older's been murdered."

Clive had his cup to his mouth. Two said, "Mr. Lovett and I think he's been murdered by somebody the police won't be able to find. Mr. Orr neither."

Crawford frowned. "Who?"

Two took a deep breath. Looked around the room again. The walls were chinked logs. They didn't hold pictures, but on the fireplace's mantel was a picture of a man in a uniform. Two nodded toward it and said to Clive, "Is that your cousin?"

Clive smiled. "No. That's George the Fifth, King of the United Kingdom and Dominions."

Two had tried to open the subject the only way she could think of. She wished she'd asked for tea.

Clive said, "Crawford, have you ever heard of the Bell Witch?"

"Lord, sir. The Bell Witch was meanness itself. Don't even talk about that."

Clive smiled. "So you know about her?"

"Some people called it Kate, but I don't know if it was a her or an it. Sometimes, it was a dog. Or a creature that didn't look like a natural animal. Let's don't be talking about the Bell Witch."

Two frowned. She'd never heard of that particular witch. Clive said, "So you do believe in witches?"

Crawford took a gulp of tea and glanced out the window. He wished somebody would come to the porch and knock on the door. Telling a white person you believed in witches was like saying you believed in voodoo. A dangerous thing to do if you wanted respect. But even white people, judges, doctors, and state representatives believed in the Bell Witch. They talked with it in groups for years. Crawford said, "I do believe in the Bell Witch. Yes, I surely do. And the old slaves used to believe in witches. But I've never seen one myself."

Two said, "Indians believe in witches, too, Crawford. And Mr. Lovett and I believe that a spirit killed Jack. We've seen him."

Crawford said, "Go chase yourself!" He set his cup down.

"Actually, it's true," Clive said. "I'm seen him several times. Other spirits, too."

"Here in the park?" Crawford's voice rose.

"Some of them."

Crawford ran his hands down the front of his pants. "That's nothing I like hearing."

"I don't think they're dangerous."

"You said one killed Older. That sounds dangerous to me."

"I don't think he's dangerous to us. I think he was protecting the animals and Two."

Crawford looked out the window again. He still wished someone would arrive. A live human being.

Clive said, "If we leave the body where it is, what are the chances that Karr will find it?"

Crawford rubbed a hand over his mouth and shook his head. "He's lazy. He won't be crossing the creek and climbing a hill."

Two said, "Will he smell it?"

"Most breezes go around that hill, over to the golf course, and, maybe, to the Bible College. Smells don't carry that far."

"What about a strong wind?" Two asked.

"That might take a smell up to the bears. It depends."

"What about dogs?" That was Clive.

"Well, they might smell it. A beagle. Even a terrier, maybe. Yes, sir. And probably from the bear enclosure."

"We'll have to move it, then." That was Two.

"You gonna do that?" Crawford said.

Two hesitated. Hearing Clive say that the Cherokee spirit was trying to protect her and the animals swayed her opinion. He could just as well be a protective spirit as a witch. And if so, she was indebted to him. She wished she'd been there to help him kill Older. She thought of Lefty and Rooster beating the botanist to a pulp. She was appreciative, but really she wanted to fight her own fights, not have men always fight them for her. There was no way to change the past, but maybe she could make up for it. She said, "I'm gonna help. If I weren't in this cast, I'd do it by myself."

Clive and Crawford looked at each other. They raised their eyebrows in unison. Then they looked at Two. Clive said, "I'll move the body. I'm just not sure where to. Maybe the cave is the best solution. It's the closest. We can blame the odor on Ocher."

Two shook her head and raised a hand. "He can't be buried with Ocher. He has to go somewhere else."

Clive didn't really want Older near where Millwood had appeared either. He said, "Crawford, you know this land better than anybody. What do you think?"

"We could carry him off into the Overton Hills. But people hunt in there. And ride their horses," Crawford said.

After that, they grew quiet, thinking. Clive walked to a window, and Crawford focused on the fireplace. Two lifted her cast into a vacant chair. It was getting dirty. Showing wear. She rubbed a smudge. Rubbed another. Pictured the turtles, encased their whole lives. Dirt on them crusted and fell off. Or was washed off when they swam. They were wonderful animals. And great warriors, according to Cherokee legend. She said, "I know where to put him."

Helping
Nature
Take
Her
Course

≡

About two o'clock in the morning, Clive found Bobby Minton, the watchman, sleeping on a bench near the bird cages. He decided letting Bobby doze on was too risky and kicked a trash container. Bobby jerked upright. Scrambled to his feet, switched on his torch, and swished it around. He saw Clive, but not who he was. He reached for his gun. Clive said, "Whoa, Minton. It's me, Lovett. Fine night."

Bobby went slack and thanked the Lord. If he'd shot the general manager, he'd be ruined forever. "I'm sorry, sir. Didn't know who ya were. Something wrong?"

"Mrs. Shackleford has called me. She's seen someone on their lawn. Could you go over? Mr. Shackleford is asleep and has a big meeting tomorrow. Don't disturb them unless you make an arrest. Whoever it was may've gone. But Mrs. Shackleford will feel better if someone is guarding their house. Obviously, you won't be missing much here." Clive raised an eyebrow.

Bobby rubbed the back of his neck. He could use a sick-baby excuse, but he slept on the bench every night. He said, "Be happy to. It's a thirty-minute walk. Trolley's not running."

"You can take my car. Do you drive?"

"No, sir, I don't."

"Come with me. I'll drive you."

Clive let Minton out in front of Maggie's house, Wayside, and drove back to the park. There wasn't an access road in front of the bears' enclosure, so they couldn't use the car to haul Jack's body up. Clive and Crawford relied on Bang On. Crawford stayed in the saddle, and Clive shimmied down the hill's slope with a rope and a torch until he saw a leg. He turned the body so the feet were facing uphill and tied the rope around the legs, not the boots, as during the war he'd learned footwear slips off during pulls. He gave Crawford the order, and hovered while Jack slid up. He adjusted his stiff legs and arms for routes around trees and over rocks. When the body reached the crest of the hill, Clive said, "Far enough." Crawford halted Bang On. Clive said, "I'm switching on the torch to get a look."

Crawford dismounted and turned toward the bear enclosure. Zana had extended a paw through the bars. Crawford said, "No chewing gum." Zana growled. She was still angry. Crawford knew she was Tom Noddy's grandmother, and figured her mood might not settle for days. He didn't step any closer, but kept talking to her until Clive said, "Crawford, I need your help."

Crawford whispered, "Lord, don't desert me." Aloud he said, "Yes, sir."

"Here're our choices. We can drag him behind Bang On or throw him over the saddle. Your saddle. You call it."

Crawford looked at Jack's body. His arms and legs were spread like a spider's. His head was thrown back, and his neck exposed as though it was about to be shaved. Fortunately, that angle hid the sight of the top of his head. Crawford scratched his cheek. Winced. Said, "He's stiff. And what's that I smell?"

"Well." Clive ran his hand down over his mouth.

"That's my daddy's saddle. Let's drag the S.O.B."

They walked Bang On, dragging Jack beside the concrete path from the bear enclosure and through the grassy concert field. They avoided the casino, skating rink, and bird and animal cages. Took the smaller paths, skirted the dimly lit larger ones, and also the playground, but they used the racing fields. They both knew the park as well as their own bellies, so had no problems and didn't see another human being until Two's form appeared in the dark. She flashed her torch. Clive flashed his. Except for the moon's waxing light, the night again enveloped them.

Two had thought deeply about what she was doing. The more she thought, the more bonded she felt to the Cherokee's spirit, and the more convinced she became that he wasn't a witch, that he had come to guard and defend. They were of the same tribe; if both alive, would be flesh and blood. That's how she overcame her natural reluctance to open a grave. She didn't know the body was still in there. She hoped it wasn't. But if it was, she was prepared to do a lot of smudging.

She held Bang On's reins while Clive and Crawford untied Jack's legs and hoisted his corpse over the barrier into the turtle enclosure.

Once inside, Clive said, "Go on home, Crawford. You've done well."

Crawford hesitated.

"Look, if somebody comes along, we can all hide in the bushes. But Bang On is a dead giveaway." He glanced at Jack's torso. He hadn't meant to say "dead" that way.

Crawford didn't like any dead body. But especially one that looked like a spider and had a cap of blood on its head. And he was still trying to adjust to the idea of ghosts in the park. But he knew for certain he'd get less mercy than the others if they got caught. He said, "That's a good point. But y'all be careful. Sleep in, Two. I'll come 'round in the afternoon."

Two and Clive didn't waste time watching Crawford go. She'd brought a pillowcase, dropped Clive's torch in it, and held hers lit. Clive dragged Jack's body into the bushes, and near the stone box grave. He let the feet drop, pulled his handkerchief from his pocket, and wiped his brow. He said, "Have you taken a look?"

Two shook her head. Swung the torch over the lid. She said, "It's broken. Somebody's been in it."

"It's probably been robbed. They may have even taken the body." Clive stuffed his handkerchief back in his pocket. "I'll have a look-see. You might want to turn your head."

Two did look up, away from the casket. The branches weren't far overhead. They were in a tight space, almost like a cave. She took a deep breath. "I can take it."

"Okay. Here we go. Heave ho." Clive gripped the smaller of the pieces, pulled it to the side and then up. He set it down carefully against the box. Two shone the light in. It lit up the feet. She moved the light to the remaining top piece. "I guess that answers that question."

"Yes. Rather. I wish that weren't the case."

Two dropped the beam to the ground. She looked at her own feet. One in a boot, one still encased. She said, "We get the world we have, not the one we want. But we can make this one better. Do ya need help with the other slab?"

"No, I've got it. I'm just going to tilt it over."

Two positioned the light on Clive's head, away from the skull that had once been a face. And Clive eased the larger slab so that it also sat on its end against the box. Neither of them looked at the head. They turned to Jack.

Two was steady enough on her crutches to help by lifting a shoulder. They laid Jack's body directly on top of the skeleton, head to head. But he was too tall. His ankles and feet stuck out over the end of the box. Clive turned him on his side, struggled to bend his stiff legs into a fetal position. While he was doing that, Two said, "We've made a mistake."

Clive stopped. "What?"

"We haveta undress him."

Clive sighed and rubbed his brow. "Blast it. I wasn't thinking. I'll do it."

"I've seen a pecker, Mr. Lovett." Two turned, wedged the torch between the trunk and a limb on a little tree, and reached for an arm to unbutton the shirt at the sleeve.

"You should call me Clive after all we've been through."

"All right, Clive. I wish we'd brought his satchel to stuff the clothes in. I don't want them in my pillowcase."

"We can use his brogans." He was removing one of them.

They undressed Jack together. Cut his clothes with Clive's pocket knife to make it easier. But Clive removed Jack's soiled smalls himself. He stuffed them into a boot. Wiped his hands on Jack's trousers, and stuffed them in on top of them. He said, "We better round up the turtles."

"First, let's build a way in and out for them."

"Right-o. We can remove the slab on the end facing the cave. That'll let them in and expel the odor toward the underground." He knelt and tried to wiggle the slab on the end.

Two grunted. Clive looked up. He couldn't see her face very well. "What's wrong?"

"We don't wanta completely destroy a grave. Can't we build a ramp?"

"We could. But we have to manage the odor."

It was a better solution. Still, it didn't seem right. Two didn't know why she'd suddenly reached a sticking point. They'd already disturbed the body.

Clive said, "I'll do it. You look for turtles."

Two didn't move. Her breathing became hard and short.

Clive couldn't see her well. But he'd heard those breaths in the trenches. He arose. Placed a palm on Two's shoulder. "I'll do it. When it's all over, I'll come back in here and replace the slab. You have my word."

Two took a deeper breath. "They dug up these people like they were potatoes."

Clive pinched the bridge of his nose under his glasses. "I'm certain they did. But that's not what we're doing. In Westminster Abbey they've always opened graves to add people. I've heard this race did the same. We'll just leave it open long enough for nature to take her course."

"For the turtles to take their course."

"Yes. For the turtles to do their work. To help Methuselah get justice for Dinah."

Two found that idea comforting. Her breathing returned to normal. She was back in the saddle. Clive removed his hand from her shoulder. He asked, "How long do you think it will take them to eat him?"

"The 101 turtles can eat a dead calf in a day. But there're lots more of them. Maybe two days for him. It'll help if the turtles aren't fed anything else."

"I can see to that. See if you can locate a couple. I'll dig this slab out."

"What are ya gonna use?"

"My pocket knife if I have to. Go on. Find me some turtles." Clive dropped to his knees. He grasped the edge of the slab once again and started pulling.

Two retrieved Clive's torch from her pillowcase and found two turtles nearby. Both with their heads and legs inside their shells. She set one on Jack's hip, another on his thigh. She found another couple of turtles real quick and set them in. She said, "We probably need just about ten. The others'll find their way by morning. They sorta cluster with each other."

Clive unfolded his knife's blade. "I'm a little worried about buzzards. Turkey vultures can't smell, but black vultures can."

Two had found another turtle. She scooped it into her pillowcase. "If we were on the ranch, I could shoot 'em."

"Probably not here. But vultures are afraid of hawks. It'll be a good time to pull my hawks out of their cages and put them on display."

"You can do that down here?"

"I can do it anywhere I please. They're well trained. I raised them from hatchlings."

Two set two more turtles in. She said, "We have the first elimination races on Sunday."

Clive was on the ground, scraping away dirt with his knife. He said, "I forgot about that. This is Thursday night . . ."

"Actually, it's Friday morning."

"Hum. That's a pity. Throw more turtles in."

Friday

≡

Crawford had already been to the turtle enclosure to set up perches for the hawks when he brought Gay around. Two asked if he'd smelled the body or seen any buzzards. Crawford said neither, and she filled him in on events after he'd left. Next, they talked about ghosts. Crawford told her Bell Witch stories, and Two told him about the Indian on the lawn and her grandmother's voice at the hen house. Crawford looked over at the unpainted wood, dirty windows, and rusty tin roof. He shivered and asked if the Indian had been around since. Two said she hadn't seen him, but expected to. Hoped to.

However, her immediate concern was smudging. She asked Crawford to come collect materials with her. But Crawford had a date with Bonita, so Two set off alone into the woods in her cart. She knew where to find what she needed, gathered it quickly, returned, and tied Gay to the trellis. She smudged her room and walked through the smoke four times. She rested in peace for about twenty minutes. Then she retrieved Gay and rode toward the turtle enclosure.

Clive was outside the pen with two Cooper's hawks on perches. As far as Two could tell, neither hawk was tethered, and Clive was either giving a lecture or answering questions from a crowd of about twenty people. Clouds covered the sun. No big birds circled beneath them. Two was content to watch from a distance, to hope the turtles were busy, and to search inside herself to pry out some guilt. The only spot she found was for not having killed Jack herself. That shocked her a little. But she figured she'd get over it.

Looking for the Indian, she skimmed her eyes over the turtle track. It was laid out in circles with strings and markers, but not yet chalk lined, and empty of people, solid or spirit. Her glance darted to small groups of trees where racing fans would stand if the sun grew too hot. The Indian wasn't around any of those. She peered closely at the copse concealing the grave. But she didn't think he'd be near there, and he wasn't.

She decided to visit the bears on the theory that he may've retreated to kin. She steered Gay through the Saturday crowd, stopped for conversations and autographs, and avoided running over any children. She arrived at the enclosure with some hope of seeing the Indian.

She saw mostly courting couples, as the den, for reasons lost to memory, was considered the most romantic place in the park. There was also a flock of little kids herded by two uniformed young women. And, of course, though the tub had been removed, the bears were there. They were still agitated, grumbling, moaning, and pacing. But there was no Indian lolling under a tree, squatting on a rock, or sitting on a limb. No Indian at all, except Two, and she didn't count herself in. She was disappointed, but wanted to talk to the bears, share their sorrow, and comfort her kin. But not in the state they were in. And not with a crowd milling.

So Two turned Gay toward Adam's lot. Except for three boys using sticks to shoot the buffalo, all was quiet there. Two disembarked under her usual tree. She didn't call Adam because the boys would hear. So she stared into the middle distance and let images and voices float. Maybe the Indian had been a trapped soul and would never appear again. He'd won a scalp. He didn't take it with him, but it was his. The winning would change him. Maybe release him. Two didn't know. But sitting there, she lost all hope of ever seeing him again, and she began to feel sad.

Eventually, the boys left and Adam lumbered over. Two rose above her feelings of loss and told him the entire story. He chewed his cud with great satisfaction.

Games

Showers kept Two in on Saturday, delayed the chalking of the race-course, and brought Clive to Chambliss to court Helen and to review with Two the elimination race rules. The turtles would be brought out of the pen in washtubs, people would pick theirs, pay the quarter fee, and get a coupon with a number. They could choose a color, red, white, or blue, for their number to be painted on the shell. Two said designated painters were important because some people, particularly children, don't paint well, and others have been known to play with paint, throw it, and get into fistfights.

She explained (mainly to Helen) that turtles run toward shade. They should be placed inside a small wire pen in the center of the circle, then the wire lifted in concert by two or more men. The scoring could vary. Sometimes, points are assigned every time a turtle passes a line from one concentric circle to the next. That method requires the officials to stand on lines with clipboards in hand. The other way of scoring is to simply have the first turtles to make it beyond a single circle be deemed the winners. The second type of scoring is easier, but since you never can tell what a turtle will do, sometimes so many of them wander around that very few make it to the farthest line. Two believed that had to do with weather. The sunnier and hotter the day, the more likely the turtles to scuttle to shade. If the clouds lingered after the showers, the more complicated scoring might be the better alternative. The track could be chalked for either method.

They were in the small front parlor. Helen left and came back with the *Tennessean*. She said, "The prediction is for clouds. Maybe even rain."

"We'll have to postpone if it keeps raining," Clive said. "But the safest decision is to chalk concentric circles and have officials with clipboards. John is off on Sundays. I should talk to him now about who we pull in."

"I'll be one," Two volunteered.

"If you want, of course. How many more will we need?"

"The course isn't that big. Probably just two judges for each circle. If ya chalk in more lines, like you're cutting a pie in quarters, they can stand on those intersections with the circles. I'll get ever'body placed. Don't worry."

Clive rose. "Thanks. I'll get cracking."

Helen offered to get his umbrella, and they both took their leave. Two picked up the *Tennessean*. She read an article about the anniversary of the Battle of Little Big Horn that quoted Sitting Bull calling Custer a fool. Two smacked her lips. Moved on to an article about Aimee Semple McPherson. The evangelist had reappeared after being gone for five weeks. She claimed kidnappers had imprisoned her in a cabin, but was unable to lead police and reporters to where she'd been held. Two was wondering about Sister's story when she heard, "Reading my competition?"

Edgar was standing in the door frame, a little damp, but with a smile on his face. He sat without invitation. Two felt pleased. She'd thought over their evening on the porch. Wondered if Edgar had considered her behavior odd. If she'd see him again. If he had a girlfriend.

He said, "It's awful short notice, but I'm off today. Are ya free for supper and the pictures? The feature is *It's the Old Army Game.* W. C. Fields. I think he's pretty funny."

The drizzle had stopped. Two wore her best silk scarf and a skirt without a split. At Woolworth's mezzanine counter, they ate fried chicken, mashed potatoes, green beans, and biscuits. They watched the people shopping on the first floor below, bet pennies on what they would buy, and saw one woman slip a lipstick into her purse on the sly. After the Fields movie and the shorts, they walked to the end of the street and admired the capitol building in lights. Then at the Transfer Station, they boarded the Glendale car and held hands during the ride. Two spent much of the trolley trip trying to decide if she should allow herself to be kissed or not. Her inclination was yes. She didn't think a romance with Edgar would really work, but he was fun, and she wanted to resurrect the parts of herself that had been so dormant since the winter. To see if they still worked.

She was still thinking about kissing when they got off at Buford Station, passed Little Elk's tree, and headed up the walk to the porch. If Edgar didn't stop her soon, nothing would happen. There was a no-kissing rule in the dorm. Two felt the situation was blocked by her crutches and was growing a little discouraged when Edgar placed his hand on the back of her neck. He said, "Could ya hold up?"

Two stopped and turned. Edgar slipped a hand between a crutch and her waist. "Do ya mind? Just a taste?" He kissed her tenderly, but urgently. She kissed him back. That continued until she pulled away. "Thanks for the evening. It's been terrific."

Edgar tilted his head. "What time's the turtle race tomorrow?"

"Three o'clock."

"I may have to work. If not, I'll see ya' there. I'll walk ya' on up."

A cluster of women that included the Montgomerys was on the porch. They all pretended they were having a serious exchange on an important subject. Couldn't look up from their conversation and couldn't be distracted. Two didn't want to get grilled and appreciated their discretion. She hurried off to her room, feeling a stirring in her body that was like . . . Well, she couldn't say, exactly. But she saw a picture in her mind of a crocus breaking through soil.

Nashville's Heartbeat

≡

The next morning, the sun rose unopposed by clouds and stayed that way. Two got to the racecourse early, scanned the sky, and sniffed the air. She saw no big birds in flight, smelled no sickening odor. The course had been chalked, and she looked it over. Then she climbed over the fence into the enclosure in much the same way she mounted horses. A couple of washtubs were already in there, and she'd brought a small bag. To keep other people as far away from the grave and turtle pen as possible, she started loading turtles in her sack, one at a time. But grabbing turtles isn't easy on crutches, and Two fussed at herself for not bringing a net and fussed at the turtles for waddling so fast. She chased one to the edge of the growth concealing the cave, whiffed a bad odor, and nearly fell over. She went after a different turtle. She'd gathered about forty-five when Randy Hoffer, the junior keeper, arrived.

Two had been setting the turtles in the tubs, and Randy and another keeper had carried the tubs to the course by the time the crowd began to arrive. Clive and another employee came with them. Randy began selling turtles, and Two painted them. She let the buyers pick their color, painted the numbers on the shells, and told the new owners to take their turtles to the hillside to wander while they dried. She had to repaint three turtles because the initial numbers got smudged. She fixed those with fluid visitors provided from Banjo lighters in their pockets.

Two was still painting when Edgar showed up. He snapped a few people holding their entries, pulled out his notepad, and interviewed some on why they picked their particular turtles. Then he huddled with men taking bets. Gambling was illegal in the park, and all over Tennessee, but side-betting was a big part of the attraction, and the park had a standing policy of averting its eyes on wagers.

The first elimination race attracted forty-two contestants. And because it was sunny, the turtles were speedy. The ten fastest survived to go on to the next round. The second elimination was held forty-five minutes later. It attracted over fifty entries. Another ten were picked to make it into the race on the Fourth of July.

People had the option of taking their turtles home or leaving them at the park. Some chose to take theirs away, but most deposited them in a tub to be hauled over to the bird cages to live until the big race. By the time the crowd dispersed, Two was splotched with paint, sweaty, and smelling too much like turtles. But no carrion birds were circling, no one had complained of an odor, and Edgar was still hanging around.

When he walked over, Two said, "Let me get downwind from ya. I smell like turtle do-do." She swung to his other side, and said, "Howcha like it?"

"It's the berries. It'll draw an even bigger crowd when word gets around."

"Ya gonna make that happen?" They'd started toward Chambliss.

"I intend to. Though my publisher isn't too hot on the park and the zoo."

"So I hear. But that hasn't stopped ya so far."

"Well, this place is Nashville's heartbeat. Generations of people have played, romanced one another, and died in this park."

Two clutched her grips tighter. "Played and romanced, not died."

Edgar put his hands in his pockets. "I wouldn't be too sure 'bout that."

Two's face flushed. "Whaddya mean?"

"Well, I heard a funny story from one of the keepers. Said somebody came up with a scalp."

Two stopped. Edgar did as well. Two tried to look puzzled. "A scalp?"

"Now, don't pretend ya don't know what a scalp is." He'd thrown his line out hoping Two wouldn't know what he was talking about. But the look on her face wasn't right.

"What exactly does 'don't pretend' mean?" Two jutted her jaw. Her eyes flared.

Edgar rubbed his hand over his brow. The lady had more temper than he'd anticipated. He hoped she wasn't hiding something. And hoped she didn't think he thought she'd scalped someone because she was an Indian. He said, "That didn't come out exactly right. No offense intended. It's just that . . ." He put his hand in his shirt pocket and pulled out his notepad. He flipped pages. Read aloud, "Randy Hoffer. Keeper. Bloody scalp. Red hair."

Two breathed out hard. She took a hand off a grip and flexed her fingers. Then she shook her head. "Oh, that! That was part of Tom Noddy's hide."

"You're sure?" Edgar raised an eyebrow.

Two flexed the fingers of her other hand. "Positive. Tom Noddy died last week."

"I read that in the *Tennessean*. But Lovett is quoted as saying there was no sign of violence and that the bear drowned."

Two hadn't read the article. However, she figured the quote was accurate. She turned and looked at the sky over the turtle enclosure. No buzzards, crows, or birds of any kind. She said, "Well, that's the public story. And I think Tom did drown. But someone . . . Mr. Lovett doesn't know who . . . cut a piece of hide off one of his legs. I don't know which one. They probably planned to scare people with it."

"Who'd do a thing like that?"

"Probably one of the crew. Just a prank. They're always cutting up."

Two paused. "Sorry for the pun. Ya aren't gonna put that in the paper, are ya?"

A prank wasn't much of a story, and even sweaty, disheveled, and on crutches, Two Feathers was the most attractive woman Edgar had seen in a long time. Maybe in his entire life. He slipped his notepad back in his pocket and smiled. "Not if ya'll let me buy ya some ice cream."

Two tilted her head and widened her eyes in a partly sincere, partly practiced, pose. Her lips separated a little. She took a deeper breath. "Could I get the turtle smell off first?"

Author's
Note

≋

I grew up in the neighborhood built over the old Glendale Park and Zoo. One of the park's trees survived on the edge of my yard, and when I walked home every day from Glendale Elementary School, I crossed through the remains of the parallel line of trees that had sheltered the old trolley tracks. One summer, in the roots of another park tree behind my next-door neighbors' fence, my neighborhood gang found a large joint bone. We called a father out, and he told us to leave the bone alone; it probably belonged to a rhinoceros or hippopotamus that had died at the zoo. In researching this book, I didn't uncover any reference to rhinoceroses at Glendale, but I did find one lone mention of a "blood sweating behemoth" in the February 23, 1926, edition of the *Nashville Tennessean*.

About a mile away from my house, on the edge of the neighborhood, was a deserted mansion. I sometimes trespassed there, marveling at its peeling wallpaper, dilapidated stairway, and at the birds flying in and out of its broken windows. I knew the mansion had been built before the Civil War, and I thought the springhouses in the hillside below it were connected to cellars under the house, and had been dug for the purpose of escaping the Yankees. I went in the springhouses more than once, but never far enough back to confirm my theory, as they were very scary. I didn't know until I was an adult that the mansion was connected to a swindle and scandal that revolved around the son of the owner, implicated other family members, ruined many of Nashville's moneyed elite and smaller investors, and caused a financial collapse that extended into seven Southern states.

I thought a spooky building concealed behind a tall wall of cane down the road from the old mansion was the bathhouse for a swimming pool in the old park zoo, not what it actually was, the remains of a clubhouse for a golf club I didn't know existed until I started researching this book. I avoided that building until I was well into my adulthood because, when I first became aware of it during 1960s Civil Rights movement, it was the site of a public meeting of the Ku Klux Klan that even our conservative, racially segregated community considered appalling.

I knew about the Bell Witch as a child. We all knew about the Bell Witch.

And I knew there were caves close by. One was on my street. In winter, I sometimes sledded down the slight slope from the cave's entrance toward the icy waters of its creek. But more often, I sledded down my street's hill toward the stream. During summers, I caught a lot of crawfish in that stream, and sometimes I followed it to its source, peered into the cave, and wondered what was in there. Its opening was too small to crawl into, but several streets over, on the way to the elementary school where my mother taught, a larger cave opened on a hillside overlooking a bigger creek. Sometime during my teenage years, I learned that location had once been the home of the Glendale bears. But I didn't know anything more about other caves anywhere around until, in researching this book, I discovered that the Glendale Park and Zoo had had a horse diving tank and that the tank had collapsed into one.

Also, until I began researching this book, I'd never heard of Buford College, although I now believe its campus became some of the yards on my own street. Neither did I know growing up that much of the most valuable residential property in all of Nashville — that along Hillsboro Road and Tyne Boulevard — had been (and still was, in part) owned by an affluent, educated African American family that had had it for generations. That area became very familiar to me as a teenager, and my first job out of college was teaching English at Hillsboro High School. But I never even heard a whisper about that family. However, once I discovered them, I couldn't leave them out. And because I felt my major African American character needed a love interest, I drew on the history of another very successful African American Nashville family.

I did know that Indian graves had been found in our neighborhood, but only above the creek running next to Lealand Lane. This bothered me as a child, even though I had no idea of the extent of the cemetery, and knew nothing about its desecration. I did learn in the fourth grade, however, that the white pioneers coming into the area proclaimed it virgin land, uninhabited and unused. Theirs for the taking. And that the taking had entailed killing a lot of Indians, and was justified by those Indians' unchristian, savage nature and unprovoked attacks. My mother, a fourth-grade teacher with a Cherokee family still very much alive in Oklahoma, had to teach that racist, faux-history year after year, even as I moved on. Or, maybe, as I never really moved on.

Acknowledgments

≡

Although the events in this book are entirely fiction, many of the characters are based on the lives of real people, three of whom have also captured the imaginations of novelists who've written before me. In those cases, in the interest of the continuity of literature and because no improvement was needed, I used the names those authors chose. Peter Taylor came up with the pseudonyms Lewis and Mary Ann Shackleford, and, thus, named my entire Shackleford family. Alfred Lealand Crabb invented the name Gale Thurston using a slight twist on the real name.

I want to thank my high school friend, Emily Jordan Noel, for her help in researching the Noel cemetery and family, and for introducing me to Robert Sharp, formerly of the Art Institute of Chicago, and Kevin Smith, Ph.D., professor and director of anthropology at Middle Tennessee State University. Both generously shared with me their scholarship on the cemetery, and Kevin provided to me as well his work on Buford College and Glendale Park. I'd also like to thank Anne Wigle-Occhipinti for sending me (a total stranger) a wealth of information on the Glendale Park and Zoo, and particularly on Clare (Clive) Lovett. I am indebted to my childhood next-door neighbor and lifelong friend, Vince "Pepper" Parrish, for tracking down leads, even when he knew I was being obsessive and, maybe, delusional. I'm also in debt to Pam VanMeter, a friend and horse veterinarian, who explained to me how unscrupulous people can get away with killing large animals.

I'd also like to thank readers who gave me insightful and necessary criticism, even though I asked them to read during the Christmas season when they all had more important things to do. In alphabetical order, those are, Laura Derr, Kim Edwards, Rona Roberts, and Martha Helen Smith. Each in her own way improved this book. I am in their debt.

I am also in the debt of my brilliant agent, Lynn Nesbit, who took a particular liking to Two and was anxious to bring her out into the world. And to Nicole Angeloro, my editor, who was not only extremely helpful but made revising fun. The publishing world is in need of more editors like Nicole.

About the author

About the book

Read on

Insights,
Interviews
& More . . .

Meet Margaret Verble

Greg Reynolds

MARGARET VERBLE is an enrolled citizen of the Cherokee Nation of Oklahoma. Many members of her family have remained in Oklahoma to this day and some still own and farm the land on which her books are set, but Margaret was raised in Nashville, Tennessee, and currently lives in Lexington, Kentucky. *Maud's Line*, her first novel, was a finalist for the Pulitzer Prize for Fiction in 2016 and her second novel, *Cherokee America*, won the Spur Award for Best Western and was listed by the *New York Times* as one of the 100 Notable Books of the Year for 2019. *When Two Feathers Fell from the Sky*, selected by *Booklist* as one of the 10 Best Adult Novels of 2021, is set in Nashville. Margaret's next novel, *Stealing*, will be published by Mariner Books in 2023. ❧

A Conversation with Margaret Verble

Q: What do you hope readers take away from your novels?

A: I hope my readers enjoy my books. Literature should be good storytelling and entertaining as well as instructive. It bothers me that so much of literary fiction is psychologically painful and sort of a chore to get through. People have choices. They don't have to read. If they do read, they should find it rewarding. And it's easier to absorb ideas under pleasurable conditions.

As for instruction, I want readers to learn some Cherokee history beyond the Trail of Tears and begin to see American history in a way that's not so Eurocentric. I also write stories where people care about each other despite racial, wealth, and class differences. We need more of that.

Q: What has been the greatest influence on your writing?

A: I grew up watching a treaty being broken. When I was a kid, the Army Corp of Engineers stole the Arkansas Riverbed from the Cherokees in trucks carrying valuable sand and gravel down the very section line I portrayed in *Maud's Line*. It went on for several years, and it infuriated me. Those trucks ran me off the road more than once, and I watched the old Indians in my family stomach that outrageous theft when I knew they had been stolen from again and again.

Q: Why do you write fiction set in the past?

A: We write what we enjoy reading. I enjoy literary fiction and rarely read any other kind. Given that, the question becomes, why historical literary fiction rather than contemporary literary fiction? And the answer is that I don't understand present times very well. I might think I do at a particular moment; then five or so years later, I look back and think, "Gee, I didn't realize that." To understand an era requires a historical perspective.

Q: What one piece of advice would you share with other writers?

A: Research is important, even if you're writing contemporary fiction. Few people have interesting and original enough life experience to write only from that. ∾

Reading Group Guide

1. Why did the author decide to begin the story of Two Feathers and the Glendale Park and Zoo with "When It Was"? What does this section reveal about the story's setting and historical context? What major themes and motifs of the novel does it introduce? Would your view of the book have been different if the author had not included it? How?

2. How is Two treated differently than the other women at Glendale? Why didn't Helen Hampton "feel like she could get as familiar with Two as she could with the other residents" (10)? How does Two cope with this? Does she ever challenge this racial discrimination? Why or why not? After her injury, why doesn't Two want her parents to travel on the train to get to her?

3. Discuss how the book creates a dialogue about racism and segregation in America. Two admits she has been treated with prejudice both on the road and on the ranch. Are there instances of this during her time at Glendale? How does racism influence the way Two interacts with other people, such as her friend Hank Crawford? How is Crawford impacted by the segregation of 1920s Nashville? How does his family's status as landowners affect this? When Crawford shares that his cousin has been beaten, how does Two respond? How does she relate to Crawford's experiences with racism and segregation, and where do their experiences diverge?

4. How does Two feel when she learns that Glendale is built upon a cemetery? Who was involved in the desecration of Noel Cemetery? What items were removed from the graves and what was done with them? How did Shackleford see his

own involvement, and how did this change as he "approached the twilight of his life" (102)? When did he notice this change? What questions does the novel suggest about archaeology, ownership, and the history of museums and collections?

5. Who is Jack Older, and why is he convinced that he's Native American, even though he's white? What did he misunderstand about his parents' farm that further reinforced this notion? Why does he think Two Feathers "seemed like his destiny" (46), and how does this influence his actions? Discuss how his character serves as a catalyst for the exploration of the larger themes of appropriation and entitlement.

6. How is Clive Lovett affected by PTSD? How do the other characters, including his boss, Mr. Shackleford, respond to this? When Clive forms a relationship with Helen, what doesn't he want her to know about him? Is he able to overcome this? How does his experience in the cave with Two change him and "[shift] earthquakelike his entire view of existence" (105)?

7. What was the Scopes trial and why was it both popular and contentious? What "two large underlying and conflicting ideas" (141) did it bring into public view? Where did Clive stand on these issues, and what does Helen think about this? What did Clive mean when he said to Helen that "if William Jennings Bryan could've seen my monkeys, he might've rethought his position" (141)? Where does Two Feathers stand on these same issues? How does the novel reconcile the two ideas?

8. Who is Little Elk and what was his life like? Why is he interested in keeping watch over Two Feathers? Why does he believe he has been sent back to this area? What makes him decide he should kill Pale Jump?

9. Discuss the conclusion of the book. Who was ultimately responsible for the death of the animals at Glendale and what becomes of them? Why do Two, Clive, and Crawford decide to hide the evidence of murder at Glendale? Were you surprised by their choice? Why or why not? Who or what do they feel they are protecting by doing this? ༺

Other Books by Margaret Verble

MAUD'S LINE

Finalist for the Pulitzer Prize

Eastern Oklahoma, 1928: Eighteen-year-old Maud Nail lives with her rogue father and sensitive brother on one of the allotments parceled out by the U.S. Government to the Cherokees when their land was confiscated for Oklahoma's statehood. Maud's days are filled with hard work and simple pleasures, but often marked by violence and tragedy, a fact that she accepts with determined practicality. Her prospects for a better life are slim, but when a newcomer with good looks and books rides down her section line, she takes notice. Soon she finds herself facing a series of high-stakes decisions that will determine her future and those of her loved ones.

CHEROKEE AMERICA

Winner of the Spur Award for Best Traditional Western

Cherokee Nation West, 1875: A baby, a Black hired hand, a bay horse, a gun, and a neighbor have all gone missing in the same corner of the Cherokee Nation. Cherokee American Singer, known as Check—a wealthy farmer, the mother of five boys, and the matriarch of her family—is determined to find out what's going on. As she knows all too well, complex alliances and simmering race and culture clashes unite and divide the people living on Cherokee land in the aftermath of the Civil War. Tensions mount and violence escalates, and the long arm of white law encroaches further into Indian territory.

Discover great authors, exclusive offers, and more at hc.com.